ZEKE
RISING

— BOOK 1 —

By: J. A. Reed

2

Zeke Rising: Book 1

Dedicated to…

My Brother

J. A. Reed

4

CHAPTER ONE: NORMALITY IS RELATIVE

Hell wouldn't have been at the top of my places-to-live list, but once you get used to it, it's not so bad. If I had to find an Earth equivalent, I'd say it's a lot like living in the Arctic Circle, except it's always winter. After the first few thousand years, the cold doesn't really bother you anymore, but just try to keep that in mind next time you say, "When Hell freezes over!" because it just makes you sound dumb and ignorant. I've never understood why humans would think Hell was hot and all fiery anyway, I mean fire was a gift to mankind from on high, it cooks your food, keeps you warm when it's too cold, and provides light for you to see through the darkness, why would you picture that as your eternal torment? I guess that's what humans do though, they take something nice and find the worst possible way to ruin it; honestly, it amazes me sometimes.

As much as I complain though, Hell's actually been getting a lot better over the last few decades. Ever since my little sis, Trini, convinced some scientist to split the atom and tear a hole between Hell and Earth, more and more demons have been taking little vacations topside. For certain larger and more powerful beings such as myself that can't fit through the fractures just quite yet, we get our entertainment watching all you humans. It's kind of like you're some sort of planetary reality TV show. To keep with terms you might understand, before the fracture watching your planet from Hell was like watching an old black and white TV from 20 feet away without glasses on. Since then, however, the pictures have been getting bigger, clearer, and more colorful; now it's like Ultra 4D super-IMAX Deluxe or whatever overly excessive, exaggerated, redundant name you're using these days.

My favorite pastime in recent history has definitely been watching Earth movies and TV shows. Normal human lives are pretty boring to me now that I've gotten used to all the scripted action, horror, adventure, *cough* romance *cough*, and comedy that's out there. I'd love to get more into reading, but since all we can do is watch, best I can do is read over

6

someone's shoulder, which just kind of makes me feel awkward. Besides, do you have any idea how hard it is to find someone that can read at the same speed as me, not too fast, not too slow, and I have to stop wherever they stop and hope they actually finish reading it. It got annoying pretty fast, so I just gave up trying.

I've had to force myself away from TV recently, though, because the biggest of the fractures over New Mexico and Russia are no more than a few weeks from being wide enough for me to finally slip through and see with my own eyes what all the fuss is about. If I were just any ol' demon, I wouldn't have to worry about it, I could just hop on over and possess any random Joe Schmo and go about my business, but I'm afraid it isn't that easy for a fallen angel such as myself.

You see, angels – all angels – have certain rules we need to follow, one of which is that an angel cannot take a human host unless the human consents. That makes it easy for my brothers and sisters still topside because what kind of human doesn't want a nice beautiful angel to show up and bless them with heavenly love, or whatever bull crap they try to spin. I've watched some of my younger siblings down here try and win over hosts, and it's never pretty. Once we reach Earth, our natural forms already start to rot and fester, our wings are burnt down to the bone, and our skin is pale and cold. That's not even the worst part, though; what really causes most humans to run screaming is the bad PR fallen angels have been getting for the past few thousand years. They say there's no such thing as bad publicity, but I'm pretty certain I have a compelling argument to the contrary.

The youngest of my siblings, the Muses, kind of cheat when they pass through. They use their powers of influence to prep a human so that when they're ready to head up, they practically hop straight into the host. They each have different methods of doing it, but each one works for them. My closest brother, Zak, didn't have that luxury the first time he tried crossing over, and he got rejected a lot, like, A LOT. As his brother, I felt really bad for him, but, also as his brother, I found each rejection immensely hilarious and made fun of him accordingly. I learned a lot of "don'ts" from watching him, so hopefully, when it's my turn I don't have to eat those words, but I'm remaining optimistic.

Not a moment later, the phrase "Speak of the devil" proved to be particularly relevant, as Zak popped in through the Nagasaki fracture overhead. He arced across the sky like a shooting star until I flagged him down and he took a sharp bank in my direction, landing right next to me mere seconds later. As an Enochian, he was noticeably shorter and thinner than me, and his face was much longer with protruding cheekbones higher than average.

"What happened?" I asked, "I thought you had a host again? What happened this time?" Last I saw, Zak had been with a young Japanese woman who had offered her service in exchange for curing her mother's cancer.

"What do you think happened?" he replied sounding rather annoyed. "Same thing as the last three hosts."

I placed my hand on his shoulder to comfort him, "I keep trying to tell you, little bro, you've gotta stand up for yourself. I mean, you don't see Megatron, Trini, or any of those guys giving up their hosts."

Zak snickered as he always did when I referred to our brother Metatron by that nickname. "I tried this time, I threatened to put the cancer back if she reneged on our arrangement, but she called my bluff."

"Well there's your problem right there, don't make it a bluff. Give that mom her cancer back. You know what, give her a little extra cancer just for the trouble." I focused on the target and created a sheet of frost particles in the air between us. It swirled for a moment before displaying an image of the former host across its surface like a portable television screen. She was in a small beat up two-door car driving her mom through the countryside near Omura. "Here, they're still pretty close to Nagasaki, you should be able to do it from here."

Zak reached up and cleared the image away with a wave of his hand, "No, no, no, it's fine, I'll find another host. It's not a

8

big deal."

I looked at him confused, "C'mon, it's really not hard, just a tumor or two," I pulled the live image back up, "Here, I'll even do it for you."

"No!" Zak snapped and dispersed the image again before I could concentrate. "I said let them go, just forget about it."

He stormed off and I just stood there, frozen in surprise. Giving random people cancer was like our second favorite pastime after watching TV, and in all that time Zak had never freaked out like that. I shook off my confusion enough to move again and flew to catch up. "So...Huh?"

"I just...It's, well..." He sighed deeply before finishing with a real sentence. "You wouldn't understand, you haven't been up there yet; you haven't had a host." I still had questions, but I let my expression convey them rather than using any words. He eventually caught on and sighed again. "With a host, you're sharing more than just their body, you share a part of their mind as well. Human emotions are much more complex than I ever imagined, so...You wouldn't understand."

"I guess then. We'll have to revisit this in a few weeks when I will understand," I said with a laugh.

Zak's eyes widened, as if he had forgotten and then just remembered again. "That's right, have you thought about what it is you wanna do first? Have you thought about how you'll get a host yet?"

"Um, well, not really, and kinda, yeah, I think so."

"So specific, thanks for enlightening me," Zak said, his words slathered in sarcasm. "But I guess a host should be the priority, so what do you mean by *kinda*?"

"Well, best I can tell, humans that are down at their lowest point are the most accepting of help, even with as many strings attached as our deal would have."

Zak nodded. "Harsh, but true, go on."

"Well...that's all I've got so far. Like I said, kinda..."

Zak spared a moment to show disappointment before doing a little *I should've expected as much* shrug and then proceeded to think on a solution to my predicament. He snapped his fingers.

"I've got it! Don't you see?" He expected me to somehow read his mind, but I was getting nothing. "Think about it, what kinda place would have those types of people in spades?"

"Hmm…Bars!" I said confidently.

"What? No. Well, kinda, but even more low. Bars have happy people too. It's…"

"Funerals?" I interrupted, making it sound like a question, but I was pretty sure I got it this time.

"What? Stop that, I'll just tell you, it's hospitals. Full of dying people and desperate loved ones, it'll be perfect."

"Oh, so I was close, just overshot a little. But hospitals? Isn't that where you found that last host of yours?" I asked.

"Well, yeah, guess I did. She was the easiest to convince so far too. Hadn't really thought of that at the time though." Zak looked up at the fractures overhead. The closest one big enough to accommodate Zak wasn't very far, but it was in the middle of the Pacific Ocean. He seemed to lock eyes with it regardless. "Tell you what, I'll go do some trial runs and let you know how successful it is. Start looking at hospitals around the American and Russian fractures, see if you find anyone you might like."

"And what are you looking for exactly? Gilligan's Island?"

If that had been directed at anyone else, Zak would've laughed, but instead he kept a straight face. "No, Australia's not far from that opening, it's a short flight."

"Right, and with the things that live there, I'm sure the hospitals will have plenty of candidates for you. Good luck down unda!" I said with my best accent.

Zak flew upward. "I'll meet you under the America tear!" he shouted behind him, and just like that he was gone.

I had some time to kill until I'd reach the American fracture, and probably even more time until I could go through it, so I decided to get started finding a host that might be willing to take me on. "Where to begin?" I asked myself pulling up a visual of the area. The fracture covered most of the southwest of the continent, but the largest cracks were located under the state of New Mexico, so that's where I started my search. "So many humans, who's it gonna be? Who's the unlucky fella?"

* * *

"I swear, I must be the unluckiest person alive," I groaned from the floor of our living room. The thin Native American rug did little to soften the hardwood beneath my backside, and the morning sun was in just the wrong spot, causing it to blind my left eye through the gap of window between the wall and blinds. I tried to shift, but all I did was blind my right eye as well.

"Oh Liam, for crying out loud you're 17 years old, stop being so overdramatic, besides, I'm sure there have got to be, oh I don't know, dozens of people with worst luck than you," my mom retorted with a snicker. She was still running around the house trying to pick up before taking me to school, so I was only getting some of her divided attention. If I had to guess, she had hit the snooze button a few times too many that morning because her long curly hair had that *I give up, I'll just throw it in a bun* look and the nametag with a *Krystin C.* sticker below the name of the small family-run diner was nearly forty-five degrees crooked.

With my vision returned, I shot up to a full standing position. "This isn't funny, Mom!" It wasn't until the millisecond after it left my lips that I realized just how whiny that sounded. I cleared my throat in an attempt to sound more assertive after that. "This is the fourth time now! And why is he always eating my shoes? I mean your shoes are right there, and look! Not even a speck of drool!"

She continued to laugh as she poured a few spoonfuls of instant coffee into a mug that said *How does Jesus make his tea?* on top and *Hebrews it* on the bottom, and then gave it a few stirs. "Well, he's your dog, he likes your scent. It's his way of saying he loves you," she ended with a mushy kissy sound.

As if waiting for his cue, the sixty-pound Golden Retriever trotted over to me looking innocent as could be. I lifted the mangled sneaker and scowled at him. "Cody! If you eat one more shoe, I'll...I'm gonna...Ugh! I wish I could have you neutered again." As if taking that as a second cue, he laid down where he sat and proceeded to lick himself. "Stupid dog."

Mom took a quick detour from her frantic path through the house to pet Cody under his wrinkled chin. "Oh, he doesn't mean that, you're his bestest friend, he wuvs you."

"Not today I don't, little heathen," I scowled, crossing my arms to resist falling victim to his innocent cuteness.

Mom stopped petting him to grab her purse and search for something that probably wasn't in there, "Oh, love him or hate him, he's still your best friend."

I looked down at the poor pile of fur and stupidity, unimpressed. "Please, I can do better."

"Oh, hush now, he's loyal. Even with how badly you might treat him sometimes, he'll always be there for you, even when I'm stuck at work. What more could you ask for in a friend?"

"How about hygiene?" With that, he resumed licking himself. "And social skills."

Mom laughed both at my comment and the sight of her wallet on the table right beside where her purse had been before. She grabbed it and threw it into the oversized bag. "Maybe all he needs is a dedicated master; he's got a lot to learn, you could try playing nice." She headed back into the kitchen to resume her morning chaos. "You can start tonight. I'm covering another shift, so it'll just be the two of you."

"Again? Can I just stay over at Greg's then?" I called out after her hoping she'd actually hear me.

"No, you can't leave Cody in the house alone that long, he'll destroy the place!" she yelled back.

"Ugh!" my annoyance overflowed into an exaggerated groan. I looked back at the four-legged anchor. "She's not helping your case."

Mom finally came to the living room overburdened with all of her belongings as usual. "Okay, ready?"

I held up the shreds that used to be my running shoe higher since she somehow missed it before. "No, what am I supposed to wear?"

J. A. Reed

12

She adjusted her purse so she could squat down and pick up the left shoe that still rested on the rug beside me. She turned it in her hand a few times looking it over. "Well, this one's just fine."

"Okay, great. I'll just limp around with only one shoe, develop severe scoliosis, and live the rest of my life in a bell tower."

"Again with the overreacting. Calm down, Quasimodo. If you would, you'd probably remember, last time he ate the left shoe, which means..." She held out the good shoe and nudged me with it a few times until I snatched it.

"Which means I get to mix-match shoes, yay, lucky me," I said with a low monotone over my shoulder on the way to fetch my older shoe from the garage. I had to step over Cody to get there, so I made sure to give him a soft nudge with my foot as I passed. "Thanks for that, idiot."

"Hurry up or you'll be late again!" Mom shouted after me. I checked my watch, and it looked like barring any crazy traffic, we still had time. It was also then I remembered how terrible my luck was, so I didn't want to take any chances. I made sure to shake out the shoe just in case any creepy crawlers decided to take up residence and as I did, Mom shouted back at me again, "Although, if you *are* late again, I'll probably have to meet with your principal again..." Her tone was...hopeful? That wasn't good.

I barged back into the living room wearing one black and red shoe, and one solid gray shoe from a completely different brand. "Mom, no."

"Looks great!" she said exuberantly, ignoring my objection completely and gesturing to my feet. "I'm sure all the kids will be doing it soon. You'll be a little trendsetter, now c'mon, can't be late again."

"Mom, Mr. Daniels is evil, don't even go there," I said, standing my ground.

"Honey, everyone thinks their principal is evil, and besides, he's single. At my age, that's really all that matters."

I walked over to her and gave her a big hug. "Wrong Mom,

you deserve the best. You deserve to be as picky as you want."
We hugged a little tighter before pulling back. "And, you know,
Mr. Flannigan's single too," I said trying to hide my smirk
because we both knew how awkward and creepy the science
teacher was.

She sniffed and wiped an eyeliner-filled tear away. "Okay,
yeah, there might be a few other things that matter too."

I opened the door for her to leave first, slung my backpack
over one shoulder, and followed after her into the bright
morning light. "Are you sure we can't play hooky today? We
could binge watch that last season of *Buffy*."

She ushered me out of the way and locked the front door,
but she paused for a second as if she was actually considering
it. "No honey, I can't afford to miss a day of work, and you
can't afford to miss school."

We made our way to the car, and I mulled over what she
said and how she said it. "Wait...did you just call me dumb?" I
asked across the hood of the little two-door Pontiac.

"Of course not, honey, you're brilliant, you know that." She
opened her door and started stuffing her purse, jacket, and
other unnecessary junk into the back seat. "Just saying, if you
don't go to school, you'll probably start doing drugs, join a
gang, get shot in the street, and die in a gutter."

"Now who's being overdramatic?" I said with my door open
and only one foot in the car.

"Just giving you a taste of your own medicine," she stuck
out her tongue and then plopped down and turned over the
engine. I stood there staring at the caricature of Jesus on the
side of the mug right in front of me. "C'mon honey, what are
you waiting for?"

"Mom?" I asked suggestively, "did you forget something?"

She looked around inside the car quickly but no light bulbs
went off. "No, I don't think so."

"Pretty sure you did. You forgot about Jesus."

She was confused for all of two seconds before using his
name in vain followed by, "My coffee!" Instead of getting out
of the car and grabbing the cup like a normal person might,

14

she just blindly reached up and tried to grab it. I saw it coming, but there wasn't a thing I could do to stop it. The knife of her hand found the side of the mug and knocked it backward. Coffee spilled out across the roof, and the mug toppled over a few times before the handle stopped it from falling off. She pulled her hand back in through the window and got out to see the damage saying "Oh shoot!" over and over again. I couldn't help but laugh at her. "This isn't funny, Liam!" and her whiny voice made me laugh even harder.

"Wow! I finally see where I get it."

CHAPTER TWO: PREPARE NOW, WING IT LATER

I could've easily flown to the American fracture in a day, but as I said before, there was no rush. I had a lot of sick humans to do research on, but that got boring if I stayed at it too long, so I also wanted to make sure to cross off some of my to-do list before I left for Earth. Sure, I'd probably come back every once in a while, but the ultimate goal was to make the move as permanent as possible.

First order of business was to see my kids before leaving. I only have ten children, and that might sound like a lot to you, but when you remember just how old I am, and consider the fact that the number of nieces and nephews I have is well into six figures, it's not very many at all. Now, don't get me wrong, I don't regret having children, well…except for maybe Stacy, I think I would've been fine if she had never been conceived, but besides that, I love my kids, it just got too weird for me to keep having offspring. See, as a fallen angel, my romantic options are limited to the souls of the damned, or my three sisters that Fell. I never hooked up with a fellow angel, though, not because of the reason you think – it's not taboo for us, it's more like the Greek/Roman Gods. We're not even blood relatives, because… you know, we don't have blood, so yeah, even if Trini wasn't a crazy little nutcase, or Aida had anything remotely close to a personality and I had done anything with them, you'd have no place to judge me. My third sister, well, Lucy's a little too powerful for me to even think about getting close to. My hands instinctually get protective just talking about it, so let's get back on track, shall we?

I still remember when I found out I'd be a father for the first time. A few of my brothers had already had kids, so I knew what I was in for and it frightened the hell out of me, no pun intended. Going back to the Greek/Roman God metaphor, in the same way their children are crazy monsters like three-headed dogs or one-eyed giants, it's not very unlike the offspring of a fallen angel and damned human soul. You humans know these children as demons, and I've been doing my best not to contribute to their rising numbers, but…well, accidents happen.

Monsters or not, though, they're my children, so I did my best to raise them right, teach them right from wrong, and all that. Of course, my youngest was born around a hundred years ago, so they all predate that *everyone's special, you tried your best and that's great, here's a trophy!* crap that I've been seeing lately. Now, do I sometimes wonder what my relationship would be like with my kids if I had coddled them more? Yes, but I just remind myself that would only be in my interest. All ten of my kids are strong, independent members of society, and I'm proud of that. They don't really talk to me much, but that's just because I was a bad father in other aspects.

Four of my kids lived in the city of Abaddon, so that was my first stop. I had already been looking for potential hosts for about a week by the time I headed for the city. My favorite at the time, a 24-year old biker that had clipped a semi on Hwy. 550, had just died. He even had the nerve to go to Heaven, so I couldn't so much as yell at him for it. He was the fourth potential I had really liked only to watch die before I could take advan…I mean, before I could help them.

With the biker off the table, I decided to take another break from host hunting and with my head off the screen, I was able to enjoy the sights of Abaddon, for what they're worth. It might be the finest city in Hell, but it's still Hell. Dark rock bricks frosted together made up the majority of the blocky architecture and the buildings all blended together like an artist's worst nightmare. As I approached from the northern sky, I could see the entirety of the sprawling metropolis – skyscrapers huddled together at the center of the city only to grow shorter and further apart in an outward ring, gradual at first, but after a few dozen miles it turned to a slum of rock piles barely worthy of being called homes.

I landed outside the city limits and walked the rest of the way in passing one of the aforementioned rock piles to see swarms of tiny demons hovering around and slithering through the cracks. It looked like a bustling coral reef in one of Earth's oceans, only significantly more disturbing. Their size told me all I needed to know, they were weak beings, the offspring of demons and the damned over many generations; whatever angelic power conceived their ancestors had been diluted almost to the point of nonexistence. I stomped my foot as I turned past them, and they fearfully retreated into the safety of their home. If they were fish in a reef, that made me like an army of great white sharks with frickin' laser beams. Even hidden in the rocks, I could've destroyed them all, but I was just messing around with them, all in good fun.

I received a lot of surprised glances walking through the slums, but by the time I reached the city center there was enough of a crowd for me to blend in. I reached a fork and had to decide who to visit first. I settled on the conclusion that my second to youngest would be the easiest to find, so I took the right and headed to his mother's house. I already knew she'd be pissed to see me, but I was used to that. I reached her place and knocked with a big grin, just to piss her off that little bit extra. She opened the door and as soon as her eyes met mine, her expression soured just as I knew it would. It made my smile bigger.

"Oh, great, it's *you*," she snarled in her thick Serbian accent. "Behemoth not here."

"Nice to see you, too, Nina. And yeah, I figured. He is forty feet tall after all, kinda hard to miss. Know where he is?" Behemoth got his name as you might expect, he was fourteen-and-a-half feet tall when he was born and only grew from there, and as I'm sure you could imagine, any woman that gave birth to something like that might not be too fond of the guy responsible for putting her through it.

"He run off with she-devil sister. Say they would start new life on Earth." I gave her a blank look indicating her answer was too vague for me to know who she meant. "Ugh, Shiva." she clarified with a heavy roll of her eyes. "Her mother here, too, suggest you run off before she see you."

Shiva, one of my daughters, may have been literally made out of ice, but she got that from her figurative ice queen of a mother, Vladimira. Back when I met her I wasn't the light-hearted sarcastic bastard I am today, but I realized my mistake a few decades too late. While Nina wasn't too far off from that same description, I actually liked annoying Nina, her reactions were entertaining to me at this point, but being on Vladimira's bad side was no laughing matter. "I'll leave, promise, but if you know where they were headed...?"

She snarled again. "Russia, all I know. Goodbye." And like that she slammed the door in my face.

I stood with my nose a millimeter from the door for a second in slight shock of hearing that two of my kids ran off to Earth without so much as a goodbye text. It was for things exactly like this that I bought them the new iPhone when it first came out down here in 2011.

I couldn't have been standing there for very long though, because I heard the sharp Slavic cackle that is Vladimira's voice through the door say, "Who was that?" and that was all I needed to turn and run until I was at a safe distance.

I stopped running when I reached the center building at the city's heart, home to hundreds of thousands of demons, damned, and fallen angels alike. I looked up at the towering structure and found the window belonging to my second child, eldest of my sons, Fenrir. I decided to text him before barging in, but when there was no reply and I grew impatient, I flew straight up anyway.

As you meet more of my kids, you'll come to realize I wasn't the most original dad, because yes, I named my boy Fenrisúlfr because when he popped out he had a full coat of black fur, snout, tail and paws just like the Norse wolf his mother's people told stories about, give or take a few opposable dew claws. In hindsight, I should've picked a different name, like Max or Lucky, because the one I gave him went straight to his head. Over the course of his life, he's made it his mission to fully embody the Fenrir of legend, going so far at times that he's actually started believing he *is* the mythological beast and that he'll bring about Ragnarok and end the world. I have to occasionally remind him that the "real" Fenrir dies during that apocalyptic myth, but with the fractures big enough for him to cross, I worry what he'll do with his misguided fantasies. I found myself hoping he was actually going to be at home and not off with his two siblings.

"I already told you," I heard through the window in my son's growly voice mere moments before I could get a visual. "You can count on me, one hundred percent, you have my full support whenever you decide to move forward on this." I stayed low outside the window and peeked just enough to see my son pacing through his room with a phone to his pointed ear.

He was on the phone, which made me a little less upset that he didn't text me back, so I decided to wait for him to hang up.

"No, don't worry about me, I know this is a big undertaking, I wouldn't expect you to jump the gun on anything. You just focus on getting everything set up, laid out, and ready for the next step, this isn't something we should rush into." Despite his throaty grumble, Fenrir had a very professional speaking tone. It was a nice sight to see as his father and gave me hope that his 'I am a God' phase might be over. Perhaps focusing on his business could keep him from you know, trying to kick off an apocalypse, or doing drugs, you know, whatever the kids are into these days.

"All right, I've gotta run. No, thank you." I kind of wondered who he was talking to, if it was anyone I might know, but I couldn't hear anything from the other end. "What?" Fenrir looked puzzled at the phone. "Oh no, that was just a text from dad, it was nothing."

Not going to lie, that got me back to being upset.

"I guess he's in the city for a bit, I'll probably just text him back tonight, say I was too busy or something like that. Usually works."

Sad thing was, it did always work now that I was thinking back. "Why that little piece of dog sh—" I whispered under my breath until my phone buzzed and bleeped the default text tone from my pocket. I covered my phone as quick as I could and ducked down, but Fenrir must've heard it.

"What the?" he said perplexed. "Oh, no, not you. I'll call you later, we'll do lunch." I heard the padded footsteps approach the window slowly with the *click-click* of his claws like an offbeat metronome. Since he clearly didn't want to see me today, I decided to respect his wish, so, yet again, I turned tail (figuratively) and flew out of there at top speed.

I looked back up to see the small figure in the window walk up, look around, and leave none the wiser.

"Now, let's see what was so important," I said quietly to myself as I fished out my phone to check my message. It was a response from my youngest, the fourth and last of my children living in Abaddon. He was running some errands nearby and said I could join him if I wanted to, so I did. One loud *whoosh,* and I was standing next to him. "Steve!"

"Jesus!" he exclaimed, dropping a bag of groceries from the start I had given him.

"Not even close. It's me, your dad," I said, laughing at my own dad-joke.

Steve wobbled a bit, as he bent down to retrieve his belongings. As far as demons are concerned, he looked more human than most, but he was very thin and frail; if all of my children were a litter, he was undoubtedly the runt. It took him a while to chase down everything that had rolled away, but before long he had everything together again and hanging from his three fingered hands. "You made good time," he said sarcastically.

I had a feeling he was madder about not helping him pick up his stuff than he was for making him drop it in the first place, so I stretched out a helping hand. Better late than never, right? "Like me to carry that for you?"

He was reluctant at first, but his arms were already shaking from the load so he handed it over. "I've just got one more stop before heading home."

He led the way, and we got started with the awkward small talk. After a few long silences, we got to talking about family, and since he had more contact with his siblings than I did, he carried most of that conversation. He told me more about

Behemoth and Shiva's Russia trip, how Leonard and Shax were adjusting after their move to Gomorrah, and that Fenrir had been blowing him off a lot lately.

"Yeah, don't worry, you're not alone on that one," I said and followed it up with the majority of the story, just leaving out the part about eavesdropping and running away. That made the story a lot shorter and less exciting than I realized it would be, so I ended up looking kind of stupid. "Yeah, um, I guess you had to be there."

We were already on our way back to Steve's house, and I hoped we could wrap up before getting there. "So, what brings you here, Dad? You don't exactly reach out to us much anymore." His tone hit me with a tinge of guilt.

"Well, I'm thinking of moving up north," I pointed up to the shimmering fractures overhead. "I hear it's warmer," I joked, trying to lighten the mood back to comfortable.

"Yeah, I guess. I made a few trips last year, but I don't know, it really wasn't for me." He sank his head and started lightly kicking a rock along our path. "But that's just me, I'm sure you'll enjoy it." I wasn't sure what to say back, so we just walked a little further. "Did um, do you know what you'll do for a host yet?"

"Your Uncle Zak asked me that. I'm still not totally sure, but I've still got some time."

"Shiva said Russia's real easy, a lot of remote areas to nab people."

"It's not that easy for me; I need permission to take a host," I explained. "I did find one potential in Kazakhstan though."

"Oh, right, I think I knew that, sorry. What makes you think they'll, you know, let you?"

I could see his house, so I tried to make it short. "Well, she just got diagnosed with breast cancer, she's going to try taking the treatment, but her doctor's an idiot, it's only gonna do more harm than good. The part I'm not too sure of is…well, she's a sort of Nihilist, she doesn't believe in anything after death, so I'll have to deliver that news softly, but at least she won't have any prejudice against me at first. I don't know, it's the best I've got so far." We were almost to the front of the house so I slowed my pace. "I'd really like to start in America, though; I'm meeting Uncle Zak there actually, guess I should get going."

"Oh, sure you don't want to come inside for a bit?" He reached for the door, and I started creeping away, but the door parted of its own fruition, and if I didn't know any better, I would've sworn an angel was on the other side. "You're late young man," she said to her son. She spotted me and her face lit up. "But with good reason I see. Good to see you, Zeke."

Hearing her say my name made my knees weak now just as much as it had the first time a century ago. I cleared my throat while also trying to remain cool. I don't think it worked, but it could've been worse. "Same, you, um, you look good, Dorothy." Her long straight brunette hair fell past her slender shoulders like strands of silk. Her milky white skin was smooth and spotless like porcelain, and she wore a shimmering red flapper dress with black boots that zipped all the way up to her knees.

Steve took the bag from my hand, and that gave me enough of a jolt to stop staring. He walked inside past his mother, and she turned back to me, placing her elbow against the door frame and leaning into it. "Would you like to stay for dinner?" her long eyelashes fluttered with each blink, as they concealed her striking hazel eyes, teasing me to lose myself in them only to have them taken away in short intervals.

The truth was yes, a million times yes, but I had to be strong. A hundred years was a long time, and we had a lot of history, complicated history. Usually, Zak was the one to smack me in the head and convince me going back was more harm than good, and the times I dismissed his warnings, he always turned out to be right. For decades, I lied to myself to believe the good outweighed the heartbreaks, but not this time. I was about to move across plains of existence, about to start a whole new life. With that new life, I wanted to start it off right, to cut out all my bad old habits and become the me I've always wanted to be. I was going to finally have some self-respect for myself. I didn't need her anymore, I was beyond that.

"It's getting late," she said, ending with a seductive smile that drew my gaze down to her bright ruby lips. "Come on, stay." Her pearl white teeth shone brighter than anything in this dark cold world, and when they reached over the bottom lip and bit down ever so gently, I lost every ounce of willpower I had managed to cling onto until that point.

"Okay," I said with a smile and was repaid tenfold with one back. I walked inside and felt her brush against me as I passed. It sent shivers throughout my body. I mean, technically I haven't started my new life yet. It could work out better this time, what's the harm after all? I mean, it's just dinner, it doesn't have to mean anything. Even though I'm pretty sure it does... Aw crap, what did I just do?

* * *

The final bell of the day rang, and as I rose from the seat, my spirits did as well. I slung one of my backpack straps as I bolted for the door but was halted by the cold shrill call of Ms. Linder: "Mr. Cole." Despite being the only Cole in that class, I still found myself hoping that when I turned around she would be speaking to anyone else. Maybe she was on the phone with a Mr. Cole. I turned and to my dismay, her death glare was locked on me and she curled her wrinkled index finger slowly gesturing. "A moment please."

As all the happy faces passed me on their way to freedom, I drooped my head, let my arms go limp, and Charlie Brown walked my way over to Ms. Linder's desk. The door clicked, marking the start of an uncomfortable silence. She had her arms crossed and the same pursed expression as if waiting for me to speak first, but it was kind of hard to tell. Her thinning gray hair was pulled so far back and tied into a bun so tight it could very well be that the skin of her face couldn't look any other way. I didn't know why she had called me to stay behind this time, so I played it safe with a simple, "Yes?"

"Why are you here, Mr. Cole?" she asked in a tone of disgust.

J. A. Reed

A dozen smart-ass retorts crossed my mind, but I'd gone down that road before; it only leads to detention, pissed off teachers, lectures about respecting thine elders, and all other sorts of hassle that's not worth a momentary giggle, so I bit my tongue on those. Unfortunately, once I started thinking of a serious answer, I realized I had no clue what she meant by her question. "Um, what do you mean?"

She sighed in annoyance and fished a sheet of paper from her desk drawer. She slammed it down, and I noticed it was my test from the previous day with a nice big red cliché 'F' at the top next to my chicken scratched name. It wasn't my first F in math, but I always managed to balance it up to a passing D eventually, so I wasn't super concerned about it.

"I…I'll do better on the next one, I promise," I said eagerly hoping that could be the end of it since I had cross-country practice to get to.

"Why didn't you do better on this one, Mr. Cole?" She flipped the page over to the back and pointed to two large red strikethroughs at the bottom. "You didn't even attempt the extra credit questions, even one of them could've turned this F into a D. So I'll ask you again. Why are you here?"

I picked up the paper and read the questions since the day of the test I hadn't bothered. I actually knew the second one off the top of my head, and the first one, with some time and a calculator, I probably could've gotten at least half credit. I tossed it back onto the teacher's desk and started feeling really upset. "What do you mean? Why am I here? Like, in school? Because I have to be, I'm only seventeen, it's not like I have a choice!"

I half expected her to escalate the situation and raise her voice back at me, but instead it was like she ignored my outburst. "How are things at home? I notice you're wearing mismatched shoes today."

I was severely taken aback by that for two pretty big reasons: first, my home life was great, and to think anything to the contrary was just ridiculous, but secondly, and exponentially more shocking, it almost sounded like she cared about me, you know, like…as a person. Before that moment, I always assumed she was some kind of demon in human form risen from Hell to torture children and, I don't know, kill puppies or something equally evil, but maybe I was wrong about her.

Once the initial shock wore off, I relearned how to string words into coherent sentences. "What? Oh, no, it's nothing like that. My stupid dog has been eating my shoes. I keep trying to wean him over to homework, but darn it, hasn't worked yet." I laughed trying to lighten the mood, but I got nothing from her, not even a twitch in the corner of her mouth, so I faded back to uncomfortable silence and rubbed the back of my neck nervously. "But seriously, everything's great at home, no issue there, just…Math isn't my strong suit."

Ms. Linder exhaled slowly and snatched my test back off the cluttered desktop and handed it out to me. "Is that really what you believe, Mr. Cole?" I took the paper and nodded unsurely. "You have potential Mr. Cole, I can see that much, it's only a matter of applying yourself. Seventeen or not, no one is forcing you to be here, you do have a choice. Every day you choose to stay in school, you chose not to answer the extra credit and fail that test, and even just now, you chose to turn around and stay after class. So, one last time, why are you here?"

"Um, because I chose to be here?" I asked awkwardly.

"Exactly, everything you do is your own choice. Fear of reprisal may help influence those choices, but the choice is still there for you to make, try remembering that next time you think you 'have' to do something, or if you think you can't." She reached back into her desk drawer and pulled out a trifold pamphlet with cheaply animated characters around the writing. "And if you like, you can choose to take this with you. It's a hotline for teens, completely anonymous of course."

I honestly hadn't expected her to turn back around to that notion, but since it wasn't completely out of left field this time, my reaction differed greatly. I tried to stifle my laugh, but a little bit squeaked out. I cleared it from my throat and took the pamphlet. "Thanks, Ms. Linder, I'll hang on to it, just in case. And if it's all right with you, I really need to…I mean, 'choose to' go to practice now." I took a few slow backward steps and she finally laxed her expression.

"Of course, you're free to go. Take care of yourself."

I smiled, gave a lazy salute with the pamphlet, and left as quickly as I could walk. Once I was into the hall, I practically sprinted across campus to the locker rooms since I was already running late. I reached for the handle, but the door swung open before my fingers could find the metal bar.

"Well, well, well, look who decided to grace us with his presence." Jay Metzger, the cross-country team captain, and all around smug, self-centered narcissist, strutted out already dressed in his running clothes. He certainly had a runner's build, but even if he didn't look the part, it was impossible to carry a conversation with him for more than five minutes without him bragging about his run times.

"Yeah, sorry about being late, I tried to get that door for you, I know how much effort that is for you, is it getting sore yet?" I asked sarcastically gesturing at his pencil thin arms. I had learned last year that he's incredibly self-conscious about how thin his arms are, and ever since, I've found life a lot more enjoyable.

His nostrils flared as he probably tried to think of a witty comeback, but that had never been his area of expertise. "Not as sore as your ass is going to be if Coach Bassett catches you changing this late." He looked at his watch and smirked. "Hopefully you can change faster than you run, of course that's not saying much for you." I rolled my eyes at him and pulled the door open, but he wasn't finished with me "Four and a half minutes, Cole, that's like what, a mile run, well, for me anyway. Sounds almost easy when I put it that way." He chuckled to himself, and I forced my way past him. I guess what I said earlier about five minutes of conversation with him was giving him way too much credit.

I took more time trying to open my locker than I did actually getting changed, but only because I rushed and had to put in my lock combo three times before getting it to work. I was a little late to the track, but Coaches Bassett and Meyers didn't show up until right after me, so my rear end was saved. Jay looked devastated when he realized I hadn't been caught and my best friend Greg noticed it too. He stuck out his fist for me to bump it with mine as we lined up for warm-ups. "Poor Metzger," Greg whispered over his shoulder to me, "but at least he's not a rat. I guess that's something,"

"Quezada! Shut your trap!" Coach Bassett shouted, and Greg turned white, which couldn't have been easy for his caramel complexion. He pinched his lips together with his fingers and took a few steps away from me until Coach seemed happy with the distance. He resumed blowing his whistle until he was satisfied we were all in place, and then a few extra times for no reason.

Assistant Coach Meyers took over from there and led us through stretches and warm-ups. In her Biology class, she was always timid and quiet, but out here on the track, she could flip a switch and become a monster. Her command voice was Earth-shattering, and since she worked with the boy's team, if she ever passed one of us on a distance run she would mock their masculinity.

She turned us back over to Coach Bassett, who returned to abusing his whistle far more than necessary. Coach Bassett was well aged but clearly past his prime. His salt and pepper hair had receded a long time ago, but unlike Mr. Smith the basketball coach, he didn't try to comb it over and just embraced it. He wore his white embroidered polo tucked into khakis just like he did every day, and given the grass stain on his knee, they were still the same pair he'd been wearing since Monday. His thick black belt was doing its best to keep his gut in, but over the years the belt had continued to give up more and more ground. Luckily for our team, despite his current physique, he was an amazing coach; he definitely knew what he was doing, and our team's record attested to that. "Listen up, ladies! It's Friday, you know what that means?!"

"Fartleks," the team mumbled together with little enthusiasm, well, except Jay, he shouted it gleefully.

"Oh, c'mon, what was that?! Try it again! What does that

mean?!"

"FARTLEKS!" we repeated with feeling, as fake as it might be.

"That's right, Fartlek Friday! Now line up, we don't have all day!" We moved as a group over to the track's starting line, but not quickly enough in his eyes. "C'mon ladies! Hustle! The longer you take, the longer you'll run!" That put some hop in our steps, and we were lined up within seconds. He looked disappointed. "You guys are no fun. Okay, minute sprint in 3, 2, 1…" He blew his whistle loud and held it until he ran out of breath.

"C'mon! Push!" Coach Meyer shouted from the back. "I'm joggin' here! Don't make me pass you!"

After the minute, the whistle blew again, "Thirty-second walk! Keep that blood flowing!" It was still early so there wasn't much need to catch our breaths, but after a few more sprints, those thirty seconds started feeling really damn short. "Two-minute jog's next! You're halfway there!"

He had already told us we were halfway done three times at this point; I couldn't tell if he was doing it to be funny, or what, but he always liked to do that.

We did three more cycles of minute sprint, half-minute walk, and two-minute jogs before he changed it up, "Two left! Push yourself!" We did the two rounds when he repeated that we had only two left. A lot of groaning answered him back, and he didn't much care for that, "Oh, I'm sorry, you want more?! All right, two more!" Three rounds later we were back to, "Two left!" and after another three he finally called, "Last one!" and meant it.

The team stumbled over to the bleachers and guzzled down gallons of water collectively. Jay was strutting around telling everyone how easy the whole thing was and laughing at some of the slower guys with his buddies. I decided to ignore it since engaging them was all they really wanted and instead went to check on Greg, who was pacing a little circle behind the bleachers with his hands on his head. "Hey, hangin' in there?"

He stopped walking when he faced me again and stumbled a

little. His long straight hair had been in a standard, albeit outdated, bowl cut before practice, but now it was a wet matted mop dripping sweat down his face. "I might…die," he said, stopping to wheeze halfway through.

I laughed and patted him on the shoulder, "I think you'll make it. C'mon, let's go." We made our way back to the locker rooms to shower, but conversation was a bit light for the first few minutes. Once Greg was able to speak full sentences without gasping for air, we were back to our usual selves talking about shows we watched, games that were coming out, whether a single pit bull could take on a hundred vicious Chihuahuas, you know, normal best friend stuff. It wasn't until we were sitting outside the parking lot waiting for our rides that the conversation got real.

"Dude, I think I'm finally done with my college essay, mind if I send it to you for a look over?" Greg asked with a begging inclination.

"Sure, but you know I'm only getting a B in English."

"Better than my C, and I've read, reread, rewritten, re-reread, and re-rewritten that thing so many times it's just a blob of words to me at this point. I need someone to make sure it's at least somewhat coherent."

I stuck out my fist, "No problem, I got you."

Greg smiled and tapped his knuckles to mine. "If you want me to look over yours, too, you can send it whenever." I unconsciously got defensive because I was nowhere near thinking about starting a college essay, even though applications were going to be due soon. "Liam?" Greg asked accusingly.

I tried to avoid eye contact and stall as best I could for a bit. "Um…Yeah?"

"You have started working on an essay, right?" he asked knowing full well what my answer would be. I resumed my attempted avoidance without success. "Liam, c'mon, you have to get started on that now. This is not the kinda thing you cram the night before it's due. Trust me, I've been working on mine over a month."

"Jesus! A month?!" I've never worked more than two days

on any one project, granted most of that crammed work was subpar, but still, a whole month on a single paper? That was absurd, no wonder I had been putting it off; I knew there was a good reason...

Greg was speechless for a few minutes until we spotted his brother's car turning into the parking lot to pick him up. "Look, I'll send you mine when I get home, that way you can at least have a format to work from."

"All right," I said with little energy.

When his brother pulled up, Greg loaded his bag into the back seat over a triple layer of fast food trash and water bottles of varying emptiness. "I'm serious, Liam. I'm going to hold you to this, I want a rough draft from you by the end of the month."

"Yeah, okay, Mr. Quezada," I said mockingly, "I guess I missed the part where you got your teaching degree."

He started to crack a smile but stopped himself. "It's for your own good, I know you won't do anything on your own." He opened the car door and climbed in but hesitated closing it behind him. "I'm afraid to ask, but...do you even know what schools you're trying for?"

I walked over and closed his door for him. "See you on Monday, buddy!" I shouted so he'd hear me through the window. His brother took off on that cue, but I was able to lip read a few choice words before he was gone.

Mom didn't pick me up for another ten minutes, so I had plenty of time to dwell on the topic of college. I had looked up a few colleges last summer, but it had all been so overwhelming. I wasn't very good in school as it was, the idea of going through four more years of that was not appealing in the slightest, and everyone said college was significantly more difficult than high school, so any remnants of desire I might've had vanished when I heard that. Not to mention, in high school you just get assigned the classes you need, and that's it. In college, you have to pick a major, which classes to take, the schedule can be all over the place, it just seemed so difficult.

I still remember as far back as middle school, teachers were pressuring us to think about college and what we would want to do for the rest of our lives. I don't know what I want to do next weekend let alone the rest of my life; there's too much responsibility in that. I know I want to run, that's about it, and getting a scholarship would be pretty easy if that's what I wanted, but anything past that terrified me. My best bet would be to just find the nearest college and start with general classes, figure it out from there.

When mom was turning to leave the parking lot she asked me how school and practice was, but all I said was "Fine." I didn't really want to think on the college subject anymore, and I knew that if I said anything I'd be stuck on that topic with her for the rest of the day; it was better to just leave that conversation to the realm of the unspoken.

CHAPTER THREE: A DEATH IN THE FAMILY

Two damn weeks, that's how long it took me to leave that wretched house again. Dorothy had gone and roped me into her web of false hope and deceptive teasing yet again, and all I could do was beat myself up for knowingly walking into it for the hundredth time, give or take.

"Zeke! Wait!" she cried after me before I could fly away.

I wanted to just take off anyway and leave that house behind not just physically but emotionally as well, yet even in that lowest of moments where I was entirely aware of the full extent of how unhealthy our relationship was I still couldn't ignore her pull over me. "Dot, I can't…" I trailed off, but I don't think there was any one ending to that sentence, nothing that could cover everything.

"I know, I'm sorry," she uttered softly, exactly as she had the hundred times before. "Maybe you're right, we can't keep doing this. Maybe we should go back to being just friends?"

I saw that question coming two weeks ago, as soon as I was stupid enough to walk into that house, I knew this moment was coming, it had only been a matter of postponing the inevitable as much as possible; although, two weeks was pretty standard. Sadly, there was no right answer to this, because I've tried it all. If I say yes, then she's happy to not lose me, and I'm miserable until we start talking again, which leads to me trying to ignore my feelings until my natural charm wins her back, and the cycle starts over again. If I say no, she gets upset, I feel good about myself for letting her go, a few months or years go by and I start missing her more and more, then one day we run into each other or something like that, the sparks fly again, I tell myself it'll be different this time, and BAM, back to square one. I had to find a way to break this destructive pattern. "Go back? We were never friends."

She was noticeably caught off guard by that one and it looked like it hurt her a little. "W-what do you mean?"

This was going to be my only chance to get it off my chest, so I tried to choose my words carefully. "I mean that from the first moment I met you all the way to this very second, I've never felt anything less than crazy about you. It never mattered how much you hated me or how many times I said I hated you, my feelings for you never diminished. I wouldn't be able to be just friends with you even if I tried. Just like how I can't seem to let you go, as much as I know I have to." She was speechless, and I was hesitating to say the words I knew had to follow because saying them out loud would be going past the point of no return and it terrified me. "So, you can't ask me to be friends, because I can't do that. If you want me back, you can ask me that. If you want to leave me on the back burner so you can get me back whenever you feel like it, you can ask that, too, but you can't ask me to be friends. I should be asking you…" Another hesitation came because despite being in uncharted territory for the first time in a hundred years, I still knew exactly how this was going to end, and it wasn't what I wanted; perhaps it was what I needed though. "…I need to ask you to let me go. That's the only way this works, you have a hold over me that I can't break from my end, but if you let go, we can both move on. So please, I'm begging you, just let me go and never come back."

She wiped a mascara filled tear off her cheek, "But I don't want to lose you."

"But you don't want me either."

A few more black droplets slid down to her chin, and she took a step backward. "I'm sorry." With nothing else, she turned and walked back into the house, closing the door behind her. I wanted to feel good, I had finally confronted the situation honestly, laid it all out to bare, and stopped denying what was wrong, but it was still painful.

"I'm done with this place." I took off and flew as fast as my burnt wings would let me straight for the American fracture.

With all of Hell zooming by beneath me, I began to calm down little by little. Dozens of cities and hundreds of towns passed, and the vastness of my infinite surroundings humbled me. There was so much I hadn't experienced in my life, and even though I had an eternity left, I knew I would still never do

J. A. Reed

34

everything there was to do. I had wasted so much time repeating mistakes when I could've been out there making new ones.

The fracture came into view over the horizon and another realization came to me – damned souls couldn't cross back up to Earth, so once I was there, it would be physically impossible to be with Dorothy. I reached the center of the fracture within a few minutes and stopped at its event horizon. This was it, it had been a while now since Enochian's could fit through, so there was a chance for me now. I only had the potential host in Kazakhstan at the moment, but I didn't care; I was ready to put Hell in my rearview mirror.

"Ugh...Humpf...Ugh, c'mon, you can...Hnnnng...do this Zeke, c'mon!" I was able to get my arm through the fracture, but after that, it was like trying to squeeze through a doggie door. I decided to take the blessing in disguise and use the extra time to find a new host a little closer to this fracture, so I freefell back down to the surface and resumed my research.

A few days later, Zak showed up just like he promised he would. He had been having success in finding hosts at hospitals, about two out of every three since he last saw me. He walked me through each one since I had been too busy to keep an eye on him. When he asked what I had been doing the whole time, I tried to leave out the little two-week blunder, but I was a bad liar and once he knew I was hiding he pressed the issue until I cracked. "You stupid idiot!"

"I know, but it's over this time, like, for real this time," I said confidently when any of the past times I would've said the same thing, except I would've been lying.

I filled him in on the way I ended things and he seemed to agree it was a good call, but he remained reserved, unsure if it was enough. "Well, you're still an idiot," he said, ending the subject. "Any promising leads though? Or did you completely waste the past few weeks?"

Glad to be off the subject of Dorothy and even more so that I did indeed have some potentials, I began filling him in on my findings over the past days. "Yes, I actually did stuff, here, look!" I quickly pulled up a screen of Albuquerque's Presbyterian Hospital. "So, I've been watching patients as they come in. There's quite a few good ones, but so far I think my favorite is this one." I zoomed in through the wall to a young seventeen-year-old boy asleep in his bed. He was lean, but a little on the slender side, definitely a runner's build. The covers made it difficult to see what plagued him, but the large bruise under his chin and stitched up forehead ruled out internal disease. "He just came in yesterday, crazy story too, he was..."

An ear-shattering wail cut me short, and both Zak and I flinched in panic. "What the...?" Zak asked, but he cut himself short looking up toward the source of the cry. A small light arced across the sky and continued to scream in the worst kind of agony. I squinted to make out who it was. "Gavin?"

"Gavreel?" Zak asked, recognizing the nickname but not quite believing it to be true. "What's he doing back here? He hasn't left Earth in years." Once Zak confirmed it was Gavin with his own two eyes, he looked at me and mirrored the same look of confusion. The sound faded, and we snapped our heads back up to see our younger brother disappearing from sight. Without a word we both took flight and charged after him to investigate.

As we chased the trail of heartbreak, I racked my brain trying to think of what could possibly be causing such a thing. Gavin had been the first of us to cross over to Earth, and in all that time he'd only come back three times.

"What do you think happened?" Zak asked, sounding worried about any potential answer. He had probably been having just as much trouble thinking of anything as I had. Luckily, before I could answer, Gavin turned downward and landed at the front door of an all too familiar house. "Uh-oh," Zak said ominously over the newfound silence. We were both stopped in midair debating whether or not we should go down there. The medium-sized building was the only speck of civilization for miles around. Even from our vantage point a mile off the ground, we could barely see the top of Gomorrah over the horizon. "Think we should go down there?"

J. A. Reed

36

If it had been purely for curiosity, I would've run for my life and acted like I hadn't seen a thing, but whatever was happening, it had to be big. "Yeah, Gavin wouldn't come back to Hell for no reason. He certainly wouldn't run straight to Lucy either."

Zak swallowed a large gulp of air before following me down to the house. We could hear Gavin sobbing quietly through the door as we stepped onto the front porch. I lifted my knuckles slowly and reached out to the cold stone door, but before they found their target the door pulled away and in its place stood the Archangel Ramiel.

He stood there staring blankly at us, so my default setting kicked in, "Hey, if it isn't the Almighty Ram!" My strange sense of humor didn't usually get any rise out of my more stuck up siblings, and Ram was no different. "So, Zak and I were just in the neighborhood." I gestured out behind me and remembered too late that there was no neighborhood, not even close. "Um, and we just thought we'd pop in, see how you and Lucy were doing, it's been like what, two, three thousand years?"

Ram turned to look behind him, and with him partially out of the doorway I could see Gavin crying in Lucy's arms in the other room. I suddenly felt bad for trying to joke around, this clearly wasn't the time. Ram turned back, blocking the view inside again. "If you come inside, you will leave that absurd attitude at the door. Do you understand?" he asked threateningly.

There was no doubt he could follow through making me pay if I didn't do what he wished, so I kicked it into serious mode because my life literally depended on it. I lowered my head in remorse and nodded.

Satisfied, he stepped out of the way again and gestured for us to come inside but stopped Zak with a gentle hand on his shoulder. "Zadkiel, if you wouldn't mind?"

Zak was understandably nervous, it wasn't everyday an Archangel asked you a favor. "Um…Of course, w-who would you like me to contact?"

"All of them."

"All of them? But…Well…We all haven't…" Zak stuttered in shock and disbelief. As the only fallen Enochian, Zak was the only one that could communicate with our brothers and sisters over such a great distance, but he hardly ever needed to use that particular talent, and he had certainly never used it to contact all of them before.

"Thank you kindly, Zadkiel," Ram said as if Zak hadn't protested at all. "We'll wait for them to arrive before filling you in on all the details." He finally turned back to me and looked down his nose. "Try not to touch anything if you can help it." At first, I wanted to be all 'Why are you looking at me when you say that?' but then I saw all the cool stuff they had in their house, and it made perfect sense. Zak stepped outside to contact the others, giving me ample time to look around.

Lining the walls of the entrance hall were several exquisite paintings and sculptures of all different eras. I had never seen any of them before, but each one had a familiar style to it, and upon closer look, signatures belonging to those familiar artists could be seen in the lower corner of each masterpiece. I'll spare dropping any names though, sometimes it's better not knowing if your favorite painter ended up down here.

When we entered the main living area, Zak was still looking completely lost after what I can only imagine were the strangest series of conversations in his life, but regardless he opened his arms for Gavin and gave him a big hug. Lucy, now with a small reprieve, looked to me. "Ezekiel," she said in greeting.

"Lucy. How many times do I have to tell you? Call me Zeke."

"How many times do I have to tell you to call me Lucifer?" she said with only a hint of a smile.

"Fair enough." I opened up and gave her a short half hug. When we pulled back, I looked around. "So, what's going on that we really need to get the whole band back together?"

"Would you believe me if I said it was for a good reason?" she asked, leading the question with her quiet tone.

I looked at Gavin as he sobbed into Zak's shoulder and knew enough to answer, "No. No I wouldn't."

J. A. Reed

38

Lucy turned away and returned to Gavin's side. "You'll understand soon enough; for now, Gavreel and I will be in the back. Don't disturb us." She turned to Ram who was still waiting by the front door. "Come get us when they're all here."

Lucy took Gavin's shoulder and led him away, still sobbing and clutching something tight to his chest. I asked Zak about it, but he didn't know. Gavin had been clutching it since they came in and hadn't let it go even when Zak had hugged him.

The same moment their door closed to the back, the front door opened and the three Guardians, Aida, Razzmatazz, and Zoof (as I call them anyway) entered in a single file. We all greeted one another, and they asked us if we knew what this family meeting was all about. We were a little surprised they didn't already know but told them what we had seen and everything that happened when we arrived. A few minutes later two of the other Angels, Nate, and Satchel, came in together and we repeated the process. Tabby came in a full fifteen minutes after the previous group and started apologizing for taking so long.

The rest trickled in one at a time spaced out a few minutes apart. Trini started getting pissed within just a few minutes of arriving and nearly left a few times, but Ram wasn't having it. Megatron was the last to show up, but we were still waiting on Cass, another Angel, and Xaf, a Muse.

"Come now, Ramiel, must we wait any longer?" Razzmatazz asked impatiently.

"We wait for everyone Raziel; do not ask again," he snapped back. Ram might've been more powerful than Razzmatazz, but if Aida and Zoof had his back it would make for a pretty even playing field.

Satchel stood and slowly placed himself between the two. "All right, let's just all calm down for a second. Castiel and Xapham can't be too far behind. I'm sure they're right around the corner." His voice was shaking a little, though.

I decided to try my hand at helping. "Yes, Satchel's right. I'm—"

"My name is Sachiel!" he snapped at me. I hadn't seen him

in a few hundred years so I forgot how much my nickname annoyed him. I guess I wasn't doing a very good job at helping so far.

"Right, yes, sorry. But I do think he's partly right. Xaf's reliable, he'll be here as quickly as angel-ly possible, but Cass? I mean, we all know he's not exactly the biggest family man. So maybe we can compromise a bit. We wait for Xaf, but if Cass is late, we just start without him. Sound good?"

There was a lot of glancing around between one another with some light murmuring, but I generally got the idea they were all on board.

"There will be no need for that," Ram said over all the debate and opened the front door again to reveal Cass; his face clearly telegraphed his desire to be anywhere but here with us.

"All right, I'm here, can you stop annoying me now?" Cass growled at Zak as he entered past Ram. Zak half stood to defend that he had only done as he was told, but froze along with the rest of us because for the first time since we all arrived, Ram left the front door and headed past us toward the back.

"Wait, where's Xapham?" Trini asked as he brushed past her. "We have to wait for Xapham," she pleaded.

"Xapham isn't coming, Trinity," Lucy's voice said, as she re-entered the crowded room.

The glaring and murmuring resumed, only louder and worrisome this time around. I too was worried and confused, but it was only when I remembered Gavin's shattered state that the worst-case scenario became so utterly clear to me.

"The last time we were all in the same place at the same time, things didn't work out very well," Lucy said, walking through the center of our huddle.

"You mean when you lead us to war against Father and we all Fell because of it?" Cass asked with equal parts rage and sarcasm. "Little hard to forget."

"Think what you will of that battle, but it was an important one, in ways none of you could understand." She shot a glance over to Ram. "But I gather us all together now for a very different reason."

"Except Xapham," Trini said, fighting back tears. "You should be waiting for him. Why isn't he here yet?" She looked longingly at the door, and I think each and every one of us wished he would walk in at the mention of his name, but he didn't.

"Because he's dead, isn't he?" I asked quietly, but the silence that fell immediately after left the words to echo around unencumbered.

"That's not funny, Ezekiel!" Megatron shouted, nearly taking a swing at my head.

"But it's true." Another wave of shocked silence fell over the room and all eyes fell back to Lucy. "I'm afraid that just shortly before you all arrived, Gavreel found Xapham's remains at his home on Earth."

The shrieking wail we had heard when Gavin returned from Earth was mimicked now by Trini and the other Muses. Zak, the Angels, and Guardians were all stunned by this, and most of them had to ease themselves down into a seat.

Cass shook his head. "No, there's no way! We…we can't be killed, and there's certainly nothing on Earth that could've caused this. You're wrong!"

Trini shouted a series of obscenities before taking deep labored breaths. "It was those Saints! They have those blasted flaming swords, it had to be them!"

"It's too soon to know anything for certain, sister. We don't know who or what did this, yet. But I needed to make sure you all knew the situation. If you're going to go back," she looked at me, "or are intending to go, up to Earth, make sure you look out for one another. I won't be able to look out for you up there."

"Are you trying to tell us not to go back?" Megatron asked outraged. As one of the biggest supporters of life topside, he would suffer the most if she were.

"No, I'm just urging caution. As you all may have noticed, we're not exactly the closest family. It took something like this to get us all in a room together, but up there, all you'll have is each other."

"Well, I guess it's a good thing I never even wanted to go, isn't it? There was no real point in dragging me back into this crap, was there?" Cass snarled at everyone equally. "Now if you'll excuse me, I'll see you all in another million years."

He was the first to leave and after some reminiscing of Xaf's finest moments, others started to bid their farewells slowly but surely. Trini spent most of the day threatening the lives of every Saint and anything that got in her way, she was definitely on the starting line of a warpath that I'd like to avoid getting caught into. Gavin had joined the rest of us and looked like he was doing a lot better, but he still clutched something close to his chest. After some time, Nate finally had the nerve to ask about it. He was defensive at first, but eventually relaxed and laid it out on a table against the back wall. They were shriveled and shrunken, but there was no doubt about it, they were the wings of a fallen Muse.

Gavin, with all of us around for support, found the strength to retell the story of how he found Xaf's body. He had apparently been acting very paranoid for the past few weeks, thinking someone or something had been following him. "I was so stupid! I should've known then. Maybe I could've done something."

"You couldn't have known. This isn't your fault," Tabby said as he comforted Gavin.

"Tabbris is right," Trini said from her brooding spot on the other side of the room. "It's not your fault, it's those good-for-nothing Saints. But they'll pay for this. And I won't kill them slow, no, we're going to make them suffer, aren't we guys?"

The look of hesitation on everyone's face was well founded. Saints may have only been the second to lowest tier of angels, but they were created for one reason and one reason alone: to fight. They had humanoid forms like the rest of us, but they could also transform parts of their bodies after any of God's creatures, making them formidable foes even for the higher tiers.

"Easy there, Trinity, we should listen to Lucifer," Satchel

said trying to calm her even a little. "Besides, there's not even any evidence to support that it was one of their ranks. We don't even know if their flaming swords can kill one of us, it's never been done."

His efforts were even less successful than mine had been earlier because Trini exploded at him. "It's been done right there!" she pointed at the feeble wings on the table. "But if you won't help me you don't have to! I'll take them all on myself if I have to, but trust me when I say this, I *will* get revenge for this. Mark my words!" After that, she stormed out and flew off so fast the house shook a little bit.

Zak and I stayed a little longer but eventually left with the last few that remained. Ram saw us out and we had one last goodbye before flying off in different directions. We swore we would try our best to all stay in touch better, but there was no telling how sincere they were about keeping their word.

When we were on our way back to the American fracture, Zak broke the long silence about midway. "So, where were we before that...unfortunateness?"

I tried to remember, but the events surrounding our little family squabble had occupied the whole forefront of my mind, so it actually took us quite some time to remember what we had been talking about. Somehow landing jogged my memory. "Right, the host thing. I was telling you about my new favorite."

"Oh yeah, that kid in the hospital, what's his story?"

* * *

There I stood, surrounded on all sides except right in front of me, but unable to move. The desert dirt beneath my mismatched sneakers hadn't seen so much as a raindrop in months, making it harder than rock. In hindsight, it probably would've been worth investing in a new pair of shoes, but I always did have a nasty habit of procrastinating buying new shoes. Breaking in a fresh pair was always the worst, so I'd put it off and keep putting it off until my old shoes were more painful than the first few days with a new pair would be.

I glanced to my left where I could see a man with one of those six shot pistols in one hand, while he slowly combed his other forefinger and thumb across his touch-of-gray goatee. I quickly wiped the nervous sweat from my brow and did my best to cool off by pinching the front of my thin shirt and fanning myself with it, but under the harsh New Mexican sun, there was little I could do now. The older man to my left finally left his facial hair alone long enough to pull back the hammer on the weapon and raise it. The shining white of his teeth broke through the shag surrounding it making a sinister looking grin and he moved his clubbed finger to the trigger. With an ear shattering *BANG!* the gun went off. I pushed off into a sprint as fast as I could to put some distance between me and the other hundred that were right on my heels, but I knew I couldn't get more than a dozen strides at that speed. I knew I'd have to slow down to save my energy for the long haul, but it had been a necessary evil to escape the cluster at the starting line.

Jay was the only other runner up ahead with me now, and as much as we disliked one another, we both knew that it would have to take a back seat until after we beat the snot out of Farmington High. They had been laughing at us all day over last year's Qualifier when they beat us out for State, but this year was our year, and today's Meet was our chance to turn the tables on those pompous snobs.

After the first mile, the amorphous blob that had been behind us finally smoothed out into a steady stream of competitors. Jay and I were still at the front of the pack, but there were at least two dozen others hot on our heels. As we passed the two-mile mark, I could feel myself slipping behind Jay, but we were past the halfway point, so I pushed myself to keep up with him. I tried to keep my attention in front of me, but the sounds of footfalls behind me were getting noticeably quieter. It was only when we hit a sharp turn in the track that I was able to see what our tail looked like. Three of the runners from Farmington were five feet behind me in single file, two from Belen about ten feet further back, and the next closest was a small pack of six, two from my team, three from Farmington, and one from a school I didn't recognize. A large gap of thirty feet or so separated them from the unending line that housed everyone else. Hopefully, Greg was in there somewhere, and not one of the stragglers trailing behind.

We neared the final stretch, and Jay shot ahead into a sprint. I tried to pick up my own pace, but I was barely getting enough oxygen as it was, so I was perfectly happy as long as I didn't go any slower. Two of the boys from Farmington popped into my peripheral vision and tried to overtake me on the left. A little part of me wanted to let them, but somehow, I dug deep and found a reserve tank I didn't know I had. The finish line had felt so close a second ago, and yet even after countless agonizing strides, it was still so terribly out of reach. With every wheezing breath, I wished my adversaries would slow down and give me some reprieve, but they only seemed to pick up speed, which meant I had to go faster in turn. Twenty feet, push yourself, Liam! Ten feet, don't stop, push through, all the way. Only five more feet, two more strides and you're done!

"Woo Liam!" Jay shouted when I crossed, making second place by a photo finish. He wrapped an arm around me and we helped each other walk to the water table and catch our breaths. "What'd I tell you? Stick with me and you'll do fine. Glad you were able to keep up."

"What are you talking about?" I would've preferred waiting until I no longer looked like death to joke, but I couldn't pass up the opportunity. "I slowed down for you, didn't want to hurt your fragile reputation." I failed to keep a straight face and the laugh lead to a few seconds of coughing, but it was worth it.

Jay laughed and coughed too. "Sure you did, 'cause you've run faster than a 14:36 5k before, I must've missed it."

I glanced back at the time clock and it had only been thirty seconds since I finished the race. "Yup, there it is," yet again he proved five minutes without bragging was too much to ask for.

"There's what?" he asked while pouring water into a tiny Dixie cup.

"Oh, nothing." I filled my cup about twenty times until

enough other runners had finished that a queue had formed behind me, but I was still incredibly thirsty. I walked around and rejoined the back of the line and looked around to see if Greg was among the faces, but he must've still been running. I only filled my dinky cup ten times the second go around before getting booted out again, but instead of jumping back in line for water, I walked over to a separate table with orange slices and bananas to set up shop for a few minutes.

Three orange slices and half a banana later, I finally saw the sweaty mop head I called Greg barreling toward the water table. I grabbed a pair of bananas, one for him and another for me, and put one in my pocket before heading over to meet him. "Yo Greg!" I shouted once I got close. He was still at the back of the line, so as thirsty and tired as he was, he was able to direct his attention to me without too much distraction. I pointed down to my pocket, "Is this a banana in my pocket, or am I just happy to see you?"

"You're so corny, dude," he said trying not to laugh. I handed him the one in my hand and peeled the other one for myself. "Cheers," he said holding his up like a drink and we both tipped ours toward each other with a nod before taking a bite. With his mouth full, he asked what I could only assume was, "How'd you do?" but all I had to work with were the vowels.

I took a second to swallow my food before replying, "Good. Real good actually, came in second right behind Metzger."

"Aw man, you couldn't've beaten him? He needs to be taken down a peg." He finally reached the water station and grabbed a cup, but he looked at it like it had just insulted his mother. "What the hell is this? How am I supposed to...? I mean really?!"

I laughed as Greg struggled to fill the cup since most of the water coolers were starting to run out; he had to tilt them just to get a light trickle. "Trust me, if I could've beaten him, I would've. If I hadn't been forcing myself to keep up with him I never would've done that good though, so I can't be mad."

"What kinda savages don't bring enough water to something

J. A. Reed

like this?! I mean c'mon, that's just evil!" he whined on, ignoring what I said, not that it really mattered though.

"Coach usually brings a case, let's head back and check," I said trying to be helpful.

He gave the other coolers a few shakes, but each time provided diminishing returns, so he gave up before long. "Okay, but if he's out by the time we get there, somebody might die, just sayin'."

We found the corner of bleachers where our team had gathered and to Greg's delight, there was still half a case of bottled water for him to go crazy with. Coach Bassett delivered the good news once everyone was there, "Well color me surprised, you actually won this thing. But don't let it go to your heads, ladies! Farmington slacked off since last year and look where it got them! So, don't expect me to go any easier on you next week! If anything, we need to train harder, we only won by two points, pitiful!" Greg and a few others groaned, but overall the high from winning kept everyone in good spirits.

About fifteen minutes later, after adequate trash-talking toward the Farmington team across the bleachers, it was time for the girls to race. I would've liked to have stayed and watched, help support our school and see our victory over Farmington complete, but unfortunately, Mom had already texted me that she was on her way to pick me up early. I packed up my bag, changed into a fresh shirt, and began heading to the parking lot to meet her.

"You going somewhere already?" a soft female voice asked from behind me. I turned around and nearly dropped my bag. Courtney Cooper, the girl I've had a major crush on since the first time I saw her on the first day of freshmen year, was actually talking to me. Her long straight dirty blonde hair was tied back into a ponytail and her race bib number 79 was all crumpled up, a superstition the girls of our school had been doing for years. "You all right, Liam?"

"Huh? Oh yeah, I'm…yeah," I babbled out of nervous fear, but once I collected myself I was finally able to use words again. "Sorry, yeah, I have to leave a bit early. Wish I could stay.

Good skill though." That was another stupid cross-country superstition we all used, because somehow saying "good luck" was bad luck, and "break a leg" was just downright wrong. I didn't agree with it, but everyone and their mother did, and the last thing I wanted was to jinx Courtney right now.

"Oh, well…Okay." She rubbed her neck, and if I wasn't mistaken, it looked like she was almost as nervous as I was. I stopped walking in hopes that we could talk a little longer, but I didn't know what else to say. Luckily, she broke the silence. "So, I heard you came in second, that's great."

"Oh, yeah, thanks. Wasn't easy, but we beat Farmington, so it was worth it," I laughed, trying to sound humble.

We chatted for a little longer, but when I checked my phone for the time, she apologized for keeping me and remembered she was running late for her own race. "Jay and some of the others are talking about doing a big group dinner tonight, to celebrate their win, and hopefully ours too. You should totally come."

"I'm sorry, I wish I could, but today's my mom's birthday, and we've already got dinner plans tonight." If it had been anything else, I would've rescheduled in a heartbeat, but my mom's birthday wasn't exactly flexible.

"Oh, of course, don't worry about it. I should get to the starting line. Have a good night, Liam." She turned and started jogging away. I almost turned away, too, but something deep inside of me told me this was my one and only shot, and if I let it slip away now, I'd regret it for the rest of my life. "Courtney! Wait!" I called after her.

She stopped and faced me, but we were still about twenty feet apart. "Yes?"

My stomach felt like it was trying to fly out through my mouth, my hands were so clammy I wouldn't have been surprised to find pearls in them the next time I open them, and my heartbeat was so fast I might've cracked a rib, but somehow, I managed to hide all of that and say, "Maybe we could do dinner or something tomorrow instead."

The corners of her pink lips curled upwards slightly. "Just

J. A. Reed

the two of us, or like a team thing?"

"I was thinking…just us?" That moment right there, that seemingly endless moment in which I had to wait for either a dream come true, or crushing rejection, was the scariest moment of my entire 17 years on this planet.

"Sounds like a date." Without another word, she jogged away to start her race, and my phone vibrated in my hand to snap me back to reality like a pinch.

A text from mom read [Here] and I looked back to the parking lot to see her little car by the nearest curb. I hopped in and buckled my seatbelt, the whole time going over my interaction with Courtney and still finding it hard to believe. When I realized I had forgotten to get her number, it was a little easier for me to believe, but I was riding such a high, even that little hiccup couldn't get me down. Instead, I just saw it as a good reason to talk to her at school the next day.

"What are you smiling about?" mom asked with a tone indicating she knew why.

"What? Nothing. I came in second today, probably the fastest I've ever run," I said, not technically lying, but also not being completely honest.

"Oh, wow. Congrats honey." She put the car into drive and made her way to the exit of the parking lot. "So, it has nothing to do with that cute young lady I saw you talking to?"

The next fifteen minutes consisted of her trying to explain the birds and the bees to me, despite telling her we learned all that in health class years ago. She changed gear eventually to try and pry information on Courtney, and I did my best to change the subject but she was relentless. "What's her last name, do I know her parents? How long have you known each other? What classes do you have with her? Where are you going to take her for your first date?" and about a million other questions that all received the same reply.

"I don't know, Mom," I said right as we pulled up to the house. "Can't you just drop it, please? I don't like talking about this stuff with you." She pouted, as I ran inside to take a quick five-minute shower and throw on some nice clothes. I was back in the car in record time, but it didn't really matter much because she was finagling her hair in the mirror of her visor.

She had a lock of hair in the front left that had turned gray a few years ago and she was fussing with it trying to make it look good. "Maybe I should've dyed it. Yeah, don't you think? I'm too young to be going gray."

"No Mom, it looks fine, gives you character, distinction. And hey, you're halfway to a really good Rogue costume for Halloween." She snapped the visor closed and glared at me for a second. Eventually she turned her head slowly back to the road and we took off for the restaurant without another word on the subject. After a minute of icy silence, I thought I'd help lighten the mood. "Did you make the reservation?"

"What?" she yelled in a panic. "You were supposed to..." I hadn't been able to keep a straight face and she had seen it. "You little stinker!" she tried to slap me on the shoulder, but I deflected her attack. "You're not as funny as you think you are."

I stopped myself from laughing more to correct her, "Yes I am, I'm hilarious." With the mood lightened, I looked around for something to occupy myself, and I caught the time in the corner of my eye. "Oh, and don't worry about the time, I made it for five fifteen instead of five."

She looked at the same clock on her dashboard and seemed okay despite it reading ten past the hour. "No, we're still good, this clock's fifteen minutes fast."

"Well, one: we're still ten minutes from the restaurant, so we would've been late, and two: that only works if you don't constantly remind yourself that it's fifteen minutes fast. You might as well have it set on time and save yourself the head math."

We continued to bicker the rest of the drive until we turned into downtown. I stopped to look out my window at the skyscrapers, although small compared to areas like New York or LA, they were impressive to someone like me who hadn't really traveled much. I had just started peeling my forehead off the glass window when something reflecting off the

J. A. Reed

skyscraper's mirror-like windows caught my attention. "What's th–"

It had been moving so fast down the windows I didn't identify it until it was too late. My eyes turned to the front windshield just in time to see the object slam onto the hood of the car with crushing force. My mom and I screamed, both out of surprise and terror because the object was definitely a human being.

My mom flinched, causing her to twist the wheel around, and slammed on the brakes at the same time, resulting in the car being whipped around and the two of us pinned to the right sides of our seats by the centrifugal force. Screams both inside and outside the car did their best to drown out the screeching of tires but failed. The whirling world outside our windows disappeared behind a veil of smoke and the smell of burnt rubber filled my nostrils.

After what seemed like a lifetime, the car finally jolted to a stop, and I was able to think again. I checked myself for injuries, but everything seemed okay.

"Oh my God, Honey, are you…" I had just enough time to look up at my mom as she panted her words, but before she could finish her sentence the smoke beyond her driver's side window cleared away and was replaced by the grill of a city dump truck moving toward us at high speed. I blacked out so fast, I don't even remember it hitting us.

CHAPTER FOUR: CRUEL WORLD

I watched Liam Cole closely over the next several weeks, as I waited and waited for the fracture to expand wide enough for me. On the bright side, his injuries weren't life-threatening, so even if it took another year, he'd still be around for me to try my luck then. I maintained occasional checkups on a few of my other potentials, including the woman in Kazakhstan, but the more I watched Liam, the more I wanted it to work out with him.

While he slept, I'd rewind time on my screen to go back before the accident and watch him in everyday life; it was a great way to get a feel for his personality, beliefs, and sense of self. While was awake, my heart would break watching him struggle with his new situation and the uncertainty of his mother's condition.

The accident they were in was rough, I went back and watched it a few times trying to make sense of it. An older gentleman in his forties by the name of Thane Varro had chosen to end his life by plummeting off the roof of Albuquerque's tallest building. Krystin and Liam Cole were unlucky enough to be in the wrong place at the wrong time and broke his fall, not that it did him a lot of good, though.

I went back and watched Thane before he jumped; his eyes were red and puffy from crying, but completely dried out by that point. His suit and tie were wrinkled and dirty with tearing on the sleeves. "God. Please forgive me," he said for last words before the final, long step down. Dear ol' Dad hadn't, of course, because Thane was taking up residence down here now. Can't fault a human for trying, though.

If that had been the end of it, I'd never even know who Liam was, but their bad luck didn't end there. His mother had lost control of their vehicle and spun out into an intersection where a fully loaded dump truck t-boned them at forty miles an hour. Krystin took the brunt of the impact, breaking a few dozen bones and rupturing a couple of internal organs; she had been in critical condition and in and out of surgery for weeks, but even now she was comatose with little sign of waking up.

Liam had come out of the accident better off than his mother, but he didn't come out completely unscathed. In addition to breaking his left leg in three places, he suffered a severe spinal injury leaving him paralyzed from the waist down. As a runner, that news had devastated him, but he was always more concerned about his mom than his own disability. I would listen to him pray to God every night as he cried himself to sleep that she would be okay. Every night my Father and so-called righteous brothers did nothing to answer his prayers, but if he could just hang on for a little longer, I was coming. I'd heal his spine, legs, and save his mother, too, not just because I could, but because I should.

"That's it!" I shouted, startling several random passersby. I was done waiting for the fracture, I'd squeeze through if I had to; one way or another I was going to Earth tonight.

I made a quick flight to my home on the outskirts of Gomorrah to finalize my preparations. It was a sizable building for one person, but I had built it myself, so I felt like I was more than entitled to reap the fruits of my labor. I rushed inside to drop off whatever belongings I had on my person since I wouldn't be needing them on the other side and made one clean sweep through the house to make sure things would be where I wanted them in case I came back down the road. I made sure my California King bed was made, but since I hadn't slept there in several weeks, it was already good to go. I checked my dirty laundry to find there was a significant amount in the hamper, but I didn't feel like waiting to get it washed, so instead, I simply froze it in a never-melt ice spell. It was a handy spell to have, even if it wasn't much use in Hell since everything is frozen over to begin with, but it had its uses. Next time I returned and had time, I'd just be able to dispel it and they might be a little damp, but they'd be preserved until then.

Once I was satisfied everything was in its proper place, I went through and frosted shut all of my doors and windows to make sure nobody else could break in and squat while I was away. Now, the only thing that could melt through that ice was either one of my fallen siblings of equal or greater power or angelic fire, but since only a normal, non-fallen, angel can control that, and if one were to even touch the plane to Hell they would instantly Fall, there was zero chance of that happening.

I finally sealed up the front door on my way outside but when I turned to head out, I had the figurative hell scared out of me. "Lucy?! What the hell are you doing here?!"

Lucy stood there on my porch blocking my path down the steps with a smirk on her face as she laughed at scaring me. "Can't a girl just drop by to say hello to her little brother?" She walked toward me slowly, brushed past me and placed her hand on the frozen doorknob. "Or should I say: goodbye."

The way she spoke the words, it wasn't a question, she definitely knew I was intending on leaving tonight. I, on the other hand, had no clue how she knew, nor why she cared, but I knew I should handle this tactfully. "Are you here to talk me out of it?"

"Not necessarily," she said eerily as she headed back to the porch stairs. "I'm here to speak my peace, what you do after that is up to you."

Deciding it would be easier to just let her have her way, I pulled over one of my patio chairs and plopped down into it. "I'd offer you inside, but, well, you know."

She looked back to the door and smirked again because we both knew she could walk right in any time she wanted to, but she pulled up the second chair and took a seat. "Are you ready?"

"Ready for what?" I asked, trying to sound innocent at first, "Ready to start this conversation? I wasn't, but I am now, thanks for the heads up." She retorted my sarcasm with an annoyed glare. "Oh, you mean ready for," I pointed up, "up there? Yeah, got a host lined up, a few back-ups just in case. Should be good."

"Should be?" she asked, turning my own words against me.

"Ninety-nine percent, I don't like to deal in absolutes. I like to remain flexible, expect the unexpected and all that jazz."

"Isn't that what lead to you being sent down here with me?" she asked, still sounding like a shrink.

"Dad acting like a spoiled little child is what lead to us here, I still stand behind our principals, no regrets on that."

I've been able to make Lucy crack a smile quite a lot, but this was a rare occurrence where I managed to get a significantly audible giggle. "He really did, didn't he? And thanks, I'm happy to hear that. I know not everyone feels that same way anymore."

I knew there were a few that fit that description, but one brother in particular stood out in spades, "Don't let Cass get to you, he's nothing but a sore loser. He was more gung-ho than anyone back then."

Lucy cracked another smile, but what I had said wasn't supposed to be funny. "He's just acting like a spoiled little child?"

I laughed harder at the mere fact she actually made a joke than I did at the joke itself, "Yes! I couldn't have said it better myself."

"Seriously though," she started, turning the tone back, "Don't you ever wish you could return home?"

I had to think about that for a while because I never really had settled on a good answer for that. Heaven was amazing, I mean that should be obvious from the name, so yeah, I always thought about going back, but after so much time, other factors became important in the hypothetical thought. Maybe it was just my own internal way of rationalizing never being able to return, but I had recently started to convince myself Earth would be better than Heaven ever was. I would probably need to spend some quality time on that plane of existence before making up my mind, but in the meantime, I did have one definitive answer. "If Dad hasn't changed, then no, never. I'd go back in a heartbeat if things changed, but we both know he's too stubborn for that."

Lucy really listened and processed my words before replying, "Sadly that's a little too accurate. Most usually don't realize, God was young and inexperienced in the beginning.

There was certainly a lot of room for improvement."

"I'll have to take your word for that, never had the pleasure myself," I said, sounding a little saltier than I intended. Lucy was an Archangel, so she had worked side by side with Father until the Fall, but I had never even seen the big guy. Despite my resentment now, he's still my Father, my Creator, and the abandonment issues are very real.

"God works in mysterious ways, as they say," she said quietly as she looked intently at the ground. "Ezekiel," she added after her reflection period ended and she looked back up at me, "I know I can't stop you from going up to Earth, but I really am worried after what happened to Xapham. It could be a long time before your older siblings can cross over, so that'll make you the most powerful of us residing there."

I was a little surprised by this because even without counting Cass, there were still Nate and Satchel, both Angels like me. Was she giving this speech to them as well, or did she believe me to be stronger than them?

Before I could voice any of my thoughts, she continued, "I know you're different from the others with your nicknames and jokes all the time, and I know you want to escape to Earth to get away from the family drama, but I need to ask, will you please watch over the others?"

So that was it. She didn't think I was the strongest, she knew I was a screw-up and wanted to make me babysit. Now, she's not wrong about me, but for a second I had thought she was complimenting me, and being wrong about that made me feel bad. "Look, I'll do what I can, but I'm not going to babysit them or anything. If they need help, I'll do what I can, but I won't just stick my neck out for them. Maybe that makes me a bad brother, but none of us are exactly in the running for sibling of the millennia either."

She sulked and drew her eyes back to the same spot on the floor, "I know, and I take full responsibility for that. I should've done more to keep us all together, but as long as you promise to do your best when and where you can, that's good enough for me."

56

She had worded it a little different than I liked, so I tried to nicely insert the little amendment, "Yeah, but only if the need arises."

She easily saw through me, "Ezekiel, it's not 'if,' it's 'when.' Times are changing. Fractures between worlds, immortals being killed, these are only omens for what's to come."

If it had been anyone else, I would've chalked it up to wild conspiracy theory, but Lucy wasn't one to say something like that lightly. "I don't want to fight in another war if that's what you're getting at. We'll still be just as far away from Heaven on Earth as we are here. We can maintain our peaceful indifference. I can, at the very least." I had followed Lucy into a war against God once before, and unlike Cass, I wasn't upset we lost, I was just grown up enough to know fighting was useless. I was heading to Earth for an escape, not to reign Hell or anything dastardly, so I wouldn't be any threat to Heaven. If Lucy wanted to dig up the past to go to war again and get herself killed, that was on her.

"I'm sorry, I didn't mean to upset you, my brother. I only wanted to know where you stood on the matter. If what you truly want is to be left alone, I will respect your wishes." She stood up and walked over to the steps leading down to the street. "And I sincerely hope they respect them as well." Before I could even process that, she disappeared into a blur.

On that note, it felt weird to just leave the same way she did, but there was literally nothing left for me to do there, I had already sealed my house with the intention of not going back. I definitely had a lot to think about on the flight back to the American fracture, none of it good though. I started trying to think from the perspective of the non-fallen angels. We had been locked up in Hell like prisoners in jail, and now we were starting to break out and roam free. I mean, sure we weren't capable of going back to Heaven, but we were still messing around with their little pets called humans. I could easily plead my case of non-violence and cohabitation, but would they even care? I might be incredibly charming and likable, but pretty much all of my siblings are dense and snobbish, it might just cancel out.

I reached the center of the fracture before settling on anything to resolve that potential issue, so I just decided to put a pin in it and worry about it some other time. I really had to focus my attention on squeezing through the fracture even though it wasn't completely wide enough for me to fit through just yet.

I started with a few stretches to limber up, but since I didn't stretch very often, it didn't help much. It kind of hurt actually, but whatever. Next step was to try and psyche myself up verbally, "All right Zeke, think thin. Think thin. Easy-peasy."

With nothing stopping me except my own hesitation, I finally said, "Screw it!" and threw myself at it head first.

I felt pressure around my shoulders as they caught on the edges of the fracture. I tried using my wings to propel me further, but I didn't have room to maneuver them, so I backed off just enough to reach both of my arms through and pull myself through. It took some work, but I got in deeper than before, only my wings were caught. I wriggled and twisted around, trying to find a way for the uneven cracks to work in my favor, but without much success.

I was just about to back out and try a different angle when I started feeling something tugging on my upper body, pulling me toward the other side. At first, it was great, I'd be through in no time with this help. Sadly the situation turned rather dire in an instant. The force pulling was no longer a gentle tug but a dense and painful pressure that wasn't just pulling me, it was stretching me. In that moment, I had a fair amount of regrets, pretty much everything that had led me to be in that situation, but I could self-reflect later, for then, only one thing mattered: getting the hell out of there. I tried to retreat back to the safety of Hell, but with my arms being crushed and stretched nearly to the breaking point, I couldn't get the proper leverage. The only other choice was to keep pushing through before any serious damage was done.

I moved my arms out to my sides, which was no easy feat as the pressure built up around me, but once they were there, I pushed out against any solid surfaces that were available. I tucked my wings into my shoulder blades as tightly as they could get and pushed with every ounce of strength left in my upper body. A sharp pain coursed through my back. The blackened brittle bones of my right wing snapped under the pressure, but it was enough to propel me through the rest of the way, and the immediate sense of relief was a great painkiller.

I was out of the frying pan, but the blistering heat of New Mexico was the figurative fire. I didn't have the slightest sense of direction in this new world where everything was hot, bright, loud and confusing. Even if I had known what I was doing and where I was going, my broken wing was causing me to spiral out of control.

This bumbling around continued for several minutes, and because I was nothing more than a non-corporeal being on this plane, I was phasing through entire cities as I corkscrewed through the air. Blurs of colors washed over me at hundreds of miles per hour, and I could already feel myself beginning to decay. If I didn't get a handle on things soon, I'd lose my window of being presentable and would have to return to Hell to heal. The next thought popped in my head, *What if I never get control? What if I just spin out of control until I rot away completely?*

I tried focusing on slowing down, but there was no effect. The more I tried, the more I failed, and the more I failed, the more I panicked. Before long I was in full panic mode, despite my best effort to restrain myself. I flailed around trying to use any outside force to help me, but everything slipped through my fingers, literally. "Help me!" I shouted, hoping Zak or any of my other siblings would hear me. I shouted over and over again, as I crossed what I could only imagine was the equator a few times over.

Then my vision of swirling colors came to a jarring halt. I was staring at a window; its frame was off-white with cross sections dividing it into twelve smaller squares of glass. There was a flower pot on the window sill that had been crudely painted yellow, dried droplets along the sides were evidence it had been painted by an amateur. Beyond the window was a spectacular view of a city's skyline silhouetted in gray sky. I knew I had seen it before somewhere in a movie but couldn't place it at the moment, I was too busy being grateful for whoever saved me. Wait, who did save me?

There was a hand grasping my head from behind, but I couldn't turn to see who it belonged to. Before I could open my mouth to say anything to my savior, I felt a rush of warmth flow from the top of my head all the way down my spine and through every nerve of my body. My aching upper body relaxed and my wing painlessly snapped back into place. My eyes rolled back, and if I had been a dog I would've been kicking my leg out that's how amazing it felt. "Oh yeah. Thank you," I moaned in gratitude, even though I had no idea who I was speaking to.

Without saying a word or releasing my head from their grip, my savior whisked me away and back to the fracture in New Mexico, but this time it was a beautifully clean arc over the gorgeous landscape. When I finally felt the hand release me, I spun around to greet the mysterious good Samaritan only to find nothing but endless desert as far as the eye could see.

I flapped my wings a few times to make sure they were in good working order, and they felt better than before, it was a miracle. I was so mesmerized by my miraculous recovery that I had forgotten why I was there and what I needed to do until some of my hand rotted through. "Right!" I exclaimed to myself. "No time to waste. Here goes nothing." I was careful, but I flew up and headed straight for the hospital.

* * *

At a certain point, I had to move past denial and accept that this was not just some horrible nightmare. My mom really was in the fight of her life, I really was going to be paralyzed from the waist down for the rest of my life, and no matter what I did, there was nothing I could do to change that.

The first week had been terrible when I was restricted to my bed and had nothing to go off except the words of my doctors, but once they finally got me into a wheelchair and took me to see her, reality set in, and it got so much worse. I'm man enough to admit I cried when I saw her lying there, practically lifeless with only machines attached to miles of tubes and wiring keeping her alive. "There's nothing we can do now, except pray," was all her doctor said to me in regards to any treatment options.

I had never considered myself particularly religious before, I used to go to church when I was younger, and I definitely believed there was more to life than what I knew, but I wasn't sure what exactly, so I never devoted myself to any one religion, but here, at rock bottom, I poured every fiber of my being into my prayers. I begged and pleaded for her to wake up and be okay, I offered everything I had to give in exchange for her, and when I was ignored night after night, I'd grow angry and curse God, but after venting, I'd go right back to praying for help and the cycle would begin all over again.

At some point, I must've passed out because one second it was dark in my room, and after blinking my eyes the room was flooded with both natural and fluorescent light. At the foot of my bed was a burly male nurse in light purple scrubs holding a chrome bedpan in one hand and my dead-weighted leg in the other.

"Oh, welcome back to the life of the living, sleepyhead," he said with a yellowing smile. Larry had been my primary daytime nurse for weeks now, so I knew him well enough.

I propped myself up on my elbows and looked around for the clock. "What time is it?" I asked once I realized the curtain was pulled closed, blocking my view of the wall clock.

He raised my leg higher to get a look at the watch face on the inside of his wrist, "Quarter past one."

"What?!" I exclaimed. Last I remember from the night before, it hadn't even been midnight yet, which meant I had slept over thirteen hours. That would've been a stretch for me under any circumstance, but since I've been here in the hospital, nurses and doctors have been waking me up two or three times throughout the night to get vital signs or administer one thing or another, so I averaged three or four hours a night with maybe a nap during the day, but never very long at a time.

"Don't worry kid," Larry said, sensing my panic. "It's not too late, let me just…dispose of this, and then I'll take you to see her."

I breathed a little easier because I usually went to visit my mom at ten every day and stay with her until around noon at which point my doctor usually made me get back to bed. While I waited for Larry to return, I reached over for my phone off instinct, but the moment my eyes caught sight of its shattered screen I remembered for the hundredth time that wouldn't be an option. I put it back down on the bedside table where I could forget about it until the next time I wanted to reach for it and begin the vicious cycle all over again. I considered just chucking it for the corner trash can, if it went in I could pretend it was a final buzzer three-pointer and that might make me feel better, but on a second thought I decided it was too much effort, so I dropped the subject and tried to distract myself some other way.

The room I was in was pretty bland; there was a second bed closer to the door, but it belonged to an older gentleman that was barely ever awake, and when he was conscious he didn't do much but watch TV from the fifties, and with the curtains, I only ever got glimpses of him from time to time. The faded beige walls were bare, save for a few cheap art prints in frames. The one in front of my bed was a cabin covered in snow and surrounded by pine trees. At times, I'd find myself looking at it and wondering what life would be like If mom and I had lived in a place like that instead of a busy New Mexico city. In a place like that, we wouldn't have been in this situation.

Before I could dive any deeper into the fantasy, Larry returned with an empty wheelchair. "You ready?" he asked before unhooking my cast sling from the hook hanging above my bed.

"Yeah," I nodded, "but I wanna try doing it on my own again today." Usually, Larry would just pick me up and set me in the chair like it was nothing, but the more I came to terms with my new lifestyle, the more I knew I'd have to eventually be able to do this on my own. That day was still pretty far away though because my attempt ended the same as each of the previous tries; after a few minutes of straining to even orient myself the right way, my arm strength would give out and I'd have to reluctantly ask Larry for help. It was embarrassing, but the thing I liked about Larry was he would make jokes others might see as insensitive, but I knew it as the opposite. Larry was the only nurse that treated me like a normal person, and not a charity case or a burden.

"Oh yeah, you missed two meals today, I can tell," he said curling me a few times before setting me down in the chair. "Let's swing by the cafeteria on the way, shall we? My treat."

"Naw, I'll get this one, just charge it to my room," I said, joking back at him.

"Tempting, really, maybe on steak night." He walked around me and started pushing me out the door and down the hall. It was busier now than when we usually made this trip, but Larry guided us through the chaos like the professional he was. "So, you party too hard last night? You slept like a rock."

"No," I chuckled, "just the usual. Guess I was just getting caught up, haven't had a good night's sleep since…since I've been here." I lowered my head as the memory of the accident flooded back into my mind.

"Well, good thing you finally got one. Just in time, too, 'cause Nurse Jackie started her vacation today," he said calmly, pulling me out of my thoughts by mentioning that good news. Nurse Jackie was his night shift replacement, and I absolutely despised her. One look at her and it was obvious, she hated her job, hated her patients even more, and she did her best to spread her misery everywhere she went.

"That's the best news I've heard all day. Don't think you should've opened with that though, it's all downhill from here now." We reached an intersection with a massive direction board. The cafeteria was labeled straight ahead and the ICU was to the right. I turned my head down that way as we passed by and continued on ahead. I knew she would still be asleep when I got there, but I felt guilty for being so late.

"Who said that's the best news I got for you?" Larry cut in again to distract me. "Ye of little faith, I thought you knew me better than that."

"Well now I'm curious, what could be better than a few nights without the she-devil in scrubs?"

"Hey now," he leaned down and hissed a whisper in my ear, "you can't be saying that so loud, you'll get me in trouble." Larry had been the one to coin that nickname for Nurse Jackie and he didn't want that fact to get out. I did the sealed lips motion and we laughed a bit before he picked back up where we left off. "And hey, you were the one that didn't want it to be all downhill from here, so clearly I can't tell you."

We reached the counter at the cafeteria and the lunch rush had passed, so we didn't have to wait very long. "I'll take the Shepard's pie please," I said to the heavyset lady behind the counter, and then turned my head around as much as I could to address Larry, "And you can't just tease me with something like that and leave me in suspense."

He smirked like that was exactly what he had wanted to do from the start, how evil of him. "And I'll have a green chile burger please," he said before answering me since the lady was starting to look impatiently at the two of us. "And I'll tell you, but later. Too many people around."

We got the rest of our meals and I directed Larry to a quiet empty corner so he couldn't have any more excuses to keep his secret news from me. "All right, bub, spill the beans!" I commanded once we were settled.

"All right, I was hoping to surprise you with it later tonight, but since I already said too much, it's on me anyway. So, with Nurse Jackie on vacation, someone else has to cover her patients, right?" I nodded since that was an obvious assumption. "Well, for the next week, you'll be under the care of none other than Nurse Sara."

My face lit up, and I couldn't help but smile from ear to ear. Nurse Sara was a gorgeous dirty blonde nurse in her mid-twenties and one of the kindest people I've ever met. She had been looking over me my first few nights after the accident and sat with me whenever she wasn't seeing other patients to make sure I was okay. When she moved to a different section, and I got stuck with Nurse Jackie, it had been horrible. "Oh my God yes! You weren't kidding, that's the best news ever!" After it escaped my lips, I had a painful tinge of guilt. My mother was still fighting for her life yet my best news ever was getting a nice nurse for a week. I'm such a terrible son.

Whether Larry saw my internal struggle or not, he carried on without missing a beat, "And since you're my bro, I've decided to conveniently forget to give you your sponge bath until after shift change. Oops." He smirked that smirk again and took an exaggerated sip of his soda.

My face turned bright red and my mind was yet again successfully taken off my previous train of thought. "Now you're just trying to embarrass me."

"Hey, you're supposed to be getting those at night anyway, I only do it to save you from the she-devil in scrubs. She's a flicker, you know."

I didn't exactly know what that meant, but given the context, I could make a pretty safe assumption and I definitely didn't want that, so I was grateful. "Yeah, but still, it'll be awkward."

"Well, it's not too late, I still could." Larry cracked the knuckles of his massive rough hands and suddenly I was no longer concerned about a little humiliation.

We finished our food over more guy talk and made our way for the ICU. I had been happily distracted up until that point, but the closer I got, the more difficult it was to maintain my smile.

When Larry parked me next to her and engaged my chair's brakes, he was somber as well, respecting the moment. "I'll come get you in about an hour, a little less time than usual, I know, but we'll need to have you back in bed by then. Is that all right?"

"Yeah, that's fine. Thank you, man."

"Anytime, kid." He patted my shoulder and left us to be alone. I heard him close the door behind him, and even though that whole wall was floor to ceiling glass, we had enough privacy for me to speak out loud to her and not worry about being easily overheard.

"Hey, Mom. Sorry I'm late, I overslept. I know, typical me, right?" The beeping of her heart monitor was the only response I got. "Let's see, what's new? T-that nurse on night shift I'm always complaining about is going to be gone for a week."

Beep. Beep. Beep.

"The one taking over is really nice, I'm sure you'd like her."

Beep. Beep. Beep.

"I actually don't know what section she normally works, maybe you've already met her here, how funny would that be?"

Beep. Beep. Beep.

"She's very pretty, a little older than me obviously, but still, pretty."

Beep. Beep. Beep.

"If you still…If you still wanted to have that talk, I'd really like to now. I could use some tips on talking to women."

Beep. Beep. Beep.

"Mom, please. Please just say something to me."

Beep. Beep. Beep.

"You're all I have Mom, please don't leave me all alone."

Beep. Beep. Beep.

I grabbed her hand and squeezed it but felt no squeeze back. I sank my head into the bedding and couldn't hold my tears back any longer. I'm not sure how much of the hour I spent like that, but when I did eventually pick my head up and wiped my cheeks, I just sat there, not sure what else to say. I spent the few remaining moments of my time in silence that was only broken when the door behind me cracked open again. With my chair locked facing the other way, it was hard for me to look around to make sure it was him. "Larry?"

"No." The voice was familiar as one of the other daytime nurses, but I didn't know him that well. "I'm afraid he had something else he had to take care of, but he asked me to make sure you get back to your room all right. Are you ready to go?"

I wiped my eyes one more time to make sure they were dry before I answered. "Yeah, I'm ready." He came over and unlocked my breaks, as I put my hand on my mom's one last time. "I love you, Mom. I'll be back tomorrow."

The trip back to my room was a quiet one; the nurse whose name I couldn't remember didn't try striking up any conversation, and I didn't feel much like talking anyway. Without any distraction, my mind began to wonder where Larry had gone, and of course, it was all of the negative possibilities. Maybe he was getting tired of me, needed to pawn me off on someone else for a while. My rational mind knew better than that, but the negative thoughts were starting to snuff that part of me out after everything I had been through.

We reached the hallway with my room and I just wanted to curl up and sleep, despite knowing I wouldn't be able to.

Larry popped out of my door and shot me his yellow smile. "Hey kid, look who I found." He gestured inside, and curiosity nearly pulled me out of my funk, but not enough. The other nurse turned my chair, and I was able to see what Larry was talking about inside my room.

"Surprise!" a large group of my cross-country teammates and coaches shouted with balloons, some flowers, and a big banner that read 'Get Well Soon Liam! We Miss You!'

I placed my hands on my chair wheels to stop the nurse from pushing me through the door's threshold; I was in no mood to see anyone, and instead, I found myself face-to-face with around fifteen of my casual acquaintances. Greg was among the group, and perhaps if it had been just him, I could muster up the courage to entertain a guest, but the wall of smiling faces only put me off more than anything else.

"It's good to see you up and about there, Cole," Coach Bassett said once the clapping subsided. Was he trying to be funny by saying that? The reactions from the rest would suggest so, but I wasn't laughing. "Now, I know after everything, you probably haven't heard yet, but we have great news: we took State! And we never could've done it without you!"

Jay stepped forward holding a State Champion medal on a red, white, and blue ribbon in one hand, and a trophy with a running figure in the other.

"C'mon buddy, these are for you," he said since I was still clear across the room. I looked among them nervously and even checked behind me to find the nurse had moved on elsewhere. I grabbed the rails on my wheels and rolled myself forward with an eerie squeaking of the tires on smooth linoleum. "Here you go," Jay said as he placed the medal around my neck. "And the MVP award." He handed me the trophy, and I read the label; sure enough, it claimed I was the team MVP.

"What the hell is this?" I muttered quietly at the golden man topping the trophy, the one with two working legs. "How the hell can I be team MVP?"

There were uncomfortable glances shared between everyone in the room except for me, I looked Coach Bassett dead in the eye until he couldn't avoid me anymore. "Well, you're an important member of this team."

I scoffed and rolled my eyes so hard it was almost painful. "Clearly not! You won State perfectly fine without me! I don't need some pity award!" I threw the trophy to the ground in front of me, and it broke into three pieces that flew several feet in different directions.

Faces ranged from shock to terror after my outburst, but I didn't care; every single person in this room knew I didn't deserve MVP even if I had been there for State, and I hated them for trying. The medal was one thing, everyone on the team got one, and I actually had contributed at my last race, so if they had ended it there I wouldn't have given it a second thought, but the trophy made it blatantly obvious they were showing me unfair sympathy.

"Listen up, you ungrateful little sh–" Coach Bassett said with a red face and contorted mouth as he just barely caught himself. "I mean, we didn't mean any ill will there, Cole."

"Oh great, you're not going to curse me out either? Just because I'm a cripple now, you're not going to tear me a new one when I clearly deserve it?"

"All right," Larry chimed in, as he took a step to place himself between us. "Young Mr. Cole here should really be getting back into bed, so let's clear out of here, shall we?"

"I think you're right," Coach Bassett said quietly, which was unheard of from a man as notoriously loud as he.

Larry grabbed the back of my chair and pulled me out of the way to make room for them to exit. I tried to avoid looking at them, but my gaze seemed to have a different idea. I looked at each one of them as they passed by. Coach Bassett had a mixture of guilt and anger, a look few besides him could pull off. Jay looked the guiltiest; the trophy had probably been his idea, but if not, as the real team MVP he felt responsible in one way or another. Greg was the only one to reach out and place a comforting hand on me. "I tried to tell them it was too much, sorry bro."

When there were only three people left shuffling toward the bottlenecked doorway, I finally noticed Courtney at the back of the pack with her head hung low. As soon as I noticed her, I immediately regretted my actions, but it was too late to do anything about it. She took slow short steps as she passed by me. "I, uh…I hope you haven't forgotten, did you still want to have that dinner?"

Whether it was true or not, my mind could only hear the pity in her words. She left it as a yes or no question giving herself an out; if I say no, she doesn't have to feel bad, she doesn't have to look like a bad person. Part of me wanted to say yes and force her to be the bad guy, but another part of me couldn't do something that vindictive. If she was going to play it safe, so was I. "I don't know right now. I don't even… I just don't know."

"Yeah, right, of course, I'm sorry, I couldn't even imagine what you're…just…when you do know, I still do, and it's not…" She looked down at one of the broken trophy pieces under the nearest corner of my bed. "I get that a lot has changed, but that doesn't mean everything's changed."

She turned and left the room leaving only Larry, my snoring neighbor, and my shame. Larry picked me up and placed me under my covers. "They told me they were your friends, my bad, sorry about that." With his half smile, I knew he was testing my current mood, but I didn't respond and he caught the hint to drop the jokes. He picked up the call button off the floor along with the trophy pieces. "Here, I'll give you some space, but if you need to talk, or anything, I won't be far. Sound good, kid?"

I snatched the call button and discarded it among the blanket wrinkles near my ankles, "Yeah, sounds fantastic."

Larry stopped over the wastebasket near the door with the trophy pieces, looked at me and nearly asked a stupid question, but saved himself the embarrassment when he dropped them inside without a word. He disappeared through the door and it slowly closed itself behind him. Safely alone from prying eyes, I pulled my pillow around to cover my face with it and muffle my groaning.

"You know, you forgot to get her number again."

The strange voice freaked me out and I dropped my pillow off the bed.

"Huh? Who are…" Hovering next to my bed, and yes, I did say *hovering,* was a pale man with yellowing eyes dressed all in black. Over his shoulder were blackened crispy bones that made up a shape not unlike wings. "*What* are you?"

"Wow, okay, good, that could've gone much worse, good." He landed on his feet and folded his wings in enough they were out of my view. "Hello, my name's Zeke, I'm an angel, and I've come to make an offer."

CHAPTER FIVE: DIDN'T READ THE FINE PRINT

The young boy's mouth and eyelids seemed to be stuck open for a long time before he blinked and rubbed his eyes. It was only after he opened his eyes again to see that I was not only still there, but absolutely real, that he began to panic. I knew it had been too easy so far. He darted for the nurse call button, but in his irrational state he fumbled and it ended up clattering to the ground in front of me.

"Well, that's a shame, guess you'll just have to hear me out now, won't you?" I tried to smile friendly, but with the decay setting in, my rotting teeth were probably not my best feature at the moment.

"I...I'll scream," he said, shuddering in fear.

"So, after all those nights you prayed for your mother, you're just going to freak out and reject the help?" I asked with a feigned insult. "Okay then, I guess I'll just go." I floated up and began phasing through the roof, waiting for him to call me back.

"Wait!" His cry sounded muffled through the concrete ceiling after my head and torso were already past the fluorescent lights. I stopped my rise and smirked victoriously, so it was definitely a good thing he couldn't see my face. I floated back down at a much slower rate and waited for him to make the next move. He remained conflicted and silent until well after I was back to ground level. "How do you know I was praying?"

"Um," I looked back at my wings thinking that was a little obvious. "You heard the part where I said I'm an angel, right?"

"Um, yeah, but...Well, you're not exactly what I imagined an angel would look like."

I laughed lightly, "I'm sorry, were you expecting a chubby little baby with a harp? Because I'm more of a percussion guy myself." The silence was clear enough to me that it was still too early to be joking, and I honestly didn't want to scare him away again, so I pulled back a bit. "Okay, I know what you mean, and I'm not going to lie to you, but just hear me out, all right?"

He nodded, and his body language loosened up showing he would give me a chance. "I am an angel, but, I'm what you would call a 'fallen' angel. But it's not what you think!" I added the last part as quickly as I could in an attempt to stop any preconceptions from forming. "There's a lot about us that got lost in translation. We're not evil or anything, at least not all of us. I'm not." It didn't work.

"Oh my God! You're the devil?!"

"No, no I'm not, technically my sister is, but the same goes for the fluffy white harp-wielding guys, and I don't see any of them here offering to help you, do you?"

My last question resonated with him a little, but he was still back in full panic mode. "M-maybe not, but that doesn't mean I'm going to s-sell my soul to the devil."

"Again, not the devil, and I don't want your soul…just…just a place to live." It was technically true, but I wanted to ease into the whole sharing-a-body thing.

"What? A place to…What?" His eyes widened when it clicked for him, "You're going to possess me?!"

Guess there was no way to ease into that. "No, not possess, more like…roommates."

"No! No, get out of here! I don't need you! Help!"

I looked over and luckily the elderly gentlemen in the bed next to him was completely unconscious, but if I didn't get him to calm back down someone outside would hear him and my chance would be gone. "Please, just stop shouting! Look, do you want your mom to wake up or not?! Do you want to ever walk again?!" He stopped yelling, "I came here to help you, I could be in any hospital talking to anyone else, but I chose you because I saw what happened to you and your mother and I knew it wasn't fair. The only reason I Fell was because of one little disagreement between us and the winning side, and for that, we got kicked out of paradise and abandoned, just like you. God got bored with humanity, he wanted to move on and leave you to destroy yourselves and we were the ones that stood up for you. So, you can reject me and live a long miserable life devoted to God, but in the end, it won't matter."

J. A. Reed

The more I told him, the more his face turned from fear to woe. I really hated dropping such a bomb on him, I really wished I hadn't had to, but all I wanted to do was help him and if telling the harsh truth did the trick, it would be a necessary evil.

"How can I trust you?" he finally muttered after mulling it over for some time.

"Trust in yourself. You've felt it, you've always felt it, the absence of God. If you let me in, I'll show it to you. We'll share a body, and I'll show you." I could tell I was finally getting to him, but there was still one push he needed to get him all the way. "If it helps, you can boot me out whenever you want to. I can heal you and your mother and you'll never have to see me again, all I ask is you give me a chance to prove to you that all I want to do is help."

There was another long silence, as he fought with the idea. "Can…can I have some time to think about it?"

Time wasn't on my side; if I didn't take a host soon, I'd have to go back to Hell to regenerate and gain my strength before I could return, and I'd have to wait for the fracture a little longer to avoid another bumpy ride. That argument would have no weight for him, but there was one that would, and it was equally pressing for time. "Your mom can't afford to wait much longer."

Liam began crying, torn by the severity of the decision. He was entirely right to have his doubts, many of my more jaded siblings probably would've made the same promises but not be as honest about them as I was, but I had to have faith that he would trust me. "Just promise me one thing," he sobbed.

"Anything."

"Just promise me that even if you're lying to me, even if you take my soul and torture me in Hell or whatever, that you'll still save my mom."

"I promise," I said, shedding a tear of my own.

"Okay," he wiped his eyes as clear as he could with one pass of his hands. "How does this work?"

It already has. Liam had opened himself up for me, and I had joined with him effortlessly and painlessly. *Whoa…*

"Whoa…" he said out loud at the same time as I said it in his head. I could feel what he felt as he could feel me; our minds were still separate, but there was a lot of overflow from both sides. I was flooded with the most severe level of emotions I'd ever felt. The grief he felt for his mother, the sense of rejection stemming from his father leaving them, love, anger, joy, disgust, and a thousand others were at an intensity that I never knew possible before that moment.

How do you live like this? I asked, unable to focus on anything through the rush. *Whoa!* In another instance, I was hit by overwhelming physical sensation. I could feel every nerve in his, or rather our, body tingling with life, and that was only from the waist up. The complexity of the mortal body as it pumped fluids, consumed energy, created waste, and countless other functions foreign to my natural angelic form made it feel like I had inhabited an entire city rather than just one person.

"What do you mean?" he asked, and I could sense his confusion even before he verbalized it.

You don't feel that? I was getting dizzy from the sensory overload, but Liam must've been so used to it that experiencing my emotions was nothing to him. *Wait, what do you feel?*

"Well, I don't know, it's weird. I…I'm getting a lot of information, bits and pieces mostly. You've lived a really long damn life. Wait! You give people cancer for fun? What the hell?!"

Anger, mistrust, and a blend of a dozen other emotions flared up and I did everything I could to keep his emotions from drowning me. *Ugh, I'm sorry, not my finest moments. Please stop, I'm sorry.* It was too much, I could tell it wasn't as strong of an emotional response as many of his others, but even that was too much for me to handle. I thought back to what Zak had told me, when he said I wouldn't understand until I had a host and he was right, nothing could've prepared me for this. *I can't, please stop.*

"Are you okay?" Liam's concerned voice echoed accompanied by the wave of respective feelings, but by now I was beginning to adjust, only I knew that it would be some time before I would be fully acclimated.

Yeah, I will be, I think, this is just all so new for me, I just need some time to get used to this.

"What?! We don't have time! We need to get to my mom right now!" Liam attempted to reach the nurse call button again, but I hadn't even gotten started on repairing his spinal injury, so he was still just as unsuccessful as he had been before.

I will, I promised I would. I just need a second, let me at least work on healing you first. I tried to push the emotions aside and focus on locating the source of his injuries, and since I could feel every fiber of Liam's being, it wasn't difficult; fixing the issue was a different story, though. With my full attention, I could probably have him back in full running shape in a few minutes, but there were more than a few distractions around me, the biggest being Liam's impatience. As if the emotion itself wasn't bad enough, he had to go and add a strong physical distraction when he dove from the bed headfirst trying to get the call button.

"Help!" he shouted while frantically pressing the button with one hand and holding a rather nasty forehead gash closed with the other. "Larry! Larry!"

Well isn't that just brilliant?! Way to go, idiot, now look what you've done. As if I didn't have enough injuries to heal already. *Do you really think they'll take you straight to your mom now that you're bleeding?*

The door opened, and Larry charged in. "Hey kid, what's wrong?"

"I can be pretty persistent," Liam whispered so only I could hear him, and I couldn't argue with that one.

Fine, you do your thing, I'll see what I can do here in the meantime. I tried to distance myself from all of the outside stimuli so I could focus on healing Liam's back, and for the most part it worked. I could kind of make out the conversation Liam was having with the frantic Larry, but it was just muffled background noise now. Almost half an hour passed like that as I focused on mending his spinal disk, which proved more challenging than I first guessed. Occasionally I would take a short break to gauge Liam's progress outside and I laughed to myself when Larry refused to take him anywhere until he could stitch up his forehead. *Told you so.* Liam didn't want to reply to me out loud, but I could feel him curse me in his mind, and that only made me laugh harder.

After I worked out a decent way to focus on my single task, I was finally able to get a solid five minutes of work done. Liam's spine was now good enough to walk on, but still incredibly tender; he would need to remain as still as possible until I could finish the final touches, but I was satisfied enough for the time being to take another break and check on the outside world. To my surprise, I came back to find we were being wheeled down the hall toward Krystin's room.

All right, Liam, I'm here. I fixed you up most of the way, but you should probably stay in the chair, your leg's still broken, and your back's not at 100 percent just yet.

"Yeah, I know, it hurts like hell," he muttered softly as he rubbed his leg and shifted in his seat painfully. It wasn't pleasant for me either, but it would take more time to finish, and I knew he'd rather take the pain than wait any longer to save his mother.

We rounded the last corner leading up to Krystin's room and saw a doctor exit from inside. Normally, that wouldn't have been a strange sight, but he was followed by three nurses and another doctor, and all five of them had the same look of dread on their faces.

"What the…?" Whether it was denial or just plain ignorance, Liam couldn't put the picture together, but I did, and once I did, he sensed it from me. "No. No!"

Liam, I'm so sorry. One of the nurses spotted us and her face turned white. She nudged the first doctor, and I could see him preparing the bad news speech. I tried to brace Liam for the impending harsh truth, but my mere attempt did nothing but piss him off even more.

"No! It can't be! You're wrong! No." I could feel rage and adrenaline coursing through Liam's circulatory system like tingling fire.

"Um, Mr. Cole, I'm very sorry," The doctor started, but

before he could say any more Liam sprung from the wheelchair and shoved his way past him. He pushed past the pain in his leg for the first few steps before collapsing at the door to her room.

Liam! It's too late! Stop before you hurt yourself even more! He ignored me and hobbled into the room until he could brace himself against his mother's bed. The tubes and wires that used to stretch from the machines to her now dangled uselessly on the ground and the familiar rhythmic tone from the heart monitor had been muted to save us from hearing the soul-crushing steady tone. *We're too late, I'm sorry.*

"No! You have to save her! You promised me! Save her! You promised!" he yelled through streams of tears over and over again. He strained to adjust his position and placed his hands over her heart, undoing everything I had healed in the process. "Do something! Save her, please!"

For the sake of argument, I tried to reach out for her, but her soul had already been long gone. There was nothing I could do. *I'm sorry, she's gone.*

"Then bring her back! You can..." Liam slowed as he searched through the knowledge I shared with him, desperately looking for something that wasn't there. "You...You can't..." He finally removed his hands and fell in a heap on the ground.

Years of getting used to human emotion couldn't have prepared me for that moment. The loss Liam felt shook me to my core and I couldn't stop myself from crying out. *P-please! Stop! I can't!*

Liam had held it in for a while, trapping the flood of pain inside where it could drown me, but once he hit the ground with nothing to catch his dead weight he finally succumbed and wailed out, "Get out! Get away from me! Go!"

Suddenly and violently, I was ripped from Liam with enough force to launch my angelic form clear of the building. With recent experience tumbling uncontrollably, my healthy wings caught me before the hospital could vanish over the horizon, but the ferocity of my banishment took quite the toll on me. I wanted nothing more than to fly back to Liam, but I could still feel residual emotion, and there were two truths apparent to me: I couldn't handle that pain again, and he was in no condition to see me right now.

I looked down at my hands to see that I had resumed my previous level of decomposition, which meant I didn't have time to wait him out on this end. Reluctantly, I turned and headed for the nearest fracture back to Hell where I could regain my strength and keep an eye on Liam from a safe distance, because one way or another, I'd be back for him; I had broken my promise, and I'd do anything to find a way to make it up to him.

* * *

I'm reminded of the saying "Be careful what you wish for." I had prayed for a miracle, for someone to save my mom's life, and an angel actually came to answer my prayers, but I hesitated. I had questioned him, panicked, and wasted time that I could've used to save her, but instead I reached her too late. I let my one and only shot slip through my fingers because I was too scared to make the leap of faith. She died because of me.

A day passed by around me, as I laid motionless in my bed. Nurses would come and go leaving trays of food or taking vitals, but I hadn't taken a bite or said a word. The sun set and rose again with my eyes remaining fixed on a single point of the wall in front of me, as I replayed the events over and over again in my mind's eye they began twisting and turning further from the truth. Every little mistake I had made from the moment the angel arrived until reaching that last hallway blew up and exaggerated making them a hundred times worse in retrospect, and if there had been anything I had done right, I was blind to it by now.

"Liam?" a voice said, breaking my trance. I looked over to find a thin woman in her late thirties wearing a dark three-piece pantsuit. Her hair was braided and twisted up on the back of her head, hardly visible because she was sitting down at my level and all of her attention was faced straight at me. I looked at her, but still didn't feel much like talking; the fact I was even paying attention was a miracle in and of itself. "I'm sorry Liam, I can only imagine what you're going through right now."

Great, more pity. All I wanted was to be left alone, but if someone was going to talk to me, I'd rather it not be half-hearted condolences. It was bad when all I had to deal with was people seeing my physical trauma, now things would be even worse, and I was even less willing to tolerate it. I maintained my silence hoping she'd either get on with what she had come here to say or leave me alone; I prayed for the latter.

"My name is Christie Merlot, I'm with Social Services, and if it's all right, I'd like to speak with you for a moment." I guess I wasn't getting off so lucky. "Does that thing work?"

Instinctually I looked up out of curiosity and found her gesturing to the TV in my corner of the room. Next, my eyes dropped to the remote on the nightstand that would've been within reach if I had any will to lean far enough over and grab it. She must've followed my gaze because she stood, grabbed it, and handed it to me.

"I'm free for the next hour, wanna see if there's anything good on?" I had been flipping through the limited cable channels for weeks and had rarely ever found something worth watching, but it seemed like a better alternative to talking right then, so I begrudgingly snatched up the remote and pressed the power button.

I needed three tries before finding the right position to hold the remote so the TV would register, which annoyed me more than it should've, but the station that flickered on was a decent looking movie channel, and despite heavy edits and commercial breaks, was probably the best I would find, so I dropped the remote right away.

"Oh, I haven't seen this one in ages. Hate the way these channels butcher good movies, though, they always seem to cut out the best scenes." Ms. Merlot took her seat back, turning it slightly to face the TV and proceeded to watch without another word.

The movie had already been playing for half an hour or so,

but just as it reached the start of its second act, the first commercial break since I had turned it on broke the narrative, as well as Ms. Merlot's silence.

"Have you seen this one before?"

I nodded with as little effort as possible because I had seen it, only once, a few years ago.

"Good, I love this movie, definitely in my top ten. Have you ever seen the TV show?"

"TV show?" I asked before remembering that I wasn't speaking.

"Yeah, it predates the movie, same cast and everything. It's just as amazing as this, but there's only one season, pretty sad really." She looked back at the TV which was only on its second commercial. "Looks like there's a DVD player in that TV; I've got the whole series on DVD at home. Maybe I can bring it in for you tomorrow. I could think of worst ways to pass time."

"You don't have to do that," I said shyly. I'm not sure what it was about her, but I was no longer getting the feeling of pity from her.

"I know that, but I like recommending good shows and movies, and streaming it on your phone would burn up way too much data." She laughed a little at the end there and I cracked a half smile too.

I pulled my phone out of my pocket and showed her the cracked screen. "I don't think my data's the real problem."

"Yeah, I suppose not then." The commercial break ended and the movie came back on. "You know, I've got the movie too. If you wanted to keep it chronological, I'd highly suggest waiting until tomorrow."

Even though I had seen the movie before, the details were a little hazy. I picked up the remote and with only my second try, I managed to turn it off. "Yeah, that does sound better."

"I'll swing by first thing in the morning then. It might take you all day to get through them all, but trust me, it'll be worth it." She stood up and pushed her chair back against the wall. "But if you don't have anything else, I'll let you get some rest."

It was strange, now that she was getting ready to leave, I no longer wanted that as badly as I did before. "Um, well," I started, not entirely sure what I wanted to ask right away. "Um, never mind."

She walked over to my side and knelt down beside me. "It's okay, Liam, you can ask me anything." She gave a closed lip smile and tilted her head ever so slightly.

"Well, I was just wondering, do you know what's going to happen to…" The end of that sentence proved difficult to verbalize without my eyes watering, so I shifted to an easier alternative. "Do you know if there's going to be a service for my mom?"

Her smile fell away along with her gaze, but she quickly regained her composure. "There's a lot that goes into that, but yes, we'll certainly take care of that over the next few days. So, don't you worry about that, for now just focus on getting better, all right?"

"Okay." I nodded my head and she said her goodbye, leaving me in the cold and lonely room, only now it seemed just a little less bleak than before. I tried turning the TV back on to find something else to watch, but after two and a half cycles through the available channels, Larry came in to take me to my physical therapy. What was left of the day and the whole night were entirely uneventful, but just as promised, Ms. Merlot returned bright and early with DVDs in tow.

We spent some time talking about the show, and thankfully she avoided giving away any spoilers, and then we moved on to discussing similar shows and movies we'd both seen. Before leaving, she tactfully shifted the conversation to ask me about how my recovery was progressing and how confident I was with a wheelchair, but once the mood began to sour, she pulled back and left me with the first episode to enjoy. I felt bad for most of it, knowing I wasn't being the easiest person to work with, but I appreciated the way she was going about it, not pushing too hard too fast.

The show was a great distraction, and I got lost in it with only minor hiccups when it came time to swap DVDs, but the handy little call button solved that particular issue quite easily. I watched the whole day and fairly late into the night and wholeheartedly agreed with her assessment of the show; it was well worth the binge watch in every way. I slept well and had a pleasant dream for the first time in a long time. Of course, the only down side was waking up to the sad reality I was stuck with.

"Good morning Liam," Ms. Merlot said when she peeked around the corner from the door. "Did you sleep well?" I rubbed the sleep out of my eyes, yawned, and nodded my head in response. She walked over to the TV and picked up all the DVDs laying out where the nurses had left them. "looks like you managed to get through them all, I assume you liked it then?"

"I think it's my new favorite show, so yeah, most definitely," I said as I stifled yet another yawn. "Thank you by the way."

"Glad to hear it." She began packing up the disks into the cases. "You know, the Middletons actually met the director once a few years ago, I'm sure they'd love to tell you all about that."

"Who?"

She had been facing away when she spoke, so I wasn't completely sure what she had said, but if I had heard her correctly, I had no idea who she was talking about; I'd never met any Middletons before.

She finished up by the TV and pulled the chair away from the wall to sit by my side. "Tony and Maria Middleton, they have a foster home out in Edgewood. They're a great couple, very well suited to your needs."

"Wait…Foster home? But I…I thought…" Honestly, I hadn't really thought of what was going to happen next, but Foster care certainly wasn't what I wanted. "Can't I just go home?"

Her eyes dropped as she hesitated to answer. "I'm afraid it's not that simple, Liam. There's…there's just a lot that goes into these things." She was clearly remaining vague on purpose, like she was hiding the full details from me. I didn't like it one bit.

"There's gotta be something I can do. My mom owned our

house, it should go to me, right? And, well I'm almost 18, isn't there something I can do? Can't I get emancipated or whatever it's called?" My life was going to be different now, I had no illusions about that, but I wanted something familiar to hang onto; I didn't want to leave my house and school on top of everything else.

She did the hesitation look again, only this time it took her longer to bring herself out of it and I knew that could only mean bad news for me. "You…You could petition for emancipation, but that would take time, you'd likely already reach your birthday before getting anywhere and…well, as for the house…" Another hesitation. "…did you know that your mother took out a second mortgage earlier this year?"

I regretted not paying attention to mortgages in Econ class now, but I knew enough to know that it wasn't good. "No, she never said anything about that. What does that…" I didn't actually want to hear the answer to that anymore. "What about…Isn't there anything? Savings? L–" I was hoping she could anticipate what I wanted to ask so I wouldn't have to say it out loud, but I found the words after a momentary choke up, "…Life insurance?" Her face told me before she could. "So there's nothing?!" I wasn't mad at her, but she was the only one there, and I had to let my frustration out some way. "Are you telling me that after 36 years, there's nothing left?! You're just going to take away everything she spent her life working to the bone to get?!"

"Liam, please." She rose out of her chair slightly and put her palms out toward me like I was a rabid dog. "Don't get worked up. Everything's going to be okay."

"No! It's not!" I shouted as tears filled my eyes. "She's gone! She's gone, and you're telling me it was all for nothing!" The tears dripped down my chin, and I stopped long enough to catch my breath. "What am I supposed to do now? What am I supposed to do without her?"

She placed her hand on my knee, and despite not being able to feel it, it did enough to comfort me a little bit. "No one can answer that question for you, but I can tell you what you're not supposed to do. You're not supposed to do this alone. It's okay to accept help when you need it, it's okay to let people in."

"Wait, what did you say?" something about that sounded familiar, but I couldn't quite place it just yet.

"I'm just saying, it's perfectly normal if you want to put up walls, keep people out, but it's okay to ask for help, to find someone you can let in and help you process all of this."

"Let someone in…" That's what the angel had said, that I needed to let him in. Sure, he hadn't saved my mom like he promised, but he had tried, and he had helped me before I reinjured myself.

"Mr. and Mrs. Middleton really are a great couple," Ms. Merlot continued, completely oblivious to the revelation I was currently having. "and they have a bunch of kids just like you living with them, I'm sure you could relate to them, and they've all gone through very similar experiences. I really think going there will do you a lot of good."

"Yeah, um, when might that be?" I asked, not entirely there since I was still thinking about the angel.

"Um, I'm not sure. I could go check with your doctors, find out when we can get you released." She stood up and took a few steps back toward the door. "Will you be all right if I just step out for a second?"

"Yeah, yeah, that's fine."

She looked back at me a few more times on her way to the door, but once she was gone, I sat up as high as I could, closed my eyes, and prayed. What was his name again? Oh yeah, "Zeke? Zeke, can you hear me?" I focused, really focused on reaching out with all of my heart. "Zeke, please hear me. I know it wasn't your fault, you did everything you could, I just didn't get to her fast enough. I don't blame you." I didn't feel anything, no response, nothing. "I'm sorry for reacting the way I did. I'm sorry I rejected you, but I'm ready now. I'm ready to have you back…if you're still willing to have me."

I opened my eyes to look around, but the room was cold and empty. Disappointed, but not entirely surprised, I sank back down into my bed. *Your timing is impeccable.*

J. A. Reed

"Zeke?!" I exclaimed louder than I should've and actually covered my mouth for a second until I could remind myself a whisper would suffice. "Zeke, you came back?"

Just now, yeah. Glad I wasn't too late. Are you ready to get out of here?

"Um, I still can't walk."

Don't worry about that, I picked up a few pointers after our first go around; I can poof us straight to your house and worry about fixing you up there. Unless you have any business to wrap up here.

"You can? Um, yeah, I'm ready then. There's nothing left for me here anyway."

Okay, and…well, I'm sorry…I'm sorry I couldn't have done this before. I was disoriented, and I didn't know…

"It's okay, Zeke, it wasn't your fault. I know you tried. You can do it for me now, so just get us out of here. We'll worry about the rest later."

You got it. Now just hold onto your…actually, never mind, there's nothing to hold onto. It was a strange sensation, but one second I was laying in my hospital bed, and the next, I wasn't.

CHAPTER SIX: FRESH START

I had been expecting to stay and live in New Mexico with Liam, but after everything he had gone through, there was nothing left for him there but painful memories. I healed him as quickly as I could, and with experience under my belt, and none of the same distractions as the first time, it only took me a few minutes. Once he was back on his feet, Liam packed a bag of nothing but a few clean clothes and a toothbrush. He passed by every single photo or keepsake that might hold any sentimental value without a second thought. The only thing from his old life that accompanied us to our next destination was his Golden Retriever, Cody. I could feel a rush of positive emotion from Liam as he gave his repaired spine a test drive hopping the fence to the neighbors yard to fetch Cody back, but the depression set back in almost immediately.

Petting the excited pup helped Liam's state again, but was only marginally better. "Can you even take him with us?" Liam asked unsurely before I even had the chance to attempt.

Yeah, another person might be harder to do, but an animal, no problem.

"Well, it's a good thing I don't have anyone else then," he said in a painful, self-pitying tone.

I didn't know what to say to him, I didn't even know if there was anything that I could say to him, but I tried. *Liam, look...*

"I know, I'm sorry, I didn't mean that. Once...once we're out of here, I'll be okay. Starting a new life, leaving this one behind, that's all I need."

I knew it wouldn't be that easy, but I could also feel the certainty he felt in saying it, so at the very least it was a start, and if anything happened, I'd be there to pick up on it right away. *Okay, just hold Cody tightly, we're jumping a bit further this time. Here we go!*

From our first jump, I knew that Liam perceived it as something along the lines of teleportation, but that was only because his mind couldn't fully handle the bending of the laws of physics. What was really happening was the same thing I had

J. A. Reed

accidentally done when I first crossed over to Earth, I was flying in my natural angelic form, only with Liam and Cody fused to me this time.

Liam hadn't stated a preference on where he wanted to relocate, only asking for more than one state between the new home and the old, so the decision had been left to me. It hadn't been an easy choice, after all, I knew almost nothing about living on Earth, and the things I did know had to be taken with a grain of salt because I learned them from watching TV and movies; not exactly the most reliable sources. It wasn't until I considered asking one of my siblings for help that I landed on my choice.

"Oh God, I'm never going to get used to that," Liam uttered sickly upon arrival, but he didn't get much time to settle his stomach because Cody started going nuts from the jarring trip too. "shut up, you stupid animal! hey, wait, is that the space needle?"

Good eye. Yeah, I know a few people here in the city, they should be able to help us get set up.

Liam attached a leash to Cody and let him run around a bit to get acclimated to all of the new smells. Once he was calm and content, Liam took a better look around. We were in the middle of a grassy field near the base of the towering landmark that had a few scattered trees about, a massive domed water fountain, and a few hundred people walking all around us. "Wow! Are you crazy? Did someone see us?"

Easy pal, calm down. No eyes had been on us until after Liam started shouting nonsense to seemingly nobody. *It's okay, humans are dumb, completely oblivious to their surroundings. Worst case: someone might think their eyes are playing tricks on them, but I'd find even that surprising.*

"Hey, you could at least say present company excluded," Liam said, and when he got more stares from passersby, he knelt down and pulled Cody closer to him and acted like he was talking to the dog instead of himself. "Yeah, we're going to need to work out a better method of communicating. Wait!" On the bright side, the people in the park were beginning to avoid us, so Liam could finish his realization in peace. "You're in my head, can't I just, like, I dunno, think what I wanna say?"

Theoretically? Yes, that would be possible, but right now I have a block between our personal thoughts for the sake of privacy. It's an all or nothing kinda thing, I'd be able to hear all of your thoughts, and you'd hear all of mine. My brother highly recommended avoiding that at all costs.

Liam sighed and continued to pet Cody as he thought. While I couldn't hear his thoughts, I could still feel his emotions, and from that get a decent idea of his overall state of mind. He was frustrated for a few short moments before a sudden realization. "Got it!" he said out loud at the same time. He fished out his broken phone and held it up to the side of his head. "There we go, now we're free to talk."

Yeah, guess that'll do it. We should get going though, the people around here still think you're crazy.

We only stuck around the park long enough for Cody to take care of business and then began walking.

"Where are we going anyway?" It was nice to be surrounded by people on the sidewalk and not get stares now that Liam was talking into a phone.

I told you, I know some people here, we're going to pay one of them a visit.

"Could you be any more vague? Besides, who would you even know up…Wait, what the hell does Megatron have to do with anything?"

*What? How do you…*That's when I remembered, the same way I could sense his emotions, he got glimpses of my memories. That could get annoying in time. *Never mind, Megatron's my brother; he's a Muse, and he's been living up here on Earth for a while now. He can help us get set up with whatever we need: money, a place to live, whatever.* Truth was, I didn't really know what else we would need. The only point of reference I had to go off was what I had seen in movies about people on the run. First, they always smashed their phones, and that part had already been taken care of for us, but after that, the main characters would find some some way to get their hands on fake IDs, and while I didn't think our situation required quite such drastic measures,

Megatron would definitely know what we did need.

"All right, I guess that's a smart move. Where's Mega–"
Liam stopped because he felt ridiculous saying that nickname
out loud. "Where's your brother at now?"

Work would be my best bet, his office is this way, just a few miles.

"A few miles?! You couldn't have dropped us off a little
closer?"

*Theoretically? Yes, but c'mon, you're a runner, and you've been
bedridden for over a month with a broken back. I don't need to be in your
head to know you could use a good run.*

A smile stretched across his face for the first time in days.
"How many miles exactly?"

*Three, but I could probably find a suitable detour to make it a nice
even 5K.*

"Start the clock." Liam put his phone back in his pocket,
gave a jolt on Cody's leash, and took off running; the rush of
endorphins was nearly immediate.

Twenty-one minutes and twelve seconds, I said trying to hold back
a laugh as we stopped in front of Megatron's office building.

"Oh shut it already, I told you to stop counting ages ago,"
Liam said angrily. "I swear, I could've done it in half that time
if it wasn't for this little moron here." He turned to Cody
where he laid out panting like his life depended on it. "You're
joking, right? You didn't even jog, how are you tired?!"

Our run, if you could even call it that, had taken us away
from the beautiful city center and closer to the industrialized
port area. The closer we had gotten to our destination the more
the city turned derelict, with the concentration of grime,
beggars, and graffiti increasing exponentially. The clean and
sharp headquarters building was the only shining diamond in
the rough.

You don't seem very tired, I said, fishing for a certain response.

"Not for a lack of trying!" he exclaimed, not the reaction I
was looking for, but I remained hopeful. "But now that you
mention it, I feel better than I thought I would. I was afraid my
legs would, oh, I don't know, be weaker or something."

I laughed to myself, deciding not to tell him just yet that I had been breaking down the lactic acid in his muscles as fast as it built up. It would've worked better if he had been able to run at full speed, but luckily, he had jogged in place at each streetlight and tried to rush Cody by jogging and tugging on his leash, so regardless, his legs would be ungodly sore in the morning. I couldn't give people cancer anymore, so that seemed like an amusing alternative. *We're about 4,000 feet lower here than Albuquerque, so maybe it's the elevation? That's gotta be it.* I laughed silently again even harder.

"Need some water?"

Liam turned to face the direction of the voice and found that it belonged to a pretty blonde security guard wearing an expertly starched white uniform top. I felt Liam's heartbeat jump up a notch as blood rushed to his cheeks, and I couldn't really blame him, she was gorgeous.

"Um, yeah. Yeah, I could use some…"

"I was asking for the dog," she sneered, crushing Liam's feelings of infatuation. "Look at the poor guy. What's wrong with you?"

Liam fumbled around with sounds that can't quite be called words while the security guard knelt down and let Cody lap up some water from her own green tinted sports bottle.

You should try saying something, that usually helps, I said, trying not to be belittling, but failing.

"Um, sorry. I'm not from around here. I, um, I wasn't expecting to bring him with me." He sighed with relief since getting those words out had been a chore.

She looked up at us and lessened her death glare. "Well, what are you doing here?"

"I um…I have a meeting with Mega–"

Oh crap, Edward Kratz, his host's name is Edward Kratz! I said as quickly as I could to stop him from finishing that nickname.

"Um, a meeting with Edward Kratz?" If I had control over my own hands, I would've buried my face into my palm. He made it sound like a question and the security guard's suspicions of us intensified.

She stood up and crossed her arms. "Mr. Kratz? Really?

J. A. Reed

And how do you know Mr. Kratz exactly?"

I coached Liam through what to say, and luckily, for once, he didn't mess it up. "Yeah, I don't have an appointment, but his brother Zeke sent me. If you call up I'm sure there won't be an issue."

Now smile, I said, praying he knew better than to verbalize that part. *But not a creepy smile, more of a confident smirk.*

I could tell the guard was at a loss. She clearly hadn't expected Liam to suddenly start being coherent. She still held onto a tinge of doubt, but she excused herself to fact check my story. When she returned, she held the front door open for us and had a defeated look on her face. "Follow me, sir."

Yes! It worked! Okay, cards on the table, that was a total gamble, Megatron kinda hates me.

"What?!" Liam shouted at me but quickly did his best to cover. "Um, what...about Cody?"

"We can hold onto him at the front desk until your business is concluded." She scratched his head as we walked through the door. "That's right little guy, I'll take real good care of you." She spoke in baby talk, but she still managed to add an insulting tone toward Liam. I was kind of impressed.

One awkwardly silent elevator ride later, we were led to a waiting room and dropped off like a child at school. The receptionist, Kristin, pulled away from her phone call just long enough to say, "Mr. Kratz is in a meeting; please have a seat, and I'll let you know when he's available." It was apparently a long meeting – a *very* long meeting – that had probably just begun because we were halfway through our fifth magazine before we finally heard, "Mr. Kratz will see you now." Kristin stood up from behind her desk and gestured toward the hallway behind her. "Follow me please."

We followed her around the desk and into the hallway. Along the walls were various pieces of art, most of it pretty good, just nothing famous. Further down the line there was one section of large frames that ditched the mediocre art in lieu of corporate headshots. Each head shot showcased the various men and women running the company in their expensive suits.

"Which one?" Liam whispered trying not to draw attention.

Second to last, that's my little brother. Well, the poor sap he's inhabiting at least. The portrait in question contained a big boned gray-haired man seated in a navy blue portly suit sporting a massive gold watch and thick glasses. It hung above a plaque reading: "Edward Kratz" on one line, and "Regional Chief Marketing Officer" on the second line. I could feel Liam get uneasy like he wanted to say something but couldn't at the moment. I took a leap and assumed what he was thinking. *Sadly, not all of my siblings are as courteous to their hosts as I am. Megatron and the other Muses usually take over their hosts completely once they get in. I don't condone it, but there's also nothing I can do about it.* The receptionist stopped in front of one of the many doors and opened it for us with a glinting smile. *Once we're inside let me do the talking, but I'll answer any questions you have afterward, I promise.* My words did little to calm his nerves, but Liam hid it well on the outside.

"Thank you," he said while passing the woman. She smiled bigger and blushed as she let the door close behind us.

"A child?" a deep throaty voice said in a grumble. "Was that the best you could find, Ezekiel?"

The man in the room with them was almost unrecognizable from the portrait we had passed in the hallway. He was well over a hundred pounds overweight, and a fair amount of that extra fat resided in his neck and jowls making his head look like a gelatinous blob. He had the same amber colored horn-rimmed glasses on, but now they were digging trenches into the side of his head as opposed to resting comfortably as they should. Liam felt disgusted, and I couldn't blame him.

"At least he's in shape," I said out loud in my own angelic voice, "You've really let yourself go little brother."

"Whoa! You can do that?" Liam asked, startled by my unexpected switch from internal speech to external.

"Ugh," Megatron grunted, "I see you've taken after Zadkiel. Why do you both insist on sharing your hosts? Doesn't the constant mortal squabbling get annoying? It's bad enough having to work around them."

J. A. Reed

"You never were much of a people person, were you?" I said, egging him on out of habit. I was supposed to be nice to him until he helped us out, but it was hard to fight my nature.

"Never mind, I see it now. You're just as annoying as them, maybe even more so." He glanced over at his computer's dual monitors and read something quickly before returning his gaze to us. "I hope you didn't come all this way just to pester me, I have work to do."

"Right, yes, sorry. I do have a good reason for being here. Mind if we take a seat?"

He begrudgingly motioned for us to sit across from him and sat back in his surprisingly strong chair. I tried to keep on subject as I told him the story of my arrival in New Mexico and the tragedy that forced us to relocate to Seattle. I ended by trying to stroke his ego, making sure to overestimate how rich and connected he was, and I even commented on my own downfalls, stressing how lost I was in this new world with no one but my amazing brother to help me. I really pulled out all the stops.

"Is that it?" he asked, nearly emotionless.

"Um, yeah?" I wasn't sure what I expected him to say, but that wasn't it. "So, can you help us?"

Megatron sat silently staring at us for a second before straining to sit up and reach his desk. He grabbed a picture frame and turned it around toward us. "Do you see this house?"

The photo featured a masterfully decorated living room with floor to ceiling windows that offered a beautiful view of the Seattle skyline. I already started to fear where this was going, but I humored him. "Yup," but I had to get my own licks in where I could, too. "My host doesn't need glasses."

Megatron tightened his jaw in annoyance and removed his glasses. The fat on the side of his head slowly filled in the gaps left behind like very old memory foam. "When I took this host, he was living in a rundown studio apartment. It took me years to build this company from nothing, influencing the right people just right, planting the seeds of ideas from behind the scenes and hoping these damn humans didn't screw it all up, as they tend to do. I worked for everything I have now, and you want me to just give you money and a place to live? I didn't get any handouts, why should you?"

He wasn't wrong, but at the same time he had plenty to spare; at this point he was just being petty. "I'm not asking for a handout, more like…a stepping stone. And a few pointers maybe? Like, with us ditching that hospital in Albuquerque, I don't know if they can track us or something. Do we need to get a new identity?"

Megatron pinched and massaged the bridge of his nose, which I took to mean that notion was completely ridiculous but perhaps not. "I can get you set up with new papers. But I'm not doing it for you, as long as you're here in my city I don't want you and that un-severed spine drawing any damn tabloid attention." He scoffed and added the rest mostly to himself, "It's bad enough Tabbris put us on the damn radar with his little *hobby*."

"Great!" I cheered. "I'm sure that'll take some time to round up, though, where should we stay until that's all taken care of?" I said, fishing for the handout.

This time he rubbed his temples, but my consistent nagging was finally paying off. "If I help you will you leave me alone?"

"For now, yeah." I couldn't make any long-term promises.

"All right. I own a condo building overlooking Lake Washington. You'll have to room with Tabbris, but it should be more than big enough for the two of you."

"Tabby? Really?" If our family had a black sheep, it was Tabby. He was antisocial, awkward, and all around unpleasant.

"There's a congregation of homeless people near Pike Place if you'd prefer? I can have Kristin drop you off–"

"Okay, fine, I'm sorry." It was obvious he wouldn't budge, and I guess I had it coming if I was honest with myself. "We'll take the condo." He jotted down an address and slid it across the desk.

Liam grabbed the paper and turned to leave, but Megatron wasn't done yet. "Not take, rent. But don't worry, I'll get you a job at our nearest location so you can afford what I'll charge you." He shot a sinister smirk at us; clearly, he was enjoying this very much.

"That sounds only fair," I said, trying to sound nice. "Thanks for your time, Megatron."

"I think it's about time you cut it with that nickname – I still haven't said how much your rent would be."

"True, but you already promised we'd make enough working for you to afford the rent, so the more you charge us, the more you'll have to pay us. Unless you're going to go back on your word...?" This time I was the one smirking.

"Just get out of here," he grumbled with a vigorous wave of his hand. Taking my victory while I still had it, we left the building like it was on fire, only slowing down long enough to trade the visitor's badge back for Cody from the front desk.

* * *

Stopping for a much-needed lunch break at a quaint little café/bakery down the road from Megatron's office, I tied Cody up and went inside to see what I could get to satisfy my grumbling stomach. The glass display that covered a majority of the counter was packed with delicious looking baked goods from cinnamon rolls the size of my head that were coated in thick layers of cream colored frosting, to croissants stuffed to the brim with various meats, vegetables, and melted cheeses, but the small squares of paper all glared at me with their high price tags. Unfortunately, it was the sad looking egg and cheese breakfast sandwich that had my name on it. I cleared out the last of my cash on the measly sandwich and used the three coins in change that came back to me as a sad excuse for a tip. The cashier shot me a fake smile with the receipt, but his eyes didn't hide the fact that he thought I was a cheapskate.

As I took a seat to wait for my order, Zeke assured me that once we got to the condo money wouldn't be an issue any longer, but it was hard for me to shake the uneasy feeling of being completely broke and helpless. My mind kept projecting my face onto those of all the homeless people we had passed in the city like some sort of waking nightmare or a premonition of my possible future. Zeke was able to feel my discomfort and offered to fly us to the condo afterwards because it would be too far for Cody to run, and we couldn't afford the bus let alone a cab. I was actually grateful for that when my order was ready and it took a significant amount of effort for me to just stand up and grab it off the counter.

I grabbed the back of a nearby booth seat, as I tried to stretch out the stiffness building in my legs and I could've sworn I heard Zeke laugh in my head, but after a quick glance around, I didn't see anything funny or out of the ordinary in the café. Besides an employee, there were only a handful of people in the shop, two guys and a girl around college age sharing a booth toward the back, a middle-aged man in a brown suit that had been behind me in line, but was now texting as he waited for his scone and latte, and a man in his eighties or nineties going to town on a slice of blueberry pie at the counter with a worn out *Navy Veteran* hat covering his thin silver hair.

Somewhat satisfied with the quick stretch, I continued for the front door, but my steps were a little on the uncoordinated side. "Have a nice day," the tattooed man behind the counter said in reaction to the bell jingling against the glass of the door, and I could hear the slight tinge of resentment in his voice for skimping on the tip. It made me feel bad all over again, but I promised myself I'd come back and tip triple just to make up for it once I could afford to do so.

Cody was waiting patiently for our return tied to the leg of a minuscule outdoor patio set that he easily could've dragged away if he had the mind to; luckily, he wasn't smart enough to know how close he was to freedom.

"Good boy," I said rubbing under his chin with my free hand as I took a seat in one of the two lopsided metal chairs. "That was a pretty crazy meeting, wasn't it?" I made it sound like baby talk to a dog, but in reality, I didn't want to wait any longer before discussing everything that had happened with

J. A. Reed

Zeke. Trying to make my end of the conversation not sound crazy would get more and more difficult, but I was willing to take that risk.

Oh, right, yeah, sorry about that. You know how family drama can be, but in the end, we are family, so he wouldn't have left us high and dry. Are you all right with the whole arrangement, though? You know, working for him and all that?

I opened the brown paper bag, fished out my sandwich, and took a big first bite as I thought on that. Getting a job to pull my weight sounded completely reasonable to me, so that wasn't an issue, but I did come to the realization that prior to the actual meeting itself, I hadn't the slightest clue how it was going to go. I had been in uncharted territory for a while now, first, my whole foundation was rocked in the accident, then came the really crazy stuff like finding out angels were real, finding out fallen angels were real, taking one on as a host, losing my... well, losing everything, and lastly, flying halfway across the country in an instant to meet yet another fallen angel. Looking at the whole thing from that perspective, the meeting was actually the most normal thing I had done in weeks. I finished chewing and swallowed the last bits of that first big bite, so I answered quietly, "Yeah, I think a job will be good for me, something to do, a distraction from...stuff."

I guess so, yeah. I don't really know, I've never really had a job, per se. I mean, as an angel I was given a purpose to fulfill, but, I'd hardly call that a job. And if it was, I totally got fired, literally and figuratively. Regardless though, I'll be right there with you, we're in this thing together!

I laughed out loud a little and was lucky enough that no one passing by gave me any strange looks, but Zeke had reminded me of a question I had been holding onto for a while and I risked saying it in the open public. "What purpose is that exactly?" I glanced around like I was about to tell an inappropriate joke, "Why did...*He*...make angels?"

There was a pause before Zeke said anything in response, and I regretted asking something that was probably far too personal, but he eventually did chime in with his usual nonchalance. *Wow, yeah, go ahead, skip all the small stuff and just make that leap. I'll tell you best I know, but I don't have the full answer for you, because Dear ol' Dad and I weren't what you would call "close," never actually met the guy, if that gives you any idea, but I do know that each of our tiers have different purposes. Take the Muses, at the bottom right above you mortals, they inspire those closest to them, filling them with positive emotions to unite them. In the beginning, before mankind was even a twinkle in the Old Man's eye, it was just us angels, so the Muses were pretty much the glue that kept us close as a family. It wasn't until humanity came around that they started spreading their gifts wider and branching out, I don't think that helped when we started dividing. Um, next up are Saints, they're easy, they're warriors, they guarded the inner sanctum where Pops spent all his time, only Archangels were allowed in there. Best way I can describe it: I pray you never come face to face with a Saint, because then you'd know why nothing but an Archangel would even try to get past them. In hindsight, that's probably why we lost; not a single Saint picked our side.*

"That didn't seem like a red flag at the time?" I asked only halfway seriously.

I was a little more concerned with doing what I thought was right, not holding a popularity contest, so excuse me for not taking a headcount before the fire and brimstone started to fly.

"Ok, I'm sorry, please carry…wait, was there really fire and brimstone, or was that just a metaphor?" Now the uncomfortable passersby were back, and I had to remind myself to watch my volume, my eagerness to hear what could only be be the greatest war story in all creation had gotten the better of me.

Of course there was, it was a crazy battle, I won't go into details, but it was intense. My hopes crushed, Zeke went on. *Where was I? Oh right, Enochians and Angels are very similar, not sure what we were really meant to do, but the general consensus is we were just made for odd job manual labor type stuff, Jack of all trades in a sort. I'm sure there are more differences between us and them, but none that really stick out in my mind. Guardians are like the overprotective big brothers and sisters, and Archangels were more like aunts and uncles than siblings, they were pretty much on the same level as Pops, I barely met any of them before the Fall, knew most only by reputation.*

J. A. Reed

"So, let me get this straight…you know what everyone else was made to do but not your own class? That sucks." I raised the last bite of my sandwich when Cody whined loudly at it. His sad eyes looked hungrily at it, and I remembered it had probably been a while since he last ate. "Oh fine, you can have it." I threw it down, and Cody lapped it up in two seconds flat.

Not just me, I don't know what Enochians do either. Well, I mean, Zak's the only one I ever really talked to, and he can communicate over a much greater distance than anyone else, that might be the Enochian thing. Ooh! They're all super goody two-shoes and real sticklers for the rules, too; I'm pretty sure that's why all but one of them sided with the others still upstairs. But just because they're all squares doesn't mean that was Pops doing, I'm sure that's just my opinion and nothing more.

"I'm starting to see a trend here. Just how outnumbered were you?"

Um, well, including me, we were…15 strong…out of 42…But that's in the past, just let it go, are you ready to leave yet or what?

Zeke had given me much more than I expected, so I was fine with dropping the subject for a while. I adjusted my footing, preparing to stand and leave, but without warning all of my muscles tensed up, making it impossible to move. I could only guess it was because of the personal nature of our last subject, but I got hit with a sudden memory flash that had been far stronger and more vivid than any I had witnessed before that moment. The memory took place somewhere very bright, making my eyes strain to adjust.

"Ezekiel, please don't do this," a feminine voice rang out seemingly disembodied. It sounded very similar to when Zeke had spoken for himself in Megatron's office. I felt a light caress on my right shoulder and leaned my cheek in to meet the hand that was there, only it wasn't me controlling my body. In fact, I was pretty sure I wasn't even in my body. "Please, just forget these rebellious thoughts and stay with me." I turned my head and kissed the hand getting a partial view behind me. Where I had expected to find the burnt skeleton wings I knew from our first encounter, I instead found a mass of glowing orange feathers more beautiful than any that exist on Earth. This memory was definitely from before the Fall, but I didn't know much more than that yet. Who was this woman behind me?

"You know I can't do that, Jo, it isn't right what they intend to do with humanity." The voice coming from me was Zeke's for sure, but there was little trace of his cool demeanor.

The mysterious woman behind me moved in closer and wrapped me in a full body embrace, but I still couldn't see her face. "It's not your place to meddle in such affairs. If you worry for the humans, let the Guardians protect them. Let the Archangels counsel Father in what is right. I fear that if you forget your place, something terrible will happen to you."

"Maybe I haven't forgotten my place, maybe I have found it. The others, they all know their purpose, maybe this is ours." I grabbed her hands and squeezed them affectionately. "This could be our purpose, won't you reconsider? Won't you stay by my side?"

The tender moment froze in complacent silence for an extended period of time, but it turned sour once the woman released her grip and whispered, "I'm sorry," in my ear. I fell to my knees, and the last sound I heard was that of wings flapping away behind me. A single quick blink later, I was back in present day Seattle.

"Who's…" I almost said her name next, but given just how personal that memory had felt, I decided to drop it for now and not push him any further too quickly. I really did want to learn more about the Fall and everything leading up to it, but there would be more than enough time for that later, once we both had time to get more comfortable with one another.

Who what now? Zeke asked confused by my awkward single word.

"Oh, I was going to say…" I stalled just long enough to make up a cover story. "Just asking, Who's Tabby, the other Muse we're going to be living with?" Not too bad if I say so myself.

Oh right, I forgot that part, or maybe just repressed it…Tabby is a special one, super weird, but don't worry, he mostly keeps to himself so I'm sure we'll barely even notice he's there. Shall we go now though? You'll finally be able to talk freely again back at the condo.

"Definitely, I'm so…" Without any warning, Zeke scooped us all up and flew us to the inside of what I can only assume was the new condo. "…Tired." I wobbled a little from the jump and had to take a seat on what turned out to be a very comfortable white couch before getting my bearings.

Sorry, I thought you would've gotten used to that by now.

"Maybe just a three-second countdown or something next time." I burped loudly, and was incredibly relieved it had only been a burp. "Much appreciated."

After my stomach stopped doing somersaults, I rose up slowly and was able to properly take in my new surroundings. The living room walls, carpet, and furniture around me all matched the white couch that had just caught me. The surfaces of bookshelves, cabinets, and entertainment centers were neatly decorated in various electronics and framed art, but not a single speck of dust. The carpet and upholstery were completely pristine and stain-free, which given the warning about Tabby's hermit-like lifestyle, was not expected.

I spun around to find a cozy kitchen tucked away in the corner of the room, the brushed silver appliances and linoleum floor giving it a pleasing contrast from the rest of the area. In the next corner to my right the wall folded away leading to a long hallway with at least three closed doors visible. Not wanting to open the wrong door and disrupt an unsuspecting Tabby, I decided to hold off on exploring that area of the condo for the time being.

My attention returned to scanning the living room and appreciating everything from the 70-inch wall mounted TV to the turnstile sitting atop more than 200 records. I bubbled up with excitement looking around at everything and the fears that had plagued me earlier that day about being homeless faded away, overshadowed by hope. "This is amazing," I said, tearing up just a little.

Hell yeah it is. Who knew Tabby had good taste? Oh, and look at that view.

I shifted my gaze slightly to my right where floor to ceiling glass doors led out to a patio overlooking the lake. With each step closer I took, more and more of the spectacular view came into sight. I parted the doors, and a cool breeze rushed over me like a wave; if any of my past worries had clung onto me this long, they were now washed away for certain. A few more gliding steps, and I reached the railing, leaving nothing left between me and the blissful landscape. Immediately below were a series of docks with small boats of varying types that rocked back and forth on the choppy water. Beyond that were miles of twinkling lights as the late afternoon sun reflected back at me intermittently with each ripple across the lake surface. In the distance, rolling hills coated in green, spots of dense gray skyscrapers, bridges packed with the red taillights of after-work traffic, and wispy white clouds that blocked a majority of the blue sky filled the remainder of the view.

More tears of joy filled my eyes, but when one of them finally succumbed and rolled down my cheek, it was no longer born from happy feelings. Suddenly, without wanting to, I realized how alone I was. My mom was gone, she would never see this gorgeous view, just as I would never see her again. More tears fell under the weight of sadness and I tried to wipe them away, but more just took up their place.

Liam? Are you all right?

"Yeah, I'm fine," I lied. I tried to push through the rough patch, but instead of getting better, my thoughts only soured further. I spiraled into worse and worse thoughts until it seemed like I was lost to the abyss, no way back up to when I had been happy. Happy? That word felt like a foreign concept now, something I've only heard of, but never really understood. My head dropped – dropped so low all I could see from my perch was the railing under my hands, and the cement pathways that lead to the boat docks. From this high up, the pathways looked so small and pointless, not unlike myself. I looked closer, and I wanted to be closer. I wanted to be down there…

Liam! What are you doing?!

"What?!" Zeke's loud voice in my head snapped me back to reality, but not the same reality I had remembered from before.

J. A. Reed

I was standing on top of the patio table with one foot reaching out over the ledge. "What the hell?!" I shouted, fumbling to regain my balance and not fall over. Shaking, I got down off the table and put my hands on my knees trying to catch my breath and lower my racing heartbeat. "What just happened?"

"Nice to see you again, Ezekiel," said a voice from inside the condo. It startled me, returning my heartrate back to unsafe levels. "Who's your friend?" He looked to be barely older than me, nineteen maybe, but if he addressed Zeke, I knew it could only be another like him.

"Of course," Zeke said out loud through me again, "Tabby, can you please leave my host alone? He's gone through enough without your twisted sense of humor."

Tabby laughed as he walked up to us. Long straight black hair fell over his face covering his right eye, but the deep purple one peered through and did a quick once over. "Aw, but it's so much easier when they're hurt is still fresh."

"What are you talking about? Did you…What did you do?" I had my suspicions, but this world of fallen angels was still new and confusing to me, so I didn't want to assume.

Tabby's a Muse, remember? He can influence people with thoughts, ideas, emotions, you name it. Tabby likes to use that gift for…well, I think you already know the answer.

"You're a monster," I spat, but that only made Tabby laugh again.

"In your opinion, maybe. I've seen your story a million times, kid; the only difference is you prayed and got Zeke instead. Often when they pray out, I'm the one that helps them." He held out his hand, "The name's Tabbris, but in public you can call me Tristan; that's my host's name."

I looked at his hand but didn't touch it. "Which room is mine?" I said, trying and failing to hold back my hatred.

Tabby smirked and lowered his hand knowing a lost cause when he saw it. "First on the right. Bathroom is last on the left. And don't worry, I'm rarely here, and when I am, I keep to myself."

I walked through him and he moved almost quickly enough

so that only my shoulder clipped his. "Good." I got as far as my hand on the doorknob of my room before he spoke again.

"What was his name?" I didn't want to give him any more attention than I already had, but curiosity got the better of me, so I looked back but said nothing. "The man who jumped, what was his name?"

In a messed-up way, it made sense why he'd be interested in that, so I obliged, "Varro, Thane Varro."

"Huh," he said surprised. "Not one of mine, peculiar. Don't see many of those." With one last shrug before forgetting about it and moving on, Tabby turned and disappeared into the kitchen, and I disappeared into my room.

CHAPTER SEVEN: THE NEW NORMAL

One long month of working full forty-hour weeks and eating nothing but instant noodles and the occasional stale pastry slotted for the dumpster at work finally paid off when I got my hands on my second paycheck. The first check only covered half of a pay period and went entirely to paying rent and grocery shopping for the aforementioned noodles, so this much bigger check was all mine to do with as I pleased. My initial instinct was to splurge it all away on video games and as many inches of television screen as possible, but Zeke in a rare moment of maturity reminded me how devastated I had been every time I opened our empty fridge over the past weeks, so our first stop ended up being the market.

As I pulled out a shopping cart and got started, I fished my new pay as you go phone out and opened up a generic note-taking app to type [Can you even taste the food I eat? I've always wondered.] Pretending to be on the phone had proven to be a decent method of talking to Zeke in public without being judged negatively, but texting felt more comfortable at times.

That would be an understatement, he said with an audible smirk. *Angels don't need food, so a sense of taste wasn't high on the list of priorities when we were created. Humans, on the other hand, I can't even put it into words. Let's just say as much as you complain about your Ramen every day, to me it's still some of the best tasting food I've ever had, so if there's better food out there, I can't even imagine.*

I had originally intended on just grabbing a few essentials, but if Zeke had never tried any foods before, I'd have to make sure and grab a few extra delicacies. Bacon, cinnamon buns, ice cream, a frozen pizza, and about a dozen other guilty pleasure foods all made their way into my cart, but after a short hesitation I returned the pizza.

Wait, why'd you put that one back?

[If we're going to do this, we're going to do this right. Just trust me]

We crisscrossed our way down each and every aisle and

eventually filled the cart more than we should have, but only because shopping with Zeke was just like what I imagine shopping with a seven-year-old is like. *Whoa, what's that? Ooh, that looks good, is it good? Wait, go back, I saw something back that way, c'mon, turn back!*

Our last pass through the store was along the deli where workers covered in white clothes, red aprons, and poofy hair nets were cutting and preparing freshly sliced meats and cheeses. What they had to offer here almost definitely trumped the processed and prepackaged counterparts already in my cart, but at this point being able to afford everything we had grabbed was already questionable, so despite the pestering voice in my head, I had to continue forward.

"Good day, sir," said a warm and bubbly voice next to the closest display. "Would you like to try a free sample?"

Instinctually, a smile crept up, but as soon as I saw that her samples were nothing but olives, it faded back away. I was just about to respectfully decline, but then the strangest thought popped to the front of my mind. So far Zeke had only been thinking of food as wondrous and delicious, but as anyone knows, there are plenty of bad eats out there as well.

"Oh, yes please," I said with realistic enthusiasm. I picked up the toothpick and raised the unappealing food trying desperately to not let my emotions toward it spoil the surprise for Zeke.

Ah, something new, bring it on! Zeke said with naive excitement.

I took one bite into it and had to remind myself this was just a momentary sacrifice for the sake of a hopefully epic prank. "That's good," I lied to the employee as she smiled up at me with her wide eyes in suspense of my reaction.

Ugh, what is that? Zeke said, disgust obvious in his tone. *Ugh, no, no, please. Please make it stop.* I chewed it several more times just to make sure the flavors would stick around a while longer before swallowing and the foul taste helped keep me from laughing. *Ugh, why? Why would you eat this? This is awful! I can't…I can't…Please, spit it out, throw it up, just do something, please!*

"May I have one more?" I asked, merely to hear what Zeke

would say.

No! No, please! I will fly us straight to China! Or…wherever! I don't even care if people see, I am not letting you put one more of those cursed things anywhere near your mouth again!

"Sure," the lady replied, clearly oblivious to my real motives, "of course you can, help yourself."

Not willing to call Zeke's bluff, which I actually don't think was a bluff at all, I put my hands back on my cart and started moving forward again. "Oh, I was just kidding, thank you though." I pulled my phone back out just to make sure Zeke got the message, [Payback for my dead legs last month]

What? That was all for…? Ok, yeah, I guess I deserved that. But mine was way funnier, I mean when you tried to get out of bed that next morning? Classic!

"I fell and…" I accidentally blurted before catching myself and calming down. [I fell and dislocated my shoulder!!! How is that funny?]

I put it back in, c'mon. And I could've left your legs that sore all day, but no, I fixed them up too. So…you're welcome.

I reached the casher line and had to wait until after loading the contents of our cart onto the moving conveyor belt; luckily, our cashier wasn't the cream of the crop, so I had time to type my response before paying and leaving. [I might have certain things to thank you for, that's not one of them. We're even now]

After you push this cart all the way home we'll be even. My wings need a rest once every seven hundred seventy-seven uses, it's an ancient angel thing, you wouldn't understand.

[I understand being petty]

"That'll be $242.12 please," The cashier said politely.

Well, there goes most of that check, hope it was worth it, Zeke added, clearly still salty toward me for seemingly nothing, and it didn't end there. Zeke was stubbornly true to his word of making me push the cart all the way home despite being able to easily fly everything home. Luckily, the store was less than a mile from the condo and pretty much entirely flat or downhill, but the principle of the thing was far greater than just the current situation. It was time to clear the air.

"I don't get it, you have the power to do these incredible things, and it doesn't cost you a thing, no time, no energy, just easy as can be, and yet you're literally freeloading in my head right now. What gives?"

You already know why I'm making you walk, but if you mean more "big picture," have you ever really thought about just how big that picture is? I had months downstairs to search for potential hosts, people just like you, people hurting in every different way imaginable, and do you know what I learned? Bad things happen. They just do, there's no way to stop that. Now yes, I could spend every minute of every day healing the sick and preventing tragedies, but that would just be treating the symptoms, not the disease.

"And what's the disease?"

Well, to be honest, that's about as far as that metaphor goes. What's wrong on Earth isn't a simple black-and-white problem. Now, I will admit, the presence of the fractures between this world and mine have done more harm than good, and the bigger they get, the more powerful beings can cross over and wreak havoc, but at the end of the day humans still hold a vast majority of control over themselves. Humans can choose to embrace the negative influences demons bring with them, or they can choose to ignore them.

I had been open to hearing his take on things up until that last bit, that last part I had firsthand experience with and knew him to be completely wrong. "Easy for you to say!" I said a little too loudly out of anger. "I felt Tabby's influence and can assure you there's no ignoring that."

That's different, he's a Muse, he was made for influencing. I'm talking about demons that are nowhere near that level.

"Maybe, maybe not. Just…just hold on." We reached our building, and I got ready to carry the first load of bags up when Zeke flew everything, cart and all, up into the condo. I tried not to get off topic so I let the fact that he didn't warn me, yet again, slide. "The point I'm trying to make, the point you're clearly missing entirely, is that I know you're not as cold-hearted as most, so why aren't you doing more good with your powers? Why are we just working at a coffee shop and living a seemingly normal life when we could be out there? We could be doing so much more with our time." Making my point had taken the focus of my attention, but I had also managed to get a few of the items that needed to be on ice put away as I had been ranting.

It took less effort to listen, so I picked up the pace and started putting the rest of the groceries away as Zeke rebuked. "Look," he said out loud now that we were safely in the privacy of our own home, "you're right about me not being that bad respectively, but neither am I Mother Teresa. If you want to waste your days away putting Band-Aids on bullet wounds, you go right ahead, but you can do it without me. I came to Earth to get away, a glorified vacation. All I want to do is just live this seemingly normal life and work at a coffee shop, figuratively speaking, of course; I don't really wanna work for Megatron forever, but you know what I mean."

As I put the last can into the pantry, I was at a loss for words. Obviously, I couldn't do any of the good I was thinking about without Zeke, and he clearly wanted no part in any of it at all. I began to question just how long I wanted to share my body with this parasite. I had been so terrified of taking on a fallen angel back when we first met because I was scared he was lying to me, but now I was scared because I knew he wasn't. Back then, the stakes had been my life in exchange for my mother's, and while I'll be the first to admit that screw up was my fault, I had to consider the stakes now. Without Zeke, I'd be homeless, jobless, and all alone in an unknown city. Somehow the stakes were worse now than they were before, and it made me feel trapped.

"What's wrong now?" Zeke asked, and while it may have actually been a worried tone, in my head it sounded condescending.

"Nothing, I just need…I just need to go for a run. I need to clear my head." I ran into my room and changed as quickly as I ever had before. What I really wanted was to be alone, and away from Zeke more specifically, but I knew that wasn't possible. Regardless, a nice long run would do me some good, and I could try my best to imagine Zeke wasn't there, and that was all I could ask for.

* * *

Liam runs too much. If he's not working or sleeping, he's running, and I have nothing against running, if the occasion calls for it, but I mean c'mon! A little variety, that's all I ask for. And I'm not the only one that thinks so either, even the stupid dog knows it's excessive. Liam used to take Cody with him on his jogs, but the little fella couldn't keep up, so instead of cutting back or anything, he just started leaving him behind and running even further without the excess baggage. Never thought I'd say it, but I'm jealous of that four-legged idiot, I wish Liam could leave me at home too.

When this all began, I had hoped it was just a phase since his legs worked again, but the more time that passed, the more he went out and the further he'd go. I quietly indulged him for a while, but it just got so boring so fast. People watching had been able to hold my attention in small doses, but after a while even that started losing its appeal. I gradually started dropping subtle hints, offering up my much faster wings more often, making sure that he knew I could keep him in shape even if he never got out of bed, and even escalated to the occasional passive-aggressive remark in hopes he would catch on, but all I ever got back was nonsense about it 'clearing his head' or whatever. I've been living in that head for months now, and I can attest, there's just as much going on up here no matter how fast his feet are moving. Regardless, I don't know how much longer I can deal with all the running. I'd talk to him about it, but he doesn't talk to me much anymore since he seems to need to go for a run every time we're home alone, and after that there are too many eyes and ears around for us to talk openly.

I finally caught a small break when we were on our way back from one of the hillier routes Liam liked to throw in every once and a while and came to a street blocked off for

J. A. Reed

construction. Liam stopped all forward momentum but continued to jog in place as he swiveled his head from left to right.

Know which way to go? I asked, but I already knew that Liam didn't know the city well enough yet to know exactly how to get back except for his usual route.

"Um…" he said quietly as he looked around for some bearing. "Left?"

If you want to get lost, yeah, sure, left. If you want to get home though, it's to the right. If you like, I can be your own personal GPS. I shifted my voice to a pretty decent British robot impression. *In five feet, turn right.* I had expected Liam to laugh but didn't get so much as a lip curl out of him, he just turned right and resumed his quick pace. *Recalculating. In twenty feet, stop being a jackass.* This at least got a minor reaction, but Liam remained silent. *Ok, seriously now, what's gotten into you?*

"Can't…talk," he whispered one word at a time between strides.

Well, do you hear that sound? Ring, ring. That's your phone, you should answer it, because we're talking one way or another, and you won't like what's behind door number two. I didn't like making threats like that, but recently it seemed to be the only way to get Liam to cooperate.

Liam slowed to a walk and took several deep breaths before reluctantly pulling his phone out of his armband and holding it parallel with the ground a few inches in front of his mouth. "What is it?" he barked.

What's wrong with you recently? You hardly talk to me anymore, and all you do is run, and don't give me more of that clearing your head business, what's really going on?

Liam dragged out the silence as he struggled with how to reply. "Look, you just wouldn't understand." I wasn't satisfied with that answer.

Are you kidding me? I'm thousands of years old, just try me.

Liam slowed down even more and remained quiet even longer than the last time. "It's just…So much has happened recently, so much I'd rather not think about. Running…It helps me not think about it all. It helps me get through the day." As hard as he tried, a few tears broke through his defenses.

Great, now I made him cry. I couldn't stick with my "running is boring, stop it" argument, so I'd have to come up with something on the fly. *I know that, trust me, I know better than most, but...but don't you think you should find a little healthier way to cope?*

"Running is very healthy," he replied defensively.

He had a good point, but I was quick to recover. *Physically? Maybe, but emotionally? All you're doing is running away...*

"I'm not running away," Liam interrupted, "what I'm doing is different."

Is it? You said it yourself, you're running to stop yourself from thinking or feeling anything. Maybe you should stop running for once and face those feelings head on. That's the only way you'll ever resolve them. Damn, that was good, that was not where I started going with that conversation, but I was so glad it went that way, much better than my original idea.

It appeared to have worked because Liam stood still, and I could feel his emotions growing the longer he remained there. Fear, sadness, loneliness and everything you'd expect to accompany it boiled up and nearly drowned Liam before he cracked.

"I can't! I just...I just can't, ok?" Wiping his eyes again, he took off into a sprint. I tried calling his name a few times, but each time he only ran faster until I gave up trying and he finally slowed back to a jog. I wasn't sure if I had made things worse, better, or made no difference at all, but at the very least I tried, and it might not be today, but eventually I would try again. In the meantime, I could work on a new, and hopefully more successful, tactic.

As Liam passed alongside a fenced-off grassy park, I was suddenly reminded of my first few minutes on Earth, the way I had been flying uncontrollably with my broken wing, and I wandered if that's what Liam felt like.

Liam? He kept ignoring me, but that nagging feeling of familiarity was only growing stronger. *Liam, can you hold on for a second?* Again, he failed to respond, but I was trying to focus on figuring out what exactly I was sensing, and then out of nowhere it hit me like a ton of bricks. *LIAM STOP!*

Liam stopped finally, but he didn't understand that I was on a whole new subject. "I'm just not ready, can't you…"

No, not that, there's a Guardian here somewhere.

"Wait, what?" Liam spun around in circles, checking every direction more than a few times, but nothing seemed out of the ordinary. "You mean, like…like you?"

Guardians are a little above my pay grade, and this one isn't fallen, but besides that, yeah, it's an angel.

"An angel…" Liam said but quietly and in a tone suggesting he wasn't paying attention to me anymore. I pulled some of my attention away from trying to narrow down the source of the Guardian's power to follow Liam's gaze and figure out where his mind had wondered off to so suddenly. I couldn't be certain, but my educated guess was the beautiful young brunette playing fetch with her full grown Dalmatian midway through the park. She had a slender build and a perfectly shaped smile framing her straight and sparkling white teeth. I had seen Liam's high School crush when she came to visit him in the hospital, and despite the hair color being different, there was no denying he had a particular type. As Liam's eyes began to tingle from a lack of blinking, the young woman glanced up and made eye contact; Liam's reaction was anything but suave. He broke off his stare immediately, acted like he was finishing up some stretches, and then ran down the pavement until a building stood between us and the girl.

Liam, you have to get in there.

"What? I-I can't, I-I don't even…"

Liam…

"I m-mean what would I even…"

Liam, listen to…

"How do I even…"

Liam, stop stammering or I'll… he cut me off again, but this time what flowed from his voice box couldn't be considered words when strung together the way he had, even though individually I recognized all of them. *That's it!* Thanks to Liam's cowardice, we were in a perfect spot to disappear, so I flew him straight back to the condo bathroom, which had proved to be a good call because even if I hadn't torn him across several blocks, he probably had been on the verge of yakking up his breakfast anyway.

After flushing the toilet and grabbing something to clean up the areas he missed the bowl, Liam was able to get whole words out again, instead of whatever made up language he had used before. "How many times do I have to tell you? A little warning next time, Jeez!"

"You were spiraling, I had to rely on a classic. Now finish cleaning yourself up, grab Cody, and then we're heading back before that Guardian goes anywhere."

Liam threw the wad of soiled toilet paper into the bowl but remained still and obviously confused. "Wait, hold on, what? Why do we need Cody?"

"Well, he's a dog, it's a dog park, you get enough crazy stares as it is. Besides, I think I'll be able to use his heightened senses to find the Guardian easier. Now let's go, they might not be there for much longer."

"Um, well, I mean, I just puked, can't I brush my teeth first?"

I sighed, debating whether fighting him on this would be worth the risk, or just an additional waste of time and somehow, I knew it would be the latter. There was one potential way of compromising, so I tried that first. "Gargle some mouthwash and you can have a piece of gum, good enough?"

"Fine, but I better not regret it," Liam threatened as he opened the bathroom cabinet. One burning shot of spearmint later we threw a leash on Cody, popped a piece of fruity flavored gum, and, with ample warning, flew right back to Liam's hiding spot. I could feel how nervous he was to peak back around the corner. "Think she's still there?"

Who, the angel, or the human? I said, purposefully trying to embarrass him.

J. A. Reed

"What? I meant…What, I was talking…well, him or her, I don't know, do angels even have genders? I don't even…there were a lot of humans, I don't know what you're talking about… Can we get back to the thing now?" I laughed at him the whole time he regressed back to babbling, but he stopped once he realized he didn't actually know what I had in store next. "Wait, what are we doing anyway?"

All right, just put your hand on Cody for a few seconds, until I tell you to stop, I'll do all the hard work, you just have to follow his lead after that. Liam did as I asked and through him I tapped into Cody's body and mind. *Wow, there's like, nothing in here.*

"I know, I have a dumb dog, sorry, is it working or not?" Liam asked as he almost peeked around the corner but chickened out yet again.

Um, sort of? Even his nose sucks. It's still better than a human's, but by a dog's standard he's…he's just awful.

"Can I let go now or what? C'mon, you were the one in a hurry," Liam whined.

I worked as fast as possible with what was at my disposal and once I distinguished the correct scent, I directed Cody to follow it to the source and told Liam he could let go. Cody sniffed a wobbly pattern into the park, and the further in we got, the wider out he would swerve each time until Liam and I were both convinced he must've gotten sidetracked.

Stupid dog. Let me try again.

Instead of kneeling and letting me reconnect to Cody, Liam pulled his phone up to his ear to speak with me. "Um, well, if he's not cut out for this sort of thing, I mean, we are in a dog park…" I could tell by his leading tone, he already had an idea of his own but was too shy or embarrassed to ask. I let him go on a little longer before making my guess. "I mean, if all I have to do is touch them, you could use any dog, right? Like…I don't know, a Dalmatian perhaps?"

I tried to stop myself from busting up laughing in his face, but no amount of self-control could've prevented that one. *Oh, oh boy, thanks, I needed that.* Liam crossed his arms pouting silently. *Oh, oh sorry, you were serious? Look, if you think you can*

*speak actual words to an adult female and get close to her dog, you go right
ahead and do that. There's a first time for everything I guess.*

I guess my words of encouragement didn't do much good
because he sunk even lower and pouted harder. After a short
moment he put his phone back up to his ear. "Look, I can...I
mean, it's not like I've never...Ok, you have a point, what
should I say?"

*Easy there, kiddo, if you knew some of my horror stories when it
comes to relationships, you would not be asking for my help. Besides, it
doesn't matter what you say, you just have to speak normal, naturally, like
you would talk to a friend or anyone else. You know, contrary to popular
belief, women are people too.*

"You're an idiot."

*Exactly my point, it's a no brainer, just talk to her like you would
anyone else, because she is just anyone else.*

"No way, she's special," Liam said as if this were the
opening of some mushy Rom-Com.

*Everyone's "special," isn't that how it goes these days? You're special,
I'm special, hell, even the dumb dog is special, but if you can't say three
words to this girl, you'll never get to find out how she's special, so shut up,
nut up, and go say three words. If you don't fail, say another three, and so
on until you get the hang of it.*

"Ok! Ok! Fine, but I still don't know what to say," Liam said
as if he hadn't heard a word I said.

That's it, Cody and I will do this without you. Liam protested, but
I convinced him to put his hand back on the dog's scruffy neck.
I convinced Cody that the toy Liam's crush had been tossing to
her own dog belonged to him, and only him. Maybe having a
stupid dog could have its uses after all.

As soon as Liam let go, Cody sprinted after the fetch toy
leaving Liam completely off guard. "Cody! No!"

"I'm so sorry," there's your first three words, you're welcome.

"You what? Oh no..." Liam was already out of time when
he took his first step chasing after Cody because by that point
his stupid little guy had already stolen the toy and was running
away with it. The Dalmatian was frozen in her tracks with a
perplexed look as her head bounced back and forth between

Cody and her master.

"Hey! Give that back! Drop it!" the young woman yelled as she pursued Cody, but she was hesitant to get too close and started looking around for the owner. Cue Liam.

"Bad dog! Drop it now! Cody! Come here!" Liam got within about twenty feet when Cody realized he was in trouble and turned submissive. He snatched the toy from below sad puppy eyes and awkwardly offered it back to the angry owner. "I'm so sorry," he said without fumbling or mumbling. She took it from him without a word but her face laxed slightly. "We, um, we used to have one just like that, Sorry again."

Wow, that was a lot of words, and only one "um," see? What did I say? You got this. But pet the dog if you can. Ok, that's it from me, you focus, you do you, I'm not even here. She said something, but I had been talking over her, so hopefully Liam had paid attention.

"Angelica? It's nice to meet you," They shook hands, and that was enough for me to know she wasn't a host for the Guardian, but the power I felt had intensified now meaning we were definitely closer. "And what's...*her* name?"

Angelica no longer looked upset but only a fraction of her smile had returned. "Yes, it's a her. Her name's Ash."

"Mind if I?" Liam asked, indicating his intentions. She nodded for him to continue so he took a knee and started petting Ash. "Ash? Like...short for Ashley?" This dog was much better than Cody in every way, so I made quick work locating the signature of the Guardian. Strangely enough, it was coming from Angelica, but I had already ruled her out as a host. I continued to look, but the power emanating from the Guardian was overpowering. Never thought I'd say it, but now that I knew where it was, I needed Cody's terrible senses if I wanted a clearer picture.

"No, short for Ashes. My ex named her, thought it was funny, what with the whole firefighters and Dalmatian thing." She whistled and patted her leg until Cody walked over and plopped himself down in front of her, which caused her to laugh a little and that smile to grow halfway back to full. "And what about this little guy? What made you call him Cody?

Seems like an odd name for a dog."

Ok, that's all I need from Ash, but grab Cody again if you get a chance. That's it, I'm gone again. You're doing great by the way. Ok, sorry.

After my little interruption, Liam answered, "I don't really remember, I was young when I got him; I guess I thought he just looked like a Cody."

"Well, they say dogs look like their owner, and you don't look much like a Cody. What's your name? You failed to mention."

"Oh, I'm so sorry, I'm Liam, Liam…um…" Liam's new identity papers came in over a month ago, but he was still having trouble pronouncing his new last name. Technically, his new name was Gaylord William Janiszewski, Megatron's form of payback if I had to guess, but Liam could at least still be a passable name of choice, given the alternatives. Liam turned his head trying to think of a way to recover without having to butcher his own name. "I don't know if that's always true, though, I mean look at him and me, hair color, eye color, nose size, all way off. I mean, at least I hope my schnoz isn't that big." Even if that transition was a bit harsh, she laughed, so it didn't seem to matter much. "Ash, on the other hand, she's beautiful, perfectly sized sniffer."

"I know, I love her so much. And that's an excellent point, there would have to be some exceptions. I mean, Ash didn't look anything like Brent."

"Well, she's your dog now, isn't she? So maybe there's still some truth to it." I can't put into words how impressed I was with Liam for that smooth move, and given the blush growing on Angelica's cheeks, she caught it too.

"Cody's not so bad himself," she retorted with the full smile back on her face for the first time since they started talking. "Where was he anyway?"

"What do you mean?" Liam asked, a bit confused, but the smile on his face wouldn't be going anywhere anytime soon.

"The first time you ran by, you were alone, then you came back and had him, where was he hiding?"

J. A. Reed

"Oh, that, um…" I debated helping him out, but he had been doing better than I could so far, so I had faith he could wrap it up. "He was…He was at home. So, you see, I go on runs after work sometimes, and he has trouble keeping up, so I just thought I'd, you know, bring him to the park after I finished."

"Oh, how far do you run? Or is he just that bad of a running partner?" She laughed again while scratching Cody behind the ear.

"Oh, he's definitely a terrible running partner, he trips over his own feet constantly." She laughed like she didn't believe him, and I couldn't blame her, if I hadn't seen him do it a thousand times personally, I wouldn't have believed it myself. "I'm serious!" Liam laughed back, "Off the leash he's fine, but if I tried to take him on a run through the city he wouldn't have a chin anymore." I immediately felt Liam's sense of regret, probably from how dark that joke ended up sounding out loud, but she laughed harder than any of the previous times, so it subsided quickly, replaced by relief.

"Well if it's a running dog you want, Dalmatians are great for that, coordinated too. Ash has way too much energy for an apartment in the city; I've been meaning to look into dog walking services or something, just been too busy." With that, Angelica hopped up to her feet, and Ash followed. "Speaking of, I should really get going but, um…how would you like to make a little extra cash?"

Liam stood up slowly and tugged on Cody's collar until he come close enough to get a hand on. I was finally able to finish my work while Liam fought his old habits. "Um, what do you mean? You want me to…? I mean, I guess I could use a running partner, but I…well, I wouldn't feel right charging you for that, though."

Channeling Cody again, I was able to see through the previously blinding power of the Guardian, but I was still unable to make out a which one of my older siblings it was specifically. Whichever one it was, they were hovering over Angelica, but not joined with her like I was with Liam, and from what I could tell, they had been there for a long time. Guardians usually floated around to help as many of God's creatures as they could, the sort of Mother Teresa types Liam would be better off with if he wanted to save the world, but if this one was sticking to just one human, maybe Guardians weren't as noble as they used to be.

"Well, here's my card, give me a call, and we can work out the details." She pulled a white business card out of her clutch and handed it out between red painted nails.

Liam took it, shaking just a little. "Thanks, will do. Have a good night."

Angelica turned and left without another word, but she did look back over her shoulder twice. Liam just stood there staring at the card until I chimed in. *She's got a Guardian angel looking over her, I'm curious to know why. I think you should do it.*

"Did that really just happen?" he asked distantly.

Yes, yes it did. You got hired as her dog walker, every man's dream, I said sarcastically just to get a reaction, because in reality, he had done very well for himself. I was so proud, they grow up so fast.

CHAPTER EIGHT: A NEW DEAL

Meeting Angelica and taking her Dalmatian, Ash, on daily runs did wonders for my overall mood. It broke up the boring monotony of work, it kept Zeke preoccupied as he tried to figure out why a Guardian had such interest in one human, and most importantly, it kept my mind off all my recent bad luck. For the first time in a long time, I felt good about where my life had lead me. Of course, there were still episodes from time to time, moments where it felt like Tabby was in my head again, even when I knew he was nowhere around.

"Yo! Liam?" The external voice broke my trance allowing the commotion within the coffee shop to come flooding back around me; the clamor and hiss of the espresso machine in my hands should've done the trick seconds ago when it was ready and not burnt, but perhaps working there so long I had grown accustomed to the noise.

"Aw hell, crap!" I threw out the ruined product and prepped a replacement. Justin Miller, the owner of the voice that saved me from getting scalded by the neglected contraption, looked at me with concern but was preoccupied taking another customer's order.

After about a half-hour, the never-ending string of customers finally lulled and Justin approached me with that same concerning look now accompanied with a matching voice. "You all right? You kinda spaced out there for a second."

Justin had been working at the shop for almost a year longer than me and had been told to show me the ropes, but in terms of pay and responsibility, he was just as far down the ladder as I was. It was nice because he had the expertise to know the best ways to get everything done, but he was also carefree enough to mess around and have fun, which quite frankly was both needed and greatly appreciated. Still, I hadn't known him that long, and he knew nothing about my past, so there were limitations to what I could tell him. "Oh, yeah, sorry about that, was just thinking is all."

"Is everything all right?" he asked, not accepting my brush-off as the end of it.

"Yeah, yeah, yeah, it's just…" I hesitated, not because I couldn't tell him what I went through, but because I didn't want too. Whenever these episodes occurred, it was best to avoid dwelling on the past and instead try to focus on all of the good instead, so that was what I did. "I met someone, or at least, I think I did, I don't really know."

A huge grin beamed across Justin's face, "Oh! Way to go, boy! C'mon, tell me more, I want details." We had to abruptly pause our conversation when more customers came through or the boss walked by checking to make sure we weren't messing around, but whenever we did have a chance, I told him about how I met Angelica, censoring the story to be angel-free of course. Once I finished, he had some questions. "Do you date a lot?" That wasn't one of the questions I expected to hear.

"I…well, I mean, not too much recently…no…" I had been getting better at lying and thinking on my feet, but I still had limitations.

Justin smiled and nodded like he had already known before he even had to ask. He walked over beside me and put his arm across my shoulders. "Liam, I'm going to give you some advice I wish someone had given me when I was your age."

He's only like a year older than you, Zeke chimed in, reminding me he was still there and listening.

"Dating sucks." Once again, not the words I expected to hear. "It just straight up sucks. It sucks for everyone, but the harsh truth is it'll suck even more for you. I've known guys like you, guys that want some cheesy Hollywood Rom-Com to just unfold before you, probably reinforced by your parents or something."

"I've never really met my father, so it's not that," I added quietly and a little unnerved with my personal bubble violated.

"Semantics," he said, waving off anything not in line with his thinking. "But what I'm trying to say is that doesn't happen anymore. No, odds are this girl is just using you to walk her dog for free. She's probably got a dozen other guys at her beck and call for all her other needs. Now, I'm not saying you can't get more out of the bargain, you're a good enough looking kid, but if you're thinking monogamy and church bells, you're going to be in for one hell of a rude awakening."

Before I could process Justin's advice or even pose any argument against it, Ben, the manager, popped out of his office and called me over. "Liam! My office! Now!"

Justin quickly removed his arm from around me and tried to act like he had been working. "Good luck kid, but remember what I said."

Now confused for multiple reasons, I just sort of stumbled my way toward the manager's office, but the closer I got, the less I worried about trying to make sense of Justin's relationship advice and the more I worried about what I could've done wrong that deserved manager's involvement. I paused at the threshold and Ben was back at his desk typing away on his computer. I took a deep breath, and then stepped across.

"Why am I getting calls from corporate about you?" he asked with a sort of low grumble in his voice that was only ever present when he was upset, albeit he was always upset.

"Um, I don't know, what did they want?" I sincerely had no idea.

Damn it Megatron, he's probably just showing off, making sure we remember that we work for him. I swear I hate him sometimes.

The manager pulled a sticky note off his desk and held it out to me. I had to take a few more steps inside to reach it giving him time to tell me, saving me from more nervous build-up. "A Mr. Edward Kratz needs to see you by the end of the day. Address is here if you need it. I'll let you leave an hour early since this is technically work-related, but if it runs long don't expect any overtime or nothing, hear me?"

Zeke was definitely right about Megatron, but neither of us were sure why he needed a face-to-face meeting, or why it had to be before the end of the day. I took the note and read it, but all it said was my new full name, except the last name trailed into gibberish scribbles after the first few letters, Megatron's host's name, and the address for the headquarters building, all things I already knew, so I popped it in my back pocket where I'd be able to forget about it. "Yes, sir, of course. Thank you."

I tried to leave, but Ben halted me with an even deeper rattle than before. "So *now* do you know why I'm getting calls from people whose titles start with a 'C' and end with an 'O?'"

It was time to see if messing up with Justin earlier was a fluke or the start of a downhill spiral. "Um…" So far, not so good. "I'm friends with his son."

Megatron hates us, though, so don't oversell it, Zeke advised, and when Ben's face scrunched up I knew that wasn't the best thing to say. I didn't want to come across as the untouchable favorite, that would mean Ben didn't hold the power, and he was clearly a man that needed to feel powerful. "Probably just wants to make sure I'm not getting into trouble here. And I can't afford to, so if you want me to stay and help that last hour, I could go after…if you prefer?"

A smirk indicated I had saved it, because as far as Ben was concerned, one poor employee review from him and I was at his mercy. The power was back in his hands, or so he thought.

"That won't be necessary, we'll manage without you. Now get back out there and tell Justin to keep his hands to himself or he's getting written up again."

"Yes sir," With nothing else stopping me from leaving, I returned to work for the rest of my shift, and when I had an hour left on the clock, I swapped my apron for my bag and ducked out before anyone changed their minds. when we were safely away from work, I typed, [What do you think he wants?].

I don't know, it could be anything.

[Well, it's gotta be important, otherwise he could've left a message, or had Tabby tell us at home]

You're thinking of him like he's a normal person. He's obnoxiously petty. He probably wants to make me do something demeaning in exchange for our continued employment and stuff. Knowing him, he'll be all "I have an itch on my back I can't scratch, scratch it or the kid's fired." Zeke exaggerated the mocking tone significantly, but the childishness of it was rather amusing, then I found myself wondering if that were actually a possibility and shuttered to think if it was.

[let's find out then, I'm ready this time] I braced myself and Zeke flew us straight into Megatron's office in an instant. The way he was sitting at his desk typing on his keyboard looked pretty much identical to how Ben had looked, and that was all I needed to start making all of the other comparisons and realizing they were basically the same person. Megatron was also power-hungry and pissed off all of the time, but infinitely more so than Ben, and as a result he was infinitely more successful because of it.

"What took you so long?" he asked, not taking his eyes off his screen.

"Oh, you know, had to run across the street for a good cup of coffee, and not the corner to the left, you guys own that one too, I mean the one…" Megatron shut down Zeke's sarcastic rant by finally making eye contact. "Easy brother, it was just a joke, your coffee's great, just overpriced."

"Have you heard about what's been happening back home?" Megatron never looked even close to happy, but he appeared to be especially ticked off today.

Zeke must've sensed something, too, because he shifted to a more civilized manner. "No, Zak's off in Australia or something last I knew, haven't heard from him in a week or so, and can't really talk with anyone else."

"That's what I'm afraid of. No one's heard from him in a while, but we're already working on that problem. The reason I called you here…" Megatron hesitated. "…it's about your daughter."

"You have…?" I started, but as usual, I was supposed to save my questions and comments for the end.

Not now. "Which daughter? Shiva? Mara?"

"Stacy," he said with the most hate filled growl of them all.

"Damn it! Not Stacy, that b-" Zeke paused to collect himself. "That kid'll be the death of me."

"You need to go handle it before she gets out of control."

"She's been out of control since birth!" Zeke defended, "Besides, I said it last time, I'm done cleaning up her messes, get someone else to do it. Get Fenrir to help, he's her big brother, she's just as much his problem as mine."

Megatron finally pushed his keyboard away and stood up. "I can't make you go, but if you don't go now, it's just going to get worse."

"Even if I wanted to, I've got a host now,"

"Take him with you," Megatron interrupted.

"What? No, I'm not taking a seventeen-year-old boy to Hell, no way. And, speaking of Liam, we have a job now."

"I'll give you a leave of absence, I can do this all day, none of your excuses can save you." Megatron crossed his arms as far as the thick layers of fat would allow in a defiant stance.

Zeke stared him down for a moment before breaking off "Fine, no more excuses, I'm not going because I don't want to, simple as that, no other reason."

The Muse lowered his head and shook it with disappointment. "Then we're done here."

I turned to leave, but Zeke rang out before I could get my second foot off the ground. "Wait, what about Zak? And...the other thing?"

He was slow to answer, sluggishly pulling his desk chair back toward him and taking several labored breaths as he lowered himself back into the leather. "No headway on...We think Zak's still in Australia, though; doesn't look like he's in trouble, just off the grid."

"That's good, well, Zak I mean, is Trini still...?"

"Yeah, she's getting worse the longer it takes us. I'm worried about her, we all are." It was starting to bother me not being able to be clued in on the context of the conversation, and I didn't know if they were remaining vague just to keep me in the dark or some other reason. I'd have a lot of questions for Zeke once they were finished.

"Look, if you need anything from me up here, I'll do what I can, but I don't want to go back, not just yet at least. But who knows, I could get homesick in a few millennia," Zeke laughed but his brother remained unamused. "But if I can do anything for Trini, I mean it, let me know."

Megatron tilted his head at us as if trying to measure Zeke's level of sincerity. "I'll be in touch, now I have work to do."

That's his way of saying "thank you." If I hadn't been so jaded I might've laughed, but that wouldn't have been a smart move, so I could at least be glad for that. With the farewells said, I resumed my departure and headed down the hall to the elevator. *All right, brace yourself,* Zeke said once the doors closed, prepping to fly us straight home, but I had another idea.

"Wait. While we're here I want to head back to that bakery place down the street, I promised I would and it's been too long already."

Oh, that's right, I almost forgot about that. Ok, fine, and I guess it's close enough, I'll let you run there.

"You'll *let* me? How nice of you," I retorted with fake offense. The elevator doors parted revealing the lobby as well as three suits waiting to board. I squeezed past them and started my jog before I had even reached the front doors. I caught a quick glimpse of the cute blonde security guard I had crossed paths with my first time around. Her look of remembrance started with wide eyes, but as I jogged past, they narrowed, and she shook her head with a grimace. I winked at her when I passed and then looked straight ahead without seeing her reaction.

I could've easily jogged the whole way to the bakery and not broken a sweat, but for the first time in a long time I could feel that Zeke had lifted his embargo on healing my legs as I ran, something he had always hoped would curb my constant need to be active, but whether this was a one-time gift or an admittance of defeat, I couldn't be sure. Regardless, I took full advantage and sprinted the, albeit short, distance in record time and ended on the other side with a meditative heart rate. "Isn't that more fun than flying?"

Don't get used to it, I'm still pro-wings and anti-legs, just figured I'd speed things along just this once. That answered my question, not what I had hoped, but neither was it unexpected. Satisfied that any further conversation could be done through our non-verbal method, I entered the shop and was able to walk straight to the register. I was disappointed to find that it wasn't the same cashier as before, but instead a very attractive young woman which meant my attempt to tip high in order to make up for last time would instead be misconstrued as just another naive guy tipping a pretty smile in hopes of getting her attention.

With no stipulation on price this time around, I ordered the most expensive and delicious-looking thing in the display, a hot chocolate with extra whipped cream, and another one of those sad breakfast sandwiches to take home to Cody since he wouldn't care what I brought him; he'd eat the paper bag and be happy with it. I didn't quite leave the triple tip I had originally intended, but I did leave a very generous one, and just as I had suspected, the girl gave me my money's worth with a shy smile and, "Oh my, thank you so much. Your order will be right up, sweetie." What I didn't expect was for the tattooed man from my last visit to pick that moment to walk out from the back and freeze as his eyes met mine, then the multiple bills dropping from my hand into the tip jar, and then back to mine.

The man made a quick glance at the register and smirked. "Yeah, I'll get right on that, go ahead and take your break."

Zeke just laughed in my head and added, *Oh yeah, he's definitely spitting in your food,* as if it wasn't already obvious. I opened my wallet back up and slowly removed a five and added it to the jar, looking nervously hopeful while I did so. His face remained sour, and his eyes darted back and forth from my wallet to the jar, so I tried pulling out a single, but a quick squint of his eyes made me abort that and take another five. That did the trick, and he smiled. "Thank you, sir! Tell you what, we'll go ahead and bump that drink up to a large for you, on the house."

Not sure how to view this other than as a trap, I politely declined, "Oh, that's all right, you don't have to, medium's plenty for me. Thank you though."

That seemed to work just fine, so I turned and found a nearby chair to sit and wait for my costly meal while trying to shake off the unsettling feeling I can only assume was similar to that of having just been robbed. As I sat there, I looked around for a bit of people watching, but the place was practically empty. The same Navy Veteran was in the same seat as last time, and a couple in the back corner that was, hopefully, a father and daughter catching up over coffee. There was a small hunched over elderly woman near the door just standing there with a colorful head wrap hiding most of her face. She must've come in after me but I didn't remember hearing the door open, and she hadn't gone up to the counter after me either.

Before I could observe the old woman any further, my order was called and I took my food back to sit down and eat. I started with the hot chocolate, mostly whipped cream in the first sip; it tasted divine as the small amount of heat melted the cold down into the perfect Goldilocks of chocolate and cream.

Liam, I'd like a word with you, please don't react, said a voice in my head, but it wasn't Zeke, it was a female voice.

Despite the voice's warning, I jolted my head up and looked around the bakery. Everyone was still going about their normal business except for the old woman, she was now sitting at the table behind me facing the other direction.

Liam, what is it? Zeke asked, confused.

"Did you hear…?" I looked around again, but there was no indication of where the voice came from. "Never mind, it was nothing."

Good, because that drink is beyond amazing. Drink faster! I'll heal any burns, don't worry about it.

I took another sip but was still a little on edge, and then the voice returned. *I asked you not to react, please. I mean you no harm, I am an Enochian, it's a type of…*

I already knew what that meant, but I only thought that to myself not expecting her to hear, and yet she replied as if she had.

So, my fallen brother has shared with you some of our world; it's good to know they aren't all lies.

I panicked, wondering if she could hear my thoughts, did that mean Zeke could as well? I couldn't think of any lies Zeke had ever told me, but I only had his word for most things, and he had been hiding something with Megatron during that meeting…

Please my child, calm yourself. Your captor cannot hear us; I am Enochian, and I am not fallen. I have made it so we can only speak to each other, he will never know as long as you act natural. Now please, continue drinking.

I took another sip and tried to put a stop to the endless string of questions flying through my mind. It took some work, but eventually I focused on only one – Who was she?

My name is Forfax, and I have come to help you. Are you fully aware of the situation you find yourself in? You are hosting your body and soul with that of a fallen angel. Do you not know the danger you have put yourself in? The danger you have put your very soul in?

I honestly hadn't thought much about that aspect since I first took Zeke on for good. I had access to bits and pieces of his memories, and besides things like giving people cancer for fun, which I made sure he stopped, he seemed like a good person. Then I remembered our conversation the day we met, the one where he told me God had abandoned humanity, and that with or without Zeke, I'd go to Hell anyway. I had believed him then, but that faith was starting to waver now.

God has not abandoned you, Liam Cole. Sadly, what Zeke told you was true – very few humans make it to Heaven these days, but that is due to the rise in demons and fallen angels on your world, corrupting humanity with their sin. I'm sure you've seen it yourself, have you not?

I thought about Megatron, how greedy and gluttonous he was, a cut-throat businessman in every sense. I remembered what Tabby had done to me right before meeting him, how that was his sick hobby that he did just for fun. Even Zeke, while not completely evil, said it himself, he was no Mother Teresa. With all of his pranks and sarcastic jokes, he wasn't even a good influence, every time I suggested helping people, he always suggested something selfish instead.

Yes, you know it, too, but it's not too late for you my child. You can still come back into the light. You can still enter paradise and be reunited with your mother.

I spit out my hot chocolate all over the table and empty chair across from me and began coughing.

J. A. Reed

Liam?! What the Hell?! Zeke asked both concerned and annoyed.

All eyes in the place were on me, and I grabbed napkins to start cleaning up while I continued to hack up the chocolate in my windpipe. The tattooed man had made his way around the counter with a washcloth and unsurely waited for me to move so he could clean up properly. "I'm sorry, so sorry. It…I…It went down the wrong pipe." I went to throw away the wad of soaking napkins and the employee took that chance to clean up after me much faster than I had been trying and then returned to his other duties. "Sorry again, sorry," I said, trying to tell everyone until they looked away and I could sit back down without being gawked at.

Seriously Liam, what was that? Zeke asked again, less annoyed and more concerned this time.

I pulled out my phone. [wrong pipe, that's all]

Ok, slow down then, jeez.

Satisfied that Zeke bought my lie, I tried to go back to thinking about what Forfax had told me without freaking out again. My mother? Was she in Heaven? I had never asked Zeke where my mom had gone, fearing he would tell me she was in Hell, but if she were, he would be able to take me to see her. If she were in Heaven, sticking with Zeke meant for certain I'd never see her again. I didn't know what to do.

Calm down, Liam, everything is going to be all right. As I said before, it's not too late for you, you may still banish the evil from within you and take me on instead; I will be able to cleanse your soul and ensure you find yourself back on the righteous path.

My brain overloaded with questions and worries yet again. Without Zeke, I would be alone, that hadn't changed, but was that really worth damning my soul? I had seen memories of Hell, and it wasn't paradise, but neither was it fire and torment, it wasn't very different from life on Earth, but that wasn't saying much. I couldn't stay with Zeke, I just couldn't, but I would need some time to sort out my life, where to live, how to afford to eat, I would need something to fall back on.

You need not make your decision now, please take some time to make whatever arrangements you need, just be weary. If my brother learns of our deal, he will take over your body completely, just as you've seen from others of his kind.

She must've been talking about Megatron and Tabby, Mr. Kratz and Tristen weren't like me, they had no control over their own bodies.

Ah, yes, nicknames used to distract you and put you at ease.

I had never thought there could be a deeper meaning to Zeke's nicknames, I had just assumed it was because most of the angel names I had heard so far were strange, like this Forfax, I could picture Zeke calling her Foxy or something like that.

I see his influence has already begun to corrupt you, she said with a sigh of annoyance in her otherwise steady tone. *Time is running short for you, but I will contact you again soon, please be prepared before I do, your mother misses you dearly.*

The old woman behind me stood up and walked outside, and after that I didn't hear another word from the Enochian calling herself Forfax.

Ok Liam, spill the beans, what's wrong? I can feel your emotions like you're about to explode. What is it? You can tell me.

I pulled my phone out slowly trying to think of a believable excuse. [It's just…] I paused again, and then I thought of something. I had been thinking of my mom, that was the actual reason I was a wreck, so the best lie would be something nearest the truth. [my mom used to bake these for me, just brought up a lot of old memories, that's all]

Oh, I'm sorry, take all the time you need, just remember what I said before, don't run from this, find a healthy way to face it and heal. If you need anything, I'm here for you. Always.

His voice sounded so sincere, and I knew he wasn't lying, but the only way for me to truly heal was to get rid of him and go to Heaven to be reunited with her. I just wish there could be a way to do that without screwing Zeke over. I still had time, though, and I was going to use every second of it to find the best way to make everyone happy.

CHAPTER NINE: DOUBLE DATE

I didn't realized just how hard it was going to be attempting to set up a fallback if I had to keep it secret from someone sharing my own body until Zeke flew us back home. I wanted to look up rooms for rent and see if I could start applying for new jobs, but that would just cause Zeke to ask questions, questions I couldn't answer. Instead, I'd have to do the best I could to make multiple different contingencies so that if one, or two, or five, don't pan out, I'll still have more.

I went to my bed to lay down and think without interruption or distractions. Over an hour passed, and I still didn't have anything good. Options for staying in Seattle could very well be numerous, or there could be zero, without knowing for sure and getting a head start, there was no way to tell. I could try locating homeless shelters or something like that, but that would be worst case, last resort. I contemplated trying to get back to Albuquerque, where I at least had friends. Greg and his mom would take me in without question under normal circumstances, but after having been paralyzed and then disappearing for months, if I showed back up out of the blue and could suddenly walk again, there was no telling how they'd react.

Liam, did you lose track of time or what? Zeke said, breaking through the music I had blasting in my room to help me think.

"Huh? What?" I actually had lost track worrying so much about my next step. I had been so lost in my thoughts in fact, I completely forgot about Zeke as well, I hadn't even thought about how to help him after leaving. As much as I wanted what was best for myself, it just didn't feel right to leave Zeke high and dry after everything he had done for me.

Aren't you going to get your daily run in with Angelica's dog? I was tempted to let you sleep through it, but figured you'd be even more cranky if you did. Lesser of two evils and all that jazz.

I didn't feel like wasting time by getting dressed and going out, but a run would probably do me a lot of good, so I heaved myself out of bed and put on my running clothes. "All right, don't wanna be late, I'm ready."

Zeke flew us right to her front door and I knocked.
Angelica was quick to answer, but she was fully dressed up in a
pantsuit and seemed to be in a rush. "Oh, you're here, thank
God! Look, I have to run out real quick, should only be an
hour, that shouldn't be a problem, right, you two usually go for
about an hour, right?"

Taken a little off guard by her frantic worrying, I stammered
a bit, "Um, oh yeah, that's, yeah, that's no problem. We can,
yeah, we'll be fine."

She pulled Ash out by the collar and handed me the leash.
"Oh, thank you, I'm really sorry about this, something came up
last minute, I'll make it up to you, I promise." Then she hugged
me and I lost all feeling in my body except a powerful tingling.

"Um, oh, of course, it's…it's no problem." I stood there
awkward as could be, but luckily, she was too busy checking
and double checking that she had everything she needed before
locking the door and speed walking down the hall and out of
the building.

Well, guess it's a good thing you didn't skip today.

"Yeah, I guess so." After the initial shock and confusion
wore off, I pulled on Ash's leash and walked her down to the
sidewalk. "C'mon girl, let's go."

Knowing Angelica would be gone at least an hour, I started
off at a relatively slower pace and chose the longer of our usual
routes. At first, I found myself wondering where it was she had
to run off to in such a hurry, and made up various different
scenarios in my head, most of them involving her with other
guys and making me a little mad, but I quickly shook those
thoughts for more pressing matters.

Even after my runner's high kicked in full force, I still
couldn't think of a good fallback for next time I met with Foxy,
and I was nowhere even close to an idea to make all parties
happy, if one even existed. As I was coming back down
Angelica's street an extra ten minutes over her requested hour,
one crazy idea popped into my head. Angelica had a nice place
from what I had seen through the doorway each day I stopped

by, and we were starting to become friends, at least I thought we were. I began wondering if I could try asking her to put me up while I get on my feet. It was crazy, and probably wouldn't work, but I didn't really have many other options.

I made my way to her door and knocked, hoping she hadn't gotten caught up with her mysterious errand. It took longer this time around, but she eventually made it to the door and opened it, still wearing the pantsuit from earlier. "Oh, good. Sorry, I was a little late, but glad you didn't get stuck waiting on me. Here, c'mon in, please."

This was the first time she had asked me to come inside. I unhooked Ash's leash to let her run in, buying me some time to collect myself. I stepped inside slowly and wiped my feet a few more times than was necessary before going all the way in and she closed the door behind me. "Beautiful place," I said, looking at all of the high-class decorations coating the walls and furniture; there wasn't a single movie poster in sight.

"Thanks, I do what I can. How was Ash? Wasn't too long for her or anything, was it?" She took off her coat and placed it in her room as she talked across the apartment.

"Oh, no, she's a champ. Like I said, it was no trouble." Not knowing what to do, I just sort of stood in the middle of the living room with my hands cupped together in front of me.

"Good, I'm so glad," Angelica came out of her room and was combing her hair with her hands after pulling it out of a tight bun. She laughed when she saw me. "You can have a seat, you know."

"Oh, that's all right, I'm all sweaty from the run, I wouldn't want to..."

"That's fine, you don't smell bad or anything. You actually smell kinda good, are you wearing cologne?" She stopped her hustling around to wait for my answer, putting me on the spot and making my nerves even worse, as if that were possible.

"Um...no..."

She smiled and then went about her business. "Well, guess it's just good genes then. Anyway, I know you said it was no trouble, but I want to thank you anyway, thank you for all you've done. Do you like Chinese?"

Any other time I would've understood what she meant, but this was not any other time. "Um, yeah, I guess, I mean, I don't really know any though."

"What?" she asked, laughing a little.

Way to go kid, she meant food, not people, idiot. Here, I'll throw you a bone just this once.

Then, with an assist from Zeke, I prevented myself from looking like a total moron. "I'm new here, I don't really know of any good places."

"Oh, ok, I thought for a second there…Never mind. Anyway, I ask because I do know of a good place, and they deliver, so how about you stay for dinner? My treat."

Obviously, I wanted to say a resounding yes, but I had a lot on my plate and dinner with Angelica, alone, in her apartment; it all seemed way too distracting. I looked down at my clothes again and saw the sweat ring stretching out around my neck down to the middle of the shirt. This was not how I pictured our first dat…dinner, our first dinner…"I don't know, I really should shower or something."

"Or something," she said and then disappeared into her room again. Before my brain could process what she had said and done, she popped back out holding a small box with clothes inside. "My ex left some clothes here, and I doubt he'll ever come back for them; you can change into these. They might be a bit baggy on you, but it's better than nothing."

Again, I was frozen from the drastic curveball she threw my way. "Um, are you sure? I don't want to impose."

"I am, and you're not. So, will you stay? Free Chinese…" She shook the box closer to me and had a high musical quality in her voice that made it impossible to resist.

With her overpowering charm, there was only one thing I could say. "Ok, fine, you win, I'll stay."

She did a little jump with glee, "Good! Here, you can change in my bathroom, right through here." She pulled her phone and a small tri-fold menu out of her purse. "Oh, but first, what do you want?"

J. A. Reed

I picked something random off the menu even though I had no idea what it was, but she said it was a great choice, so I stuck with it and hoped for the best. I went into the bathroom and locked the door.

Liam! My Man! Look at you, I hope you're ready. Honestly, I didn't know you had it in you.

"What?" As soon as the word slipped I turned to the door, expecting Angelica to have heard me and come asking if I was okay, but she didn't. Instead, the only thing I heard from under the door was her ordering on the phone. I was careful to maintain a hushed whisper after that. "What are you talking about?"

Dude, she totally wants you. Walking her dog didn't mean anything, but dinner, alone, in her apartment…That, my boy, means a whole truck load. Do you need me to fly you to a pharmacy real quick?

"What? No, stop it. She's just…wait…. Do you really think?"

Honestly, there's no telling for sure until you make your move, or she makes hers, but if I were a Magic 8-Ball, I'd be saying "Outlook Good" or maybe…wait, I can't remember what else 8-Balls say…oh well, outlook good is a good one. Just, you know, don't screw it up.

"Why would you say that? Don't say don't screw up, that's a terrible thing to say to a person. Good luck, break a leg, good skill, anything else. Oh God, I'm going to screw this up, aren't I?" I turned on the sink and splashed water in my face. I never understood why that was a thing in movies until just that second.

First of all, don't drag my father into this, and second of all, you got me, an ace in your pocket. I'll help you out, I'm really good at reading people and body language. I'll let you know when to push for the romantic, when to pull back and play hard to get, I got your back, man.

I grabbed a hand towel and dried off my face, giving myself a good once over in the mirror to make sure there was no visual evidence of my momentary freak out. Satisfied, I began changing into the clean clothes, but felt incredibly awkward as I did, finding it difficult to overlook the fact that they had once belonged to her ex. I stepped back as far as I could from the mirror to get a full body view in the borrowed outfit and "a bit baggy" was an understatement. The neck hole of the shirt was so large one of my shoulders could almost fit through it like how women used to wear their sweaters in 1980s workout videos. The belt was nearly useless since it was about two or three holes too few, and I had to roll the legs up to allow myself to walk.

Um…well, personality is what's really important, right? Zeke said in a tone that worried me even further.

"Well, on the bright side, I'm not worried anymore, now at least I know *for sure* nothing's gonna happen. It's a weight off, really."

Oh, c'mon Liam, I was joking. She's the one that gave you those clothes, if it becomes a deal breaker for her, then she's crazy.

"Liam?" Angelica's voice rolled through the cracks of the door, sounding very close to the other side. "Are you still changing?"

"Um, just about finished, one more sec," I replied, still nervous to face her in such a raggedy fashion.

"Ok, well I'm going to change really quick, so don't come out yet."

My heart pounded in my chest, and as the sounds of cloth moving and colliding with the ground painted a mental image in my mind's eye, it only raced faster. "Oh…Wow…" I whispered as my fantasy continued to portray what was happening right in front of me with nothing but an inch of hardboard in the way.

This is it, go in! Zeke encouraged enthusiastically. I shook my head side to side, my vocal cords paralyzed in fear that I might be heard and disrupt the moment. *No, this is it, this is your moment! She wants you to come in, pun definitely…*

"Shh!" I hissed at a high enough pitch that the sound shouldn't have left the bathroom. "No, that's a terrible idea."

"Sorry, I'm almost decent," she called out, and it made me weak in the knees to the point that I had to grab the countertop to prevent myself from falling down.

I turned back to the mirror and took several deep breaths,

J. A. Reed

waiting for Zeke to chime back in, but he was oddly silent. I pulled out my phone and typed [What's wrong? You butthurt again?] but there was no response. I turned on the water for the noise and whispered, "Zeke, c'mon, that was terrible advice, you can't be mad at me." Still, there was nothing. "Fine, pout. You're so childish…" I turned the water off, and the silence that followed was deafening. Zeke had been quiet before, but this felt like something else, something more. It felt like he was gone, but that was crazy, right? "Zeke? Zeke, you're scaring me, stop kidding around, man."

A knock at the front door startled me, and I turned. "That's the food, hurry up in there, ok?" Angelica's footsteps echoed further as she left the room and down the hallway. As light as her feet were, each reverberating sound danced along the acoustics of the bathroom filling it with sound and exaggerating the newfound emptiness I felt. Was Zeke really gone, or was this some sort of sick joke of his? I had lived seventeen years without Zeke, so surely this new feeling had been there before, but the sudden contrast made it impossible to ignore now. I began debating my deal with Foxy, wondering if this was what my future without Zeke would be like, but at the same time, there was so much more at stake than just a momentary feeling of loneliness. When I heard the front door shut, I lunged for the handle to lead me out of that suddenly claustrophobic restroom and hoped that with Angelica as company I could shake the feeling of abandonment.

Angelica set down the bags before she turned her attention to me, but once she did she failed to restrain her amusement regarding my attire. "Oh, honey," she said in the sad sort of way, "I'm so sorry, I didn't…I'm sorry." She said the words, but her constant giggling made me wonder how truthful they really were.

"Hey, you're not allowed to laugh, you're the one that insisted, remember, this is all your doing," I laughed through most of that not being able to keep a straight face, and afterwards, a part of me hoped Zeke would finally speak up, happy that I took at least some of his advice, but he didn't, and when Angelica turned to get plates out, my smile faded.

"Go ahead and sit wherever you like," she said from the kitchen while reaching on tippy-toes into one of the cupboards. I glanced over at the table where there were six seats to choose from, and I found myself wondering what Zeke would suggest. Would he tell me to sit at the head of the table, or along one of the sides? Or would he tell me to rush into the kitchen and help her get the plates down, making a move on her right there, something I obviously wouldn't do, but I could imagine him saying that in my head. He didn't though.

I had been so lost in my head that Angelica beat me to the table, setting two places on opposite sides of the table and effectively taking the choice out of my hands. "Are you ok? You seem a little...distant."

"Huh? Oh, no, it's...it's nothing."

She took her seat but kept her eyes on me. "Oh, yeah, right, you do an excellent job pleading your case. Seriously, you can talk to me, we're friends, aren't we?" she said, fishing to know my viewpoint.

"Um, yeah, yeah we are, it's just..." I took my seat to buy myself a little extra time of stalling. I wanted to tell her my predicament, even if it was only a half-truth hiding the celestial portion and just coming clean about the difficult choice of picking sides, but there was still a small portion of me that was worried Zeke was listening, waiting to know what I had been conspiring behind his back. I settled on easing into it, "So, I have this roommate, Zeke." So far, not bad, close enough to true.

"Oh, yeah, I think I heard you say his name in the bathroom, did he call you or something?" She broke apart a set of chopsticks and began serving herself as she listened.

"Um, yeah, but he...well, he kinda hung up on me..." Also, very close to true, if not a little contextually odd, but I kept going. "See, we haven't been getting along too well recently. I moved in with him after...after my mom passed, and I didn't really know anyone else. He took me in, gave me a place to live, hooked me up with a job,"

"Wow, he sounds like a really good guy, what are you two fighting about, though?" I paused again to serve myself some food and thought about how she was right, he was a good guy, in appearances at least. The more I talked about him, the less I wanted to turn my back on him, but none of that changed the fact that as long as I remained with him, I'd never be reunited with my mother, and Angelica wouldn't be able to give me real advice unless I could find a way to put those stakes into terms she could understand. "Well, just the other day I spoke with… with…well, it was kinda like, an attorney. It turns out, my dad wants to reach out, but he really hates Zeke, really old bad blood from a big family squabble, I'll spare you the details." Bringing my father up wasn't ideal, but it was probably important to maintain the parent/child relationship to express how important leaving Zeke really was.

"Oh, well, sorry to hear that, isn't there some way for them to reconcile? I mean, what could be so bad they still hold a grudge?." Suddenly her eyes widened, and she lowered her chopsticks and covered her lips as if she regretted letting those words slip through them. "Sorry, sorry if I'm over stepping here,"

"No, you're fine, I don't know a whole lot about what happened between them myself, I just know it was bad, like kicked out and disowned, bad."

"Wait, is Zeke like, your older brother…? Or uncle? I thought you said he was just your roommate." She was beginning to see the flaws of my lie, and I wasn't sure which way to go.

"No, more like a family friend, I guess. I don't know…I didn't meet him until my mom was sick." As I said it, I could already see how that would cast doubt over Zeke as the one to side with, and accurately so. It was great to finally be able to open up about the whole situation, it was allowing me to see everything in a new, clearer light.

"Well, where was your dad in all of this? What happened that Zeke had to be the one to take you in?" Suddenly my analogy was falling apart even more. I had used my father to represent both my mother and Foxy, which was starting to mix up my dilemma.

Just as I was about to try and clear it up further, I realized something – she wasn't entirely wrong. Foxy and everything she represented had never been there for me, but Zeke was. Just like my actual father, they were completely absent from my life, so what do I really owe them? The only thing they can give me now is my mother, which is a very generous gift, but there aren't any other redeeming qualities on their side as far as I'm concerned. I still needed to convey the importance of seeing my mom again, but she wasn't wrong about them not being there when I needed them most, only Zeke. "My dad, he left us when we were young, but if I take his side and…and end up living with him, sure I'll never see Zeke again, and he might end up hating me for it, but I'll get to be with my family. And not just him, but the rest of my family, family that *was* always there for me, family that I miss more…more than I could ever say."

Angelica took a bite of the last piece of orange chicken on her plate as she contemplated the heaping pile of drama I had unloaded on her. "Wow, that is a pickle, isn't it," she said only half there, the other half still mulling it all over.

"I'm so sorry, I didn't mean to vent like that."

"No, no," she cut me off, "it's good you did, that sounds like a lot to keep bottled up inside, you needed to let it out, I'm glad you did, I just…Well, what do *you* want to do?"

I had really been hoping she was going to be the one to tell me, but after seeing how therapeutic talking the situation out had been, maybe putting the rest of my thoughts into words would work just as well. "Um…I don't know, it's a huge decision and I only have a few days to decide. The…um…the um…the attorney, yeah, that's it, she needs my answer soon."

"Well, short notice like that must suck, but you've got to be weighing the options so far, right? What have you come up with so far?" Yet again, she put it on me to figure out; or maybe she just needed more information to help me decide.

I finished my plate and went for seconds. "Um…Well, I

definitely want to see my family again, I already know that's my priority one right now, but…" As much as I knew what the next words were, I didn't want to say them.

"But you don't want to lose Zeke," Angelica correctly finished for me. I rubbed my eyes with the tips of my fingers trying to keep any tears locked behind my eyelids. When I pulled my hand away I looked back to her and nodded gently in my way of nonverbally thanking her.

"Right. He's done more for me in a few months than anyone else ever has, or ever could, but…but I'm worried. My…my father, or rather the attorney…or whatever, they did remind me that they know him a lot better than I do, and that he's not always as good of a guy as he has been to me, that if I stick with him, he'll be a bad influence, and honestly, I know they're right about that, but at the same time, I don't think it's really *as* bad as they try to make it sound."

Angelica scrunched up her face in confusion. "You're losing me a little, what makes Zeke so bad? Is he into drugs or something?"

"Um, not necessarily, it's not like that, it's just…my dad is very religious, yeah, like, super into his faith, and Zeke, he…he kinda lost his a long time ago,"

"Was that the fight?"

"Yeah, basically. Anyway, my father, he looks at Zeke and thinks he's the devil." Feeling like I had skirted a little too close to the truth I started nervously laughing as I poorly backtracked. "Well, not literally of course, I mean, that's ridiculous…"

"Um, right. Anyway, it sounds to me like you can either get your family back but lose a friend, or keep your friend and lose out on being with your family, but why not just reach out to your family without going through your father?"

"It's not that easy, they live really far away, I can't have both, that's the problem."

"It…it's been a long time, what if your dad and Zeke could reconcile, I mean, have you even tried?"

I didn't know much about the Fall, but it really had been a

long, long time ago, and I hadn't tried that. I knew that I wanted a way to make everyone happy, and maybe that could work. "I'm not sure if Zeke would even want to go back to be honest, I haven't told him about any of this, I was scared of what he would think."

"Well there's your problem right there, talk to him about it, see if there's a way to compromise before you try tearing yourself apart between them." She smiled at me, and I smiled back. Then, I remembered he was already gone. I pulled out my phone and looked at it, hoping that Zeke would finally break his silence with a "Gotcha!" or something equally childish, but the emptiness was still there. "Do you want to call him now? I wouldn't mind at all if you did."

"No, no, that's all right, I have a feeling he wouldn't answer even if I did." I looked back up at her and forced a smile back on my face. "It can wait until after dinner anyway."

"Cheers to that," she said, and raised her glass. I did as well, and only in that moment did I no longer feel crushingly alone. If Zeke came back, great, but if he didn't, I started to think I'd be ok with that too.

* * *

One minute I'm providing Liam with excellent, Grade-A romantic advice, and the next I'm dangling off the edge of a roof by the neck of my angelic form. "Whoa! Whoa! What's the big ide…Eve?"

Evangeline, one of my older sisters in the Guardian tier, glared up at me past her outstretched arm with burning green eyes. Her divine body was easily a foot taller than my own but also far more sleek and slender; every inch of exposed skin was bronzed to perfection, chocolate-colored hair with little twists down either side of her soft face framed it elegantly, and thin plate armor of celestial metals covered her torso with some slight overlap onto her extremities. "Still using those silly nicknames, I see. I thought you would've grown out of that by now."

I looked down at the multi-story drop below my feet and couldn't help but laugh a little. "Oh, Eve, if only you knew!" My voice sounded muffled with her thin fingers digging into my neck, but I made due. "I'm actually far more immature than I ever was before. You can drop me and see for yourself, I'll cheer the whole way down and shout 'Again! Again!' afterwards."

She rolled her eyes at me and threw me back to the rooftop where I glided down softly. "The fall might not hurt you, but I certainly can," she said, trying to maintain some form of intimidation over me.

I hopped up onto the closest refrigeration unit to have a seat and overly exaggerated stretching out my neck. "Well, after a *Fall* like mine, everything else is a piece of cake, but how about you do us both a favor and skip the scare tactics and just tell me what you want?" I lifted my hand to rub my sore throat and could already see some rot beginning to form. "And how the hell did you separate me from my host?" I knew a host could banish me if I didn't take full control like most of my siblings, but I had never heard of being removed from outside influence; of course, I was still new to this whole host thing, there was a lot I still didn't know.

Her eyes did a quick up-down glance in my direction and produced a face that screamed *pitiful* before answering. "It took no effort at all, the bond you...no, not bond, what you have with that human is weak, barely a connection at all. Regardless, it's easily within my power to protect living souls from evil's influence."

I put my hands over my heart and faked hurt, "Oh, ouch! Words hurt you know, Eve. And besides, it's not my fault, we're still in the storming stage, proper team building takes time, effort, and SYNERGY!" I ended with my best cheesy company training video impression and laughed because I knew she wouldn't.

She rolled her eyes even harder now. "How about you do us both a favor and skip the class clown routine and just let me tell you what I want?"

I hopped down, intrigued. "Using my own words against me? I can respect that. Please." I zipped my lips and bowed; I was withering away by the second after all.

"You've inhabited that poor young human long enough. I let you slide before, but now you've crossed a line, I won't let your evil spread to another."

With my thumb and index finger, I unzipped my lips, "Ok, enough with that word, I'm not *evil,* not all fallen angels are evil, I expected this from them, but not from you. If I had to put it into words, I'd say I'm…" I thought for a better synonym, but my mind drew a blank. "…not uptight? What's a good word for that? Um, like carefree, it's close, but I think I can do better."

Remaining steadfast she quickly fired back, "You have fallen from Grace and escaped Hell. I know exactly what you are, and I suggest you crawl back down while you still can."

"If that's what you really want, why did you fix my wing when I escaped?"

Eve took half a step back and shock flashed across her face briefly before she could overcome it and resume her hard stare. "I didn't think you saw me; you were in pretty bad shape."

"I didn't, just an educated guess. I mean, there aren't very many Guardians to choose from. Honestly, though, three times in as many months, didn't think you'd be that easy to track down." Yet again I was fully aware of how many buttons I was trying to press in a row and enjoying it for as long as I could.

I could tell by her body language I was starting to get closer to the right buttons, but she resisted the urge to lash out. "So, was that why you've been following my human? To get to me?"

I wanted to keep her on the defensive, to be the one asking the questions, for now at least, and her particular choice of words gave me the perfect opening. "Oh, *your* human? I was wondering what was going on there, does she even know that she has a celestial stalker?"

She folded her arms across her chest, it was working. "I'm not stalking her, I'm guarding, as is my job, something your lowly tier would know nothing about."

Her increasingly harsh insults were like a Geiger counter for

locating sore spots, and with that last one I was definitely onto
something big. "Ok, all right, my apologies, I just want to keep
my host happy, and he's taken a real shine to your human, a real
schoolyard crush, so, safe to say we'll be sticking around for
a…"

Before I could even finish poking the bear, she swooped her
long slender arm out and snatched me up by the throat again
while expanding her massive wingspan of green fire out to
block off the entire skyline. The feathers made of pure
energetic heat flickered and licked the chilly night air, and as
they curled inward on me, the rotting edges of my skin began
to accelerate with sizzling blisters. "You will stay away from
her!" Hot emerald flames poured from her eyes as she shouted
angrily.

I guess I had found the tipping point, oops. "Ok, ok, easy
there, no more angels need to die, I'm sorry, I'll go in peace,"
Let's just say it was a good thing that angels don't have
bladders.

Eve's eyes returned to their standard green, and her wings
ceased their vice grip motion toward me. "What are you talking
about? angels don't die, that's impossible."

I was happy to have the slight reprieve, but more so I was
surprised word of Xaf's fate hadn't reached upstairs, especially
since Father was all-knowing and everything. Guardians were
high in the ranks, but I guess he was still keeping his secrets
within the Archangel circle even after all this time. I didn't want
to be the one to break the news to Eve in her already agitated
state, but I was already past the point of no return. "I…I'm
sorry, I guess I assumed you knew. Xaf's gone. Gavin found
him a few months ago, or…what was left of him I should say."

Eve retracted her wings and nearly collapsed, only barely
catching herself on the railing at the building's edge. "That…
That can't be. What…What could…"

"We don't know yet," I said preemptively, "Trini's blaming
the Saints, and quite frankly I can't think of another
possibility."

Eve was slow to stand up, but she continued to slouch and

support some of her weight against the chipped metal bars. "No, they would never, they rarely leave their posts guarding the inner sanctum, and they are forbidden from crossing over to Earth. No, it must have been a demon, or another one of you fallen." Her voice was beginning to develop a low rumble as her anger returned, but there was still time to show her reason.

"One of us would never turn on our own, you have to know that. And no demon is that powerful, trust me, I fathered a few of the stronger ones and even they could never hurt an angel, fallen or otherwise."

Her eyes narrowed and I felt myself tense up defensively. Apparently, I made a mistake somewhere. "You say none of your blasphemous traitors could've done this, and yet you accuse us? We cherish life, *all* life! Even you and your kind are protected, as you already know." She gestured to my right wing.

"That may have been true millennia ago, but what about now? We're not trapped in Hell any longer; I know there are more than a few downstairs that are still bitter over the war, and if you're any indication, you guys have your own prejudice against us. Is it really so far-fetched to think someone hates us more than you do?"

She looked like she wanted to be mad, but once my words had time to resonate with her, she knew it was at least possible. "Regardless of how we feel, Xapham was still family to all of us, the others deserve to know of what happened." She hesitated, "I'll…I'll find out if anyone knows anything when I deliver the news, but I still think you should look down below for the true culprit."

Satisfied that we were no longer fighting, I tried to bid my farewell before my form could rot away completely. "Megatron and the others are all over that. As I'm sure you could guess, they're very motivated to find the truth, no matter what that is."

I tried to phase through the roof and back into Angelica's apartment, but Eve wasn't fooled. "This doesn't change anything, I still want you to stay away from her."

I mouthed a few curse words before I turned back. "Ok,

J. A. Reed

fine, but I'm curious, what makes her so special? There are billions of humans, why follow around just one?"

"I could ask you the same thing, why the boy? Or do you not even know?"

"Mixture of right place, right time, and a fair amount of researching on my part, I can't let all that go to waste. I mean, do you even know how long it takes to break in a new human?"

She didn't laugh, but neither was she annoyed by the return of my joking nature. After some internal debate, her body language softened. "You do leave the host in control, which is more than I can say for most of your kind, so I suppose I'll let it slide for now." She rose up slowly. "But only if he accepts you back, which if I read him properly in there, might not happen."

Before I could refute, she flew off like a bullet. "What? You're crazy...he'll take me back, Liam freakin' loves me," I said to the empty space out of spite. "And that's right! You better run!" I turned and descended through the building before she could have a chance to hear me and turn back to call me out on my insult.

"Cheers to that," I heard Angelica's voice seconds before I peeked my head through the wall to see Liam clinking glasses with her. She was smiling and laughing, so apparently, he hadn't screwed up in my absence.

I watched them exchange glances over their plates, but I was running out of time to either get my host back or retreat back to Hell where I could heal and it didn't look like the coast would be clear for a long while. I looked around for a suitable distraction, and when I settled on one, I snuck by and into the kitchen.

"So, how long have you lived here?" Liam asked right as I knocked over a few dishes in the drying rack.

"Only..." Angelica's answer was cut short by the deafening clatter of the plate and bowl I helped get off the countertop and find the floor. "What the...? Damn it, sorry, I need to get that, just one second."

I flew back around as she left the room and knelt down to

clean up the shattered bits of ceramic. "Shhh, it's me," I whispered, hoping I could keep Liam from blowing his cover.

"What are…" he quieted down, "what are you doing? Why did you leave?"

"I didn't!" I hissed. "I was basically kidnapped, but hurry up and take me back, I'm falling apart here! Literally!"

"Yeah, I get how this thing works now, I just…I…"

"What the hell?" Eve was right, he's hesitating taking me back, but why? "I don't have time to argue, just take me back and we can talk about this after dinner."

"Can you find Ash for me please? I wanna make sure she doesn't come in here until I can clean it thoroughly!"

"Yeah, no problem!" Liam shouted back, "I…can't we just…ok, fine."

Without needing any more, I dove headfirst and melded with Liam again, and while it hadn't been as painful as the first time, it did throw me off a little more than I had prepared myself for. *Thank you, now we can stay if you like, but apparently, we have some things we need to discuss.*

"Yeah, I'm done here anyway." he whispered just in time before Angelica came back to the dining room drying her hands on a dishrag. "Um, I think Ash is still in the back, but I'm pretty stuffed, so I think I should get going anyway, it's getting pretty late."

"Oh, ok, um, yeah, I'll show you out." She turned back to drop the dish towel and then walked me to the door. "Thanks for staying though, I'm glad you did, even though I pretty much kidnapped you." She laughed nervously, but Liam seemed too preoccupied to acknowledge it, and she ended up looking embarrassed. I could've saved him by letting him know what he was missing, but he hesitated taking me back, so I'll hesitate to help him.

"Um, right, thanks for dinner, normal time tomorrow?" Liam was still distant, and Angelica could tell.

"Um, yeah, same time I guess. Goodnight…" Liam left, still lost in his own mind that he ignored her, and once I heard Angelica close the door, I flew us straight back home for a much-needed heart-to-heart.

CHAPTER TEN: GOING FOR A STROLL OUTSIDE

Zeke got us home so fast, I hadn't been able to prepare an argument, an angle, anything at all really. He, on the other hand, wasted no time whatsoever. "Ok, no more running, no more avoiding, something is going on between us, and we need to hash this thing out right now, right here."

Angelica's advice resonated in my head, all I had to do was open up and tell him all about Foxy's deal, my mother, and how torn apart I was by the whole thing, but before I could open my mouth, Foxy's warning followed up on the coattails to provide the counter argument. There was only one chance for me to get this right, and if I blabbed about my side deal and was wrong, Zeke would be able to take me over completely and I'd be lost, just like all the other hosts I had met. I needed more information; I needed more time. "Ok, fine, but it's a two-way street. You still have way more secrets than I do. I want to know where my mother is."

I had caught him off guard with that question, and due to that, had to wait in the most uncomfortable of silences for what felt like days before he found the words. *Her....She was already gone when we got there, but I felt...I can't be certain, but...it felt like...*

"Heaven or Hell, Zeke!" I shouted louder than I had intended, but he was taking too long and needed a fire lit under him. "Just tell me!"

Heaven! All right! She's in Heaven.

Foxy hadn't lied, but neither had Zeke...so far. I needed more.

"Good, that's good. Now what about me? If I drop dead right now, which way am I going? Huh?" I was coming off a little more aggressive than I meant to, and Zeke replied in kind.

That's an easy one, you're on the highway, not the stairway, but are you trying to blame me for that? Have you forgotten what I told you back in the hospital? God gave up on humanity thousands of years ago, everyone, no matter how good, or just, or devoted they are, all get sent away. Souls going upstairs are rarer than lottery winners, so I don't know what your mother did to get in, but there's no way to follow her, there never would've been for you, with or without me.

I found the couch and lowered myself into it, stunned by that information. Zeke basically confirmed what I already believed, but in a far larger scale than I ever knew possible. I had thought that as long as I was good, kindhearted and giving, I could earn my way into Heaven, but now things were different. Foxy's deal wasn't just the best option, it was the only option. I had to take it.

Don't be sad, Liam, Hell's actually not such a bad place, Zeke said trying to be supportive. *Any and all historical figures are there; they usually hate meeting fans, but I could get you an in.*

"What's Heaven like?" He might try to downplay it to spare my feelings, but I had to know as much as possible, I needed more of a reason to support my new decision and maybe it would make me feel like less of a piece of crap.

I...I don't think you should bother yourself with... he started, trying to save me from knowing what I was missing out on, but he had no idea.

"Please, I what to know where she is, I want to know she's at peace." It wasn't a lie, I just hid the fact that I also wanted to know where I would be going. He bought it.

Ok, if it'll put your mind at ease, I can show you, close your eyes.

I closed my eyes, and Zeke shared a memory with me. There was a slight familiarity between this memory and the dozens I had accidentally gleaned from his time in Hell, but as if it were being screened through a completely different filter. The size and scope of it were the same, but where Hell was cold, dark, and dingy, Heaven was warm, bright, and glistening. There were towering structures like palaces littering the landscape and each window was filled with a twinkling light as if warm fires lie within every room. To my left was a city, thousands of towers that grew larger and taller the closer they reached to the center, building upon each other stretching further into the sky than should ever be structurally possible. At the heart of the great city rested the pinnacle of beauty in this world, and from Zeke's memory I knew it to be none other than the inner sanctum, the literal house of God. From my distant vantage point, I could see seven bright red shining stars orbiting around the sealed keep.

Silhouetting the holy city was the expansive sky, which was lit up with every color of the rainbow as if sunset and sunrise were happening simultaneously from every direction. I turned and found more of the same stretching on for eternity, but the clouds and colors were twirling and flowing like a Vincent van Gogh masterpiece. I felt the water build up in my eyes but was having trouble telling if they were my own tears or Zeke's. I opened my eyes and was back in the condo, breathing heavily and desperately trying to dry my cheeks with my sleeves.

I'm sorry, Zeke apologized, *I haven't thought about that place in a very, very long time.*

"You still miss it, don't you?" I had been emotional when I saw his memory, but I could tell that a great deal of what I had felt stemmed from the memory and not myself. Zeke had told me about our first bonding back in the hospital and how overwhelmed he had been by human emotion, but apparently angels could have strong feelings just fine on their own.

Of course I miss it; it was paradise. If I could go back, I would in a heartbeat, but it's not that simple.

There it was! Zeke actually wanted to return to Heaven; if Foxy knew that, there might be a way to make all of this work. It was a longshot, I had no doubts about that, but God and angels were all about forgiveness, so it had to be possible. I could save Zeke and be reunited with my mother all in one fell swoop, it was like Christmas. "What if it was simple? What if there was a way for you to go back?"

There's not though, it's impossible for either of us. See? This is why I didn't want to show you, I didn't want to get your hopes up for something impossible.

"Ok, but imagine for a second that it was possible, what then?" I asked, just trying to hear him consider it.

"But it's not!" he shouted at me, mad enough to use his out loud angelic voice. *There's no going back for me, and you'd have better luck getting struck by lightning while being eaten by a shark, so just drop the subject and be happy your mom is at peace.*

"But…" I started a counterpoint, but Zeke wouldn't have it.

No buts! You don't know my Father, he's stubborn, he would never admit he was wrong, he would never take me, or anyone else, back once he's decided to cast them aside. I'd show you with memories, but I don't have any, I never even met him! I could feel the argument drift away from Heaven and twist into his personal feelings against God.

"Are you sure he won't forgive you? Have you ever tried? His whole thing is about forgiveness, isn't it? Maybe there is a way for you to go home and you've just never considered it before."

Ugh! No, he is not all about forgiveness, that's all just PR and half-truths given to Man by Tammy and Barty Boy, his goody two-shoes little Muses, and half of that's been altered in one way or another over the millennia, so whatever you think you know about him, I assure you, you know nothing. So, it doesn't matter how badly I want to go home, I can't, not ever! So please, can you just drop it?!

There it was again, he did want to go back, but he was so blinded by the pain of rejection and unresolved feelings of abandonment that he couldn't even allow himself to consider the possibility. Factor into that trying to stop me from dreaming what he believed to be an impossible dream, and his outrage became completely understandable. Sadly, with this new glimmer of hope, came more questions and uncertainties. Foxy hadn't exactly said the nicest things about Zeke, but she only ever compared him to his more abrasive siblings. Maybe if she knew him the way I did, she could see that he wasn't like the others who Fell. There was still no guarantee Zeke could be saved, and if things between him and his Father were really that bad, Zeke might not accept an offer unless some sort of compromise could be made. I needed to find Foxy, and I needed to do it without Zeke watching my every move. I needed another kidnapping or something. Speaking of which, "Ok, I'll drop it, but next I wanna know where you went during dinner. All you said was that you were kidnapped. Pretty sure there's more to that story."

Ugh! Zeke sighed loudly, *Can't we do this another time? I'm tired, being out in the open for so long took a lot out of me, I need time to recover.*

"You're the one that said we needed to talk, and I have more questions, like what were you and Megatron talking about in his office? What ever happened to that Guardian angel you were looking for? Who's–?"

Enough! Jeez, enough, ok, Megatron wanted me to go back to hell and keep an eye on one of my kids, The Guardian we were tracking was the one that kidnapped me, and she demanded that we leave Angelica alone, so tonight was the last we'll be seeing of her, and no more questions for tonight, I need some rest.

"Wait, what?! Zeke, what do you mean stay away from Angelica? I can't just–"

You can, and you will, now I give you permission to go, run, do whatever you like for the next twelve or so hours, because I need to heal, so I'm going dormant.

"Wait, you can do that? Why have you never…Zeke?" There was silence, but not nearly as deafening as it had been when we were separated, instead, I could still feel him, but it was faint. "Zeke? Can you hear me?" No response. "Zeke, I just wanted to let you know, you're ugly, and you smell bad." I waited for a response, but he was out like a light. "Ok, this is perfect, just have to find Foxy, strike up a new deal, and he'll be none the wiser. Perfect, now…where do I find an Enochian…? And why am I talking to myself?" I looked around and luckily Tabby wasn't home, so there hadn't been any witnesses to my goof up.

With only twelve or so hours to spare, I rushed to my room and dressed warmly for heading out into the rainy night. I ran all the way to the little bakery, which had been harder than I anticipated with all of the necessary layers. I asked for a water cup and rehydrated while I waited for Foxy to reveal herself to me. An hour passed by and neither the old woman nor the voice in my head returned, causing me to worry. What if she's rescinded her deal? What if I took too long to decide and I'm doomed to go to Hell?

I waited another excruciating thirty minutes, and my only company was increasingly negative thoughts until the shop asked me to leave so they could close up. I looked up and down the street lost, unsure of which way to go, or if I should stay and wait longer. I picked a direction and started walking slowly, but I had already cooled down from my run to get there, so I had to bundle myself up in an attempt to stay warm.

I was so confused, where was she? I tried praying to see if she would hear me, but there was no sign of it working, so next I ducked into an alley and tried talking to her aloud. "Fox… Farfox? Or, sorry, Forfax! It's me, Liam. Zeke's gone dormant or whatever, so it's ok to come out! I've thought about the deal, and I want to take you up on it, but I want to try and help Zeke too. I know you think he's beyond saving, but please, I know it's not too late for him."

I repeated my message various different times in multiple different ways, but still I was ignored. Spirit broken, I wandered around quite a bit longer heading in the general direction back home, but when I got too tired and cold to keep going I turned into what I had thought was a restaurant, but had turned out to be a bar.

Not caring that I wasn't supposed to be there, I just sat down at the counter anyway, catching the attention of the bartender immediately. He strutted over. "I'd ask for an ID, but I think we both know you can't be in here, kid."

"I'm tired, can't I just get a club soda or something?" I pleaded, but his neck tattoos and foot-long beard suggested he wasn't the kind to cave from a sob story, but before he could have me thrown out, a slender feminine hand reached out from over my shoulder and pressed a hundred-dollar bill onto the bar.

"Make that two club sodas, and a little privacy."

The owner of the hand and money pulled the nearest stool even closer to me and slid gracefully onto it with long smooth legs. She shot me a sultry smile causing my cheeks to turn the same deep red of her silk cocktail dress that hung perfectly over her ample frame. "Nice to see you again, Liam."

I was frozen in shock for a long moment, moving nothing but my eyelids. as I tried to blink fast and often enough to reassure myself what was happening was real, but eventually my brain started working again. "Foxy?"

Her annoyed sigh sounded exactly like the one I had heard in my head the first time I suggested that nickname, only this time I was able to witness the facial reaction that accompanied it. Even annoyed the soft features of her host's face under golden curls couldn't look anything other than stunning. "I'll file that under my brother's influence, so I'll let it slide. Have you come to a decision?"

The bartender returned with our drinks buying time for me to collect my thoughts. "Anything else I can do for you, angel?" he said with a flirtatious smile.

"Just the privacy I requested, *human,*" she shot back with a heated glare.

The man's smile fell away and he nervously walked away trying to play it off like he had other work to do, but was not convincing whatsoever. She turned back to me with renewed softness. "I know he's gone dormant, you can speak freely, my child."

I lowered my head and only made occasional but brief eye contact as I spoke my peace, "I...I wanted to know if there's any way to help Zeke; he won't allow himself to admit it, but I know he wants to go back to Heaven, and I can assure you, he's not a bad guy, I just...I really want to help him, I need to help him...after everything he's done for me."

"You still wish to help the fallen angel? That's unexpected. Perhaps there's some truth to what you say then; perhaps there's hope for redeeming him as well, provided he's willing to atone for his past transgressions."

I lifted my head up at this glimmer of hope. "I'm sure he will, once he knows there's real hope, I'm sure he'll do whatever he needs to."

Foxy turned her head in an inquisitive notion. "What do you mean? Has he not already expressed to you his wishes to repent?"

The glimmer was beginning to fade, but I was determined to breathe life back into it like a campfire ember. "No, it's not like that. He has told me he wants back, that he regrets the Fall, it's just, he's under the impression it's completely impossible, so he refuses to torture himself with hypotheticals. But trust me, once we show him it's possible, he'll embrace it completely, I know he will."

Foxy remained silent for some time and I wasn't able to read her well enough to know if she was doubting my assurances, or being swayed by them. "Very well, but you will not be able to save him, that decision must be his and his alone."

"Yes. Yes, of course." I said, just happy that I'd kept the hope alive this long.

Foxy pulled a bar napkin toward her and traced her thin index finger along it leaving scorched writing behind. "I want you to meet me at this location tomorrow, but do not reveal my presence to Ezekiel until then." She finished the directions and slid the napkin to me but held her fingers on it as she continued her instructions. "I will approach him, and I will offer him the chance to turn his back on Hell and return to the light. You may do your best to convince him, but you must make him believe that you will respect his decision either way. If you're right, there will be no trouble, and you both can be saved, but should you be wrong about him, we can't risk him taking full control over you."

She finally released the napkin, and I peeked at it before folding it into my pocket. "Don't worry, He'll come with me, and regardless, he'd never—"

"If you're wrong about one thing, you could be wrong about more. Please, for your own safety, don't give him cause to think you might betray him. If you're wrong and he rejects Heaven, banish him as you did before, and take me instead. I'll be able to protect you from him." I lowered my head again, and she sensed my discomfort. "I know you don't want to abandon him, and in all likelihood, you won't have to, but you have to remember that I know others of his kind; I know what they are capable of. All I want is to make sure you're safe."

I picked up my soda and drank half of the glass in one go before the carbonation made my eyes water, or at least I let myself believe it was due to the carbonation. "What time do you…"

"I'll be waiting for you all day, take your time, prepare however you need to, there will be no rush." She grabbed a couple more napkins and passed them to me. "It's going to be all right Liam, it'll all be over soon." Foxy stood up, hesitated, and then walked away and outside. I stayed and sipped on the remainder of my soda until there was nothing left but melted ice. The bartender periodically shot me a few sideways glances, either debating how long a hundred dollars bought me before kicking me out, or waiting for Foxy to come back, but I decided to get up and leave before either option could take place.

The walk back home was long, but the cold didn't seem to affect me as much this time with so much on my mind. I found myself relating to Zeke in a new way that scared me. Throughout my conversation with Foxy, and even before that, I had convinced myself that Zeke would never refuse Heaven if the possibility were presented to him for real, so I hadn't been allowing myself to consider hypotheticals. Tomorrow, Zeke would get his chance to have what he believed for so long to be impossible, and in doing so, I would get that same chance. If he could embrace this new chance, then I wouldn't have to, but if he refused, then I would have to do the unspeakable.

I got home late and walked past Tabby in the living room watching late night television but paid no mind to him. I entered my room and fell face first into bed. I couldn't sleep, but there was something I could do. I couldn't ask Zeke to do what I was unwilling to do, so I vowed to myself right then and there, that no matter what happened, I was open to the alternative I had previously thought impossible. I would fill my head with that thought, hoping and praying that it would spill over and influence Zeke's decision when the time came. If Zeke made the wrong decision, then he wasn't who I thought he was, and I would be able to turn my back on that stranger, but I did know Zeke, so I wasn't worried. Tomorrow I was going to get my soul back, my mother back, and Zeke was coming with me, or Ezekiel would be out of my life forever.

J. A. Reed

There were no longer any down sides in this situation that had tormented me for what felt like forever. With my mind now at ease, I drifted off into the most peaceful slumber I had known in months.

* * *

I emerged from my dormant state in the morning shortly after Liam had woken up, but before he was awake enough to get out of bed. It was our day off from the coffee shop, so there was no rush to go anywhere, but I was feeling refreshed and energized, so I announced my return with gusto, *Rise and shine, sleepyhead! Forecast is only partly cloudy, which for the Pacific Northwest is one of the finest days you can ask for, let's go out, do something fun!*

Liam rolled over and moved some of the clutter blocking his view to the bedside clock. It was a quarter past noon, much later than their usual ten o'clock wake up call. "Ugh, who are you, and what have you done with Zeke?"

What did you do last night? How late did you go to bed?

Liam dozed off for a few seconds before waking back up and answering like he hadn't missed a beat. "Went out, found a bar, pretty girl bought me a drink."

I laughed a little at that and wished I hadn't missed it. *Did you go back to Angelica's? Or are you just a player now?*

Liam rubbed the sleep out of his eyes and heaved himself up into a seated position. "No, not like that, and it was just soda, don't worry, I'm still a good kid." He stretched and yawned big.

I don't care about that. Hell, Tabby leaves his liquor cabinet unlocked; if you wanted that I could hook you up.

Liam chuckled, still pretty groggy, "Naw, I'm good, my body is a temple." He laughed again.

You mean our body, and I've never really been a fan of temples. I laughed back, but Liam just rubbed his eyes again more vigorously trying to wake up enough to stand. *But seriously, what do you want to do today, besides going for a run, if that's possible?*

Liam stood, wobbled for a second, and then seemed all right enough to move. "What about a hike? I found out about a trail outside the city while you were MIA last night, supposed to have a great view."

A hike? Really? We need to start broadening your horizons, get you some new, less strenuous hobbies, but sure, why not. Baby steps I guess.

Liam sluggishly made his way to the kitchen where he proceeded through his average morning routine. As eggs and sausage fried on the stove top, he pulled out Cody's dog food and poured it into one of those funny looking bowls that helped to prevent him from scarfing it all down too fast, but the dog was as determined as ever to try. He agitated the sizzling pan occasionally while packing a small lunch for the hike until the amazing smell told him it was done, so he flicked off the heating element and popped off to the bathroom for a quick second as our breakfast cooled down to a more manageable temperature. As he ate, Cody was still chasing down the last little bits of his own meal that were perpetually outsmarting him. "I think we should leave Cody behind on this one," Liam said between bites, "at least until we've had a chance to check it out for ourselves first."

Agreed, I said wholeheartedly, *don't want a repeat of Zoo Loop, that was a nightmare.* I had to admit, though, even if we had done the Zoo Loop trail alone first, we never could've guessed that Cody would be able to wriggle out of his collar and try making friends with a tiger, but that's only because we both continually underestimated the idiocy of our furry friend.

Liam choked on a piece of scrambled egg as he laughed from remembering that day. "I doubt we'll ever get a repeat of that, but yeah, you know what I mean."

Liam finished breakfast and took the plate and pan to the sink. *All right, ready to go?* I asked, making sure to prep him before taking flight.

"Not just yet, I'm going to clean up a bit first." Liam then began running the hot water and squirted a few pumps of dish soap.

What? Now? You can do it when we get home, it needs to soak anyway.

"No, it's fine, besides, I've actually started to notice, it's easier to wash them right away, before it dries up and sticks, it'll just take me a second." As if Liam's sudden urge to break tradition wasn't odd enough, his tone and demeanor made it feel like he was trying to hide something from me.

Everything all right, Liam? You seem a little, I don't know, off. I tried to see what emotions I could sense off him, but there was nothing strong enough for me to pick up, which was a good sign I guess.

"Yeah, it's just…well, it's later than usual, new hike, not sure how long or late we'll be. Just want to leave it clean in case Tabby comes home and we…and we're not here." Liam's speech was broken up and monotone, but I just shrugged it off as being distracted by the fact he was wrist deep in suds and sausage grease.

I impatiently waited for him to be satisfied with the state of the kitchen and get changed, where yet again he insisted on frivolous details like making the bed and putting all of the dirty clothes inside the hamper rather than on the floor beside it. *All right, 'Mom!' You know when I said to find a new hobby, this isn't what I had in mind.*

"Oh, stop your whining. I promise, this won't be a regular thing, if we wake up tomorrow at a more reasonable time, it'll be back to business as usual." Liam pulled out his phone and pulled up a map of the trail he had in mind for the day and pointed to a portion about halfway up the trail. "Now fly us here, we can hike the rest from there."

Childish giddiness filled my voice, *What? Really? You mean we don't have to hike the whole trail?*

"It's not too late; if you want, we can start here." Liam moved his finger way too far across the screen.

No, no, you can't take it back now, first spot, coming right up! Liam barely had enough time to let out a single snicker before I pushed off and flew straight up, got the lay of the land, spotted the point on the trail, and rocketed down to a secluded spot out of sight of any other hikers.

"All right, let's get moving." Liam tightened the straps on his backpack and started up the trail. The scenery was very beautiful, far enough outside the city that the air was clear and smelled of pine and cedar. Gray clouds scattered the lower sky and the moisture level was just shy of precipitation. The compacted trail was wet but only rarely were there spots soft enough to form mud puddles and they were easily avoidable. "Having fun yet?"

I had to admit, I was. The past months had been nothing but working and running through the city, it was refreshing to just walk through the beautiful sea of greens and browns spotlighted in sporadic beams of sunlight. *Eh, it's all right,* I said, holding back to make sure he wouldn't let it go to his head.

He laughed, knowing exactly what I was doing. "Well don't worry, we're almost to the top, you'll definitely enjoy that view, I promise."

We continued on for a few more miles, and I found myself incredibly thankful the we started halfway up the trail, because as beautiful as the trail was, boredom was slowly creeping over the horizon. Just as I was beginning to contemplate when to resort to are-we-there-yet level of tactics, the end of the trail came into view. A few more dozen yards, and we reached the apex where we stopped. The sun was still high overhead, and the clouds had rolled away just enough to leave a massive chunk of crystal clear sky over the landscape ahead of us. Shimmering blue water twinkled like a sea of precious stones and wind blew through large spans of grass making it appear just as lively and free-flowing as the lake beside it.

Wow... I knew when I came to Earth that I wanted to have the sorts of experience that had been impossible in Hell, but this was beyond my wildest dreams.

"Beautiful, isn't it?" Liam said, just as awestruck as I was.

Make sure you thank whoever suggested this place. And say what you will about Dear ol' Dad, but damn, can he make something beautiful.

"You're not wrong, but after you showed me what Heaven looks like, don't think this holds a candle. Close, but not quite."

With that, the moment was ruined, and if Liam dredging up

the reminder that I'd never see Heaven again wasn't bad enough, just the simple fact that he ruined such a nice moment made me even more mad. I tried to forget about it and take the moment back, but it was gone and trying only caused an exponential downhill spiral until all I wanted was to just go home. "Thanks for the salt in that wound," I said out loud to accentuate my displeasure. "Let's just go home."

"If that's what you wish, there may be a way," a feminine voice said from above and behind us. Liam spun around and our eyes spotted something descending from the dark clouds as they rolled back in. She was still some distance away, but as she floated down closer I could make out more and more detail. The first thing that was obvious were her blazing wings that burned in a faint bluish hue indicating she was an Enochian. As the details of her face came into focus I recognized her slender features immediately, but even if I hadn't been so stunned and could've spoken when she first emerged, there was only one female Enochian, which meant there was only one angel that it could be.

"Foxy?" I asked once I found my voice again.

"Yes! I knew it!" Liam whispered to himself, but there would be time to figure out what he was talking about later.

"Foxy, what are you doing here? If this is about Eve, I already told her–"

"I'm not here on anyone else's behalf brother, I'm here to ask you if you're ready to repent your sins. I'm here to offer you a chance to return home – isn't that what you want?" She stopped a dozen feet above the ground with the sun at her back forcing Liam to squint, limiting our visibility.

"What? What are you talking about? Why don't you come down here? Let's talk like normal people." There was something fishy about this whole situation. Why was she here if not for the same reason as Eve? Why was she being so distant and cryptic? Most importantly, how did she know I had been thinking about Heaven so much recently, and what was she trying to do in exploiting that?

"Haven't you spent enough time being down, Ezekiel?

Aren't you ready to rise back up? I want to help you brother, but you must allow me to help you. Release your human host, embrace your true form, and I can usher you back into paradise."

"Leave Liam out of this! And I'm not doing a thing until you explain yourself!"

Liam lowered his head and spoke quietly for me to know he was speaking to me directly. "Wait, Zeke, it's ok. All this talk about Heaven, if you can go back, don't worry about me, you've already done more than enough for me. I'll be fine, you should trust her."

Not so fast, Liam. Something feels off about this. The non-fallen don't just casually approach us fallen and make promises like this all willy-nilly. No, I don't know why, but she's lying, this might have something to do with what happened to Xaf.

"No, she's a freakin' angel. Angels don't lie, they help people," Liam said in a pleading tone. His blind willingness was only making my sinking feeling worse.

Is that so? Name one person that's been helped by an angel, just one.

"Angelica!" he said defiantly without skipping a step. I knew I shouldn't have told him the truth about my kidnapping.

Ok fine, name two! You can't. Angels aren't what you think they are, I've tried to tell you this a hundred times. Why are you on her side anyway?

"I'm not! Whatever you decide, I'm with you 100 percent, but I really, truly, honestly believe that this could be the best thing for both of us. You could go home again, you could be happy. And I…I could see my mom again…"

Suddenly it all became crystal clear, the reason Liam had been talking about Heaven so much recently; he knew she was there, and I had been the one to tell him there was virtually zero chance of him ever getting in to see her again. *Wait, did you know about this?*

"What?" he said, crippling terror rushing through him so strongly I could easily feel its tingle down his spine. "What, no, of course not."

What did she promise you? Your mother? Damn it, Liam, she's played you! You've done exactly what she wanted, we have to get out of here right now!

"Foxy! He knows!" Liam cried out in trembling fear, but fear directed at me. I was frozen in shock.

"Then do it now! Before it's too late!" Foxy cried back to him.

I finally collected myself enough to speak, but I still couldn't think fast enough to act. *What? Liam, what are you doing?*

"I'm sorry Zeke, I tried, I really tried." He fell to his knees and screamed out; I could feel him willing me out of his body forcefully. By the time I knew it was happening, I tried to cling on, but just as Eve had said the night before, our bond was weak, and there was nothing for me to hold onto now that he no longer wanted me.

My freshly healed angelic form flung out behind Liam, tumbling along the rocky path several feet before sliding to a halt. I held out my hands in front of me and immediately began to notice the decay settling in again. "Liam, what have you done?"

"Offer yourself to me now, my child," Foxy said, her light blue eyes burning hungrily at Liam. "I can cleanse your soul."

"Liam, don't! She—"

Before I could finish my warning, he shot up to a standing position and threw out his arms toward her. "Save me!"

"Liam! No!" Foxy's angelic form propelled itself into Liam's body like a meteor and produced a shockwave that flung me even further along the rocky ground causing bits and pieces of my deteriorating flesh to rip and peel with each scrape.

After my body came to an abrupt stop against a rather large rock formation, I heaved myself up and tried my best to peer through the haze of dirt and pollen as it slowly drifted away with the breeze. I spotted Liam's back where he stood, still in the same spot as before, only now it was marked with deep sections of earth gouged out around him. "Liam?" I said both confirming and pleading. "Liam, if you can hear me, banish her. Do it now, before it's—"

"Too late," said Foxy's voice from Liam's throat. She turned his body around to face me, and his eyes blazed a blue hot fire that licked out high above his eyebrows before calming back down to within the confines of the iris.

"Let him go!" I ordered. "He has nothing to do with this!"

"He aligned himself with the likes of you, his life is forfeit, just like yours." Foxy reached behind her back, and when she retrieved it, there was a rose gold sword hilt in her grasp. My jaw dropped in disbelief, but as more and more of the flaming sword appeared into view, the more I had to believe what I was seeing.

"Where did you get that?" The only flaming swords in all of existence resided in the hands of the Saints, seven swords for seven Saints, and none of them would ever separate themselves from their sword for even a second. "You...You can't have that."

"And you can't have this world!" Foxy screamed. She forced Liam's body to carry her closer toward me one menacingly slow step at a time. "Look at you – even the very air around you is trying to banish you back to where you belong. It wasn't enough for you to be a blight on the good name of angels, was it? Now you're trying to spread your corruption to these pitiful creatures, where will it end? Once you've had your fill here, you'll start trying to break back into Heaven, and that is something I cannot allow! You and your filth need to be put down!"

I kept backing away from Foxy, but the faster I tried to backpedal the faster she approached. "*Put down?* So it was you! You killed Xaf! Have you gone mad? Xaf never hurt anyone, he never even..."

"Xapham was just as guilty as the rest of you!" She raised the sword up to drive the point home. "More evil, less evil, it makes no difference. Xapham had to die because you *all* have to die. He was easy pickings, it made for a good start, but one by one you'll all fall by my sword. Metatron won't be able to protect the other Muses forever; Zadkiel will come out of hiding eventually, and after I kill you, a full-fledged Angel, I'll know for sure that I can wipe out the rest of them."

I looked around for something, anything, to defend myself with, but there wasn't so much as a stick, and she was wielding a flaming sword tried and proven to be able to kill an immortal being. My only chance was to either talk my way out or turn tail and run. Zak had always joked I could talk my way out of anything, so I guess it was time to put that to the test. "You've got one hell of a weapon, that's for sure, but do you really think you'll be a match for the likes of Aida or Ram? What are you going to do when Lucy crosses over, huh? I mean, think about the long haul. What's your endgame?"

Foxy stopped, which at first was really good, but then she laughed the most eerie laugh I had ever heard outside of a horror movie. "Lucifer and Ramiel will be dealt with should they ever try and leave Hell, but the rest of you are mine, and with this tool of purification at my side, even the mighty Guardians will fall before me." Her angelic wings shot out of Liam's back and with three hefty beats she was back in the air towering over me. "But for now, I'll have to settle for target practice."

I guess Zak was wrong. As Foxy brandished the sword intimidatingly, I pivoted on the spot and pushed off with all my might trying to find the nearest fracture to retreat where she couldn't follow. I was several states away from the nearest crack, which would only be a couple minute's flight, but Foxy's far superior wings were nearly twice as fast as my shriveled-up ones, so with each dash I made for safe harbor she was there to cut me off. After a few tries, she didn't even seem to be trying to kill me, only toying with me. If I couldn't outrun her, I had to think of another way to escape, but I was fresh out of ideas and all alone. Alone? That's it! Megatron! She said it herself, he had been able to protect the Muses so far, he might be able to help now. It was a long shot, and showing up unannounced with an insane killer hot on my tail was incredibly risky, but it was the only bad option I had.

Once I changed my tactic and headed back to the city, I bought myself a short reprieve. Foxy had stopped to see what I was trying to do next, but her delay in my pursuit actually caused me to worry more. What if she wanted me to lead her to Megatron or the others? Luckily, I didn't have to worry about that for very long because before I could reach Megatron's office Foxy finally decided to stop playing around and began swinging the fiery blade for kill shots. I did my best to dodge and weave around in the air while continuing for Megatron, but she was beginning to make fewer mistakes as she got a feeling for the sword, something she likely didn't have to worry about against Xaf.

Molten hot pain erupted through my right leg as Foxy's sword made contact with my right knee and I fell from the sky crashing onto a nearby rooftop. I turned over and grabbed my injury tightly, trying desperately to stop my whole leg from splitting into two distinct pieces. "Foxy! Wait! Stop!" I begged and pleaded as she landed gracefully in front of me, twisting Liam's mouth into a sinister grin.

"You gave me quite the challenge, Ezekiel. I suppose I shouldn't wait so long with the next one, I'll kill the rest quick and clean, just like Xapham."

I tried to back away, but I was already pressed against the brick edge of the roof, and my injury was too severe for me to even consider running as an option. Despite the fact I knew it was useless, I gave begging one last ditch effort. "Please, Forfax, please don't do this."

"Goodbye, brother." She raised the sword high above Liam's head with both hands, but before she could drive the blade down, a rush of wind and blazing green flames swept her off her feet and high into the air. "What are you doing, sister?" Eve held Liam and Foxy, still bound together, by the throat in one hand, and the wrist wielding the Saint's blade in the other.

"Release me!" she cried, writhing to break free but powerless against Eve's superior strength. As I sat on the ground watching, I should've just been happy to be alive, but instead I was only able to dwell on the sad truth that Foxy had a stronger bond with Liam in a few minutes than I had after months of being with him. She had nearly killed me and all Liam did was sit by and watch. Where had I gone so wrong?

J. A. Reed

"I will not release you until you have calmed down Forfax! I will not let you kill our brother! He is hereby placed under my protection; do you understand me?"

Foxy continued to struggle, but she gradually moved less and less until she realized her efforts were truly wasted. She took a few heated breaths and she kept Liam's face contorted with rage, but the words that came out were the one's Eve had been looking for. "Fine, I swear, the fallen will not be harmed."

"Good, now I'm going to release you, and you're going to leave, agreed?"

"Agreed," she sneered.

"But what about the sword?!" I called out, hoping Eve wouldn't allow such a dangerous weapon to remain in the hands of a murderer, but I was too late.

"The sword is mine, that's not negotiable."

"But, Eve! She killed Xaf!"

Eve looked back at me with shock and horror all over her face. "What? Forfax, is this true?"

Foxy floated up and backwards far enough to stay out of range should Eve try anything against her again. "I'll leave Ezekiel alone for now, but should he or anyone else come after me, all bets are off."

"Forfax, wait!" Eve shouted after her, but Foxy turned and rocketed off through the storm clouds and out of view. "No…" Eve said quietly under her breath. "That can't be, Father would never…No…"

"Eve, sorry to interrupt, but…I could use a little help… again…" I tried to keep my voice steady, but the pain in my knee was becoming more and more unbearable by the second as the rot ate away at the cut.

"Oh, of course, I'm so sorry." She dropped to my side and with a single touch all the pain was gone, but there was nothing she could do to halt the festering that had already taken place. "You need to go back to Hell and heal, there's no more I can do for you here."

"Well, if you want to help, I could use a lift," I said jokingly now that I could think without the blinding pain.

"Sure thing," she laughed back, but I could tell she was worried about my condition despite my light-hearted attitude. "Perhaps on the way you can tell me what on Earth just happened?"

"Sure thing, she tricked...she tricked Liam." Even before Eve started flying the sky above her was spinning. "She's...she's crazy, killed...she killed...now she's...kill us all..."

"Ezekiel? Ezekiel! Stay with me! We're almost there, but I can't come through with you, you have to stay awake! Ezekiel! Keep talking, stay with me!" I could hear her, but it was really hard to keep my eyes open.

"She...Liam...He...Liam..."

She said something else to me, but I couldn't make out most of it. She shook me pretty hard too, but my eyes, they were so heavy. "ZEKE!"

"Huh? Wha...?" My eyes popped open and all I saw for miles around was barren desert and Eve kneeling over me.

"Thank the Lord, Ezekiel, please, go through now, back to Hell, you'll be safe there."

"You called me Zeke," I said with a dopey smile.

Eve rolled her eyes, and that was the last thing I saw before I reached out to touch the fracture and fell back down to Hell. I wrapped my wings around myself as I began to free-fall toward the ground and abruptly lost consciousness before I even reached the ground, which I can only assume was a good thing, because I'm sure that landing would've hurt like hell if I had been awake to experience it.

CHAPTER ELEVEN: FAMILY MEETING

I drifted in and out of consciousness for what could've been hours, or days, or longer, I couldn't be sure. The first time I opened my eyes I saw a blurred swarm of demons around me staring at me with a mixture of confusion, curiosity, greed, worry, and pretty much everything else across the spectrum. "Isn't that an angel?" I heard one voice murmur amongst the low chatter. "What happened to it?" said another. "He just fell from the sky," chimed in a third.

"I need..." I tried to sit up, but just getting my head off the cold hard ground was an insurmountable feat. "I need to..."

"Shh!" hissed one of the members of the crowd. "He's trying to speak." The hushed voices quieted but didn't dissipate completely.

"To save...Liam..." I drifted away again after that.

My eyes opened again, but nothing made sense around me. The twinkling light emitted by the fractures were far below me, the sky was covered in dust and ice, and a large obstruction was swaying back and forth in front of my eyes making it difficult to gain my bearings. "Wha...? Where?" I groaned.

"Shh," said a calming voice from right beside me. "Just rest, you'll be safe soon."

"Where...taking me...?" I tried to swallow mid-sentence but failed and lost a few words in doing so; still, it did at least give me some much-needed sense of direction – I was hanging upside down, slung over a shoulder belonging to the calming voice. I never heard a response to my question, but after an extended blink, I was suddenly laying on my back in a strange bed. I used every ounce of strength I had left to lift my head a few inches off the velvety soft pillow and look through the open doorway where I could see the same back that had carried me before filling the large open space.

"What were you thinking bringing him here?" a quiet voice whispered from beyond the massive stranger.

"Where else was I going to take him? He's an angel."

"I fail to see how that's my problem," the quiet mysterious

man hissed with annoyance, but after a short pause, his tone lightened up a little. "Fine, he can stay until he can walk, then I want him gone, do you hear me?"

"Of course, father. Thank you."

The longer I attempted to maintain my raised posture, the more painful it became until I couldn't help but groan audibly from the strain.

"Shh! Is he awake?" the less than thrilled man asked hopefully. I saw a hand reach over to shove the helpful one out of the way, but before I could see either of their faces, I collapsed back into the marshmallowy softness of the bed and linen and its overwhelming comfort stole me away; I was helpless to resist.

Despite the deep level of my sleep, it was anything but peaceful. The events on that mountain played out in my dreams over and over again, and each time I tried to change the events for the better, the outcome would be worse and worse. It was a heartbreaking, soul-wrenching type of torture that could only be considered my own personal Hell, but so much worse than the real thing.

"Liam!" I shouted when he died at the end of my dream, but this time I shot up in my bed and had actually made that outburst in real life. I sighed a breath of relief that the nightmares were over, but it was short lived. "Liam?" I called out, hoping that I was wrong and had dreamt the whole hike as well as the replays.

"Ezekiel?" said a familiar voice from the hallway outside. Cass entered in a rush with a tarnished brass serving tray covered in clean bandages. "Good, you're awake!" He set the tray down on the bed but not too close to me. "Can you move? Have you fully healed yet?" With his eagerness, I realized the voice I had heard before passing out was none other than that of my own brother.

"It's nice to see you too, Cass." I looked around the room and noticed the walls were very bleak and boring, definitely Cass's room. "What am I doing here?"

"That's what I would like to know," Cass said, trying to hide his worried tone, but a sliver had snuck through.

"I…I have to go back," I tried to pull the covers off and stand, but my movements were sluggish and labored, and as much as Cass wanted me out of his house, he could tell now wasn't the time for that. He pushed on my shoulder gently which was enough to knock me back down and drive the point home. "Ugh, I have to go back for Liam, she…she took him." Saying it out loud broke me down all over again.

"Who took who? What are you talking about, Ezekiel? What happened to you?" Cass lifted one of bandages on my shoulder and just shrugged at the state of healing which was blocked from my view, but given how I felt, I didn't think it was great. He pressed it back in place with a slight sting, confirming my suspicion.

"Foxy! She tricked him."

"I swear, you and your nicknames," he muttered under his breath. "You mean Forfax? What does she have to do with this? And tricked who, this 'Liam' you kept muttering in your sleep?" he asked, unsure how the dots connected with the limited information.

"Yes, Liam, she got inside his head, turned him against me. He's in trouble, I have to get him back."

"So, losing your host? That's how this happened? That hardly explains the state you were in when you came to us," he added with a patronizing tone, "Why didn't you just return before the rot took over as badly as it had? Are you just that stubborn?"

"Why are you asking if you clearly don't care?" I snapped, tired of wasting my breath.

He stood up and took the tray with him. "You wouldn't still be here if I didn't care, but since you seem to be okay now, fine, you don't need to tell me anymore, just get some rest." He checked a few more bandages the same way and seemed satisfied enough to leave them unchanged, so he set the tray on a nearby nightstand and headed for the door.

"She didn't just take Liam for no reason," I said hoping it would get him to stop, and it did. He turned back toward me.

"She wanted to weaken me. She wanted to kill me, just like she killed Xaf."

He seemed mostly unfazed, but he did break eye contact by looking down and away. "Are you certain about that?"

"She confessed to it, right before she tried to kill me with a flaming sword."

"A flaming sword? Really? I know you have a terrible sense of humor, but don't joke about Xapham's death like that!" Cass shouted angrily, but the look on his face didn't match his tone, there was fear in his eyes.

"I'm not joking about this!" I shouted back, defending my honor. "Think about it. It's the only thing that makes sense, what else could've killed an angel?" Cass stepped toward me and raised a hand to about hip level before opening his mouth, but no words followed, and he froze in place struggling to come up with an argument, but only produced a lingering silence.

When he finally did move, it was as if all of his tensed muscles relaxed at the same time leaving him to sink back down onto the bed. "I know it's been a long time, but things couldn't have changed that much in our absence, could it?" he finally asked, as if already knowing the answer to his own question.

"It wasn't just us either," I said, taking advantage of another silence to drop another bomb. "She said she'll kill all of us. She didn't even seem to be afraid of Lucy or Ram, she said they would be 'dealt with' should they ever try to leave Hell."

"Should they try to leave?" he asked, hope rising in his voice. "Well then that's it, isn't it? If we just stay down here, we don't have to worry, right?"

"Like hell we don't!" Cass and I both jumped due to the outburst coming from the hallway. Megatron squeezed through followed closely by Trini, and Gavin followed up the rear. "I just heard what happened, I'm..." He paused when he looked at me laid out on my back. "...I don't think 'glad' would be the right word, but it's good to see you didn't die."

"It's nice to see you too, little bro," I said back with affection that was obviously only pretend. "And does word really travel that fast?"

"Of course not!" Trini spat, offended I wasn't kissing Megatron's feet as she did. "Little happens in Seattle without us knowing about it; we've got ears and eyes everywhere."

"Oh, good, nice to know there was an audience to my celestial beatdown. Maybe next time you can tag in."

"Listen here you…" Megatron started, but Cass stood up and flared up his wings between the two of us.

"Enough! If all you're going to do is bicker, you can do it somewhere else!" He looked back and forth between us waiting for one of us to try and say something. I knew Megatron was too pompous to be the bigger man, so I nonverbally complied first. He was quick to back off second and motioned with his hand for Trini to as well. Satisfied, Cass lowered his wings. "Good. Now, Metatron, what do you want?"

"I just came to speak with Ezekiel, to see if Forfax said or did anything that could help us find her again." He tried to keep a proper, respectful tone, but I could tell he was still heated just below the surface.

"Well, how much did you eavesdrop from the hallway?" I asked, also failing to convincingly portray respect.

He slowly exhaled through his nose before speaking, the obesity of his host making it whistle unevenly. "Just that she wants to kill us all, so please, from the top."

I told them all the story. I started with Eve's kidnapping, wondering if that was the moment Foxy took advantage and turned Liam, but regardless she was important to the story later. I filled in the missing pieces from my recovery time as best I could, certain that Foxy's deception was completed in that time, and then wrapped the whole thing together with the events from the mountaintop, all the way through to Eve helping me through the fracture. "And then I woke up here, that's everything I know."

"With a few added assumptions I noticed," Gavin chimed in. "What makes you think your host was tricked?"

"Yes, I agree. You should've just taken him over completely like I told you to from the start," Megatron added.

"What does it matter?!" Trini yelled, stunning the rest of us in silence. "Why are we wasting time on the stupid host?! Where did she go?! How can we find her?! What are we going to do about that sword?! She needs to pay for what she's done!"

"She will, Trinity, don't fret, but we need to be smart about this. We can't defeat her as long as she has that sword, we need to get it away from her before anything," Megatron said, trying to calm her down.

"And then drive it right through whatever empty cavity used to hold a heart and burn her out of existence!" she yelled with a cackle, clearly not calmed down.

"We're not doing anything until we get her away from Liam," I stated, making sure they knew that part was not negotiable.

"There are bigger things at risk here than one puny human," Gavin scoffed.

Megatron caught Cass's look as things were beginning to escalate again and tried to cut it short with a more tactful tone. "He's right Ezekiel, this is bigger than one soul."

"You're going up against an Enochian, she's stronger than the three of you, so unless you think Cass here's willing to break his little one-man boycott, or you can find Zak in time, you're going to need me there when you try to take her down." They looked to Cass, but it was useless, we all knew he had no stake in this, nor did he want one. Once their eyes turned back to me, I continued. "Exactly, so we do this my way, Liam's a strong kid, and he's had plenty of experience banishing angels, he's practically a pro. All we need to do is reach him and separate them."

There was an awkwardly long silence as they tried to think of another option, but without me, they knew they'd be outmatched. "Well," Megatron started, breaking the tension, "in theory, if Liam's the one actually wielding the sword when they separate, it should stay in his hand, but that's still a stretch; it's going to be dangerous."

"What if you're wrong about him?" Gavin asked, bringing his terrible argument back up. "What if we can't get him to banish her because he doesn't want to?"

"He'll want to, I can reach him, I know it." By the looks they gave me, they weren't convinced. "But, if that's not enough, I can reach out to Eve, she helped before, and she was able to pull out of Liam before by force."

"Please," Trini scorned, "Forfax is one of hers, she's not going to turn her back on one of her own."

"That's right," Cass said breaking his long silence from the sidelines, "Last time that happened everyone on the wrong end Fell, whether we regretted it or not."

There was another silence as Cass rained a pity party over the whole parade, but in that quiet moment, something clicked for me. "I think I have an idea," I said it quietly, mostly to myself, but in such a small room they were all able to hear me.

"What? What is it?" Megatron asked, his interest piqued.

I tried to stand up again, and got a little further than last time, but only so far before Cass tried to stop me again. "Calm down, Ezekiel, you're still not strong enough to…"

"Then help me up, I need to see the sky." The three Muses exchanged glances, then together as one came over and helped me to my feet. "Ow, no, it's all right, I'm ok," I grunted as Megatron and Gavin supported most of my weight on their shoulders. "Cass you're a genius."

"What's this idea?" Trini shouted as she rushed ahead of us to open the front door.

"That depends…" I said, simply to stall long enough for me to make sure I could find what I needed.

We emerged through the front doors and looked up to a clear view of the glistening fracture lines racing across the sky.

"Wait, why am I a genius?" Cass asked while he followed us to the yard, curiosity getting the better of him.

I ignored him as I scanned the fractures looking for the perfect spot. "C'mon, c'mon, I know there's got to be… There!" I freed one of my arms from Gavin and pointed to a small, lonely speck, not much bigger than a star.

"That?" Trini asked with equal parts confusion and disappointment. "What good is that going to do us? We can't even fit through a fracture that small."

"We don't need to go up through it, we just need to come down through it." I explained, hoping they would catch on from there.

"Oh, well, ok," Gavin said, only partially catching on, "But that's like, what, an escape plan? How's that going to help us stop Forfax?"

"Oh, poor simple Gavin, my plan is so much more than that. Here, let's get back inside and I'll explain everything." I put my arm back around him much to his displeasure after my little attack on his intelligence, but as soon as we pulled a one-eighty, Cass stepped over to block the entranceway. "Um, Cass? Excuse us."

"Nope, I said you could only stay until you could walk."

I looked down, over to Gavin, over to Megatron, and then back at him wondering if he had gone blind. "Cass, buddy, this isn't walking."

"Close enough, now off with the lot of you, I'm done helping." He crossed his arms, further reinforcing his position.

"Fine, I've got a place we can go, it's not far from here," Megatron said with a sneer.

The two lifted me off the ground under their combined wing-power, but Trini stayed behind to have the last word. "I should *really* hope for your sake that you never need our help with anything, because we're going to remember this."

I could hear her wings flap off the ground behind us as we flew farther away from Cass, followed closely by his shouted response, "I've survived this long on my own, I'm good!"

Cass's dismissal of us wasn't anywhere close to a surprise, so I didn't have to dwell on it for long; instead, I used that flight time to formulate the finer details of my plan in my head so that when it came time to fill in the Muses, it would be perfect. It was going to work, it had to work...

CHAPTER TWELVE: NEXT STOP, KAZAKHSTAN

*BEEP! BEEP! BEE…*My hand slammed the off button atop my analog alarm clock, the tiles reading *4:45* still shaking from dropping into place. I wanted nothing more than to simply flip my pillow over to the cool side and ignore my problems and responsibilities, but sadly I knew better.

I heaved myself up to a sitting position and rubbed my tired eyes before groaning my way to a standing position. I stumbled my way through the darkness, but with full night vision, it wasn't difficult to navigate the familiar path to the bathroom. I closed my eyes once my hand felt the light switch to protect my sensitive eyes from the harsh fluorescent bulbs until I could gradually transition through varying degrees of squinting. Within a few seconds my pupils shrunk to the appropriate size and I could finally see myself in the mirror without issue. I was beginning to wear my age very poorly; at only twenty-nine, the circles under my eyes were way too dark, and the stress and worry lines etching their way across my face were beginning to outnumber the laugh lines. "What happened to you, Natara?" I thought back to the young, beautiful blonde woman that used to live in that mirror, long silky strands of hair full of color, eyes as blue and vibrant as serene oceans far away, and skin smooth and white as porcelain, but that woman was gone, only living on through hours of hard work and make up.

I had been performing the same morning routine for so long by now I had it down to an exact science. First, I would turn on the hot water in the shower, and as the cold water was forced from the pipes, I began washing away any oils or leftover makeup from the previous day with a swab of alcohol. Once I spotted steam rising over the shower curtain, I loosened my hair out of its messy night bun and stepped inside. Two pumps of shampoo, three pumps of conditioner, and one sudsy washcloth later, I shut off the water before the last few drops of hot water could run dry. With the easy part over, and my hair wrapped up in a towel to dry, I got to work applying my face for the day. Starting from the foundation, I used a generous amount of concealer, then the eye liner, mascara, bronzer, a touch of blush, and finished with a full body coat of lotion. Satisfied with my makeup, I removed the damp towel from atop my head, releasing a cascade of moist hair down past my shoulders and let my blow dryer do the rest.

With very little time remaining before hitting the road to work, I ripped open the rickety fridge door to grab a bagel for the road. "Ugh, again?!" I exclaimed once I saw the nearly empty bag. It felt like I had just gone shopping, and my day was already overbooked, there was no way I could fit a grocery run in today. I grabbed the whole bag and shoved it in my purse, deciding to delay that particular problem for another time.

Traffic on the way to work was slightly worse than usual, turning my five minutes early into stress-fueled road rage because I could not afford to be late again. Luckily, I made it to my desk just as the bell was ringing. "Good morning, class," I called out, trying to shake away the stress and not let it show in my voice.

"Good morning, Miss Karim!" the room full of eight-year old children chimed back to me in an almost melodic unison. The rest of that morning went swimmingly, watching, listening to, and interacting with those happy-go-lucky children where the biggest problems were having to share and learning their multiplication tables, it all just helped me focus on the good in humanity as opposed to all of the bad in the world. They were so young, so innocent, and while I was in that room with them, I felt like I was as well.

"All right, children, it's recess time!" I called out as the clock's second hand neared the twelve. They all cheered as if I had just announced the best news in the world, and it only made me smile wider. The bell sounded, and like a minor stampede they all bolted for the door past me.

One of the smaller blonde girls turned short of the exit and bounded back to me with springs in her steps. "Miss Karim! Miss Karim!"

I knelt as she approached me. "Yes, Claudia?"

"I drew this for you!" She pulled a thick white page from

behind her back and handed it out to me. I grabbed it and looked at the adorably crude stick figures and immediately could tell it was me surrounded by the whole class. The words *We luv you Miss Karim* were sprawled out along the top of the page among some clouds and the sun.

"Aw, thank you so much, dear. I love it!" She shyly giggled and then ran for the door after her classmates. I looked at the drawing a little longer before placing it on my desk, and then locked up the room to head for the faculty lounge.

"Natara," Nurse Vera called to me when she saw me enter. "How's your morning?"

"Good," I said on reflex while I headed to the vending machine to buy a packaged sandwich for lunch. That last bagel had managed to tide me over so far, but my stomach was beginning to demand a refill. "You?"

"Not bad, uneventful, so that's good. Few sniffles and tummy aches, nothing major." She paused while I paid the machine and retrieved my meal. "Care to join me?" she asked hopefully.

"Um, sure, ok." I already knew what she had in store for me, and I would have rather avoided it, but I didn't want to be rude either. I took the seat opposite her and unsealed my sandwich.

"So, have your symptoms been progressing at all?" she asked trying to act casual.

"They come and go; today's been a good day so far." I know she's a nurse, but I didn't like to talk about my condition openly. "How's your husband? Is he back at work yet?"

"Yeah, his insurance wouldn't cover his medical leave any longer, he really shouldn't be back at the mill for another month at least, but, what other choice do we have." She was trying to play it off, but I could tell it was something that had been weighing heavy on her. "Luckily, the church has been very generous to us since his accident; they've been praying for our family a lot."

I had been trying to deflect and avoid the subject of religion, but I should've known that she couldn't help herself.

When it came to Vera, everything ended up leading to religion. "That's good, I'm glad that's helping," I said, unsure how else to respond to that.

"You know, this Sunday they're holding baptisms for new members, if you wanted to, you could come with us and just check it out." They say the definition of insanity is doing the same thing over and over and expecting a different result, and yet she continued to try and convert me away from Nihilism.

"Oh, no thank you, Sundays are when I like to get caught up on housework and errands and such. Maybe next time," I lied, just trying to postpone another week or two.

"Natara, honey," she leaned forward and placed her hand on mine. "You know you don't have very many 'next times' left. Please, before it's too late."

I grabbed the top of her hand with my free one, rubbed it a bit, showing my appreciation in her caring, but then removed it because as much as she was trying to help in her own way, it wasn't the kind of help I needed nor wanted. "Thank you, Vera, it really means a lot that you care about my well being so much, but I just don't believe the same as you do, please respect that."

She began tearing up, exactly why I had always beat around the bush with her before as opposed to addressing it straight on, but now we were past the point of no return. "But what if you're wrong?" she pleaded. "I don't want to see your eternal soul go to Hell when there was something I could've done to save you." We were starting to get strange looks from the other teachers around us, but Vera didn't seem to care.

I shifted my position and cleared my throat before replying in a whisper, hoping to avoid further attention from eavesdroppers. "If I'm wrong, then I'm wrong, and I'll face that, but I'm not going to let fear change me, or what I believe. And this isn't on you, this is my decision, don't punish yourself for that." This time when I put my hand on hers, it was to consul her.

She appreciated the gesture, and after a moment removed her hand from the table and wiped a few tears from her cheeks.

J. A. Reed

"Ok, but I'm still going to pray for you, that's what I believe in."

I laughed quietly with a smile. "All right, that's fine. I guess we'll call it insurance."

After the bell rang, we parted ways, and I returned to my class. The rest of the school day was uneventful, completely normal, but after work I had my weekly oncology appointment which, sadly, was beginning to feel just as normal as anything else in my hectic schedule. The mammogram was still painful and uncomfortable, but I was to the point where I had all the steps memorized and instead of the nurse walking me through it, we would just chit-chat about our weeks.

At the end of the visit, the doctor asked me to sit down and delivered the latest in the long string of bad test results. I blocked out most of the big words I didn't understand like "metastasized" or "carcinoma" and instead only focused on the treatment information. A 22 percent survival rate didn't sound promising, and the list of side-effects nearly doubled that number, but the doctor convinced me it was at least worth trying, and that if things got too bad I could stop at any time. In hindsight, I wished I had told him to take his treatment and shove it where the Sun don't shine.

* * *

BEEP! BEEP! BEEP! BEE…My hand slammed the off button atop my analog alarm clock, the tiles reading *4:00* still shaking from flipping into place. I wanted nothing more than to simply flip my pillow over to the cool side and ignore my problems, but merely thinking about the amount of effort that would take nauseated me. Speaking of which, I leaned over the edge of the bed and coughed up a thick white mixture of stomach acid and God-knows-what into the small plastic lined bucket strategically placed there.

I tried to heave myself up to a sitting position, but as weak as I was the best I could do was slide my lower half off the bed next to the bucket and sit against the side of my mattress while

I caught my breath. I rubbed my bloodshot eyes before pulling and climbing my way to a standing position using my bedside dresser as a ladder. I limped my way through the darkness while clutching the sloshing bucket in one hand and bracing my other shoulder along the wall, hoping to make it to the bathroom without collapsing. I closed my eyes once my hand felt the light switch to protect my sensitive eyes from the harsh fluorescent bulbs until I could gradually transition through varying degrees of squinting, but the light was unrelenting, forcing me to keep my eyes practically closed the whole time. Within a few minutes, my pupils shrunk enough that I could finally see myself in the mirror with only some issue. I didn't recognize the stranger looking back at me. The yellow skin sagging off my bones was covered in dark spots and everywhere I used to have a wrinkle had been replaced with deep gutted trenches large enough to hold marbles. "What did you do to yourself, Natara?" I thought back to the aged, ordinary blonde woman that used to live in that mirror, long, full hair that spent more time on her head than in the sink, blue eyes full of life and wonder, not pain and tears, and naturally colored skin which still retained its elasticity, but that woman was gone, and no amount of hard work or make up could bring her back.

I was four months into my treatment and all I had to show for it was the exterior deterioration because the cancer in my left breast seemed perfectly capable of resisting any similar effects and was in fact spreading faster than ever. The doctor continued to strongly advise against me halting my treatment, but I didn't know how much more of this I could take. I had been performing the same new morning routine for so long by now I had it down to an exact science. First, I would turn on the hot water in the shower, and as the cold water was forced from the pipes, I began washing away any bile from my tongue and teeth from the previous night with my toothbrush and floss. Once I spotted steam start to rise over the shower curtain, I loosened the knot of my chemo scarf and stepped inside. I sat on my hard-plastic stool, shaking under the stream of water and just allowed it to wash over me, occasionally lifting a sudsy washcloth to my skin, but each attempt to reach a new spot proved more strenuous than the last. Halfway through washing myself I shut off the water because the last few drops of hot water had run dry. With the hard part only halfway through, I next had to struggle to dry off before freezing to death. Once I was dry, I wrapped my head back up in a new chemo scarf and I got to work applying my face for the day. Starting from the foundation, I used a generous coat of specialized moisturizer for sensitive skin, followed by drawing on my eyebrows, struggling to attach fake eyelashes without any real ones as a guide, light peach lipstick, and finished off with just a touch of blush. Unsatisfied with my appearance, but knowing it was the best I could do, I left the bathroom, trying not to cry and wash away the eyelashes.

With very little time remaining before hitting the road to work, I walked right past the fridge, knowing it was empty, but with no appetite, I didn't care about that.

Traffic on the way to work was practically a standstill, but the principal didn't even want me coming into work at all, so no one would be mad if I were late. I made it to my handicap parking spot just as the bell was ringing, and the longest part after that was just getting out of my car; the walk to my classroom wasn't even a hundred feet. "Good morning, class," I called out as I entered, trying not to let my voice shake.

"Good morning, Miss Karim!" the room full of eight-year old children chimed back to me in an almost melodic unison.

"Good morning, are you all right?" Mrs. Omarov asked with concern. She was an elderly woman who had retired from teaching two years ago but stayed on subbing when needed and had been the one covering my class when I needed to take off sick. "Yes, thank you, I'm all right." I hoped that would remain true throughout the day.

The rest of that morning went well enough once I was able to take my seat. Watching and listening to the children was easy enough, but interacting with their energetic and youthful spirits was the biggest problem. They were slowly learning that they needed to be easy on me, and with Mrs. Omarov's old age, it was a lesson they could continue to work on even in my absence, but they were so young, so naive, it took multiple reminders before they started catching on. After recess, they were even more riled up, and the way that I used to look upon them with wonder and joy was gone; my illness had turned me callous, and I no longer wanted to drag myself into work for them, but instead just waste away my final days in peace at home. At the end of the school day I dropped off a letter explaining my wishes to return to sick leave with the principal and blew off my next chemotherapy appointment to head home and fall asleep, hoping that I'd never wake up. If this was what a normal day looked like from now on, I wanted it to be my last.

* * *

With my strength regained and most of the details of our trap for Foxy fleshed out, I only had two errands left run, the first of which was to acquire a new host. I had checked in on my former potentials, most of whom were dead, but one, a young woman in Kazakhstan near the Russian fracture, was still alive, but there were risks with attempting to join with her. There hadn't been time to vet any other potentials, so I preceded with the Hail Mary and flew through the fracture into the cold wilderness of Central Asia.

I flew as fast as I could straight for Natara Karim's house before my angelic form had much time to start deteriorating. When I arrived, she was swaying slightly in a wooden rocking chair, gazing out across her back porch.

Her head was wrapped up in a thin layer of cloth with blue, orange, and purple wisps across a black base, and it was tied in a thick knot down and behind her left ear. Draped across her shoulders rested a thick yarn knitted blanket with holes big enough to see through to her white blouse underneath. A thick gray wool blanket scrunched up in her lap had one of its four corners dragging back and forth along the wooden floor just far enough away from the curved legs to avoid getting rolled

J. A. Reed

over.

"Um, excuse me, Natara Karim." I said, unsure exactly how I should make my presence known.

She stopped rocking with a sharp creek and glanced over her right shoulder at me. I shuffled uncomfortably, wondering how she'd react to me in my natural state invading her home, but a quick laugh wasn't among my guesses. "I guess Vera was right after all. Who would've guessed?"

After a short period being frozen in confusion, I walked over to her side and she didn't move except for resuming her slow gentle rock. "Oh, no, it's not what you think. I'm here...I need your help."

"I'm tired, I'm afraid I'm not in much condition to be helping anybody..." She glanced up at me again. "...or any... whatever you are." She turned away again, as if my presence was no different from that of a cat, or a sock on the floor. "I'm...complicated. I'll tell you as much as I can, but time isn't on my side."

"Then go ahead, state your case, I've got all day, or I don't, you'd know better than I."

I looked down at her and examined her closely, she was indeed very short on time, but easily had another week left in her, sadly not much longer than that. "I'm a fallen angel, but I'm not evil like most people believe. There is a Heaven, and there is a Hell, but it's not black and white, there are good, decent people on both sides."

"And I'm going to Hell?" she asked, zero wavering in her tone.

"Given that only about one in a couple billion go to Heaven, yeah, I think it's safe to say, but it's not all bad, I've lived there for a few millennia, and I turned out all right."

She looked up again. "Your face is melting."

"Oh, yeah, that's in part why I need your help. You see, unless a human voluntarily allows me to bond with their body, my natural form cannot exist on Earth, or else, um..." I pointed to my disappearing mug, "face melting."

Natara lowered her gaze yet again and rocked in silence for

nearly a minute. "You said in part, why else are you here?"

"I…I had another host before, a young teenage boy, American. He…He was taken from me; I need to save him."

"Was he taken against his will?"

"Well, not technically, but he was tricked, fed lies to turn against me, and now he's trapped, but if I can get to him, I can save him." I wanted to be completely honest, but I needed to make sure it didn't sound like I was the bad guy.

"How can I trust you're telling me the truth? How do I know you can be trusted?" Despite the words, her voice was still and calm as it had been the whole encounter.

"I'm sorry, I have nothing but my word, and that's all I have left. I could offer to heal you, cure your cancer, but I don't want that to come off as a bribe or anything like that; it would just be the very least I could do in exchange for your invaluable help. All I ask is for twenty-four hours; after that I'll either have my friend back, or I won't, and if it's the latter, then there will be no reason for me to stay on this plane of existence."

Slowly, Natara removed her hands from beneath her wool blanket and braced them against the chair's arms. Shakily, she lifted herself up and slowly pivoted around her right leg to face me. She lifted her boney arm to my face, but phased right through me. "fallen angel, huh? Are there others?"

"Y-yes, some Fell, like me, but not all of them." I shifted uncomfortably as she continued to examine me while close enough to kiss me.

"I was wrong, I never believed in you, or even life after death, why?"

"Um, I…I don't understand." What was she trying to ask, or was she just so close to death she was starting to spout nonsense?

"Why doesn't the world know of your kind? Why so many religions and zero proof for any of them? Why make a world full of life and not even let them know you exist for sure?"

"That's a bit above my pay grade, but that's complicated, and I'm sorry, but this isn't the time. I can tell you more on the way to where we're going, share some memories with you, but even I don't have all the answers."

She peered into my eyes the whole time I spoke, only blinking after I was finished. "You have honest eyes."

"Um, thank you. Does that mean you'll help me?" She was still uncomfortably close, but if she was about to let me in, she could be as close as she wanted to be for all I cared.

"Twenty-four hours of my help, of using my body, and you'll cure my cancer? That's the deal?"

"Yes, that's all I need, and I'll give you anything within my power, anything else you want," I said, a little too much desperation escaping with my words.

"I don't want anything except my life to return to normal, before this horrible disease and so-called treatments. Can you make me forget the last four months? Erase all of the pain that has broken me?" I hesitated as I tried to think if that was something I could actually do or not. She noticed. "Don't worry, if you can't do it, I'll still help you, it's what the old me would've done."

"I…I'm not sure, but as I said, anything within my power. If I can't take the memories, I can still take away the pain, you'll be able to find the old you again, live a nice, calm simple life, just as before. I promise."

"I would like that, and I believe you, I'll help you save your friend."

With her permission given, I merged with her body, and it wasn't nearly as jarring as it had been with Liam the first time, but I could feel Natara's numbness, the broken feeling she had described and it nearly broke me as well.

"Are you all right…? I never got your name."

Zeke, and yes, just a little shaken up. What about you, are you all right?

"No, but you already knew that, didn't you?" she said softly. "Now, clock is ticking, let's do this. Where to?"

Ever been to America before? Oh, and I guess I'm supposed to tell you to brace yourself for this.

With step one taken care of far easier than I ever could've imagined, I made the flight around the globe in about six minutes, and despite telling Natara to brace herself, she didn't do it properly and ended up throwing up over the majority of the Atlantic. When we landed she had to drop to one knee. "Please…don't do that again."

Sorry, I tried to warn you, you'll get used to it soon though. Well, soon-ish. Anyway, I've got to visit a…well, I guess you can call her a friend.

She took a few deep breaths and spit on the cement floor a few times before standing up and gaining her balance. "Where are we?"

Seattle, Washington. We need to go inside this building. I had taken us straight to Angelica's apartment building, the second errand I needed to run involved speaking with Eve. I didn't know how much she would be able to help us out, so the plan didn't rely on her very much, but her help would make taking Foxy down almost too easy, so I had to try.

"Um, ok, why are you telling me?" She asked, looking around the foreign city landscape.

Well, you still have control over your body, all I'm doing is the flying.

"Why? I'm giving you twenty-four hours, have at it, unless you can't, but that would seem unlikely."

Oh, um…yeah, I can, I guess. You're cool with that?

"Yes, that's what I said from the beginning, and now that we're sharing a body, I can see parts of your mind, I know you were telling me the truth, so go ahead, take over. And why are people staring at us?" Liam had started getting so good at avoiding the one-sided crazy person conversation, I had almost forgot what it was like to get those looks.

Ok, here it goes, um…hold on. I had never taken full control before, but I concentrated and tried until her arms began listening to my commands. "Hel…hello? Testing, testing, one, two, three. Ok, I think I got it." It was strange hearing myself as a woman with a Kazakh accent, but I guess it would be better than sounding like a man given my current outward appearance.

Good, now go on, I'll just watch I guess, Natara said, now the one only I could hear inside our head. I walked up the stairs and found Angelica's door. *So, who is it we need to see here?* She asked as I knocked softly using her own thin hand.

I looked around, nervous to answer out loud in the empty hallway. "She's a friend of a friend," I whispered as quietly as possible, and it was a good thing I had because right then the door swung open and Angelica looked at Natara's sickly body with both worry and confusion. I totally forgot to start healing her, so that one was my bad.

"Um, hello, I'm sorry, can I help you?" she said unsurely.

"Um," I stuttered in Natara's own voice, then realized I had also forgotten to think of a good excuse to hang around long enough to catch Eve's attention. "I'm looking for on old friend of mine, she...she used to live here," I lied, and normally it would've been a terrible lie, but Natara's physical appearance helped sell my poor performance. "Her name's Evangeline, is there any chance you can help me find her?"

"Oh, I'm so sorry, I never met the previous tenant. I'll occasionally get some mail with the name Charles Lindbergh, if that name means anything to you...?" She trailed off, not sure how else she could help.

"Oh, yes, that was her husband's name." All I needed to do was stall, so this was as good of an excuse as anything. "Do you still have any of it with you, I can give it to them when I find her."

"Um, yeah, I think I've got them in a pile around here somewhere." She almost turned to retrieve it, but stopped and turned back to me. "Um, how do you know them exactly?"

It sounded like she was trying to vet me, make sure I wasn't up to anything nefarious, but what harm could I do with a few random bills and direct mail advertisements?

Answer her, I'm curious to know some of the story anyway, Natara chimed in.

I indulged since all it meant to me was more time to attract Eve's attention. "Oh, well Eve's practically family, we were raised together, it was kinda like a large group home. Sadly, after I left, we weren't able to stay in touch, but she recently reached out, said she's still here in Seattle, I thought that meant she was still here, but..." I looked around what little bits of apartment I could see around the door and Angelica, "I guess not."

She looked at me, the thin frail host obviously close to the end of her life, and whatever doubts or mistrusts she had before vanished. "Right, let me just find those letters, and I hope you find her," Angelica turned inside and disappeared out of sight in search of the letters.

Ok, now what parts of that were true, and what parts did you alter? I have some guesses, but...

"Shh," I was starting to understand Liam's pain every time I bugged him in public. "Not now," I leaned inside and got a better look without the obstructions from before. "Eve? Eve?" I hissed in a whisper, hoping she was watching. "Meet me on the roof, we need to talk." I was hoping for a sign she was there listening, but I got nothing. "It's important."

"Sorry, did you say something?" Angelica popped back around the corner with a stack of about a dozen envelopes in varying sizes.

"Oh, no, just admiring your home, it looks so different than the last time I was here," of course the last time I was there was with Liam barely a week ago, but I couldn't very well say that.

"Thank you, would you like to come inside? I could make some tea, or lemonade or something."

If Eve had heard me, I didn't want to make her wait on the roof for too long, but if she hadn't, I needed to stay a bit longer, I wasn't sure which way to go, so I left it open ended a little longer. "Oh, that's so sweet of you, but I wouldn't want to intrude."

"Oh no, it's no problem at all, please." She opened the door all the way and gestured for us to enter, and I guess that made the decision for me. "That's a beautiful accent you have by the way, where is it from? Russia?"

I entered and looked around trying to find Eve. "Oh, Kazakhstan actually," I said, only half paying attention while still scanning the area.

"Oh, sorry to say I don't know much about that area. Is it nice?" Angelica lead me to the dining table and then headed into the kitchen to prepare refreshments. "Oh, and I only have chamomile tea, will that be all right?"

I sat down and only now started to realize just how damaged Natara's body really was. I started working on healing her, hoping it wouldn't be visually apparent until after leaving Angelica's place. "Yes, that's fine."

Ok, I know you can't really talk, but what are we doing in here? I thought we were supposed to meet this Eve person on the roof.

I looked around the table and found a pen. I picked it up, flipped over one of the junk mail envelopes, and wrote [Need to make sure she's here first]

All right, fine, but keep the conversation interesting at least.

Angelica returned from the kitchen where a kettle sat heating up on the stove. "Tea will be ready in a minute. So, um, how do you think you'll find your friend now if she's not here?"

"Oh, well she was the one who reached out first, I think as long as she knows I'm looking, she'll find me again." I slowly covered up the ink I had just written before Angelica could see it and ask more questions.

"Hopefully, yeah. What is it you...I mean, if you don't mind, why are you looking for her now?" I could tell she was dancing around the obvious, so I threw her a bone.

"Oh, well as I'm sure you noticed I'm not exactly in good health, it's ok, you don't have to beat around the bush." I laughed and she joined in, glad it wasn't uncomfortable any longer. "But yeah, I'm looking for her help in...making arrangements. See, there's..." I tried to think of a good analogy for Liam in this situation. "my younger brother, our father left us when we were young, and his mom passed just a few months ago, so I'm pretty much all he has. He's...he's in a bit of trouble right now, trusted the wrong girl, fell in with the wrong crowd I hate to say, and Eve, she's got experience in situations like his."

"Oh, I'm so sorry to hear that. And I'm sorry I couldn't be more help," The kettle began to whistle and Angelica looked torn between comforting me, a complete stranger, or starting the tea. "Um, excuse me, I'll just get that real quick."

I'm sure we'll find her, Zeke, try not to worry, Natara said, just as sorrowful as Angelica, and as if following the trend, Ash scampered over with her big puppy dog eyes and put her chin on my leg. I pet her, but it just didn't feel the same petting her with someone else's hand. I had to save Liam, I just had to.

"Ezekiel?" I looked up with a jolt and saw Eve hiding in the far corner of the room. "What are you doing here? And who is…"

"Long story," I said as loud as I could without Angelica hearing from the kitchen. "Meet me on the roof."

"I thought I told you to leave my human alone!" Eve was able to be as loud as she wished in her angelic form and not worry about startling Angelica, but Natara wasn't as safe.

Whoa! Who is that? Why is she so mad at you?

I almost continued the argument, but Angelica returned from the kitchen with two cups suspending strings off the sides. "Would you like any honey, lemon, milk, or anything?"

"Oh, no thank you. Actually, I should really get going, I'm so sorry." I stood up and tried to back away from Angelica and closer to the front door.

"Oh, um, are you sure, I'm sorry, was it something I said?" Eve flew closer and hovered right behind Angelica with a menacing glare as a constant reminder that no matter what, I needed to leave. Now.

"No, no, no, you were great. It's just, I just got a text from my friend, she wants to meet, right now, so that's all. You were such a great host though, I'm sorry I couldn't stay." I was still backing away toward the front door, and I don't think it helped convince Angelica of my sincerity, because I was fairly certain I was coming off deathly afraid.

"Um, ok, well, good luck with everything. Have a nice time catching up with your friend." Angelica still looked worried and confused, but she went ahead and opened the door for us to leave.

"Oh, I'm sure we will, we have a lot to catch up on, after all," I said once back in the hallway, taking a moment to turn back and glance up at Eve for emphasis. "And we're going to our favorite rooftop restaurant, I just hope I can make it there in time."

"Oh, well if you need a ride I could—" The door slammed shut of its own accord and I could hear Angelica cut her offer short with a startled yelp. Eve blasted through the door and carried Natara and myself up through the heart of the building and halted a dozen feet above the roof.

"Hey, you brought my host with me this time, thanks for that," I joked to try and lighten the situation.

What was that! What the hell is going on! Natara shouted in my head hysterically.

"Why are you back?! You should've stayed away!" She repeated her previous intimidation tactics of the burning eyes and enclosing wings, but having seen it all before I wasn't afraid. Natara on the other hand, let's just say it was a good thing she didn't have control of her body, especially the bowels.

"I had to come back for Liam! And you're scaring the crap out of my host – can we please just talk like civilized angels?! For once!"

Eve maintained her hold of us for a second before her heaving breaths began to slow. She lowered us to the hard surface before releasing us, shrunk to a more appropriate height, and tucked her wings away. "I'm sorry about Liam, but you're only putting yourself and others in danger by being here. You barely escaped alive last time. If I hadn't been there…" She hesitated, not wanting to think about what we both knew would've happened.

"That's why I'm here, I have a plan to stop Foxy, but I need your help."

"Stop it right there." I was expecting to debate with her a little before winning her over, but instead she straight up shot me down. "I can't help you anymore. I have orders straight from the inner circle – I'm forbidden from interfering with Forfax until they come to a decision on how to deal with her."

"What?! She killed Xaf! If they know, what's there to think about?!" I knew there was a lot of bureaucratic red tape going on upstairs, but if anything required immediate action, it should've been this.

"Look, Ezekiel, I'm sure you want to see Forfax pay for what she did, I certainly do, but if they say they need time, then we have to give them time. Justice will be served, I promise you that."

"But what about Liam?! He doesn't have time, he'll be dead before whatever closed-door meeting going on upstairs is even close to finished!"

"And if you don't like their decision, what? War again?" she asked, dredging up ancient history.

"That…that was different. It was a split decision at the table, I just agreed with the side I thought was right," and I didn't say it out loud to her, but it was the side I still think should've been right.

"Look, all I'm saying is this is the time for patience, not rash calls to action. So, whatever you think you need my help for, please, don't try and accomplish whatever foolish thing it is without me." She walked over and put her hand on my shoulder. "Just go back and wait this thing out, please, I don't want anyone else to die."

"Neither do I." I lifted my hand and removed hers from me. "And that's why I need to save Liam. Now if you won't help me, please, at least tell me where I can find him."

"She's still got him, he's safe with her as long as you stay away," she tried to argue, but I didn't believe that for a second.

"Where are they, Eve?" I repeated, determined as ever.

"It doesn't matter where she is, she's after you. The longer you stay, the sooner she'll find you, and I am forbidden to save you if you provoke her, so please, for the last time…" With all of the information I needed, I took Natara and flew away. Eve wouldn't help us, and that would make our attack much more difficult, but not impossible, and now I knew that all I had to do was wait, and Foxy would come to us, right into our trap. During the flight I finished healing Natara, and before the night was out, I'd get Liam back…or die trying.

CHAPTER THIRTEEN: IT'S A TRAP!

I flew high above the Earth looking down, trying to find the exact spot that Megatron had chosen for us to meet, a spot as close as possible to the speck I had pointed out earlier from below. Using rough eyeball estimations, it didn't take me that long to narrow down my search area and eventually pinpoint the meeting spot, a small abandoned quarry outside of Baxterville, Mississippi. Covering maybe two hundred feet in diameter and three hundred deep, this particular quarry was little more than a big whole in the ground. Greenery had overtaken the single road winding down a major portion of the wall, and years, maybe decades, of rain water had collected into an odd shaped stagnated pool that covered 40 percent of the quarry's floor.

"Guys? I'm here!" I called out to the apparent emptiness. There was eerie silence for a little too long and I had begun to worry, but then the green lake began to ripple. Two strangers emerged from the water and rose until their feet were lightly touching the surface. "Who the hell are they, the B team?" I asked sarcastically.

"Mr. Kratz is too valuable a host to risk damaging," Megatron said from a younger, thinner host's mouth.

"And since it looks like you failed to enlist the Guardian," Trini added with her usual sharp quip from the lips of a short haired woman with angular cheekbones and dark-tinted sunglasses, "the level of danger is even higher."

"We don't need her," Gavin added as he emerged from the grassy slope next to Tabby, both in brand new hosts as well. "As much as I hate to say it, Ezekiel's plan is a good one."

"Speaking of, did you check out the fracture? Will it work as well as I hoped?" I asked fearfully.

"It's deep, more than 2000-feet deep, but there's a cavity around it, it'll work perfectly," Gavin answered.

"A few cracks reach close to the surface, but if we're going to retreat, we'll still need to dive down." Tabby added, his lack of faith in our chances showing up through his choice of words, but Megatron was quick to nip that in the bud.

"We're not going to retreat because this is going to work. Sword or not, there's five of us, and one of her." He looked around at his fellow muses and they all lowered their heads like wolves submitting to their alpha. "Good, now let's go over it one more time. Ezekiel?"

"It was my plan, why do I need to go over it again?" He gave me the same stern look, which didn't work on me, but just to speed things along, I caved. "Fine, while I'm doing all the hard work, you four will be hiding in the surroundings. I'll convince Foxy to face me *mano a mano*, and after she releases Liam, you four pounce on her, get the sword away, and Bob's your uncle! We're home free!"

"And if she refuses your challenge? Does this mean you're finally ok with losing the human?" Trini asked, only slightly less pissed off than usual.

"No, if she won't let him go then I'll reach out to him and he'll banish her before she can kill me. You guys are not to make a move until they're separated, understand?" I put my foot down, but wasn't sure if the message sunk in even after so many times repeating myself.

"Fine, we'll wait until the right moment," Megaton said, and as their shot caller, it was all I needed.

"Good, now, time for your portion, send the word." Megatron, with his wide array of eyes and ears, was in charge of leaking my location out in hopes it would reach Foxy, and if Eve was right about her and she was indeed hunting for me, once the word was out, she shouldn't be too far behind. Megatron sent the others to their hidden positions and then pulled out his phone. He flipped it open, placed a speed dial call, and held it to his head.

"Yeah, it's me. Give the word." He snapped it shut immediately after that and crushed it between his fingers, the small bits of plastic, metal, and silicon raining down into the putrid water. "Now for your *hard part*, and do try to act busy, don't want to telegraph to the world that this is a trap." With that, he began sinking back into the water where he had come from.

"What am I supposed to do? You picked this stupid hole, there's nothing to do here!" He smirked as his head passed below the emerald glass and disappeared from sight. "I hate you so much, stupid little brat."

I managed to kill about a minute-and-a-half looking around the quarry for anything of use, but there was nothing except for grass, dirt, and water. I spent a few more minutes just kicking around larger rocks until I noticed a rather large stick perfect for poking stuff. The poking stick managed to help another few minutes roll by, but eventually I ran out of things to poke. Frustrated, I threw the stick into the small lake and watched as it floated there, spinning circles slower and slower after each revolution.

"It wasn't very smart of you coming back here!" a familiar voice called from high above me. I spun around and there was Liam suspended by burning blue wings contrasting the warm colors of the sunset behind him.

"Foxy," I snarled, "It wasn't very smart of you to murder one of our own."

"We've already done this dance, Brother. You try to insult me, I talk instead of killing you quickly, you get saved by Evangeline, but oh, wait, that's right. Evangeline can't save you this time, no one can. This time, it's just the two of us, unless…" Controlling Liam's head, she scanned the surroundings. "…you brought your friends. More for me to kill, how thoughtful of you."

Crap, she wasn't supposed to be able to see them. I could still salvage it, though. "Let Liam go and you can have me!"

"What? Why would I do that? I can take you no matter what I do, why would I accept a deal from you when you have nothing I want?"

"You want to know if you can take a higher tier Angel. Last time I was caught off guard, wasting away without a host, don't you want to know if you can take me in my prime?"

What are you doing? Natara asked, sounding a little worried, *Please tell me you're just tricking her and not actually trying to face her one on one.*

"You have no idea what's going on here, do you?" she laughed. "A chance to face off against, what, three, maybe all four Muses *and* an Angel all at the same time sounds much more fun. And as for your precious host here, I already have orders from above not to harm him, so if the only thing you want is him safe, then you're in luck. He's never going to be safer than with me in here, and I certainly wouldn't risk his safety by giving him back to the likes of you."

"What? No!" My whole plan was crumbling apart around me, and all before we could even get halfway through the steps needed to get Foxy in position. I had to try my luck with plan B, I had to convince Liam to banish her on his own. "Liam! Listen to me, Liam! You have to fight her!"

"Yell all you want, Ezekiel, Liam's listening to every word, but he'll never break my hold over him. If you have any last words for him, I suggest you say them now, before I make him watch me kill you and that filthy host of yours."

"I thought you had orders not to harm the hosts?" I asked, slightly off topic, but important all the same.

"Not all hosts, just this one. Did you really think I would let the tarnish of your kind remain behind to spread through the bloodlines? Even if I don't kill her with you in there, I'll still find her. She'll get the same choice as all the others; either take your own life and face judgment at the pearly gates, or I take it for you with my flaming sword and burn away your eternal soul, leaving nothing behind." He pulled out the flaming sword and brandished it at us. "Zelda Wilson, Thane Varro, Kenton Shoffner, they've all chosen the former, but I'm looking forward to the day I get to see what this beautiful weapon does to a mortal."

Wait, did she say Thane Varro, I knew that name, wasn't that…"You! You caused the accident!"

"What acci…oh…oh this feeling, it's so strong." She began to waver a bit in the air and grabbed at Liam's chest. "Such misery but also so much rage. Humans and their emotions, such a weakness. Enough of this, time to—"

Without warning, Megatron exploded from the pool beneath Foxy and latched onto Liam's legs. "Now!" he cried out and the other three followed in suit, each desperately trying to grapple a separate limb.

"No! Liam!" I shouted, trying to halt the attack, but they didn't care, they were fueled by vengeance and didn't care about one simple human the way I did.

Foxy circled the air above the quarry as she tried to fling her attackers off, but Liam's overpowering emotions appeared to be doing a great job distracting much of her attention.

"Gavreel!" Trini shouted right before biting Liam's right forearm with all of her might, causing him to drop the flaming sword to the ground. "The sword!" she yelled through bloodstained teeth.

Gavin released Foxy's left arm and dove for the sword at a full free-fall with wing beats periodically building up even more speed, but high above, the remaining three Muses were having trouble containing Foxy without their brother's help.

"Fools! You can't stop me!" Foxy used her now free left arm to pull Trini off and held her at arm's length by the throat. "You're no match for me, sword or not!" Foxy brandished her wings and they burned even brighter than before. She swung them out and created a cocoon around Liam's body, burning Trini's host to ashes and leaving behind nothing but her angelic form.

Gavin reached the sword and heaved it up slowly as if it weighed a hundred pounds. "I got it! I'm coming!"

"Wait! Don't hurt Liam!" I called out after him, but Gavin was already rising back into the fray before I could get all of the words past my lips.

Up above, Foxy had flung Trini like a bola and she disappeared over the horizon. With both hands free and only two Muses left clinging onto her, she easily pulled Megatron and Tabby off and burned away their hosts in one swift move. She held onto the two of them and fell straight down, barreling toward Gavin while using his two siblings as shields against the threat of the flaming sword.

Gavin panicked, dodging and pointing the sword away from the meteor of angels screaming past him at Mach one. "Stop standing there and do something!" he yelled down to me, furious.

Foxy slammed into the ground of the quarry, throwing up a cloud of dirt and droplets of green water all around me. "Retreat! Take the sword and go!" I yelled at him as my plan crumbled around us. Gavin hesitated, looking down at the smoking hole where the fate of his faithful leader and hated enemy were unclear. "She can't hurt us without it! Just go!"

"Um, yeah, right." With that quick reminder, he turned and nose dived into a patch of Earth just outside the walls of the quarry.

I began fanning away the dust so I could find Foxy, Megatron, and Tabby. "Hello? Any survivors?"

Be careful, Natara reminded me, *even without the sword, she can still burn me away. I'd rather not be cremated today.*

"We have her sword; I just want to find my brothers and leave, don't worry, I won't let…" I saw Megatron and Tabby lying on the ground through the ash and dust, but there was no sign of Liam or Foxy. "…anything happen," I finished. "Guys, are you all right?" I rushed over to them while making sure to keep my eyes peeled for any surprise attack.

Megatron and Tabby were very weak from the crash and falling apart fast, but Megatron managed to lift himself up on one arm. "Ezekiel, you have to…stop…her…" He collapsed before saying anything else.

"Gavin's taking care of it, I have to get you two home." I picked them up, one on each shoulder, and sank through the ground toward the fracture underground. I passed by many small cracks that were branching off the central point of origin, but they were both still passed out and unable to cross over on their own, so I went straight to the source, a massive spherical cavern 110 feet in diameter filled three quarters of the way with murky water. "All right guys, time to wake up, you have to cross over now, Gavin should already…"

"Ezekiel!" Gavin's voice cried from behind me, within the

cavern. I turned slowly, worried about what I would see. Gavin's voice was a bad indication, because he sounded like he was in major distress, and the fact that he hadn't crossed over through any of the cracks between the surface and here was an even worse sign that something was terribly wrong.

My fears were well-founded, and the scene was well lit by both blue wings and red sword. "Gavin, no," I winced to myself. Foxy, via Liam's body, had the tiny Muse gripped tightly by the wings in one hand holding him out to face me, and the flaming sword back in the other hand's white knuckled fist. "Let him go, I'm the one you want."

"Wha...?" Megatron said, regaining consciousness. "Gavreel!" he shouted once he got his bearings.

"Wait your turn, Metatron," Foxy pointed the tip of the sword right against the small of his brother's back threateningly. "Unless you want to die that badly."

"Take Tabby and go," I said, hoping Megatron would listen to me for once in his life.

"I can't just..." he started, but I wouldn't have it.

"Fight another day, Tabby needs you, now take him and go!" Megatron looked at his unconscious brother as he withered away, and begrudgingly grabbed his hand and winked through the crack back to Hell. "All right, they're gone, it's just us now, let Gavin go, you don't have to do this."

Foxy laughed long and hard, scaring Natara and myself to the core. "How many times do I have to tell you? How long until it burns through that rotten skull of yours? I want you *all* dead, every single abomination wiped from the face of existence. The others ran, but they cannot hide forever, and this one, this one's out of time."

"Please, Eze–" Gavin reached out weakly for me, but before I could even blink, Foxy plunged the flaming sword through Gavin's back and up through the chest. Raging red flames consumed him outwards from the wound slowly as a shriek of pure agony filled the small chamber.

"No!" My scream was drowned by the mighty death rattle which lingered in echoes even after Gavin was gone, nothing but a pair of broken wing bones left behind between Foxy's fingers. She casted them aside like trash, vanishing into a fracture with a light glint, and just like that, we were alone with nothing but our hatred. "I'll kill you!" I lunged at him, not caring if it was pointless or not.

Zeke, wait! Live to fight another day! Natara tried to reason with me, but watching her kill another of our family drove me off the edge and I was blinded by revenge.

"Finally! A challenge!" Foxy sneered with glee, only provoking me further. I tackled her, grabbing for the sword first and tumbling with her all the way through the layers of lime and sandstone back to the surface inside the city of Baxterville.

"Make peace with Father, because I'm going to tear you limb from limb!" I said through gritted teeth while I fought for control of the sword.

She managed to throw me off, and I slammed through the wall of a nearby brick building. I was quick to my feet and faced her through the hole I had just created. "And hurt your precious human? I'd love to see that," she challenged through Liam's grin. The nerve of her was enough to make my blood boil.

I looked around and realized I must've crashed into a hardware store because I was surrounded by walls of tools. I grabbed a crowbar that had fallen to the floor by my feet, brandishing it menacingly, "I'll heal him after I'm done."

I lunged at her and swung faster than she could predict, catching the side of Liam's skull with the thick iron tool. She stumbled back, spit out some blood, and smiled. My next swing was blocked by the flaming sword and within seconds the crowbar turned to molten metal and dripped between my fingers, burning Natara's skin, but I easily halted the damage.

I dodged a swing of the sword and grabbed a pointed shovel, but it proved just as useless as the crowbar. Foxy continued to cut down every weapon I produced, and despite getting the occasional hit to land, she merely laughed as all they accomplished were superficial injuries to Liam, and Foxy remained unharmed.

Backed into a corner, I only had one more tool of potential use within reach, a massive pitchfork. "A pitchfork? Really, Ezekiel? Way to play into the stereotype."

"What can I say, I'm a fan of the classics," I said breathing heavily after our prolonged standstill. "Now stop trying to chit-chat, I've got places to be." I swung with the wooden handle like a Bo staff, and as I hoped she blocked with the sword. As the wood turned to ash, I flipped the now much shorter weapon around and stabbed right into the wrist holding the sword. Foxy cried out in pain, but I didn't end there; I twisted on the forks, breaking the forearm in multiple places and caught the sword before it hit the ground.

"Ugh! No!" she yelled, trying to stagger backwards, but I delivered a swift kick right to the chest and sent her flying into a rack of nuts and bolts, a sea of metal bits cascaded down around her like a glittering waterfall. I stepped up and over her as she clutched the broken limb tight to her chest and struggled to move within the tangled web of broken shelves. I heard the sounds of sirens approach and caught the flickering of red and blue lights alternating outside in the cold post-sunset darkness.

I grabbed Foxy by the neck and flew us up and right back to the quarry where we could be alone. Once there, I threw her to the ground and held the sword to her throat. "Let him go…" I said weakly, but determined.

"You can't do it, can you? I bet if it was just me, you wouldn't have wasted your breath, would you? You would've struck me down on the spot, but him…" She tried to stand up and I kicked her back into the dirt, even though it hurt seeing Liam in so much pain.

"I said let him go! I'll let you live if you release him, or else…or else I *will* do it. I'll kill you both if I have to." I tried to sell my bluff, but even I wasn't convinced it was a real threat.

"Then do it, kill us both," she said, not even slightly afraid. I raised the sword higher, making the tip touch the skin of Liam's neck, causing it to redden and blister.

I'm sorry Zeke, but if Liam is the man you told me he was, he'd want you to end it.

Natara was right, he would want me to stop Foxy after everything she's done in his name, but I just couldn't finish the deed. I lowered the sword and screamed at my own failure.

I thrusted the sword into the ground beside us before jumping on top of Foxy and pummeling my fists into her face, Liam's face, over and over again, screaming as I did it.

After several hits, the pace of strikes slowed until eventually stopping. With the rage poured out of me, my vision returned and the horror of my handiwork was laid out in front of me. Liam's swollen, bleeding face twitched on the ground beneath my fists, still under Foxy's control, but from my vantage point, I was the monster.

"M…my…" Foxy tried to choke out some words, but I couldn't make them out, so I leaned closer. "My turn."

Blinding blue light emitted from Liam's face blowing me off and across the quarry. By the time I tried to stand, Foxy and her fully healed host stood on my chest, pushing me back down to the ground. The flaming sword lit the area again after being freed from the ground, once again in the hand of the Enochian. I could feel a crack in the boundary between Hell and Earth just a few feet beneath the surface below me, but it was just out of reach, not that it mattered anymore, I had given up hope. There was no saving Liam, and my foolish attempt to save him would cost Natara her life as well. "I'm so sorry," I said to her, and to Liam, but only Foxy responded.

"Save it, I don't want your apology." She lifted the sword high over her head.

It's okay Zeke, I'm prepared to die, you have nothing to be sorry about, Natara whispered in my mind. I surrendered, and awaited my fate.

* * *

"Wake up, little human," a voice said, slowly rousing me back to consciousness. "I have a surprise for you, something I would like you to see." I tried to rub my eyes as I came to, still very much groggy, but my arms couldn't move. "Look at him, so stubborn," the voice continued, and with those words my vision came back into focus. I could see a thin blonde woman in her late twenties standing several dozen feet beneath where I hung in midair.

Huh? What the…? What's happening? I blurted, confused about where I was and what was going on.

"You've been asleep for a while, but you remember, don't you? You're helping me," She waited for me to remember, but everything was still so fuzzy. "You betrayed Ezekiel, took me in so you'd have the power to stop him."

*What? No! I…I would never…*I tried desperately to remember what had happened before I fell asleep, and without warning, it all came flooding back like a tidal wave of horrifying regret. The back-door deal with Foxy, the promise of seeing my mother again, and learning the dreaded truth on that mountain top, it all came rushing back to me and I would've cried if I could. *I'm so sorry, Zeke…I'm so sorry.*

"Don't pity him child, He'll be put out of his misery shortly, enjoy the show."

No! Please, don't hurt him! Foxy! No! I screamed as loud as I could, but with my mind separated from my body, no words escaped my lips. Instead, as my body descended from the sky, looming over my former angel companion with his new host, the other's voice flowed from within me once again, only this time loud enough to carry down into the quarry below.

"It wasn't very smart of you coming back here!"

Foxy, this isn't right, you don't have to kill anyone! I said, trying to reason with the only being that could hear my voice trapped within our shared mind space.

"Foxy," Zeke's voice growled with malicious intent.

I continued to try and get Foxy to listen to me, or at the very least be super distracting, but she just continued to taunt and toy with Zeke. It wasn't until she revealed her orders to keep me alive that I finally stopped yapping and changed gears. *Wait, what?* Unsurprisingly, Foxy continued to ignore the little voice inside her head.

"Liam! Listen to me, Liam! You have to fight her!"

"Yell all you want, Ezekiel; Liam's listening to every word, but he'll never break my hold over him."

Like hell I won't! I raged, trying with every ounce of strength I had to banish Foxy just as I had done with Zeke twice before, but Foxy gave no quarter, her hold over me absolute.

I kept fighting regardless of how fruitless it appeared to be, but two of the words out of Foxy caught my attention and I halted all attempts to fight momentarily. "Thane Varro."

What did you just say?! I asked desperately, because I very much wished that I had misheard.

"They've all chosen the former, but I'm looking forward to the day I get to see what this beautiful weapon does to a mortal."

*No…No, you didn't, that can't be…*I denied, not wanting it to be true, but Zeke confirmed my worst fear.

"You! You caused the accident!"

"What acci…"

You killed my mother! I screamed with the full force of every emotion I had bottled up inside over the past months.

"Oh…oh this feeling, it's so strong."

I'm going to kill you! I cried out again, channeling my wrath into Foxy, letting all of the hate boil over and overwhelm her as I had done before with Zeke.

My body began to waiver and I tried to move, but I hadn't broken through, only managing to disorient her with my rush of emotion. She panicked and grabbed at my chest, trying to stop it at the source.

Suddenly four beings sprung from hiding places around us and latched onto each of my limbs, and I rooted for them to tear me apart and save me from this body snatcher. They managed to free the flaming sword from my grasp, but the deep bite mark on my wrist stung like hot pokers through my flesh. Even though I couldn't control my body, I could still feel the pain inflicted upon it, but that didn't change my mindset one bit.

The tables turned in Foxy's favor very shortly, and I had to watch as she burned away their hosts one by one by one in rapid succession until only one remained.

I watched as the surviving Muse, Gavin, ran away with the sword. Joy rose up inside me, thinking that meant Zeke would be safe from threat of death, but with one dash of blinding speed, Foxy caught up to him and easily ripped the sword back from his grip. Even in the subterranean darkness of the water table her wings burned and sizzled until the last host boiled away just like the others, but this time, Foxy didn't allow the poor Muse inside to escape.

What are you doing? Let him Go! I cried as I felt Gavin's windpipe breaking between the fingers of one hand, and the licking flames surrounding the sword inch closer in the other. *Don't kill him! I...I thought you wanted Zeke?*

The slow movement in my sword hand ceased, making me believe I finally said something Foxy was willing to hear.

"Call to him," she said, moving the flaming sword closer to Gavin's neck, energized bubbles coursing their way up his face leaving blisters in their wake.

"They'll already be back in Hell by now, it's–" Foxy pulled Gavin in close and busted open his nose against my forehead. As Gavin floated through the murky water Foxy released his throat just long enough to get a stronger grasp of his wings right at the base.

"You had better hope that's not true, or I'll send you back to them in pieces." Foxy scanned the area, but however she viewed the world was not relayed through my eyes. Once she settled on a point, she dashed deeper underground until we broke into a spherical cavern filled most of the way with water, and air hot enough to melt my clothes.

"Ezekiel!" Gavin shouted in warning, but Zeke didn't run, he turned to face us instead.

No Zeke! Run! Just Run! Even when Megatron woke up, Zeke merely told him to leave without him, that stubborn jerk. *You can't stop her, run!* I wished more than anything he could hear me, but I was completely powerless.

I still held out hope that he would fallback with Megatron,

but after he was gone Zeke stood firm to face Foxy.

"All right, they're gone, it's just us now, let Gavin go, you don't have to do this," Zeke said with purpose, but I knew better, Foxy wasn't letting anyone else leave alive. She went off on a sadistic rant, proving what I already knew, and I could see it in Zeke's expression that he knew what was about to happen as well.

"Please, Eze–" Gavin begged, but the sword in my hand cut him short, and I couldn't look away or even close my eyes as he burnt away in my hands.

No! I screamed in unison with Zeke.

"I'll kill you!" he shouted, his rage now on par with my own.

He will kill you, even if it means killing me, I told Foxy, because as much as I cared about Zeke, avenging my Mother meant more than anything to me, even my own soul.

"Finally! A challenge!" Foxy sneered right before Zeke tackled us full bore, bringing us back to the surface.

Zeke continued to threaten Foxy, but she just used me as a human shield, taking blows that only I could feel and laughing in his face about it. He managed to defend himself against Foxy's sword, but every weapon he chose melted like butter beneath the heat of celestial fire, until the pitchfork. It was the most painful moment of my life when he dug the forks through my arm and twisted, breaking bones and nearly causing me to pass out again, but my desperate need to witness Foxy fail kept me clinging on.

"Ugh! No!" she cried, and I laughed.

That's right Foxy, you lose. I'm going to enjoy seeing you die.

Zeke flew us back to the quarry and slammed me hard into the ground, as if I wasn't already hurting enough.

"Let him go…" he said, sword to our throat.

No, just kill her Zeke, please. I begged, but Foxy heard me and knew his answer.

"You can't do it, can you?"

*Stop doubting him! He'll do it, he has to…*I said, partially doubting it myself.

"I said let him go!"

You know she won't let me go, just please, kill us both!

"Or else…or else I *will* do it."

Finally! Yes, you know you have to, please, do it now! Please, hear me somehow! But he didn't hear me.

"Then do it, kill us both," Foxy said, knowing he couldn't.

Zeke raised the sword, but when it plunged down, it found its mark in the dirt more than a foot away. He instead took the bony small fists of his host and pummeled them down on my head with extreme force not capable by any human. White stars and rivers of red blurred my vision, and crackling cartilage popped sending sharp pain throughout my nervous system. Right when I thought I couldn't survive another blow, the hitting stopped.

Kill me, I begged, hopping the next impact would be from the flaming sword and end Foxy's life as well as my own, but there were no more, Zeke was finished.

"M…my…" Foxy said, choking through the mess that was left of my face. The aching and shooting pain stopped, forcing me to feel relief even though it was a terrible sign. "My turn."

Bright light emitted from every break in my skin and a beautifully warm sensation filled my body as I could feel my muscles, bones, and blood vessels mending themselves back together. By the time the light dimmed and I could see again, I wished my eyes had still been blinded by my own blood, because in my hand was the sword, and at the other end of it, Zeke.

He let you live! You don't have to kill him! He's a good person, please! I continued, knowing it was stupid, but I couldn't allow myself to get through it any other way, I had to try everything I could.

"I'm so sorry," Zeke said, defeated.

Don't be sorry, I'll find a way to stop her, I don't know how, but I'll find a way. Part of me was glad no one could hear me that time, because I didn't want Zeke to know I made a promise I couldn't keep.

"Save it, I don't want your apology." Foxy said, still ignoring me. I was only conscious for one reason, watching Zeke die, I knew that now.

I watched as Foxy lifted my foot, lowered it down hard on the neck of Zeke's new host, and raise the sword.

No, please, there must be something you want more than him, please, I'll do anything!

"Goodbye, brother." She lowered the sword, and it pierced the host's solar plexus.

No, I whimpered, no more strength left to cry out when no one who mattered could hear me anyway. *I'm so sorry, Zeke.*

I watched the light slowly fade from her vibrant blue eyes, but in the moment before the flames reached the lips, they curled upwards, as if to smile. In another instant, it was gone, as was everything else; only a pile of ashes remained, quickly swept away in the breeze.

"It's done, he's gone. Thank you for your help," Foxy said coldly as she put the sword away.

You're a monster, I retorted weakly, no fight left in me. *But you win, now please, kill me and let me be with my mother again.* If there was to be anything even remotely close to a silver lining on this wretched moment, it had to be that, unless Foxy was going back on her word.

"I have orders to keep you alive, remember?"

*No, you can't, you promised…*I started, but before I could finish Foxy separated herself from my body and floated out in front of me.

"When you eventually die, you will go to Heaven, but that day will not be today nor will it be anytime soon. Just be glad of that, human."

"Wait!" I called out, but Foxy flew up and away like a speeding bullet. After I came to terms with her being gone and not coming back, I looked down and checked to make sure I could move my own body again.

With that short moment of triumph, I remembered what had just transpired and fell to my knees beside the pile of ashes left at my feet. I picked up a handful of it and tears dripped down my cheeks into the remains. "I'm so sorry, Zeke. I should've done more, I never should've trusted her in the first place. You tried to tell me, and I turned my back on you…for that, I'm sorry. I…I don't know what to do without you. I have no one, nothing…"

I let the black flakes float off my hand with the wind between my fingers. "I am so sorry, please forgive me."

The sun was still down, and the hot humid air made my skin feel slimy and gross, but it was warm enough I wasn't shivering. I walked over to one of the grassier corners of the quarry and curled up into a ball on the softest patch I could find. I closed my eyes and tried to forget everything, if only to get some sleep and dream of a better world, a world with Zeke still in it.

CHAPTER FOURTEEN: HOME AGAIN

Getting out of Mississippi with nothing but the clothes on my back was no easy task. Took me three days of begging and two nights sleeping on hard concrete before I found a kind-hearted big rig trucker named Roy willing to take me as far as Dallas.

"So," Roy said, a little over an hour into our projected nine-hour trip in an attempt to break the long silence. "How did you end up so far from home?" His tone was weary, like he was just testing the waters and would back off quickly if I gave him a good reason to do so.

I had been replaying the recent events over and over again in my mind as I peered through the glass window, watching the telephone poles whip by one after another. "Long story…" I whispered, just loud enough for him to hear at first but trailed off in the end, hoping that would squash the subject for good. I was nowhere near in the mood to talk about how royally I had screwed up, and even if I wanted to, this truck driver wouldn't be able to understand angels being involved. I was better off just remaining silent and torturing myself quietly.

"Well, we've got nothing but open road for about 400 miles, and I'm all out of books on tape, so I could go for a good story about now," Roy said with charisma that was wholly wasted on me. I adjusted my body to turn further away from him, sending the message I had heard him, but still wasn't interested.

Three more awkwardly silent hours passed before Roy spoke up again, this time from outside the parked truck while filling up the gas tank, "Are you hungry? Want something to eat?"

I turned toward him for the first time since getting into the truck, but hesitated. After a short internal struggle between my stomach and head, the former won in a landslide. "Yes, please."

"Ah!" Roy cried out triumphantly, "It speaks! Maybe next time I can get more than two words from you though." I immediately regretted letting my stomach call that shot, but after another grumble, it felt like a minor sacrifice. "Why don't you come inside, pick out whatever you'd like, my treat."

I hopped down out of the truck and headed inside, used the restroom while I was at it, and grabbed the biggest, juiciest hotdog I had ever seen, but I had a sneaking suspicion that three days of nearly complete starvation was making it look more appetizing than it actually was.

"You want some chips or a drink to go with that?" Roy asked once we entered the line for the register. I scanned the room until I found the gallon water bottles and grabbed one, trying not to drop my precious hotdog as I reached into the chilling refrigerator. I returned to Roy, now on deck for the register. "Water, huh? Not soda or anything like that?"

"I don't drink soda," I said before stopping myself.

"Yes," he whispered with quick fist pump after successfully getting extra words out of me, but he moved past the victory immediately. "Good to know, soda's bad for you anyway, not like that hot dog, though, right?" he asked sarcastically.

I let slip a corner of my mouth before I resumed my pity party frown, and Roy caught it, but instead of another gloating comment, he just smiled and approached the counter.

Roy waited until we were back on the road and the hot dog was working its way through my digestive system before showing the strings attached. "So, I think I know how you can repay me for lunch."

"What?" I asked, still maintaining a defensive posture, but looking over at him now.

Roy kept his eyes on the road as he explained, "In exchange for that hot dog, I want at least thirty minutes of real conversation, and by conversation, I mean you talking, and me listening, maybe throwing in a clarifying question here and there, but still, mostly you."

I pouted for a while but eventually decided it would be easier to just waste half an hour on superficial topics and go back to beating myself up in peace. It worked. I told him I liked running, talked about a few movies that we both liked, but every time a subject started hitting too close to home, I immediately switched to a safer one. After thirty minutes, I turned back to the window and fell silent again.

"So, what brings you so far from home?" he asked again, this time hoping our new rapport would lead me to answering.

"That was thirty minutes," I stated plainly.

"Thirty for the hot dog, another twenty for the water," he said with a lingering smirk.

"Oh, you've got to be kidding me!" I exclaimed.

"Nope, serious as a heart attack, kid," he said, smirking like a fool.

"Why do you care so much? You don't know me."

He laughed, not exactly the reaction I would've guessed. "I was young once kid, and I've met a lot of kids just like you over the years, trust me, you're not the first person to be going through whatever it is. And whatever it is, keeping it bottled up is only going to make it worse."

I turned back to the window, even more depressed than before he had said anything, because he was so very wrong. What I had just experienced, no living person had ever experienced before, not even close. I was completely and utterly alone.

"C'mon kid, just give me something, anything," he pleaded.

I rolled down the window and chucked the half empty gallon jug out the window, watching it tumble down the highway in the contoured mirror outside.

Roy slammed on the breaks and the truck screeched and skidded to a crawl. "What the hell?!" he yelled in disbelief before pulling the wheel with both hands to park the truck on the shoulder. "What the hell is wrong with you, kid?!"

"Now I don't owe you any more conversation," I said as my final words to Roy, and with a terrified look in his eyes, he dropped the subject for good.

Once we made it to Dallas, Roy hooked me up with another driver heading to Albuquerque and made sure to warn him about trying to pry for information, which led to a far less eventful drive. The only time I opened my mouth was for the final directions to my old house.

J. A. Reed

When we pulled up there was a fence surrounding the property with a giant *FORECLOSED* sign written in bright red letters. "Are you sure this is the place?" said the driver, who's name I hadn't bothered to learn, as he eyed it with suspicion.

"Thank you," I said in a grumbling monotone while stepping down from the cabin. The driver was still perplexed by the whole situation, but he quickly shrugged it off and pulled away.

I staggered over to the fence and placed my hands on it, peering through the metal links and up at my former home. Untamed weeds had sprouted several feet up between the cracks of concrete slabs making up the curved driveway and windblown trash was stuck to all of the west-facing fence walls, making it initially obvious the house had been neglected since the last time I was there.

I climbed the fence quickly but didn't stick the landing very well, stumbling and just barely catching myself with my right hand. I rubbed my throbbing palm and walked further up the driveway. Happy memories stabbed at me like knives, riding my bike after spending a long day around town with my friends, pulling out the camping chairs every Fourth of July to watch the spectacle our pyromaniac neighbors would throw together, getting bigger and bigger each year, and the closer I got to the white oak front door, the more clearly I visualized how my mom used to pull open that very same wooden slab to greet me after school before I could even get halfway there. Once my feet came to rest right on the front step, it all hit me like a ton of bricks: this wasn't my home anymore, but it was all I had left.

I wiped my cheeks before reaching for the doorknob to check and see if it was locked, which it was. I knelt and riffled through the rocks to my left until I found the semi-buried false rock hiding our spare key inside. I slid the key into the lock, and despite a bit of stick, I managed to force it open and the door pivoted on its hinges, kicking up a cloud of dust.

I fanned my hand through the air once I stepped inside. The setting sunlight trickled in from the back side of the house through the uncovered sliding glass door and reflected off the small floating particles in the air. The whole house had been stripped except for the occasional small odd and end. Our dark painted particle board bookcase was where we had left it, but the shelves were empty, and one of them had broken causing it to slant sharply on one side. A large cardboard box sat in the middle of the dining room full of small miscellaneous items such as picture frames, a lamp, a few less desirable DVDs, a small plastic ratchet set, and one of my old childhood baseball bats sticking out at an awkward angle.

I walked over and peered down into the box, but just a mere glimpse of the pictures in the frames caused me to step back. I decided to distract myself by searching the rest of the house, starting with the guest room. I opened the door slowly, not sure what to expect on the other side. It was stupid of me, but I found myself hoping to find the room untouched. I wanted to see the futon against the right wall covered in my mom's old throw pillows that had been demoted from her own room. I wished that our L-shaped desk would still be there covered in little nick-nacks including some of my finer school projects. The door creaked open and revealed a vacuum cleaner, nothing else. I couldn't say I was surprised, but my heart sank a little deeper nonetheless.

My room down the hall was similarly empty except for a section of floor where all of the house's blinds had been taken down and stacked. I spent a little longer in my room, walking around and checking out my closet for anything I might want to keep, but it was picked clean of valuables and all that remained was trash and dust.

The hallway bathroom suffered a worse fate than any other room so far because even the shower head and light fixture were taken. The toilet bowl, which used to be kept in pristine condition, was now caked with dark rings at both the former and current water levels, and everything beneath the surface was tinted sickly yellow.

My eyes were drawn back to the box and the picture frames when I came back from the hallway, no more distractions left on that side of the house. I walked through the massively empty living room, the box remaining in the corner of my eye as I passed by it, as if calling to me on a subconscious level. I forced my head to turn the opposite direction and look out into the back yard, but it was just as unkempt and raggedy as the front had been. I looked back as if a Siren song were emanating from within the four cardboard walls, unable to resist the pull.

I took a step toward the box but caught myself. There was nothing but pain in that box for me. Instead, I felt the need to finish my walkthrough of the house, but all that remained was the master bedroom. I placed my hand on the door but hesitated to open it. There was nothing but pain in there as well, in fact, there was nothing but pain in this entire house. Every room, every inch of that house held a thousand reminders of better times, and even the worst of them were fond memories compared to everything happening now. If I were smart, I'd turn and run from this place. I didn't know where I'd go, how I'd get there, or what I would do once I was there, but anything new had to be better than this heartbreaking pain, right?

I wasn't smart, however, because I opened the door and what I saw in there was worse than I ever could've imagined. Unlike the rest of the house, this room was full, but nothing inside had ever belonged to my mother. Piles of dirty rags that could hardly still hold the title of clothes were strewn about and a lumpy mattress pad had been laid out with soiled and wrinkled sheets crookedly covering it. A grimy coffee table sat unevenly near the bed covered in food wrappers, crumbs both large and small, something that looked like a glass vase, but wasn't designed for holding any flowers, and multiple mounds of garbage. Even the walls looked foreign after being covered in spray-painted tags.

Looking at the horror of what had become of my mother's beautiful room ignited a rage deep in my core making my blood boil. I didn't know if these squatters were still coming around or if they had moved on, but regardless, they were going to pay for trashing my house. I stormed over to the box in the dining room and pulled out the baseball bat, catching another look at the pictures inside. One of the bigger photos in clear view was a family portrait of my mother and myself when I was fifteen. She stood behind me in a black dress with her hair professionally done and perfect makeup, resting her hands on my shoulders. I was sitting in one of my father's suits, tailored to fit me at the time, with a dark blue tie she had taught me how to tie.

If I had seen that picture thirty seconds ago, I might've broken down and cried, but now it only fueled my anger. I turned back to the vile room and warmed up by swinging the bat into the palm of my hand. As soon as I entered the room, I came out swinging. My blind rage had started with the nearest thing I saw, but the bat did little against a mere pile of dirty clothes, so I switched up and kicked the pile around a few times. Wanting more, I changed my focus to the coffee table, and more specifically, the glass fixture upon it. I took a running start and connected with it hard, sending shards of glass and dark water fanning out across the room. I had stumbled a little in my follow through but came back and brought my bat straight down onto the table a few times, screaming to let out all of the emotions I had been holding inside.

When the table was only a pile of splinters, I heaved tired breaths, but I still had plenty of steam to let off, so I turned to the disgraceful paint job. I chose the biggest tag and started swinging my bat at it as if it were a sledgehammer. I hit a stud a few times, but soon I was caving in the drywall and making that wall disappear bit by bit. When the bat started feeling too heavy to swing with enough force, I threw it away and started ripping the wall open with my bare hands, still screaming and crying as chunks of wall fell before me.

"Freeze!" a voice called out over my shoulder, but I was too furious to listen.

"Put your hands in the air, now!" a second voice said.

I still didn't pay much mind to the voices, but the simple fact of hearing them, combined with my heart bursting through my

J. A. Reed

chest and muscles burning with fatigue, I slowed down and fell to my knees.

"Put your hands on your head, slowly!" the first voice said. I looked over my shoulder to see the voices belonged to two police officers with weapons drawn. For a moment, I felt like Tabby was there with me as I contemplated making a sudden move, but I was too tired, and too mentally broken to do much of anything. "I said hands on your head, son," the officer stated again, only this time a little softer.

My breathing was still labored but had gone down considerably. I turned back to face the empty wall and exposed studs, slowly put my hands on my head, and heard the sounds of clinking metal as one of the cops approached me. Cold steel clasped around one of my wrists, and as my hands were forced behind my back and restrained, I went limp. My mother was gone, my home was gone, and Zeke was gone. Everyone and everything I cared about was gone, so I no longer cared about what was going to happen to me, I just didn't care about anything anymore.

* * *

Nonexistence sure did look a lot like Hell. Cold rocky vastness, twinkling shatter pattern in the sky above, even Zak was there.

"Ezekiel?" Zak asked in surprise. "He's awake!" he then called, not nearly as soft as before and I jolted up to a sitting position.

"Zak? What are you doing here? Where are we?" I looked around and it really did look a lot like Hell, in fact, it looked *exactly* like Hell.

"Ezekiel, you fool!" Lucy's unmistakable stern voice stung my eardrums and I instantly tensed up.

"I didn't do it!" I spit out on pure instinct. She appeared into view from my blind side and knelt next to me. "H-hey sis...please don't hurt me," I nervously stuttered while proudly cowering and groveling.

"What were you thinking provoking Forfax like that? I asked you to protect your brothers, now…now Gavreel…" A tear welled up in her eye but didn't fall.

"It wasn't…his…fault…" Megatron painfully muttered from behind me. I spun my body just enough to get a good look around and found Ram trying to keep the badly injured Muse from getting up. "Get off me Ramiel! I'm…ugh, I'm fine." He shoved the far stronger Archangel away weakly and sat up with great difficulty. "I'm the one that altered the plan, Gavreel's death is on my hands."

Trini rushed to his side and helped him to his feet. "No, you can't blame yourself, we did everything we could." She then turned to me and a familiar level of hatred burned in her eyes, "You on the other hand, you just stood there as we were slaughtered! You could've caught the sword! Gavreel would still be alive if you hadn't chosen that damn human over him!" She turned to Zak. "You should've let him die like the rest of them."

I patted my hands to my chest where I remember Foxy holding the flaming sword, but there was no hole, no wound, not even a scratch. I looked up for answers, but the only attention I was receiving was from Trini, and that wasn't the kind of attention I needed at the moment.

Lucy stepped between us with her back to me, as I stumbled to my feet incredibly confused about the whole situation around me. "Trinity, please just calm down. Fighting each other is the last thing that we need right now. We're all hurting, some more physically than others, so I'll need help getting the wounded back to my place. Trinity, take Metatron."

"Obviously," she spat, "everyone else just stay away from us." Her head swiveled back and forth along the room, mistrust in her gaze.

"Ramiel, has Tabbris woken up yet?" Lucy asked before going any further.

"No Ma'am, but I'll take good care of him." He scooped up the small Muse into his arms like a sleeping child.

Seeing the injured frail little guy finally made Zeke realize there was a noticeable lack of hosts among their group. "Natara?" I asked myself in a hushed whisper. Foxy had killed all of their hosts, and I remember her having the sword over me, but I was somehow still alive; what about Natara?

Lucy continued around the room without hearing my hushed voice. "And Zadkiel, you'll come with—"

"I'm fine Lucifer," he said with annoyance in his voice. I began stumbling around looking for Natara, but there was nothing for miles around, nothing but us few angels.

"No, you're not," she spat back at him sternly.

"Well I can fly just fine, I can—"

"Can you all just shut up for a second?!" I shouted. "How did I get here? Why am I not dead? And where's Na…where's my host?"

Everyone froze in worried silence as eyes danced between Lucy and myself, then they all rested upon Zak. He stepped forward nervously. "I…I came as soon as I could, Zeke."

"Ugh, you deal with this," Trini scoffed with indifference, "I'll meet you all at Lucifer's." She took off with Megatron in tow and left me in even more suspense.

"Zak, what happened? I mean, what, did she die? Where is she, though, I have to see her." The faces around me sank lower and only worried me more. "What's wrong? What aren't you telling me? Was she taken? What happened?!"

"She's…she's gone…" Zak said, his head level with mine and regretful tears on his cheeks.

"Gone? Gone where?" I asked, although I think my subconscious already knew the answer.

"When I found out what you were doing, I came as fast as I could, but the fracture was too small to fit through," I didn't see the relevance at the moment, but I was too afraid to speak up. "You were so close to the edge, all you needed was a few more feet, but it was underground, I was so close to you but felt so powerless to save you." Zak was stepping closer as he spoke through heartbreaking emotion. "I wanted to save her, too, you have to believe me, I did, but…but there was nothing I could do."

"But you saved me, didn't you? Why couldn't you…!"

"I didn't save you, Zeke, she did." He cut me off and I couldn't find the words for a rebuttal, so I let him tell me. "I spoke to her through the fracture, I told her how close you were, how all I needed was a few extra feet to save you. She sacrificed herself and banished you out through her back where I could catch you and pull you back through."

"What do you mean she sacrificed herself? What did Foxy…" That's when my conscious mind caught up. The flaming sword. "No! She can't be!"

"I'm sorry, Brother, she's gone." The hosts burned away by wings were dead, but their souls still lived on, the flaming sword on the other hand was so much more powerful. Just like Xaf and Gavin, Natara had been erased from existence, she was gone forever, her very soul destroyed. I thought back to her final words, *It's okay Zeke, I'm prepared to die, you have nothing to be sorry about.* I wished those words could consul me, and I knew she had been a Nihilist, spending her whole life believing that there would be nothing after death, but I still felt responsible. If I had only left her alone.

When I came back to the real world, Ram and Tabby were gone, leaving only Lucy, Zak and myself. "We should really get going, boys," Lucy said once she felt the mood shift enough. "And I'm taking a look at that arm when we get there; I'm not taking no for an answer."

I looked down at my arms to see they were perfectly fine when Zak answered her, "Fine, whatever, just go." I tried to get a good look at his arms, but one of them was tucked out of sight. "I need a minute alone, if you don't mind?" he asked Lucy, worried her overprotectiveness of him would affect her answer.

"You have one, don't be late," her eyes threatened him as only she could, and then she lifted off the ground and sped away.

"What's wrong with your arm, Zak?" I asked, legitimately concerned as to why he was hiding it, but I got no reaction to quell my concern.

"Natara, she wanted me to tell you something before… before the end." I froze, a thousand fears scrolling across my mind, imagining only the worst insults and regrets. "She said, 'don't forget your promise, live that normal life for the both of us,' I hope you know what that means." With time running out for him, he didn't stick around for any follow up questions. I was stunned for longer than I should've been before I thought about whether Lucy's threat included me, so I snapped out of it and took off as fast as my blackened wings would carry me.

Flying high over all of Hell after such a near-death experience was calming, but it also gave me too much time to think. My mind raced from every regret I had since first heading up to Earth. I wondered if Gavin and Natara would still be alive if I had just stayed down here where I belong. I wondered if Liam would've been better off without my meddling. I pulled up a view of Earth and looked for where he was at that moment. It was dark and cold in Mississippi, and Liam was curled up in a ball shivering in his sleep at the bottom of the quarry where so much had transpired. I couldn't even be happy to see him freed from Foxy's control, he looked so miserable and alone. I waved away the image before it could make me even more sick to my stomach. I never should've come into his life, all I did was make things worse for him, worse for everyone.

I landed in Lucy's yard and followed her into the house where the rest of the angels were gathered.

"We can't keep meeting like this, Lucifer," Aida said with determination.

"We can't risk going to Earth any longer," Nate said, trying to be helpful.

"If you all had listened to me in the first place, this wouldn't have happened," Cass hissed at me, possibly angrier at himself than anyone for not doing more to stop us at his house.

"Enough!" Lucy bellowed, halting all of the bickering. "Forfax has taken two of ours now, we cannot afford to be attacking one another."

"Well, clearly we can't afford to attack her either," Cass said, the only one brave enough to break the silence.

"Killing one of our own, it's a sin," Razzmatazz said with slowly building hope. "Surely Father will intervene, right?"

Lucy and Ram exchanged looks. "The inner circle is..." Lucy started, "complicated."

"Psh, that's an understatement," Ram added, "If we want anything done within the next 500 years, we're on our own. And that's if—"

"Ramiel," Lucy cut him off with a sharp snap.

"He's right though," I added, Lucy turned her gaze to me, but lessened it, so I continued. "I spoke with Eve, she said the inner circle 'needs time' to decide how to handle it, but I'm not buying it."

"Evangeline? Does Jophiel know you've been talking to her?" Zak said, completely dismissing the serious tone of the room.

"Zadkiel! Arm, now!" Lucy shouted, making him flinch and regret drawing attention to himself. He took a few steps closer to her and she pulled him down onto the couch. She pulled away layers of clothes he had been using to hide his right arm, and when she pulled the final layer away, we were all able to see why Lucy had been so worried. Zak's arm from the elbow all the way down to the fingers looked like it had been skinned to the bone. The little bits of muscle and sinew that were still attached looked like they had been squished under a vice grip and mashed into the bone.

"What the Hell did you do to yourself, Zadkiel?!" Satchel shouted as soon as he noticed it.

"It's nothing, it looks worse than it is," he tried playing it off, but I knew what had happened.

"That's from pulling me in, isn't it?" He avoided my eye contact, only confirming my suspicion. "Zak, I'm so sorry, I didn't know. Will it heal?"

Lucy slowly rotated it and analyzed the injured limb extensively. "Aesthetically, no, the void between worlds doesn't return what it takes, but in time, full mobility should return." Hearing that felt crushing, but at least he wouldn't lose the arm.

I hated myself even more that yet another close friend of mine had to pay a permanent price for my stupid decisions. I still felt terrible, but I tried to remind myself that it wasn't as bad as it could've been.

Lucy wrapped his arm back up and he sulked away back to where he had been standing before the spotlight had found him. Aida saved him by bringing the focus back to the matter at hand. "I think some of us would rather get back to our own lives here, so can we decide once and for all what we're going to do about this whole mess?"

Without missing a beat, the room exploded into arguments for both fighting back and hiding away. The split felt very even, but I remained silent, unsure of whether or not I could trust my own judgment to make the right call. Lucy, being the only other quiet bystander in the heated room, locked eyes with me. I tried to look away by finding Ram, but he was locked in a screaming match with two of the Guardians. I could still feel Lucy's eyes burning a hole in my head and for some reason I got mad about that. Her eyes were looking at me the same way they had outside of my frozen house, when she asked me to lookout for the Muses on Earth. I had tried to tell her then that I wasn't responsible enough for that sort of job, and I had proven to be right in the worst possible way, so why was she looking at me like that again? I tried to give Liam a better life, but all I did was make it worse. I tried to avenge Xaf, but all I did was get another one of us killed. I promised Natara I only needed twenty-four hours, but instead I made them the last hours she would ever know. If it hadn't been for…wait…

With all the screaming and arguing, I stepped aside into the corner of the room and tried to hear myself think. I wasn't the common denominator in everything, Foxy was. Foxy had turned Liam against me, had killed Xaf before I even went to Earth, and had caused the accident that killed Liam's mother and paralyzed him. Foxy was the reason for all of the deaths, not me. I looked back at Lucy, and she had a smile on her lips, as if she had been waiting for me to catch up with what she had already known.

"Wait!" I yelled, but no one stopped to listen. "Wait! Listen up!" I got their attention slowly, one or two at a time, but when all eyes were on me, I continued. "I have an idea!"

"I hope it's better than your last idea," Trini snarled.

"Actually, it's pretty much the exact same idea, only this time, it's going to work, because this time, you guys are going to listen to me." Trini quickly lost her spunk and it was replaced by genuine remorse. "This time, I want you guys to stay behind down here."

"What? You're not going out there alone!" Zak said defiantly.

"Glad to hear you say that, 'cause I'm going to need you with me, Foxy thinks I'm dead, so I'll need you to call to her and lure her out."

"What about the sword?" Cass asked, trying to hide his concern.

"I can help you with that," Lucy said, standing slowly and walking over to me. "You should've come to me first, but I'll need a few days."

"Perfect, that'll give us plenty of time to prepare everything."

The angels that weren't around for the last strategy meeting were understandably confused. "What are you talking about? What are you going to do?" Zoof asked, intrigued.

"I could use all the help I can get, if you all want to help?" I asked, hoping to end the arguing and move forward as one. Unanimously, they wanted to hear what I had in mind, so I sat down and outlined my idea for them all and, with helpful input and suggestions all around, my original idea blossomed into a clear-cut, fool-proof strategy. By the end, we were all working together like we never had before, because we all knew that this time, together, we would succeed.

CHAPTER FIFTEEN: FAMILIAR FACES

I had never been arrested before, but I assumed it's much less of a hassle when you're not missing and presumed dead, and, if I had to guess, having a perfectly forged false identity didn't help my case very much. I probably could've avoided all the extra heat if I had been picked up literally anywhere else, but when a paralyzed minor gets abducted from his hospital room, the cops of that city tend to remember that sort of thing, fake ID or not.

Booking and processing might have gone smoothly if there had been any form of next of kin for me as well, but the missing persons report had been filed by the city, so I had to sit and wait all night, and pretty much the whole next day as cops placed phone call after phone call trying to find someone that could both confirm my identity, as well as assume custody of me. During those gruelingly boring twenty-something hours, I had been transferred a dozen times between an isolated holding cell and interrogation room two. Most of the trips to interrogation proved fruitless for the detectives, but for their last attempt, they tried a slightly different approach.

"Four and a half months," one of the two detectives assigned to my case stated as he read the file in front of him. "What happened that day in the hospital? Who abducted you?" I remained silent with my arms crossed, slouching low into the cold metal of the bolted down chair.

"We're just trying to help you, son," the second detective said, playing his *good cop* persona effectively, but I remained steadfast. "It's okay, Liam, if the ones that took you are hurting you, we can help keep you safe."

"Or should I call you…" the clear bad cop hesitated as he flipped to a Xerox of my fake ID, "Gaylord William Janiszewski? Wow, the boys downstairs told me it was a *good* fake; I think you should get your money back, kid." After referencing *downstairs,* all I could do was think of Zeke.

"Easy now, Shepard," good cop said, trying to reel in his partner, "He's the victim here. Liam, son, who supplied you with this new identity? Was it the same person that took you?"

"The same person that gave you your legs back too, huh?" Bad cop continued questioning me as if I had just committed murder. "How exactly does a paralyzed seventeen-year-old just vanish from a secure and monitored facility such as Albuquerque's Presbyterian Hospital? There's no evidence of anyone going in or out of your room from the moment social services arrived, and your doctors found your bed empty. And now, months later, you show up destroying your former home with a new identity and smelling like you haven't showered in a week. Oh, and how could I forget, walking too!"

Bad cop shot out of his seat so fast he sent the metal chair clanging against the wall behind him and it rattled until resting on its side more than five feet away. "Shepard! Calm down! Now!" good cop said, standing up as well and physically pulling him backwards. "Maybe you should go get some air, don't you think?"

Bad cop looked at me a few times as he considered his partner's suggestion, "Fine, whatever, he's all yours," He left the room treating the door as roughly as he had the furniture.

Good cop straightened out his suit, sat back down, and cleared his throat. "My apologies for him, he, um, he has a loved one confined to chair, so as you might imagine he has a vested interest in your case, but that's no excuse, so I'm sorry." Hearing that, I laxed my arms a little and adjusted myself slightly higher in my slouch, but remained quiet. "I'm Detective Ryder by the way, Jake Ryder, it's nice to meet you."

He offered out his hand, but I only looked at it, "Liam," I said quietly, my voice breaking a little from going so long without use.

He lowered his hand and smiled, "Liam, it's nice to meet you, now if it's all right with you, I'd like to ask you a few questions about what you've been up to, is that okay with you?"

I had to give him credit for trying, but nothing had changed, anything truthful I said would be dismissed as insane. I considered a few lies, but none of them were very good, and each one could easily fall apart under close examination. The only idea I could think of that was fool proof was also the worst one of them all, the stereotypical soap opera special, "I don't remember,"

"You don't remember what, son?" good cop asked unsurely.

"Anything," I said, slightly louder, but still very under my breath. "Last thing I remember was..." I hesitated and considered options for my last memory. If I claimed the accident, then they might tell me about my mother's passing, and that wasn't an experience I would ever wish to live over. I ended up deciding on the last thing before Zeke showed up, making the lie much easier to maintain, "I had met with someone from social services, a woman, Ms. ..." I actually didn't remember her name, it had been nearly half a year after all. "It's all a bit fuzzy," I said grabbing my head and just going all in. I waited to see whether or not he would buy my story.

His expression clearly conveyed his mixture of disbelief, confusion, doubt, and what I can only describe as *holy crap, this kid is serious*. "Uh...Um, o-okay, let me just, um..." He began flipping through my file as if the answer were in there, but obviously it wasn't and that flustered him in the most hilarious way, but I didn't even come close to laughing. Without Zeke, I didn't know if I'd ever be able to laugh ever again. "Well, um, what's...what is the first thing you do remember since the day you disappeared?"

That was surprisingly a good follow up question, one I hadn't prepared for. I decided to stick with the basics. "I um, I remember waking up somewhere in Mississippi," My eyes started watering up thinking about what happened there, I wished in that moment my lie could come true, and that I could forget everything about Zeke just to make the pain go away.

"Mississippi?" he asked with more confusion, "How did you get to Mississippi?"

"I don't remember," I shot back without hesitation.

"How did you get back to your house?"

"Hitchhiked."

"How long ago did your memory return?" He still sounded

hesitant about that really being my story, but I figured the more I answer, the more he would believe me.

"I don't know, five, six days maybe."

"Where in Mississippi? What city?"

"I don't know."

"At what point did you regain the use of your legs?"

I rolled my eyes, he wasn't going to pull a fast one on me like that, "I told you, I don't know! Why am I here anyway?"

"We're trying to help you figure out how you went missing," he was beginning to sound less nice and more defensive, good.

"Well, I'm not missing anymore. Problem solved, can I leave now? I'm eighteen now, I'm an adult, with rights." The last thing I wanted was a lawyer, but hopefully if I ranted about rights and freedom they might just let me go.

"How about destruction of property then?" he said, trying to turn the tables back on me.

"It's my house, my property, what else you got?" I was fully up right in my chair by this point, so when I crossed my arms again, it was more defiant, and less closed off.

"It's not though, it belongs to the bank now," he flipped to a page in the back of my file and rotated it around for me to see. It was a multi-page contract full of fine print that I didn't understand, but the header was clear enough. I didn't care about that though, I shoved it aside. "Liam, look, I want to help you, but your case, it's not a usual one, I'm going to need you to bear with me and help us to help you."

"You can't help me…" I said quietly under my breath like before, even slouching back down a few inches. "No one can."

"Not unless you let me in?" I heard after looking away, and unless I was crazy, it sounded like Zeke's voice.

I jolted my head back around, "What did you say?" I asked desperately.

"I said, not unless you let me," he ended one word short, but perhaps I had only heard what I wanted to hear, I hadn't had much sleep that week, it was possible I was beginning to go delirious.

"I'm tired, can I–?"

"Yeah, of course," good cop said, catching my drift before I could even finish my thought. He pulled out the handcuffs from his belt and fiddled them nervously. "I'm sorry, but you'll have to—"

I put my wrists out, "That's fine."

He took me back to my cell and removed my restraints. "I'll do what I can to get you out of here as soon as possible, but are you sure you don't have anyone you'd like me to call for you? Any friends? Extended family? Anyone?"

"No, everyone I love is dead," With that I turned my back and took a seat on the thin lumpy mattress, but compared to the streets of Mississippi, it was a luxury, so I curled up and tried my best to sleep.

I honestly couldn't tell you if I had fallen asleep or not, and if I had, I couldn't tell for how long, but loud rambling voices down the hall stirred me enough to get my eyes open.

"Look!" a predominant and familiar male voice shouted over the others, "We just want to know if he's here! His name is Liam Cole!"

Hearing my name caused me to shoot upright. There was more rambling of voices cutting each other off, so I couldn't make out much more, but I stood up as I tried to listen and made my way as far as I could, pressing myself against the steel bars. My cell was too far in the back of the station, I couldn't see anything, but saying my interest was peaked would be an understatement.

I stayed there, cheek pressed between the bars waiting to see a face I could match to the voice, but after fifteen minutes, the only familiar face to turn the corner was not one I had expected. "You? What are you doing here?"

"So, you do remember me; I heard you were having memory issues," Ms. Merlot said while slowly approaching my cell. "Do you happen to remember how you got out of the hospital? I was in quite a bit of hot water for that you know, our office prides itself on *not* losing track of our wards."

"Sorry, can't help you, everything after you left...it's gone." I waited to see her reaction, but her face didn't move at all.

Unsure what to say after her lack of engagement, I shifted gears and lashed out a bit, "What are you doing here anyway? I'm eighteen now, I don't need Social Services anymore."

"Don't you though?" she asked very matter-of-factly. "You may be legally an adult, but you haven't even graduated high school, what sort of work do you think you'll qualify for? Where will you live, do you even know the price of rent in this city?"

I hadn't thought about that, the arrangement with Megatron in Seattle had taken all the guesswork out of such things, but she was right, that wasn't the way the world really worked. "I... I'll figure something out," I lied, trying to stall.

"Or, you can ask for a little help," she said, finally warming up her expression, but despite her good intentions, all I could focus on was the fate of the last person I asked for help. All Zeke had ever done was help me and be honest with me, but I betrayed him, and that betrayal cost him his life.

"Look here, mister!" I heard the loud commanding voice echo down the halls again, "We are not leaving until we see our teammate!"

That last word gave me just enough context to match the voice with a name, so I called out to him. "Coach Bassett?!"

I don't think he heard me, I wasn't nearly as loud as he was, but Ms. Merlot turned back to look in that direction as if also waiting for a response. "Ah, yes, your running team has been annoyingly persistent since your disappearance. It's been sweet."

Another bombshell dropped on me. I had always assumed my life here had just vanished along with me, but clearly that hadn't been the case. A warm fuzzy feeling began to spread outward from my core, but it was quickly cooled off by the realization that whatever hardship they had gone through looking for me, and worrying about me, had all been there because of me. It was my choice to disappear with Zeke, to change my identity and run. I could've called, written, posted online that I was okay, but I didn't. I had allowed selfishness to blind me to the vacuum I had left behind.

J. A. Reed

"If you like, I can get them through to see you," Ms. Merlot offered sincerely.

"I…" They would have questions just like the cops, questions I would have to lie through. If I did see them, I didn't know what I would do, it might be better to just send them away, force them to forget about me once and for all. "I don't want to see them."

"Liam, they're your friends, they care more than most of the families I've seen, you should…"

"I shouldn't have left them, I shouldn't have put them through the past four months, I shouldn't have…I…" The more I said the thoughts in my head out loud, the more difficult they were to say. Eventually I gave up trying to speak through the choked-up tears.

Ms. Merlot stepped closer, but with the bars between us, she couldn't make any physical contact to console me, "You can't control how others react to your actions, sometimes people are just going to feel the way they have to feel, no matter what you do, or don't do. Now, I don't know what happened to you, or what you've been through, but look at you! You're walking, that's a miracle in and of itself. And while you might be down right now, some good clearly came of it, even if you can't remember, right?" She wasn't wrong, before Zeke showed up, things were bad. I had just lost my legs, which meant I couldn't run, and I never would've been able to process the loss of my mother in that chair; I had needed an escape, but didn't that only make what I did all the more selfish? "Now, I don't know if you actually forgot everything, or if you're just trying to protect yourself, but there are dozens of young men and women out there that care about you, and that means if you speak, they will listen. Don't get me wrong, I'm not saying you owe them anything, and they won't demand answers if they really are your friends, but I have a feeling you need them right now, so even if it's only for a minute or two, I really believe seeing them will help you."

I froze. She was right, they did care about me, and all I wanted in the world was for someone to care for me, the way

Mom and Zeke no longer could. I didn't say yes, but I did give a slight nod, and she recognized it as enough. She then turned and gave a similar nod to the officer down the hall and he disappeared for a few minutes. When he returned, there was a cascade of fourteen thru eighteen-year-olds as they jogged toward me with beaming smiles. "Liam!" they all shouted at different intervals followed up by a million questions that primarily focused on what I had been doing, or how I was walking. Seeing them was good, but it was all a bit overwhelming.

Luckily, Coach came to save the day. "Hey! Ladies!" he then turned to Ms. Merlot and some of the female runners and much quieter added, "and, um, ladies," Then, with the whole hallway quiet and frozen, he continued, "What are we?! Savages?! Give the boy some space! He's an outlaw now! Probably knows a hundred different ways to break out of here and kill us with a paperclip or something!"

Everyone laughed at this, including me to a lesser degree. It was refreshing having him crack jokes at me again. "Thanks Coach, but I only do victimless crimes." I smiled and got a few more laughs myself.

"Yeah-yeah-yeah, whatever, now with the tension cut, tell us everything! Spare no detail!" Coach licked his lips in anticipation of a juicy story, but I had to let him down.

"There's not much to say – one minute I was in my hospital bed, the next, nothing, only thing I remember after that was waking up in the middle of nowhere in Mississippi."

The team broke ranks again to blurt out questions: "Mississippi? What's there in Mississippi?" "Amnesia? I thought that was one of those Hollywood myths?" "But dude! You're legs! What about the legs?!"

The corners of my mouth crept upwards again as Coach Bassett tried to restore order a little less successfully than last time. "All right! That's enough! We came, we saw, we run! Back to the bus Ladi…everyone." Ms. Merlot was giving Coach one hell of a stink eye, and it seemed to really affect him.

"Wait!" I said as a few of them began to walk away, "Greg,

can I have a sec?"

Coach looked between us and sighed, "All right, you can have a minute with your boyfriend, but then it's sprints all the way back to the bus, you hear me, Quezada?!"

Ms. Merlot cleared her throat and intensified her stare at Coach, "boyfriend?"

His tough bravado melted into a whimpering pleading look for forgiveness, "Boy, who's a friend...that's all I meant."

Her glare remained unchanged, she was good at that. "And you educate young people?" She stood there, eyes unblinking as he slithered away with the rest of the team, then she stepped back to give Greg and I some privacy.

"Dude! I've missed you," Greg said, unsure if he was allowed to reach through the bars or not.

"I've missed you too, man, you...you would not believe what I've been through."

"Wait, so you mean..." he looked around for eavesdroppers, and then finished in a whisper, "You mean you remember?"

I wanted to tell him, but I couldn't, he'd never believe me, and even if he had, I didn't want to get him mixed up in all of this angel business, so I lied to my best friend, "Only bits and pieces, but it feels more like a crazy dream."

"Damn, well, maybe I can help you make sense of them, you know, when we're roommates," he ended with a strange giddy sound that I think only he could ever manage to produce.

"What do you mean?"

"My mom said if you ever came back, we could take you in, and that was back when she thought...well...the whole chair thing, but that means now, we won't have to get any ramps installed, it's even better!"

"What? Are you serious?" I couldn't believe it, just what I always wanted, I never thought it would've been possible.

"Yeah, and I'm sure you could get caught up on everything at school and come back," he said, still overly gleeful.

"Whoa, hold on now, don't go and ruin it for me by talking about school," It was mostly a joke, but there was a nugget of truth, I really didn't want to go back to school. It was a small price to pay though. "But seriously, all right man, I look forward to getting my life back, even if it's going to be a little different."

Greg's smile slowly faded away, and his eyes found a nice spot on the floor, only occasionally braving to meet mine. "Oh, yeah, before, it all happened so fast, I never got a chance to say…sorry about your mom."

"Thanks, it still hurts, but…I think I'm getting there." We stood in awkward silence for a while, each waiting for the other to say goodbye first. Eventually, I decided to chance it, "Prison goodbye?" I asked, hoping he would know what I meant. I put my hand up between the bars, but not passing through. Greg put his hand up to match mine, leaving a gap as if there were invisible glass. We lowered our hands at the same time.

"Was that as weird for you…?" he began to ask.

"Yeah, let's never speak of this," I said, affirming his suspicion, and then he walked away awkwardly. My back was to the bars as he was leaving, but a high pitched girly yelp startled me and drew my attention back.

"Courtney? You scared the…I mean, um…hi, didn't see you there," Greg said, his face wearing his embarrassment.

Courtney crept around the corner, equally embarrassed by the look of it. "Hey, Greg, um, I'll see you back at the bus," she said, implying that she needed a moment alone with me.

"Oh, yes, of course, you two…I mean, um, coach said sprints, so…yeah…" and Greg took off down the hall sprinting, we heard a few people yell at him to slow down and watch out, but within a few seconds, we couldn't even hear the pounding of his shoes.

"Hey Courtney," I said, not sure how else to respond to her showing up like this.

"Hey Liam," she said, also clearly out of her comfort zone. "It's good to see you, I…we've all been really worried about you."

"Thank you, that means a lot to me, but I…I was okay." For the most part, I had been; it was just recent events that had made me regret ever leaving, before that was actually pretty great, but I wasn't supposed to remember that. "How uh, how have you been though?"

"Good, good, I've been applying for scholarships and such, that's kept me pretty busy, but, well, the reason I wanted to see you before we left, I realized a while back, I never gave you my number."

"Uh…yeah, I, um…" I stammered, not sure how to react. I still had feelings for her, but I had also been growing closer to Angelica back in Seattle, which was so far away now without angel wings to do the heavy lifting. Luckily, my "impossible dilemma" stammering looked exactly like my "nervous around pretty girls" stammer, so she just reached out and handed me a slip of paper.

"So, even if you go vanishing on us again, you'll always be able to text me," she smiled a joking laugh, and I joined her.

"Okay, I promise, I'll text, what's the rule again, three days, or is it five?" I joked back.

"How about as soon as you get out of jail? Ugh, if my dad could see me now." With one last adorable snicker, she raced off to join the rest of the team.

"So, aren't you glad you talked to them?" Ms. Merlot said from the far corner where I had forgotten she disappeared.

"Yeah, I am actually, thank you."

"Don't thank me yet, you are still behind bars after all. Don't worry though, I can get you out of here in no time, then I'll draw up the paperwork for Mr. and Mrs. Quezada, and you'll be moved in before bed, how does that sound?"

"That sounds amazing, I really can't thank you enough Ms. Merlot." The warm fuzzy feeling was returning, and this time, it was settling in for the long haul.

"I need to see to your release, so how about you just promise not to disappear without a trace this time? That will be all the thanks I need."

I laughed, that wasn't likely to happen anymore, "Definitely, I promise, not going anywhere this time."

She whistled a pleasant tune as she left, so I closed my eyes and hummed along.

"Holy Hell, you get way too many visitors."

"Zeke?!" My eyes shot open, and out of the concrete wall materialized a wonderfully familiar sight for sore eyes.

"I thought they'd never leave, look at me, I'm falling apart here." He jokingly complained as he peeled off a chunk of forearm and slapped it to the ground.

"You're alive?! But…"

"It's a long story, but I'll explain on the way, if you'll have me back?"

"Of course, yes! Yes! Come on in," I went for a hug, and as I did, he joined with me again, making the warm fuzzy feeling double, filling in the hole he had left behind.

Ah! It's good to be back, fits like a glove.

"It's good to have you back. I missed you so much, you don't even know."

Easy with the emotions there, killer, I get the idea, now calm down before I start crying. But before we go, I heard what your friends all said, I'm totally cool with it if you want to stay, get your old life back.

I thought on it for a second, but then memories from Zeke began to overflow and saturate my mind, memories of the last few days, how he survived, how he lost Gavin and Natara, how he had the perfect way to get back at Foxy. I wasn't going to miss that chance for payback, not for anything. "I wanna come, I need to see this through with you, but…when it's over, yeah, I'd like to stay in touch." I looked down at the paper with the phone number on it and stuffed it in my pocket.

Oh, I see, I won't tell Angelica if you don't, wink-wink.

"Did you just say, *wink-wink?*" I questioned, ignoring the more serious problem of liking two different girls in two different time zones.

I can't wink in here, I have to say it, duh. Eye roll.

"Whatever, let's just go."

All right, you ready to break out of prison?

"Oh, that's a good point…Well, the social services lady said she's…oh," I remembered the last thing I promised her, "Oh, she is going to be *so* pissed, yeah, let's just go now."

Zeke laughed, a laugh I had almost forgotten the sound of

until now. *I like where your minds at. All right, hold on!*

CHAPTER SIXTEEN: FIGHT FIRE WITHOUT FIRE

"Woo! It feels good to fly again!" Liam shouted. as we raced across the Pacific.

Yeah, I'm sure it's great, but when we land, I have a favor to ask you.

"What is it?! Why don't you just ask me…!" before Liam could finish screaming his question over the rushing wind, I landed and we abruptly stopped. "…now…" he finished anyway.

All right, now I'm going to need your help taking down Foxy, I have a pla—

"Yeah, I know, I kinda already saw the whole thing, you really need to get a lock down on your memories," he said in a way that sounded a little pompous for someone who constantly failed to do the same with his emotions, but this wasn't the time to start arguing again.

Right, ok, well, for this to work, I'm going to need to take control, I immediately panicked, fearing he would associate it with the feelings of being trapped under Foxy's control, so I continued to spurt out a series of assurances. *It will only be for a little while.*

"Zeke…"

I promise I'll hand the reins right back over after it's done.

"Hey…"

I can't imagine what Foxy put you through, but I promise I…

"Zeke!" Liam finally called out loud enough to jolt me out of my downward apologetic spiral. "It's ok, you can drive this one, I trust you."

I felt him relax and just as I had done before with Natara, I worked my way in until Liam's body responded to my commands. "I…I'm sorry Liam," I said out loud through his own mouth.

You're sorry? You have nothing to be sorry about, I was the one who…I…I betrayed you. If Liam had still been in control, I'm sure he would've fallen to his knees he sounded so helplessly remorseful. *I watched you die. I killed you.* With that, I could no longer keep his tidal wave of emotion back and succumbed to them, falling to my knees just as I had predicted.

"Liam…I…" I didn't know how to answer. For so long I had blamed myself for everything that had happened to him, but now it seemed he had felt even worse than I had. "Liam, I don't blame you, Foxy played you, she lied to you, highlighted my faults, used the mistrust both of us had, it wasn't your fault."

It was though! he yelled, refusing my consoling. *You told me on that mountain! You told me not to trust her! I didn't listen, and now… now I've killed…those hosts, I burned them to ashes, just innocent people caught up in something they didn't even understand, and…and…your brother, your other host, you survived, but…they're gone now, forever, and that's all my fault…*

"No Liam, it wasn't your fault. I led Gavin and the others info that fight, but you know what, it wasn't my fault they died either, I've been beating myself up about that ever since it happened, but not anymore, Foxy killed them. Foxy killed Xaf, she killed…she killed your mother, and she killed those people in the quarry. She's the one responsible for all of it, and she's going to continue hunting my family, and anyone else that gets in her way, but we can stop her here today."

"You're bloody well right we can!" an Australian voice called out from somewhere over my right shoulder, and I turned to face its direction. "G'day, mate! How ya going?" the tall blonde-haired man said with a cheeky smile.

"Zak?" I asked, because even though I knew it was him in that host, I had never heard him do a convincing Australian accent like that before.

"Dan Kelly's the name, and huntin's my game. Your brothah here tells me we're after an angel today," he rubbed his hands together in anticipation.

"Don't worry Zeke," Zak's voice said from inside his host, "Dan's going to be much more capable than I ever could be, I'll be flying shotgun on this one."

Hey, that's not fair, why does his host get to fight and I have to be stuck in here watching? Liam pouted at this new development. *And how can I do that? The whole "talking out loud" thing?*

"Hold on," I said to Zak/Dan with an outstretched finger as

I took a quick sidebar with Liam. "Look, I didn't know about this either, but…I mean…look at him," Dan was incredibly fit looking and his jawline looked sharp enough to cut rocks in half. "And you can't talk out loud like we can, sorry, you're just going to have to wait until we're done if you want to say anything."

He…he doesn't look so tough, I could take him, Liam said, sounding unsure but trying to act tough.

"Who are you trying to impress? I'm the only one that can hear you," I reminded him.

No one, shut up! Liam squeaked. *Don't we have work to do?*

I couldn't help but laugh as I turned back to the duo still waiting easily within earshot of everything on my end. "Sorry, it's good to meet you Dan, I'm Zeke, and this," I said pointing to our shared face, "is Liam Cole, but that introduction will have to wait. Has Zak filled you in on everything?"

Dan pointed to his temple, "As if I'd been in the room myself, 'ell of a thing, right?"

"Good, are you ready to go then?"

"I was born ready, mate," he said with another big grin, and then, with a little help from Zak, took off and flew high into the sky. "Criiiiiikeeeeey!" he yelled gleefully, as he disappeared into the sky.

Does he actually enjoy that? What kind of monster…?

I flew after them but couldn't let Liam's comment go unanswered, even if it meant screaming over the rushing torrent of air, "I seem to remember you enjoying the ride a minute ago!"

That…that was different, it was more nostalgia than anything, and it took me months to get through it without yakking. But wait a second, it's not that bad back here, it's kinda smooth actually, I should let you fly up front more often. Now, how would you put it? Kicks legs up. He gave a relaxing sigh and a little laugh, pleased with himself.

"Ha ha!" I said, clearly fake, "We're here!" I slammed into the ground of the quarry, the same spot I had lost Natara. "Zak, or Dan, whatever, are you…?"

I looked over to find Dan vomiting on the inner wall, using

it to brace himself. *Yes! Ha! Told you! He is insane!*

"Fully sick, mate!" he shouted as he turned back and wiped his mouth with his wrist. "We gotta do that more often."

"Are you sure he's up for this Zak?" I asked, questioning this host's sanity just as much as Liam seemed to.

"He's fine, trust me, it's going to take more than a little nausea to stop him," Zak said reassuringly.

"Bloody right it will! Now, let's dig, shall we?" Dan pulled out a collapsible military-grade shovel from a leather holster behind his back and snapped it open. "Sorry, mate, only got the one."

I watched as he stabbed it into the ground where I had been less than a week prior; the image of him with the shovel brought back flashbacks of Foxy swinging the flaming sword down toward me. I had to turn my back and try thinking of something else, anything else, but it was difficult.

*I know...*Liam said softly. *I feel it too, being back here...it's not easy, is it?*

"No, no it's not, but it won't be for long."

This is going to work, right? I don't want...I don't want to watch anyone else die.

"No one else is going to die, this is going to work, I know it will. Then, how about we take a vacation?" I laughed, making a stab at the meaningless topic that had helped divide us before.

I don't know about that, I work in Washington, and go to school in New Mexico, the commute's going to be a mess, not sure if there's time for a vacation.

"Good point, I'll drive though, that should help. But I'm serious, it doesn't have to be anything big, I just want one day, one calm, relaxing day, I...I owe it to a friend..."

Ok, sure, we can do that, no problem.

"Oi!" Dan called out, "Tag out, mate!" he said, holding out the shovel over a half-dug hole.

We finished digging the rest of the hole and took one last breather before hitting the point of no return.

"You're not worried?" Dan asked, directed at all three of us, "I mean, from what I hear, this chick's pretty dangerous. I mean, I'm not worried, I've tangled with far worse, but you, Zeke, right? You've hardly limped away from her going on twice now, you really think third time's the charm here?"

I really didn't want to be reminded of my previous failures, but maybe it was better to dwell on them now, as opposed to in the thick of it and allowing it to be something Foxy could use against me. The first time, I was caught off guard, but Eve had been able to manage her easily. The second time, I was able to take her down, but couldn't deliver the final blow. This time, she didn't have Liam, and while Zak was no guardian, his help combined with Dan's experience was bound to be much more valuable than what the Muses had offered, so the only worry was whether Foxy would stand and fight, or run scared. If she was smart, she would run back upstairs where we could never reach her, but I knew she would never go for that, because she had given us that same ultimatum, and here we were, just as dumb as ever.

Um, Zeke, I think he was talking to you, Liam interjected, pulling me out of my own thoughts.

"What? I know that. Oh, sorry, yeah, this is going to work. I beat her before, so with your help, our little care packages on their way, and Liam here safe, we've got this…moderately easily…" I added, just being realistic.

"Right, just make sure to keep your head in the game, but let's get this show on the road, shall we?" Dan asked, itching for something more exciting than digging half of a hole.

"I'm ready when Zak is, this whole thing hinges on him after all," I said, a joking level of impatience in my voice.

"Hey, I'll call her when you're in position, let's go now, out of sight," Zak retorted back. We both laughed and turned away to take our respective places. I hopped down into the freshly dug hole and crouched low enough my head was below the surface level. Dan dragged over a flat sheet of woven tree branches he had whipped up frighteningly fast, and laid it overtop of me, like some sort of bizarre reverse pit trap. I was actually grateful for Dan knowing how to do that, because without him I would've been hiding in that gross green cesspool.

My view from below the branches was limited, but Dan began circling my hiding spot while Zak silently reached out and attempted to communicate with Foxy. As an Enochian, he would be able to reach out to her virtually anywhere, but she would similarly be able to talk back without ever having to show her face. The success or failure of our entire strategy hinged on Zak's baiting skill. I wished I could hear what he was saying to her.

I wonder what he's saying to her, Liam said, as if verbalizing my own thoughts. *You know him, what do you think? Yo' momma jokes? Attacking her personal hygiene? Telling her where she can shove that glorified fire poker? Hey, speaking of which, do angels even have as...*

I didn't want to risk talking out loud, so I simply silenced Liam with a symbolic finger against my lips and a very low "shh…" A part of me felt like he was completely justified in his annoying questions, paying me back for my usual antics when the tables were turned, but another part, a much larger part, couldn't wait to go back to normal and pay him back tenfold.

"Forfax!" Zak shouted, alerting us to her presence. "Come to shut me up, have you?"

Wow, that was fast, I guess you rubbed off on him more than I would've guessed. I had to agree with Liam, I'm not sure I would've been able to do much better, and I'm notoriously annoying.

"What is wrong with you people?!" Foxy shouted with flustered rage.

"'You people?'" Dan asked, his accent a strong contrast to Zak's.

"Silence mortal! My quarrel is with the decrepit parasite within you, your death will be no more than a side effect. Zadkiel! Are you ready to die?" I saw red light penetrate through the branches overhead, indicating the sword had been drawn. "Wait, you're not alone…" she said, a tinge of worry in her voice. "Do you really think you can lay a trap for me twice? In the same place no less? You fools really do deserve to go extinct. Come out!"

This possibility had been expected, but Foxy didn't need to know that. I grabbed the lid over my head and shoved it over to the side slowly. "All right! You got me," I said with a smirk as my eyes met hers.

Disbelief overwhelmed her, "What? This isn't possible, I... I..."

"Killed me? I know, crazy, right? I hope you kept the receipt for that thing," I gestured to the sword which was no longer raised but just dangling by her side. "Because I think it might be defective."

"I...no! I don't know how you're still alive, but you won't escape my grasp a third time! And don't think that host will save you, orders or not, you will die this day! Release your hosts if you wish them to live, or don't, I really don't care!" Foxy gripped the sword in both hands and held it high above her head, massive red flames exploding out of it, filling in the gap between her bright blue burning wings, turning the entire section of sky around her into a wall of fire, some sort of intimidation technique perhaps? If so, it didn't work. "Fall before the mighty power of my flaming sword!" she shouted, as if we didn't clearly see the sword she was trying to show off, but I knew that this was the cue for Zak to reach out and tell Lucy to send the package.

I prayed that my timing wouldn't be off and make me look stupid. "That's not a sword..." I said...but then nothing happened. "Zak...?" I asked, trying not to move until I could deliver the punchline.

"Oh, crap, sorry!" he said nervously. After a few awkwardly silent seconds, a flash of light erupted from the bottom of the freshly dug hole, and a large circular block of ice popped out in front of Dan. As he grabbed it, another flash produced a long thin blade of ice in front of me and I snatched the hilt. "*That's* a sword," My offensive attempt at an Australian accent made Dan glance sideways at me.

"If you had just asked, I would've said it for you, you Yank," Dan said, slightly more understanding than I would've guessed.

J. A. Reed

"But I have the sword, you have the shield, it wouldn't have made sense if you said it," I argued, but my eyes remained locked on Foxy, waiting for her to either fight or flee.

"What happened to keeping heads in the game? Lucifer's never-melt ice is strong, but we still don't know how long it'll hold up against that sword," Zak chimed in as a voice of reason.

"Well, only one way to find out, mate." Dan, ignoring reason, lunged upward with the power of Zak's wings and shield bashed Foxy hard across the face. "Crikey! She was supposed to block that, oh well, if at first you don't succeed," Foxy tumbled in the air a few revolutions before shaking off the hit, and when Dan lunged a second time, she was ready. She slashed, but he was able to deflect the blade with the shield and follow it up with a swift kick to the gut, sending her flying again. He used that time to examine the damage done. "It'll hold, but not forever!" he called back to me, still where I had started. "Now, what say we tag-team this one, mate?"

Zak wasn't kidding, this guy really knows how to handle himself, Liam said in awe.

"Wouldn't miss this super-powered beat-down for anything Aussie, just make sure to save some for me." I launched after Foxy and slashed at her, but she parried and our swords remained locked as neither one of us gave up any ground. The licking flames slowly etched away the outer layer of ice, turning it immediately to boiling steam between us. With my weapon integrity in jeopardy, I reluctantly pulled back and regrouped with Dan. "All right, brute force won't do the trick, time for a little finesse, what do you say we change up the scenery a bit?"

"I know just the place," Dan said with a grin, "And I'll stick with brute force, it's working for me." Dan went on the offensive again, but after his first attack missed, he had to resort to hiding behind the shield as slash marks turned its surface into a maze of tiny rivers running water down to the lowest point where a steady drip began to fall.

I circled around while her focus was on him, and swung for her leg, but she saw me coming and dodged. The momentary distraction was enough for Dan to escape her pursuit and tactfully retreat. Foxy took the bait and chased after him at full speed, but her energized wings made her much faster, enabling her to catch up with him over Africa. I raced to catch up but wasn't gaining any ground. All I could do was watch the aerial battle from a distant third position.

Dan blocked and bashed while going at top speed, but Foxy was able to maneuver herself all around him, changing up the angles of her attack trying to get past his guard, but his defense was seemingly impregnable. *His shield can't take that assault much longer, what's he thinking?* Liam asked in a panic.

"Dan!" I shouted, trying to get his attention so he would slow down enough for me to catch up, but we were moving too fast, the sound couldn't carry far enough. When we reached the Australian outback, he finally landed and I was able to catch up. "Dan!" I shouted again, now that he could hear. "We're supposed to stick together, remember?" I dove in front of him and took a hit with the side of my blade, saving what little remained of his ice shield.

"Don't sweat it, mate, we've got home field advantage now," he said as I blocked more of Foxy's attacks and he was free to catch his breath behind me.

"Our weapons are made, ugh! Of ice you moron! It's hotter, hmph! Than Hell here!" I said as I fought Foxy's enraged onslaught.

"Oh, that's a good point, my bad, mate." He jumped back in and split the job of blocking, making it much easier on both of us. "I'll just follow your lead then, yeah?"

I waited for Dan to connect a strike and stun Foxy. "Now! This way!" I yelled and we both took off simultaneously heading north.

"You're not getting away from me again!" Foxy yelled as she sped to catch up with us, but this time with both of us flying in tight formation, she had trouble attacking despite her superior speed. "Those won't protect you forever!" she shouted as more and more pieces of shield fell away. My sword was beginning to chip as well, but Dan's shield had been taking the brunt of the damage, so he was the one in the most danger.

We landed less than gracefully on one of the frozen chunks of rock in Alaska's archipelago, where I hoped the cold would help our ice weapons survive at least a few extra clashes with Foxy's flaming sword. "All right, so, we've managed to not die, not sure how much longer we can continue saying that, mate. Any ideas?" Dan asked as the two of us stood side by side resting as best we could while Foxy did the same no more than twenty feet in front of us.

"I…I guess I could stab her, I don't know." I said, breathing heavily.

"Will that kill her?" he asked, genuinely curious.

"Um, it definitely won't, but it could slow her down."

"Crikey! Slow her down? Really?" Dan sighed, severely disappointed in my answer.

"Haven't you ever seen The Holy Grail? That could work nicely," I said, half joking, but half considering it a possible option B.

"Enough of this," Foxy said, her eyes igniting into a sapphire blaze. She flicked the sword around and stabbed it halfway down into the ground, causing red-hot flames to erupt from the new hole in the permafrost and subsequent cracks that traced their way outward from that point. Her wings shot up into the air and added to the inferno as the ground shook and the whole island began to melt.

Stop her! Liam shouted. With her hands still on the buried sword, I took my chance and thrusted my blade at her, but with one flick of her wing, she batted it away and out of my grip. Defenseless, she swept at me with her other wing, which could burn away Liam just as easily as she had done with the other hosts back Mississippi. Just when I thought the fiery feathers were going to reduce Liam to ashes, Dan jumped between us and took the blow himself. *No!*

I got knocked back, landing only a few feet away from my ice sword. It was dangerously close to a fissure in the ground, the spewing flames making it sweat, but there was a much more pressing matter. "Dan?! Dan!"

"Oi…" I heard, but it sounded weak. I looked toward the sound and found a smoldering heap on the floor moving slightly. "Shield's gone, mate, sorry."

I sighed a huge relief, I had thought he was gone, but the wet shards of ice melting into tiny puddles around him confirmed the shield had taken the blow and saved his life. "Zak! Get him out of here!" I called as I raised to my feet.

"Good idea, mate, I'm buggered, you can drive here on out." Dan passed out, but his head shook awake a moment later as Zak took over control.

Zak jumped up, "Zeke! Get the sword!"

I turned back to where I had seen it, and more cracks were etching their way through the earth toward it, causing a pool to form underneath it. I flew low along the ground at full speed and snatched it up, pulling straight up afterwards to get as high away from the flames as possible. "I got it, now go!"

"I'm not leaving you!" Zak shouted back, as he flew up to join me. "We're in this together."

"You don't have anything to defend yourself with, just go, there's a fracture nearby, I'll meet you on the other side." He looked at me defiantly, but knew it was for the best.

"I'll see you there, don't be late." Zak sped away with Dan's body and vanished further down the tail of islands.

"Cowards, all of you!" Foxy yelled as she pulled the sword out of the ground, putting an end to the firestorm. "What about you, are you going to run, or are you going to use that thing?" She gestured to the thin slice of ice that used to be a respectable sword. I grabbed the blade in both hands and concentrated, rebuilding it with my own never-melt ice. It filled back out, but my ice was nowhere near as strong as Lucy's, so for all I knew, Foxy's sword might be able to slice clean through it. Regardless, I wasn't going to run this time, and I made sure she knew that. "That's more like it," she said with a sinister grin.

I taunted her, trying to keep the fight in the air where her wings would be less effective weapons. She lunged at me, and I blocked her attack carefully, keeping an eye on the state of my weakened sword. It survived the block, but much more of it melted away than before, giving me probably a quarter of the durability I had begun with. It would have to be enough.

I continued to gloat her as I flew half-speed in the direction of Seattle. "C'mon! Mighty righteous angel such as yourself, why can't you kill one little ol' fallen? Huh?"

She screamed and shouted insults as she desperately tried to land a killing blow, but with a weapon capable of surviving more than one hit, I was managing much better than our last duel. I was beginning to get tired, but so was she, all I had to do was make sure my sword lasted long enough for me to reach my destination.

"Why are you so upset anyway?" I asked when she lessened her assault to catch her breath a bit. "Daddy didn't love you enough? Because if that's it, it's not good enough, we all have that baggage."

"You wouldn't understand my reasoning, Father's will is above your comprehension!" she shouted angrily, followed by a few more fruitless strikes.

"But you're just an Enochian, so my comprehension should be a little better than yours, are you sure you didn't miss interpret something?" The more I spoke, the more pissed off she became, which helped keep her off balance, and it was entertaining to me, which helped keep me on balance, a real win-win.

"This sword was given to me straight from the hand of Gabriel, the messenger of God himself, there is no doubt in the divinity of my mission!" I may have made a mistake. Foxy found her second wind behind the conviction of her words, and it granted her a level of strength she hadn't possessed thus far. Foxy's rejuvenation combined with my own shock of the possibility that our execution could have actually been an order given from the top of the divine hierarchy caused me to lose the upper hand, resorting to desperate blocking that was more flinching than anything resembling skill.

I had almost reached my destination, but if I turned to run, I would ruin everything, I had to keep all of her attention on me, but that was also the biggest problem. "Foxy," I asked as one large beat of my wings pulled me backwards, missing the tip of her sword by centimeters. "Wait, let's just talk about this," I desperately wanted to go back to her sloppy angry, not this new empowered rage. "Gabriel, he, I mean…" Foxy cut me off with a massive downward slash that I had to block with both hands, one on the hilt, the other bracing the upper portion of the blade, not that it mattered too much though, the power behind her attach pushed me down a hundred feet. As we fell, I had time to finish my thought, but I had only ever seen Gabriel a handful of times, so I wasn't sure how to. He, along with most of the Archangels back before the Fall, never liked to interact with us lesser angels, so I had virtually zero ammo to use against him.

Foxy continued to push all of her strength downward as I did everything I could to keep my block at arm's length, but my elbows were shaking under the strain. We were falling at an alarming rate toward the Earth, despite my crispy wings trying with all their might to keep us above the clouds.

As we reached closer to the lowest cloud below us, I noticed the extended clash of fire and ice had resulted in her sword buried more than halfway through my own. I knew I needed to do something soon or she would break through and continue on through me, so as soon as the mist engulfed us, I pulled hard on the hilt while simultaneously pushing the tip of my blade as far as my reach would allow. With her sword stuck in mine, this caused her to get pulled along with it until I was the one with the metaphorical high ground.

My blade finally succumbed to its wound and broke along the grove the flaming sword had started. The top half of the sharpened ice tumbled through the air at a slower rate than our fall, making it appear to fly upward and disappear into the cloud. With only a hilt and less than a foot of blade left, I couldn't block another attack like the last one, so I just went for the offense. I straightened my body with the remains of my sword outstretched in front of me and freefell straight down, plunging the flat broken edge into Foxy's abdomen. I was not

256

expecting her to smile about that. Apparently never-melt ice swords don't hurt angels, noted.

Foxy used her free left hand to grab my right, preventing me from pulling the sword out, and raised the sword for a final blow that I wouldn't be able to block or escape from. I acted on pure survival instinct, grabbing her wrist to ensure the sword stay as far away from my vital parts as possible, at least for a little while longer. We struggled as the ground grew closer and closer by the second, her desperately trying to kill me, and me simply trying to live long enough to crash.

Another smile worried me. Foxy stopped flapping her wings to resist the plummet, but instead stretched them out and allowed the whipping air to drag them by, encasing us both in a cocoon of blue fire. Just one good strike from those and Liam would be toast, but luckily, my sword was still securely embedded in her gut, with just slight movements of my wrist I was able to control her movements, like my very own rudder. I forced a head over heels tumble, keeping the wings to our sides and making it too disorienting for her to strike at us so close inside her reach. The only down side was it made me equally discombobulated, so whenever we would eventually impact the earth, it was a roll of the dice to see who ended up on top, and who would be crushed.

Foxy gave up her attempt to burn Liam away and pulled her wings back, revealing a swirling world of alternating brown and blue. I pulled back with my wrist, halting the tumble just in time to make sure she was the one to be crushed upon impact, but even on top I didn't fare well myself. I bounced hard, getting at least ten feet off the ground the first time, probably about five feet up after a second bounce, but then just tumbled along the rough, dry dirt for a hundred yards crashing through thick sagebrush all along the way. When I eventually slid to a halt, I just laid there motionless.

*Ow...*Liam groaned painfully.

"H-hurts a lot more in the front seat..." I replied in the same tone.

Where's Foxy?

"Not dead, sadly." It took me a minute, but I eventually grunted and groaned my way to a slouched seating position and looked back along the trail of busted bushes and agitated dust, trying to make out any sign of Foxy. "I don't see her, maybe she got knocked out."

Maybe she ran, if she realizes where we are..."

"She won't run, she's too pissed to run, let's..." I readied my hand and prepared myself for the agonizing pain that would result from standing, but before I could even move my legs, blue flashes of light ignited in the distance like a shimmering mirage. "Damn it."

Are we in position? Liam asked, slightly panicked.

I looked around quickly, "Yeah, as good as anywhere else." Foxy flew over, looking unscathed from the impact and landed right in front of me, wind blowing steadily from directly behind her kicking dirt and dust over me. "You've got something, right there," I said, gesturing to my own stomach for my joke, but regretting the movement it took.

Foxy pulled the broken hilt out as painlessly as it had gone in and tossed it over her shoulder, burning it to vapor with her wing. "Did I get it?" she asked smugly, as if that would make me stop joking in my final moments.

I laughed, but even that hurt. "Yeah, yeah, you got it. But can I just ask for one thing? One last thing before you finish me off?" Her face was straight, but I could tell she was debating hearing me out or just finishing it quickly. A slight nod was her only indication of the answer. "Could you take like two steps to your left?"

"I should've known, even in the face of death, you're still just as immature as ever. I think I'm going to enjoy killing you more than any..." The broken tip of my ice sword clattered to the ground about two steps to Foxy's left. She looked at it, up at the cloud that had blown over head, and then back at me. "Really?"

"Um..." I said, not sure how else to react.

Foxy took the two steps and picked up the blade shard. "Did you really think that was going to work? After everything, why did you think this would even hurt me?"

"No, I had no idea, I'm just as surprised as you," I said honestly; it was a hilarious coincidence, but not at all why I asked her to take those two steps. "But thanks for taking those steps like I asked, I really appreciate it." I reached over and plunged my hand into the fracture to my right, her left, and parted it open, "Now!"

"What?" Foxy said, completely caught off guard. She dropped the ice, but before it could even hit the hot New Mexican sand, the massive fracture flew open and seven different arms reached through and latched onto Foxy. I pushed through the pain to jump up and grab the sword from her as she panicked and desperately tried to break free from the grip of Tabby, Trini, Megatron, Zak, Satchel, Nate, and even Cass, all of the fallen angels that were capable of passing through the large fracture. "No! Let...go! No!" Foxy cried as she squirmed and struggled, but she wasn't strong enough to break free from such an overwhelming onslaught.

I stood back, watching her struggle as I held the flaming sword in my hand once again. She didn't have Liam this time, she didn't have any host, so there was nothing stopping me from using it if I wanted to. I held it up to her.

When she saw it, she stopped pulling away from the arms as hard, but there was an apparent internal struggle as to which outcome would be less miserable, neither option had appeal. "Please," she begged looking at me, "Please, just kill me."

"I would like nothing more, trust me." I raised the sword, as if to strike, and I saw relief in her eyes. I couldn't have that, now could I? I quickly lowered it and rubbed my chin. "Although, I'm not a monster, I can't kill family, and besides, these guys are a hell of a lot more pissed at you than I am, I think I'll let them decide what to do with you."

"No! Please! Anything but that!" she screamed in a blood curdling screech. Zak and the others finally pulled her through the fracture, and as she passed the plane, her brilliant blue wings flared up with black smoke and extinguished, leaving burnt, crisp, boney remains in their place.

"Enjoy the family reunion, Forfax!" I yelled as it sealed up behind her. I held up her sword and looked it over in my hand, a symbol of the victory that day.

"What happened to 'Foxy'?" Zak said as he emerged from the fracture, the screams of the aforementioned cutting in and out as he passed through.

"She's not good enough for a nickname," I stated plainly, "Dan awake yet?"

"Yeah, I dropped him off at home before heading here, he'll be okay, I told you he was good though, didn't I?"

"A little headstrong, but yeah, I think he'll balance you out just fine, are you going to keep him?"

Zak laughed, "He's not a dog, but yeah, he's willing to put up with me, so I think he'll be sticking around for a while."

I looked at the sword one last time, and then held it out to Zak. "You'd better get this to Lucy, she'll know what to do with it, and you're starting to blister, just so you know."

Zak took it carefully, "Yeah, I'll make sure she gets it. What about you, don't want to pop down for a bit, see how long Forfax keeps screaming before she breaks?"

"No, sounds fun, but no thanks, we're pretty busted up, think I'll just get us home and heal."

I don't want to get out of bed for a week, speaking of, you fly, I think I need to pass out now.

I laughed a bit and looked away from Zak so he would know I wasn't speaking to him. "All right Liam, sounds good. And it's good to have you back, if I haven't said that already."

It's good to be back, and thank you, Foxy, or Forfax I mean, thank you for stopping her, it means a lot to me.

"It was my pleasure buddy, she'll pay for what she did, now get some rest, you've earned it." I waited for him to pass out before turning back to Zak, "I mean, I did all the work, but yeah, sure, good job."

Zak laughed again, "You're ridiculous, I'll see you around, brother."

He disappeared back down, and Forfax was still screaming, which put a smile on my face. We had won, and she had gotten what she deserved, she became what she hated, Forfax was now a fallen angel, just like us, but unlike us, she wouldn't be free to roam or cross back over. Hell for her would be what it had been meant to be for us, a prison, a punishment for her crimes. I almost felt sorry for her. Almost.

CHAPTER SEVENTEEN: A NORMAL DAY

*BEEP! BEEP! BEE…*My thumb slid the large red X on my phone screen to silence the alarm and sleepily with one eye open, I checked the time display to see it read *8:00.* I tossed the phone back down on the bed and rolled onto my back to stare up at the ceiling, watching the fan blades overhead as they rotated slowly cutting through the tiny specks of dust in the air only visible within the beams of morning sunlight that made it inside through the gaps in the blinds.

I rubbed the sleep from the corners of my eyes and then stretched my entire body in the most amazing way possible, groaning louder than necessary and yawning for a good twenty seconds leading into every muscle relaxing simultaneously and staring straight up once again. I watched the fan spin another ten slow revolutions before swinging my legs over and placing my feet on the warm carpet. Still seated, I reached out for a bottle of water on the nightstand and gulped down three quarters in one go before halting for a breath, but finished the rest shortly thereafter.

I made my way to the bathroom, yawning again along the way and closed the door behind me. I turned the hot water handle over the sink and touched the water between two fingers to test its temperature, but it was still cold, so I side stepped over to the toilet, lifted the seat, and emptied my bladder as I waited, the sound of the flowing liquid aiding me in accomplishing the same. After one of us ran out, I returned to the sink and washed my hands under the now scalding water. I turned it down and dried my hands, pausing afterward as I locked eyes with the reflection staring back at me. While time had only aged my face half a year, I didn't recognize the person staring back at me, but it wasn't anything physical. I still had the same dark blue eyes, the same light brown hair just as messy and unkempt as ever, at least when it was this early in the morning, and my tan had lessened from my time in the Pacific Northwest, but there was something intangible that had turned the teenager I used to be, into the man I saw today.

J. A. Reed

I grabbed the corner of the mirror and pulled it out of the way revealing my toothbrush, tooth paste, and various other hygiene supplies. I twisted the hot water back on and carried on by brushing my teeth, and when that had been accomplished, I undressed and made my way into the shower. I made sure to wash and scrub all the important areas, but I took my sweet time, performing a mini concert thanks to the amazing acoustics, and only called it quits when the hot water started running low.

I toweled off, made my way back to my room, threw on a clean set of clothes, pulled my phone off the charger, and headed out the door. A quick trip up north brought me to my favorite breakfast joint, where I was able to jump the line for tables by grabbing a counter seat and ordered the usual. As I waited for my waffles, sausage, eggs, and hash browns to arrive, I got caught up on my social media feeds, checking to see what all of my friends and acquaintances had been up to since I last checked up on them. I checked on the news and politics, one bite-size snippet at a time, but spent most of the time laughing quietly at pictures and videos that held no real substance.

The server delivered my meal and I lowered my phone to thank her with a smile. The waffle was a little undercooked for my liking, but I didn't let that take away from the overall deliciousness of it all. My plate was clean in a matter of minutes, and I flagged down my server with a finger and mouthing the words 'check please.'

I struck up a conversation with an older married couple sitting beside me as I waited, telling them about how much I loved coming in for breakfast, and they told me about the daughter they were visiting in the area. After I paid and started saying goodbye to them, the woman started asking questions about my relationship status, which I answered hesitantly until I found out she wanted to set me up with said daughter. Her husband began dismissing her, telling her to "leave the poor boy alone," and I laughed at how they were the embodiment of a bickering old married couple. I thanked them for the offer and good conversation and excused myself as they carried on their argument, three tangents from where it had begun by the time I left earshot.

Another quick trip back south and I met up with Greg. He asked where I had disappeared to, but I answered vaguely enough to satisfy his curiosity for now. We spent the next hour catching up on recent events at school and reminiscing as we packed up his mom's car with all of his hiking gear, tossing in his dad's old stuff for me since I was short on personal items in that state, and then hit the road for our favorite trail. Along the way we made a stop in a small neighborhood slightly out of the way to swing by the address in my GPS. When we pulled up a quick text was all it took for Courtney and one of her red-headed female friends to struggle through the front door carrying equipment of their own. I hopped out immediately, but was only able to meet them halfway and provide an extra hand, at which point it didn't matter beyond the thought that counted. Courtney hugged me, one of those lingering hugs that borders on the thin line between friendship and something more, and then introduced her friend to mine. I caught a glimpse of her father eyeballing me from the living room window, his arms crossed over his chest and a grimace that only intensified under his thick mustache. I quivered a bit and instinctually took a step further away from his daughter until we were in the car.

The rest of the trip didn't see a minute of silence between all of the conversations, Caraoke, and a ton of laughter, which all helped the hour drive pass by like a breeze, and it was especially nice sitting in the back with Courtney. As the drive went on our body language went from hesitant and holding back to expressive and comfortable. Occasionally I would catch a glance from Greg in the rear-view mirror watching us together and as soon as he would catch me noticing, he'd grin at me embarrassingly.

We parked the car and geared up for the hike, still equally as chatty and boisterous as we had been in the car. Courtney pulled me aside first chance we were alone and told me her friend liked Greg, and that she wanted to give them some space, and I confessed I was perfectly fine keeping her company. She laughed nervously, enjoying my charming intentions. The rest of the hike took a slightly more serious turn, our topics of discussion shifting from casual safe subjects to deep, real issues such as family life, future goals, philosophical debates, and only periodically the random funny story to keep the mood light and entertaining. We would hear snippets of conversation from Greg and Courtney's friend, most notable of which was catching her name, Katherine, which I hadn't known until that point, and we had created a whole side conversation about whether Greg's insistent talking about video games was going to ruin things for him, or if things would work out for them in spite of it all.

We reached the waterfall slower than most of the times Greg and I had gone alone, but neither of us would complain about the extra time we got to spend with Katherine and Courtney respectively. We ditched all of our gear into a heap, only pulling out the collapsible chairs and picnic lunch we had brought. We sat back to eat, relax, and engage in more conversation between all four of us, but as soon as Greg scarfed down his portion, he eagerly pestered us all to go swimming in the medium-sized pool at the waterfall's feet. He stripped down to his board shorts before any of us could finish eating, but his constant begging put a spring in our steps to join in the fun sooner rather than later.

The water was cold, but after plunging in for the initial shock it became rather refreshing. We swam around for hours, splashing water at each other, chicken fighting, and all of the other fun that could be expected; Greg even tried to start a round of Marco Polo, but instead we all ganged up on him and dunked him under while his eyes were closed. When joking about climbing all the way up the waterfall and jumping off came around, I was the only one brave enough to actually do it, but in my defense, I was the only one with someone looking out for me. Courtney was a little worried that I would get hurt, it was sweet of her.

After we tired of swimming we took some time to air dry

and started a small fire to help it along and keep us warm as the sun grew lower in the sky. I convinced Courtney to climb back to the top of the waterfall with me, assuring her that the view would be worth it, and that I wouldn't push her off; the latter required repeating every ten seconds, and my laughter didn't do much to lessen that frequency. We reached the top and saw green trees, brown mountains with white tips, and a sky that was beginning to make the shift from cool blues to warm reds and oranges. Courtney told me she wished we could stay and watch the sunset, but none of us wanted to make the hike back in the dark. I told her we should come back someday, just the two of us, and camp for the night. She kissed me before I could lean in first. It was amazing, but a part of me wished it had just been the two of us up there, that for just that moment I *didn't* have someone looking out for me.

The drive home had been much more laid back than the first trip. Courtney leaned her body against mine, and I wrapped my arms around her as she fell asleep. I stayed awake, staring out the window as the sky quickly darkened and the stars and moon failed to light up the surrounding wilderness. I replayed the day in my head over and over again, and not a single regret, just the wish that everyday could be as perfect. Streetlights started popping up, signaling we were getting closer to the city, and with that my smile faded away slightly. Soon we would have to drop off Courtney and Kat, and I would have to say goodnight. After that, all that remained would be a short drive back to Greg's, and then the day would be over. There was no telling what the next day would hold for me, for us. angels, demons, Heaven, and Hell, tomorrow they would all come flooding back into my life, and nice relaxing moments like this would become a rare luxury.

I snapped out of my thoughts when the car jolted to a halt and Greg announced it was time to part ways. I walked Courtney to her door while Greg waited by the curb, trying to convince Kat he would be more than happy to drive her home as opposed to waiting for her brother to pick her up. We took our time saying goodnight, and when I kissed her again, I didn't want to stop. Luckily, Courtney had a stronger will than I, and she disappeared inside, keeping her wide cute smile in view up until the door closed completely. I went back down the steps and waited with Greg and Kat until her ride picked her up. I could tell Greg wanted a goodnight kiss as well, but he was too nervous and hugged her instead. She asked him to text her in the morning, and he nervously laughed and promised he would. Kat's brother scrunched up his face like he had just ran over a skunk at their whole exchange before peeling out of the street and whipping around the corner, out of sight.

We talked about the individual conversations we had with each of the girls, comparing and commenting lessons learned and jobs well done until we got back to his house. He sluggishly carried his things back into the garage and then went straight to his room and plopped face first into his pillow. I went to the bathroom, washed up, brushed my teeth, and milked every second of normalcy while I still could. I finally ended up in bed at exactly midnight.

That was a great day, Zeke said softly. I nodded my head, not wanting to speak out loud or blind myself with my phone screen. *I hope we can do things like that more often.*

"Me too," I whispered. "Goodnight."

Goodnight, we've got a big day in the morning.

CHAPTER EIGHTEEN: IN MEMORIAM

Liam woke up bright and early as the sunshine through the curtains lit the room more than his closed eyes could ignore. He groaned at the sight of early numbers written on the clock nearby and tried to cover his head with the blanket, but I reminded him that we had places to be.

"You can fix my spine, but you can't help me wake up in the morning? What's wrong with you?" Liam complained as he stretched out across the partially deflated air mattress.

"What?" Greg rolled over in his bed and looked down over the edge at where my air mattress rested on the floor beside him. "Who are you talking to?" He had one eyebrow cocked in an inquisitive glare at me while his eyes occasionally darted around looking for the answer.

Now you done messed up! I proclaimed, not helping whatsoever.

"Um…" Liam stammered with a severe case of brain farts. "What?" he said, stalling for time.

"You said something about fixing your spine, and waking up. Who were you talking to?" He adjusted himself into more of an upright sitting position and his face changed from a confused curiosity, to an interrogative insistence. "You know, you've still never told me how you're able to walk again, what happened to you while you were away?"

He knows too much! I said jokingly, but keeping that fact to myself to mess with Liam, *Kill him!* It was hilarious to watch Liam struggle with holding back the gut reaction to yell at me while Greg was watching him so closely, and I got to feel the flooding conflict of emotions as they waged a war inside him. I held back my laughter as long as I could, but broke sooner rather than later. *Ok Liam, I was just messing with you, we don't have to kill him, calm down, now, I've been toying with a cover story for a while now, just repeat everything I say.*

I started talking, and Liam repeated aloud, "Ok, I guess I can tell you, but you have to promise not to tell anyone." Greg's expression changed again, only this time it was juvenile excitement, and he threw his covers aside to make room for his legs to twist around and he sat crisscross applesauce like a kindergartener at story time. "There was a doctor at the hospital, I never got his real name, he went through at least a dozen aliases while I knew him."

Wait don't repeat this part! I yelled, trying to cut him off before we got any further. *You need more emotion, stop repeating everything I say like you're reading at a fourth-grade level, put some feeling into it, son!* I directed. *Ok now, let's continue.*

"He was working on some experimental, and very controversial, new procedures, real fringe science type stuff, and apparently my case fit one of his criteria perfectly. He drugged me and smuggled me out of the hospital to his own personal lab where he experimented on me, nothing crazy, it wasn't like torture or anything, and I was kept drugged or asleep for most of it, so it's all a bit fuzzy. Eventually, when I started walking again, he couldn't keep me asleep all the time, and that was when I started planning my escape!"

"Whoa, whoa, whoa, hold on," Greg said waving his hands around to force Liam to pause my story, "What? No way? There's no way that can be true."

"I know that it…sounds ridiculous…" Liam put extra emphasis on the last two words just for me, since during this whole ordeal there hadn't been a free moment for him to address me directly.

Oh, c'mon, it gets better, we're still only in act one! Wait until you get to the height of your story arc! Oh, and the twist at the end is going to blow you away!

"Seriously though," Liam started, totally off script, "Craziest dream I've ever had, guess it was so crazy I was even talking in my sleep," he laughed it off and then rolled across the mattress to stand up. "Anyway, I've got some errands to run today, I'll probably not see you until later tonight."

Greg remained on his bed with his legs folded up like a pretzel but his face was frozen with disappointment. "Wait… Huh…?"

Ok, fine, it can be a dream, but can we at least finish telling him my story? I worked really hard on it, and look at him, poor little guy is devastated, throw him a bone.

"Yeah, but you know how dreams are, I've already started forgetting pretty much everything about it, but oh well, what are you going to do about it? Bye!" Liam turned and left the room, pulling his phone out to type a message for me as he popped into the bathroom. [That's payback for the 'Kill him' comment, just not sure if it's enough…]

Damn it, Liam! Stop ruining all my fun! If you wanna to get back at me, do it some other way. Liam laughed quietly while his hands were preoccupied, but a few shakes later he was done and headed for the front door.

[Let's just go before Greg tries to chase us down.] When Liam pulled the front door to close behind him, I utilized the transitional area where there would be no witnesses to whisk us away and begin flying southeast. When we passed over and past the Gulf of Mexico, Liam looked over his left shoulder confused. "Wait! I thought we were…!"

We are, I just want to check on Zak, he should've reached out to everyone by now, just want to make sure he's all right.

Despite my efforts at sounding nonchalant, Liam must've noticed a hint of the worry I was feeling. "I'm sure he's fine! Maybe Dan isn't much of a morning person either!"

Once we reached the coast of Australia I slowed us down and pointed out the lack of a morning sky *Think you're forgetting about time zones there, guess you really are a high school dropout.*

"Oh just shut up," he retorted immaturely. I laughed, but didn't waste any more time before calling out to Zak. My range was limited compared to my Enochian brother, so it could take quite a while to cover the whole continent and find…

I'm here, Zak's voice said in my head, which was technically the same as Liam's head, but only I could hear him.

Where are you? You were supposed to call the others together ten minutes ago.

Shh! We're a little busy at the moment, and since when do you care about ten minutes?

*I…it was just…*I didn't want Zak to know I was worried, but my hesitation only confirmed it for him.

Ha ha! he said in a sort of tone meant to make fun of me, *you were worried about little ol' me? That's so sweet,* more tone that just made me regret all of my life decisions, *but seriously, shut up, meet us here, we're at a fishing boat north of you, we should be done when you get here.*

Zak severed his connection and I could no longer hear him, which was a good thing at that point, I was beginning to get tired of him rubbing my foolishness in my face. *Ok, I found them,* I said, heading north, *Keep an eye out for a fishing boat.*

There were dozens of boats between us and the horizon, and it was hard to tell which ones were fishing boats, and which were some other kind of boat in the dark, except for the cruise ship, that one was easy to distinguish. "Wait!" Liam called out, "I think I see it!" He pointed out at a boat much more east than north, but the large net full of fish silhouetted by the deck lighting was a dead giveaway that it was indeed a fishing boat, and then the sounds of screaming men helped me think it was the right fishing boat.

Might not be the best idea to just fly over and land right on the deck. You might want to plug your nose for this.

"Oh son of a…" I hurled us straight down toward the inky black ocean surface and protected Liam's body from the brunt of the impact. I was much slower in water than the air, but we still moved at a pace faster than any human could swim. As we approached the boat, several large objects impacted the surrounding water's surface forming inverted mushroom clouds made of thousands of tiny bubbles, and when they cleared, I could tell the objects that had fallen off the boat were people.

What the hell is going on here? I thought aloud again.

"Ah-ink-air-ee-o" Liam said, or rather tried to say, but whatever he thought he had said merely sounded like gibberish underwater.

At the very least, all of the commotion and other bodies in the water would provide us good cover to approach the boat, so I swam us right up to a patch of netting on the side. Everyone who had jumped was doing the opposite, swimming as far away from the boat as they possibly could, not a reassuring sight if I'm completely honest. *Get us up there, I wanna see what's going on.* I told Liam, since he had control over all of the appendages except for my wings.

He listened and began climbing, only to stop at the top when we were close enough to peek over the edge. There were only four men left visible on the brightly illuminated deck, and Dan was one of them. There were two men laying on the ground, one twitching slightly, the other as still as a statue. The last man was on his feet, but cowering with his back to the wall of the cabin. Between him and Dan rested a rather large octopus colored light brown with bright blue rings all over its head and tentacles. It flailed around with its slimy limbs trying to feel for something, and the more it moved, the more the cowering man's condition degraded.

"Easy there, mate, just breathe," Dan said as he slowly crept with slow and soft steps closer toward both of them, "It's ok, he's more scared of you, trust me, we just need to get him back in the water, and everything will be righto."

This only caused the man to panic even more. "B-b-but my men!" he stammered.

"No wukkas, mate, it's a big ocean, they'll be fine, let's just focus on this little fella, sound good?" Dan was really close to the man now, but then one of the tentacles zigged instead of zagged, causing it to find the poor man's ankle.

"Ah! Get it off!" the man yelled as he flailed and flinched, causing himself to merely reel in the creature more.

"Crikey! Fine, we'll do this the hard way." Dan lunged at the octopus and grabbed it by the bulk of its head and rolled forward, using his momentum and twisting motion to wretch it's grip off the fisherman. He tumbled a few more times as he manhandled the cephalopod to keep it from entangling him at such close range. A series of Australian expletives added context to the grunts and groans as Dan tumbled and rolled end over end across the course decking. Liam was beginning to peek his head higher and higher over the edge as Dan rolled toward the far side of the vessel, and when both man and beast plunged overboard, he popped up all the way. "Dan!"

J. A. Reed

Zak! We called out the names belonging to our respective species simultaneously. The freaked-out survivor managed to find the door leading into the cabin and didn't hesitate hiding inside. Liam ran straight for the spot Zak/Dan fell, but all we could see over the edge was a large spot of agitated water from their impact reflecting the night sky. "Are they all right?" Liam asked, sounding a bit worried himself.

Zak? Zak, can you hear me? I called out, not caring if I sounded too worried anymore. There was a long, painful silence as the water slowly calmed, but nothing emerged from below except fewer and fewer bubbles. *Zak?*

Liam tuned back to look at the two men on the ground, now neither of them were moving. "What was that thing?" he asked, the worry in his voice growing exponentially the longer they were under water.

An explosion erupted from beneath the water and a torrential downpour followed behind it. Something inside flew up and over where we stood and impacted the deck hard enough to rock the whole boat, nearly making Liam lose his sea legs. "Bloody 'ell!" Dan shouted, drenched from head to toe, but with a massive grin across his face. "Always wanted to tangle with one of those; bugger nearly snogged me, though, that wouldn't have been good."

"What the hell?!" Liam yelled, and I agreed, how was he so happy about what we just saw?

"Oh, g'day mate," he said, finally noticing we were there. "Crikey! Almost forgot about these two, mind giving me a hand?" Dan rushed over to the man that had been frozen solid since we arrived and placed his hands on some reddish exposed skin below the elbow. "Hurry up, mate, get that one there, left calf."

Liam, confused, moved in short nervous bursts, looking around for some sort of guidance or assistance. When he eventually reached the man, the same red discoloration could be seen through a torn pant leg. "W-what do I do?"

"Not you, mate, you're buddy up here," he tapped on his own temple a few times before putting the hand back on the wound.

"Zeke?" Liam asked, both to Dan and for me to explain.

Oh, um, yeah, put your hands on it, I'll see what I can do. Liam was hesitant to touch the stranger's wound, but he did, and through the contact I was able to discern what was wrong. The octopus must've delivered some sort of neurotoxin, and it was causing paralysis that was just beginning to affect the man's diaphragm, which, if he wanted to breathe, was a very bad thing. I focused on breaking down the toxin and reversing the paralysis just in time to keep him from suffocating. When I finished, I let Liam know he could let go, and when his hands came off, the red faded away and the proper color rushed back into place.

"Crikey, that was close, we nearly lost him," Dan said as he wiped either salt water and/or sweat from his eyes. "Let's go before they come 'round."

"Wait, what were you two even doing here?" I asked out loud while I could.

"My job," Dan replied with a snap. "That innocent little fella got caught up in that fishing net, it's my job to make sure dangerous animals like that get back to where they belong, and don't kill anyone along the way."

"That's a real job?" Liam asked, "You mean you actually get paid for that?"

Dan sighed, "Yes, it's a real job, and no, I'm not going to be on the stupid telly for it, damn Yanks."

"Jeez, sorry, you don't have to bite my head off."

"Don't need to, here in my country, we've got a thousand things that'll do it for me," he laughed, no longer upset about Liam's ignorant comment. "All right now, I believe we have prior arrangements, sorry for the delay, my bad, let's dash, shall we?"

Zak's wings shot them up into the air and off, leaving us on the rocking boat with nothing but two men slowly regaining consciousness, and a lot of questions. I felt like we could both relate with how Greg had felt when Liam just bolted on him that very morning. I obviously blamed Liam for lumping me in with his bad karma.

J. A. Reed

I quickly decided to just ignore it and used my own wings to chase after them. During the short flight back to the States, I heard Zak's message as he broadcasted it to all of our fellow fallen. *Sorry for the delay. But today's ceremony will continue as scheduled. Please meet at the quarry above the Salmon Site fracture. Remember, everyone will be in attendance, so be on your best behavior, that's an order straight from Lucifer herself.*

Zak/Dan landed first, and before we could catch up, Megatron and Trini landed in their angelic forms. After we reached the quarry, the rest of my siblings appeared one by one, all without hosts except for Zak and myself. The only ones missing were the three Guardians and Lucy, but only because they still couldn't cross through to Earth, and they were still ensuring Forfax's accommodations were sufficient in making sure she wouldn't be going anywhere anytime soon. I looked over to Zak though, and he nodded, confirming that they were watching from down beneath us.

"They're late," Megatron grumbled as he noticed his arm beginning to blister.

"They'll be here," Cass said, sounding hopeful, but also a bit worried as he noticed his own deterioration.

"Hey, Ezekiel!" Trini shouted across the way at me. "What's with the meatbags? You see any other hosts around here? Beside Zadkiel of course, but you two are basically joined at the hip anyway, so I'm not surprised there."

"Oi!" Dan shouted, triggered by Trini's lack of respect. "Why don't speak to us if you're going to throw words about! In case you nodded off and missed the whole thing, Liam and I were the *meatbags* that helped get us here, you knocker! So, either play nice or you can take your rubbish and piss off! Twit."

Trini didn't take too kindly to a human speaking to her like that, but once she took a step in his direction, a bright column of light fell around the quarry. Everyone staggered around and raised their arms to shield their eyes as they tried to look up at the source of the light, but most lost focus on that as they noticed the decay on their extremities began to reverse.

"What the...?" Megatron said aloud.

"How...?" Cass added, but never finished past the first word.

With Liam still joined, I was able to continue peering through the light between his fingers without distraction. I saw glimmering movement, which as it grew closer I could tell there were four distinct colors, purple, blue, orange, and green. The colors separated even further as they grew closer, but they also grew brighter, causing Liam to shield our eyes even more.

"All right!" I shouted as loud as I could, "We get it, you made an entrance, now can you dim the lights a bit?! Jeez!"

With that, the light dimmed down to a reasonable level, and we were all able to look up at the wall of angels, every single one of the non-fallen save for the Saints and Archangels. Apparently dear ol' Daddy couldn't be bothered to give up those in his inner sanctum, or even those guarding it. On a second look over, there was one Guardian absent as well, but that hardly mattered in the overall scheme of things.

"Sorry, forgot you can't handle the light anymore," Eve said, adding a smirk afterwards. "It's safe to come out now Ezekiel, Zadkiel."

I'm going to step outside for a bit, but don't worry, you'll be perfectly safe here. Might want to stick close to Dan though, just to be sure.

Liam swallowed a big gulp of spit he had gathered from being too afraid to swallow over time. "Um...ok..."

Don't worry, I mean sure, last time we were all in the same place, we tried to kill each other, but as long as no one looks at each other wrong, or breathes wrong, or mentions whether or not eating shellfish is a sin, we'll be perfectly fine.

"Wait! What?"

I didn't stick around long enough to clear up which side was which; maybe that would teach him to always let me finish what I start, like my cover stories. *That's* how you get payback.

* * *

Even after the non-fallen angels put their wings away, there was a warm glow about them, making it easy to distinguish them from their fallen brothers and sisters. Movies, television, and other modern media had me believing they would have those little golden circlets floating a few inches above their heads, but the best comparison I could make would be those old style stained glass window depictions you see in churches and cathedrals.

There were two Muses I didn't recognize, easy to distinguish from the other class of angels by their small stature. They were sticking close to one another and shifted nervously with sideways glances across the quarry at Megatron and the other fallen Muses. Megatron paced a small line in the dirt as his attitude flowed through the whole spectrum of emotions. There was a point he shot them repeated death glares, other times he turned his back on them as he willed his eyes to dry themselves, and even a short laugh followed by him shaking his head side to side. Eventually, the two unknown Muses gingerly approached Megatron and his entourage of all that was left of their kind. I was too far away to hear anything they said, but it must not have been about shellfish, because it resulted in heartfelt hugs between the rival groups.

The rest of the angels were a little more difficult to tell apart than Muses, but if I looked closely enough, I could make out the Guardians because they were huddled together around Eve and shared her muscular build and height. The last time I had seen Eve, she was standing between Foxy and Zeke, saving him from being killed by my hands, so I wanted to approach her and thank her, but with the other two Guardians on either side of her, and nothing else around but other powerful celestial beings, I decided to stay back and continue to observe silently.

Zeke and Zak mingled their way around the quarry, but even with the two different tiers side by side for comparison, Angels and Enochians were nearly indiscernible from a physical standpoint. Zeke was slightly taller, but the group of fallen and non-fallen that weren't obviously Muse or Guardian all ranged within a few inches of one another. Zak had a slender look with angular facial features, which I was able to use to point out a few others with similar features, but all in all it was still just a guessing game at that point.

While trying to figure out who was who, one of the Angel/Enochian potentials turned her head to face me for the first time since I started really paying attention and was shocked to realize I recognized her. "Jo?" I muttered out loud by accident.

"Who?" Dan whispered to me, keeping his eyes on the potential time-bomb in front of us.

"Huh? Oh, sorry, it's nothing." I had only seen her in Zeke's memory, but looking across the open space I felt like I had known her too. I looked around to find Zeke again, and noticed he had finally spotted her as well. His face drained of color and he nervously shifted to put her at his back. I looked back to her, and she just continued to chat with what I assumed were two other Angels, and now that I had a clearer look at her, I could safely say she wasn't Enochian either.

My eyes continued to dart back and forth between Zeke and Jo, and it was a little sad to watch. Zeke constantly switched between actively avoiding Jo, and shooting hopeful glances her way while she just went about her business as if he were invisible. Jo never so much as turned her head in his direction, and the longer she avoided him, the more depressed Zeke grew. Even when he tried passing by directly in front of her, her eye contact didn't so much as twitch away from the person she was engaging with in conversation.

Suddenly a pair of bright purple wings ignited within the mass of gathered bodies and flapped softly as they lifted one of the non-fallen Muses up and over the others. He gently hovered over the pool of water and whipped back around to face the crowd that had now quit all side conversations to turn their attention to him.

"If I can get everyone's attention, please? Thank you. Now, I know we all know why we're here today, and I know there really isn't any procedure or customs for something like this, because none of us thought anything like this could ever even happen, and I certainly never expected Xapham to be the first target of anyone's anger such as this. Xapham was by far the best of us, and I speak for both Bartholomew and myself when I say we were beyond devastated the first time we lost him, and the pain of his loss now dwarfs that which resulted so, so long ago. It saddens me to think of all the time we lost, because despite the unfortunate turn of events back then, he never deserved this. No one deserves this, not fallen, not human, and despite my current feelings, not even the one responsible for such a heinous act."

The crowd shifted uncomfortably as the two sides eyed each other uncomfortably.

"I would just like to remind everyone," Eve said over the awkward silence, "we are not here to dredge up old arguments or reopen old wounds, we're here to mourn our brothers, our brothers that would never have wanted to see more fighting among family. You'll do well to remember that."

The various looks of suspicion, anger, or disgust all vanished from the faces in the crowd, replaced by matching looks of sorrow.

"Evangeline is correct," the floating purple-winged Muse said with a courteous nod for the welcomed exposition. "Xapham and Gavreel both cared more about others than they did themselves, and even though the two had different ways of showing it, there's no doubt in my mind that they would want to see us together again interacting civilly and peacefully. I would like to turn the floor over to Metatron now to say a few words, and then anyone else who would like to say a few words may follow him should they choose."

Megatron flew up to take the spot over the pool and the vast contrast from bright fiery purple wings to burnt skeletal ones was difficult to ignore. "It's difficult to talk about Xapham and Gavreel, and know that they are gone forever, part of me still doesn't believe it's possible, but then I look around, and I realize there is a part of them that's still here, in all of us. As Tamiel said, Xapham really was the best of us, he cared more about all of us than he did himself. When…when we first divided amongst ourselves, I sided with him not because I believed in what he believed, but because I trusted his judgement, and I'm not trying to bring up the painful past, but that's the only and best way I can think of honoring him, right or wrong doesn't matter, all that matters is that neither Hell nor Earth will be the same without him in this, or any other, world." He cleared his throat and tried to keep his eyes from watering up before shifting gears. "Gavreel, on the other hand, couldn't have been more different. He was shy, kept to himself, but was fiercely loyal to those of us that were close to him; I fear that was his downfall though. He took the loss of Xapham harder than any of us, and I should've known better than to bring him here that day, I should've…"

"It wasn't your fault!" Trini shouted, cutting off his downward spiral before he could get any further. She flew up and put an arm around him, shooting a judgmental look out toward the group. "I can't say much to a mixed crowd such as this, but I will say that we all know who's at fault for this," her eyes glanced upward and her face turned even more sour. Foxy was imprisoned down below, so it was pretty clear she was talking about someone else. "We are appreciative for all of you that came out to show your support. Our differences aside, I at least know that everyone of you that came out today are sharing in our pain, and we truly thank you for your support in this time. As for–" She turned her head up again, but Megatron interrupted her.

"Thank you, Trinity, I'm all right now, I can take it from here." He looked at her with a stern, unflinching face, and with only a roll of her eyes, she did as she was told and flew back down to where she had been before her borderline blasphemous interruption. "Where was I? Ah, yes, I remember Gavreel used to say that if there were ever a way to bring us all back together, that it would be Xapham's doing. I know that this wasn't what he meant, but that's just the way life works, you can't control what happens, or how it happens, all you can do is try and make the most out of what you're given. We may have lost our brothers, but we got our family back, even if it's only for today. Tomorrow we can go back to hating each other, or ignoring each other, but for today, we mourn together, as one family."

When Megatron floated back down, everyone – fallen and non-fallen – applauded and embraced his meaningful message. Eve waited for the cheering to die down before brandishing her blazing jade feathers and commanding the attention back to her. "Before we carry on any further, I have a small announcement to make. Many of Xapham's former hosts suffered untimely deaths for their connection to him, as well as many other hosts that were forced into our conflict, each losing their lives at this very spot alongside our brother. In honor of Xapham and Gavreel, the souls of those lost will be granted access into Heaven for their sacrifice." She turned to Zak. "If you would relay that for me please."

Before Zak could even react to her request, seven wisps of white energy rose from the ground throughout the quarry. "I think she heard you," Zak said, stepping back to make room for one of the rising souls. They danced around as they slowly rose up the column of angelic light beaming into the quarry and gradually took humanoid shape, but they disappeared into the sky before becoming clear enough to tell who each wisp represented. I knew one of them was Thane Varro, and it was hard to feel good about him going to Heaven, even though I knew it hadn't been his fault, there was still a part of me that would never forgive him for what had happened to my mother.

Mom... Only right then did I realize after all this time, I had never properly stopped to grieve the loss of my mother. I had cried for her, I had lashed out in anger, I had even made a deal with something worse than the devil in an attempt to reunite with her, but all that time I had been stuck in denial, believing that Zeke or Foxy could bring me back to her someway, somehow. I had never actually dealt with it as I should have, and that was when it clicked; this funeral wasn't just for Xaf and Gavin, but for all of Foxy's victims, and my mom definitely fit in that category, albeit secondhand. If she hadn't already been in Heaven, she no doubt would've been the eighth soul in that group. This funeral was just as much for her as it was anyone else. I crossed my arms below my belt, lowered my head, and began to pray for her.

"But there's one more we must recognize," Eve called out, halting my prayer for a second to listen. "While those humans gave their lives unwittingly, there was one who went above and beyond. She gave not only her life, but her soul to save one of our own, something we will never be able to repay. I'd like to ask our brother, Ezekiel, to come up and say a few words for that brave soul, because none of this would've been possible without her."

All eyes turned to Zeke, including Jo's. He froze a bit, unprepared for the spotlight so suddenly. He nervously shuffled through the mass of angels, locking eyes with Jo as he passed her, but only for a split second before they simultaneously darted their eyes anywhere except toward each other. He finally found room to extend his wings and floated up to take Eve's spot over the still, algae-infested water.

"Natara Karim...was her name," he started off nervously without direction, clearly not prepared for such a public speech. "I only actually knew her for less than a day, but before that, I had watched her closely, observed her over the course of her life, as I did with all of my potential hosts." Zeke's eyes looked up from his nervous sunken-head posture to meet my gaze. I had always gotten the feeling that he knew more about me than he led on, but I never knew the extent of that knowledge until now. "She was a strong, fearless, amazing woman. No matter how many times life dealt her a bad hand, she would put on a smile and push through knowing that with little more than a positive attitude, persistence, and a heaping pile of patience, she would come out the other side better for it."

The more Zeke spoke, the more I felt like he was talking about my mother, and the fact that he was still looking at me didn't help that feeling dissipate.

"Natara may not have been a mother, but she did work as a teacher," Zeke said to the angels before returning his attention to me, "and like any mother, she loved her children unconditionally. She understood that her job wasn't to watch over them and protect them from the harsh world forever, but to teach them, and prepare them for the world without her."

My eyes teared up, and I tried to fight what Zeke was trying to say, but it was as if he knew my mom just as well as I did, and everything he was saying about Natara was equally true for her, if not even more so.

"But then she got sick," Zeke broke eye contact with me and didn't look my direction again. "She fought against the disease with every ounce of strength she had, but over time it continuously beat her down faster than she could get up. It took this brave, amazing woman and turned her into a broken shell of her former self."

I figured he had chosen that point to look away from me to end the comparison, but memories of my mom in that hospital bed flooded my mind again, the wires and tubes everywhere making her almost unrecognizable, it felt like I was reliving it all over again.

"But even when her spirit was broken, even at her weakest, lowest point, that strength she had was still in there, buried so far down she couldn't see it any more, but it was always there. I know because I saw it, I felt it, right at the end, just before she shoved me out of the way and saved my life, I felt what she felt. She wasn't dying to end the pain, or avoid an eternity she never believed in, she did it because she knew it was the only way that one of us was going to survive, and she did it gladly." Zeke's eyes found their way back to me. "If her family or loved ones knew her the way only an angel could, they would be beyond proud of her."

Light applause followed as Zeke drifted back down to his previous spot in the thick of the crowd. I took a few steps to catch up and talk about what he had said, but a Guardian with familiar green eyes blocked my path before I could make it very far. "Kind words, wouldn't you say?" Eve asked with a tone indicating she meant more than just the words she used.

"Yes, very, I'd actually like to ask him abou–"

"He sure did seem to spend an awful lot of time on family and children for a single young woman, wouldn't you say?" Again, she meant more than just what she said.

"I…" I almost dismissed her question again, but if I did she was bound to interrupt me and just ask the same hidden question in a new way, so I decided to try my hand at turning the tables. "How about you stop beating around the bush and just ask me the real question that you wanna ask me?"

Eve smiled at this. "You're pretty bright, for a human." I tried not to take offense. "Very well, do you know why he spoke the way he did, focusing on your mother's traits more than any others?"

For a moment, I thought she was trying to trick me again, but the more I thought about the answer, the less I knew the answer. I looked past Eve and saw Zeke and Zak talking with another Enochian. "Um, no, not really."

"Allow me to explain then," she said, drawing my attention back. "We Guardians have a certain unique power, just like every tier of angel. Many think it's just as simple as protecting all of Father's creations, but that's our job, not our power."

"Well, what is it then?" I asked when she paused for me to do so.

"We feel," she said plainly. "When Zeke joins with you, he puts up a block to keep your emotions at bay, am I right?"

"Yeah, something like that," I said, unsure where she was going with this whole thing.

"Well, we Guardians, we don't put up blocks, and we can feel anyone or anything around us." I got unbelievably nervous at that. "You're nervous, and that's understandable, but don't worry, I only wanted to speak with you to enlighten you about the two things that you already know, just can't bring yourself to realize."

"What I already…? What? I…huh?" That was where she lost me, but luckily, she knew just how lost I was, and just how to guide me back.

"Zeke is your best friend."

"What? No, that's not…that can't…" I said, not believing it. I had betrayed him. Sure, Foxy was the one responsible for all of the pain leading up to this funeral, but I had still betrayed him, I had betrayed my…my best friend. She was right, he was,

J. A. Reed

but there was no way I was the same to him. "Ok, say you're right. He deserves better than me."

"Oh, hush now, you can't measure a friendship off the mistakes, we all make mistakes, even angels. One thing I can measure, however, is a bond. The first time I saw you two, the levels of mistrust and resentment made freeing you of him effortless, but when I arrived today, I don't think I could've pulled him from you even with the help of my brother and sister." She glanced over at the other two Guardians she had walked away from before intercepting me. "A bond like that, it can't be one sided, and it's incredibly rare to find, you should consider yourself lucky to have found it."

A warm fuzzy sensation shivered through my skin and I felt my face warming with blush. "Th-thank you," I said, unsure how else to react to Eve's words of enlightenment. She turned and started heading back to rejoin her kind when I remembered her choice of words earlier. "Wait!" She stopped. "You said two things, what's the other thing?"

She turned slowly, regret on her face like she had hoped I would've glossed over that part. "I don't take interest in many humans, almost none in fact…" She trailed off, waiting for me to put the pieces together.

"Right, you pretty much only stick around Angelica, what does that have to do with us?" I asked, hoping I was starting down the right path.

"Exactly. What *does* that have to do with you?" she crossed her arms and narrowed her eyes at me like a disapproving parent, it reminded me of Courtney's father.

"Wait, are you saying she likes me?" I asked, hopeful thinking raising my voice a few too many octaves.

Eve took the few steps back toward me slowly and menacingly, her green eyes ablaze in their sockets. "I keep a *very* close eye on whoever's going to be spending time with my human, so you be *very* careful around her."

I thanked God I had emptied my bladder before we left and not there on the spot. "Of course, I would never–"

"I know about your little girlfriend in New Mexico, too,

make sure you remember that as well."

"I can have friends," I said, even though that wasn't where my mind started, but that's where it was at now. Angelica and I had been friends for quite a while, and for as long as I was with Courtney, it would have to stay that way. Eve must've felt my sincerity because she backed off and no longer looked like she would kill me for looking at her wrong.

"Hey! You two!" Zeke said, running over to join us with Zak following at a slower calm pace. "So, we're all thinking of flying up to Maine for some dinner, Charmony says she knows a place we can all spread our wings, I don't really know, but she said it's cool. Wanna come?"

"Sure," Eve said without enthusiasm.

"Liam? Wanna come or want me to take you home?"

"I'm down, I've always wanted to go to Maine, I hear the lobster is to di…"

"What?!" Eve said, resuming her fiery rage, only this time it was far worse.

"What did he just say?!" yelled another Guardian from across the quarry.

"Oh crap…" I said regretfully, I had completely forgotten about the shellfish warning.

"Liam!" Zeke said with wide eyes, "I told you not to…"

"I know! I know! I didn't mean to!" One by one the non-fallen began surrounding me, wings raised high, burning the air within the quarry in a mixture of rainbow shades. I backed up until I met the wall of dirt and had no place left to run. My knees shook so violently I collapsed under my own weight and landed hard on my backside.

I closed my eyes and waited for whatever would happen next, Zeke to sweep in and save me, the angels to rip me apart, whatever.

"Gotcha!" Zeke's voice said, not at all one of the options I was expecting. I opened my eyes and saw all of the angels smiling and laughing at me.

"Wha-?" I said, very much confused.

"Ezekiel here thought it would be funny to pull a big family prank," Eve said, sparing me any more time in the dark.

"Many of us were skeptical to indulge him in such a juvenile request," one of the Enochians said.

"But today of all days we're trying to be a family again, so we caved," added Tamiel, the Muse that had delivered the eulogy.

"Watching humans squirm is rather enjoyable; I see why you enjoy your pranks so much now, brother," pitched in a voice I hadn't been able to match to a face, which was worrisome because he sounded like he needed psychological help.

Zeke walked over and offered out his hand while wearing a massively cheeky smile, "All in good fun, right?"

I wanted to be mad, but even I had to admit he got me pretty good. He had set me up with the shellfish early, made his rounds convincing everyone to get in on it, and then tricked me into setting it off, well played indeed. "All in good fun," I confirmed with a smile and took him by the hand. He pulled me up into him and we joined back together seamlessly, like it was natural for us to be that way. "And I don't know how yet, but I'll get you back for that."

Bring it on buddy.

TO BE CONTINUED…